GENERATION
OF VIPERS

Peter Cawdron

thinkingscifi.wordpress.com

Imprint: Independently published

ISBN: 9798408329861 — Paperback

For my son, Sam

O generation of vipers,
who hath warned you to flee from the wrath to come?

Matthew 3:7

ANGRY
ANDY
ANDERSON

"I was right!" Andy yells, slamming his palm on the desk and shaking the close-up camera. Out of the corner of his eye, he sees the image wobble on the live-feed monitor. It's no accident. Emotion is theater. Anger is art.

"I was right, goddamn it!" he shouts. "And that exposes a problem. One helluva big problem, if you think about it."

He turns to face one of two dozen cameras mounted on the thin black scaffold surrounding his desk. Andy's automated broadcast algorithm picks up his motion and switches angles. The red LED above that particular camera glows, letting him work the shot. Andy doesn't need the monitor set in front of and slightly below his desk to know this is a compelling view. If anything, glancing down at that would distract his audience. After all these years, it's still a temptation he has to fight. He'll catch this shot later on the replay.

Andy keeps his eyes up, narrowing his brow and clenching his teeth. The muscles in his jaw swell, giving him a chiseled look.

"What could be wrong about being right? The problem is—it exposes a fatal flaw within our character. We all want to be right, but thinking you're right isn't good enough."

Andy's a pro. He's a method actor. In private, he likens himself to

1

Joaquin Phoenix, only this isn't fiction. Oh, once it was. A couple of years ago, he'd sell his soul for a buck. He'd explode in rage and sell godawful vitamin pills off the back of his show. Now, the stakes are higher. His *Hour of Raw Power* is still fueled by rage, but it's no longer unbridled. These days, it's a trap. His goal is to coax viewers into thinking for themselves—and that's not easy. Most people flatter themselves. They think they're strong and independent, but they follow along like sheep grazing in a field. If the herd starts trampling the grass by the gate, they rush to keep up with those in front.

"Being right is an illusion. It's a mirage. Being right makes us over-confident," he says, teasing a quarter of a million people watching his live stream. By this time tomorrow, he'll have topped a million hits on his channel, bringing in some sweet advertising revenue, but he no longer sells snake oil. There are no more herbal cures or overpriced tactical jackets for sale.

"Being right is not good enough—not for me!"

Andy's a sheepdog. It ain't the bark that gets the flock moving, it's staring down the sheep, cutting off any avenue for escape. The only way to herd a flock is to dance around the fringes, teasing them. Try as they may, those damn sheep are only going one way—his way.

"You see, life ain't about being right or wrong," he says, wagging his finger. He's pacing himself, drawing his virtual audience closer. "That's the thing that trips us up. Everyone wants to be right. Everyone! Absolutely everyone! No one wants to be wrong. They want to pat themselves on the back. They want to congratulate themselves on being so damn clever. They want a reward from others—recognition. But there's a problem. Seeking validation is a sign of weakness. It's a flaw that can be exploited. It's a blind spot.

"If you're right, anyone that disagrees with you is wrong—and that's a trap for young players. Life isn't lived in black and white. Life ain't a quiz show where you can buzz in with the answers. And if it was, the title would be—*Who Wants to be an Asshole?* No, life is bigger than right and wrong. It's not *what* you think that's important, it's *why*."

Andy sets his right elbow on the desk. He aims his fingers like a gun, pointing down the barrel of the nearest camera. His eye tracks along his index finger like the sights of a Glock.

"*How* did you come to your conclusion? That's what I want to know. That's what matters. Being right or wrong isn't as important as how you got to be right or wrong in the first place. Sounds crazy, huh? But it's true."

After flying into a mock-rage, Andy needs to look thoughtful. He slows his tempo, breathing deeply.

Andy pulls his hand back into a loose fist. He touches his knuckles lightly against his lips. It's contemplation. Hamlet never looked so composed. Back when Andy started his vlog almost a decade ago, he would fire off thoughts like the door gunner on a Blackhawk shooting into the desert. Fire enough rounds and you're going to hit something—that was the mantra. These days, Andy's a sniper. One shot is all he needs. Three words. That's all he needs to hit the mark.

"Beliefs are overrated."

Andy rocks back in his chair. It's time for the storm to rise over the ocean.

"Your beliefs are irrelevant. So are mine. I don't care what you believe. I don't care whether you think you're right or wrong. What I care about is *how* you got where you are today—and that's what you should care about. Your beliefs should bother you. Your opinions should bug you. You see, I was right about Comet *Anduru* and it didn't make a goddamn bit of difference. I was blinded by my pride. The problem was—I was right for the wrong reasons."

He shakes his head, gritting his teeth and screwing up his face. His anger is staged, and yet on one level, it's real. He works himself into a frenzy. Spittle flies from his lips. His finger jabs at the camera like a boxer working a speed bag at the gym.

"Right and wrong don't mean shit! *How* the *fuck* did you get to that point? That's what I want to know—because that's what will tell me something about you. Dunning and Kruger—they knew. Only a fool thinks they're smart. Only a fool ignores others."

Andy flares his nostrils.

"Only a fool revels in being right!"

To him, people are like deep-sea game fish. Andy knows how to play a marlin. Amateurs will grab the rod and wind like crazy at the first bite. Oh, they might get lucky. Most of the time, the line will break or the fish will rip the hook from its mouth. But not Andy. He knows how to play the game. He lets the line run. He tugs a little, draws his rod in, sets the hook and relaxes. He knows he's got to work to land a big fish.

Arguments aren't won by logic. People are convinced by emotion, not reason. And people get weary. They get worn out. In the end, they'd rather give in than fight—just like a big old swordfish. For years, Andy used this technique to fish for fools and sell pills with the nutritional value of dirt. Now, he plies his trade to expose conspiracy theories. He wants people to think, not believe.

He leans forward on his desk, rocking over on his elbow. He gets close enough to whisper to the main camera. The lens and focal point are such that his face will distort slightly, but that's deliberate for effect. It's a trust play. He's inviting his listeners into a secret. His voice is low and deep. His speech is like gravel being turned over in a concrete mixer.

"Confirmation bias, baby. That's what I'm talking about. No one convinces you of anything you don't already believe. All they do is fan the flames. I'm telling you, beware of easy answers. Beware of black and white. Beware of right and wrong.

"It's not *what* you believe that's important, it's *why*. Don't ask yourself what you believe, ask yourself why. How did you get to that point? That's the trick. That's the ploy. That's the angle. That's the game. That's the goddamn secret they don't want you to know. That's how they play you."

He leans on the armrest of his chair, knowing his computer system will switch to a wide-angle shot taking in the wall screen behind him. The Stars and Stripes flutter in the wind. The red, white, and blue are computer-generated, but it doesn't matter. Everything everyone has ever seen online is manufactured. Even photos are lies—they frame

4

reality rather than capturing it. Besides, reality is boring. If it wasn't, reality TV wouldn't be so heavily scripted and carefully edited.

"I was right," he says, tapping his chest. "Comet *Anduru Kumārayā* was the Prince of Darkness. We watched that *fucking* thing. All of us. We saw it skim through the clouds of Saturn."

We watched is a trigger phrase. It's an audio key that's been preset in his production software. Whenever he says those two words, the image behind him changes to a bunch of preloaded video clips.

A thin yellow flame streaks across the nightside of Saturn, passing inside the rings before heading back out into space. It's a special effects re-creation that may or may not be accurate, but who cares? It's captivating. That's the point of using it. The size of the planet is imposing. Golden clouds swirl within the gas giant.

"We watched as that damn thing passed Jupiter," he says, reading cues from a teleprompter.

The video clip cycles.

The image of Jupiter appears as it was captured by a space telescope. The shot has been upscaled, making it indistinguishable from his fake imagery of Saturn. The clouds on Jupiter swirl like cream being stirred into coffee. There are hints of orange, brown, red and white folding on top of each other within the gas giant. A thin yellow streak skims over the clouds, leaving a dark black trail billowing through the thick atmosphere.

"We watched as *Anduru* passed over the Gulf of Mexico, causing fifty-foot waves to pound the coastline from Tampa to New Orleans and on to Corpus Christie. The lowlands of Mexico were flooded. Millions were stranded in the subsequent power outage. Hospitals struggled. Infrastructure collapsed. Tens of thousands of people died."

Notes scroll in front of Andy, streaming down his teleprompter at a steady pace, allowing him to focus on the main camera. They allow him to maintain eye contact with his audience while following a script in this portion of the video. His '*we watched*' phrase continues to trigger different video clips behind him. Their purpose is to mesmerize the audience. They provide him with an air of authenticity. This isn't the

5

local drunk leaning on the bar, rambling on about the latest conspiracy theory. This is Angry goddamn Andy Anderson!

"We watched as NASA launched a deep-space Orion from Kennedy. And we waited. It took weeks before *Anduru* came to rest between Earth and the Moon. The world ground to a halt, waiting for First Contact.

"We watched the astronauts in their tiny tin can. They drifted over an alien artifact larger than most asteroids. They talked. They planned. They rehearsed. They prepared themselves. And all the while we waited here on Earth.

"We watched as *Anduru* split open. Cracks appeared in the dark husk, breaking into gaping chasms. It made no sense—not to us. *Anduru* defied our expectations. No one knew what to think.

"We watched as the Orion explored the darkness. The craft was attacked. It was dragged inside the alien pod. The astronauts were thrown around the cabin. We saw the panic in their eyes. We felt our hearts race as the Orion's solar panels crumpled. The craft slid sideways, being pulled in toward a monster hidden in the shadows. We saw claws reaching for them.

"And we watched them escape and destroy the pod. We learned it wasn't intelligence or curiosity that brought this goddamn thing to our world, it was hunger. NASA used a drone to position a thermonuclear warhead inside *Anduru* and destroyed it from within.

"Through it all, we watched and we watched and we watched—until we could watch no more."

The phrase *watch no more* is the audio signal to switch back to the US flag.

Gentle waves roll across the digital equivalent of fabric. The pure white stars set on a navy blue background are comforting. The red and white stripes are reassuring. There's a sense of continuity, familiarity and consistency in them that defies the chaos of *Anduru*.

"I was right," Andy says softly. "I told you about this months before it happened. I told you they were coming for us. I was right—and that's not good! It's bad—flawed. It's one helluva problem. A big problem."

He takes a sip of water. Unlike every other motion he's made during his recording, this one isn't calculated. His throat is parched. His voice starts to break.

"What's wrong with being right? Why is it bad? Because being right is etched into our DNA. We all want to be right. You want to be right. I want to be right.

"Even when I'm wrong, I think I'm right. But being right is as dangerous as that fucking demon crawling up from within *Anduru*. Being right brings with it a sense of superiority, invincibility, 'cause no one can tell you you're wrong. Being right is a fool's paradise!"

Andy scratches the stubble on his chin. It's been three days. He should shave more often.

"How did I know *Anduru* posed a threat? That's the real question. How? The answer is—I didn't. I guessed. Oh, back then I wouldn't have admitted that to you. Back then, I would have told you it was instinct, insight, foresight, intelligence—that I just knew.

"Don't you see? Right or wrong, it doesn't matter. It's *how* you arrive at your conclusion that matters. I guessed. How fucked up is that?

"And this is what we do. We hear a bunch of arguments, a bunch of points thrown together by someone else, and we rush to a conclusion and think it's our own. It's not. It's theirs—and you don't know if they're lying or not.

"It doesn't matter whether it's an alien spacecraft, vaccines or election results we're talking about. What matters is—do we rush to the conclusion we want to be true? As that's always a mistake. Whether we're right or not is irrelevant. Sometimes we're right. Sometimes we're wrong. What's always relevant is *how* we got to that goddamn conclusion.

"I don't care what you believe about aliens, viruses, vaccines or election results. I care about *why* you went down that dead-end road.

7

Why did you jump at that like a dog chasing a tennis ball? Why can't you see it for what it is? A distraction. A diversion. It's something to keep you panting while avoiding any real depth. The tendency to react— to go with our instinct—is flawed. And it gets exploited by assholes all the time."

He points at his oversized belly, saying, "The gut, man. Don't think with your gut. Don't go on intuition. That's the lesson here. That's what I learned from *Anduru*.

"These scientists, these astronauts and astronomers and engineers you see on TV, they don't go with their gut. They question shit. And that's what we all need to do.

"If you think you're right—*cool*—of course, you do. We all think we're right. I think I'm right too. But don't stop there. Ask questions. Look for answers you don't like. Stop and think. Challenge yourself to go deeper. Maybe, just maybe, there's more to learn. Be willing to change your position. Instead of jumping to a conclusion, jump to a bunch of goddamn questions."

Andy pauses. He rocks his head, imitating someone looking both ways when crossing the street. He puckers his lips, playing up to his unseen audience.

To one side of him, there's a bank of computer servers with blinking network lights. On the other side, panels of acoustic insulation cover the inside of his garage door. He hasn't opened that door in years. He doubts the electric motor even works anymore. The damn thing has probably seized. But as he turns in those directions, he squints, making as though he's looking for something in the distance.

"Look both ways when you cross the road, baby. Don't run out into the traffic!"

Andy narrows his eyes as he stares at the main camera in front of him.

"Be willing to learn, not confirm."

That's it!

That's the soundbite for today.

That's what he wants his subscribers to take away with them.

Andy smiles and hits a button on the floor with his foot, triggering the software on his computer to play music, lower the studio lights and roll the closing credits.

JORGE

Thin wispy clouds drift high above the Gulf of Mexico, catching the first rays of dawn. Fine strands of gold and purple wind their way around the edge of the clouds. The dark of night gives way to the coming day. The stars fade. The horizon lightens, revealing an azure blue. Saturn is still visible in the west, awaiting the brilliance of the sun before being banished by the coming day.

Jorge lowers a pair of binoculars. One of the loadmasters gave them to him during the evacuation from Vera Cruz. As they're military-grade, the view is crystal clear. They're far better than the battered old pair he had on his first boat.

Ever since the alien encounter, Jorge's made a habit of tracking Jupiter and Saturn whenever they're visible at night. His daughter Maria taught him how to mentally trace the arc of the Sun and Moon in the sky, imagining the path of the ecliptic.

Jorge doesn't like big fancy words like ecliptic. He can't get his tongue around them. Maria used a dinner plate to explain. With a lump of rice in the middle representing the Sun, she placed a couple of meatballs out toward the edge, explaining they were the planets—and, except for Pluto, they're all on the same flat plane. It still took Jorge a while to get his head around the angle of the ecliptic as it passes overhead. Why doesn't it go straight? If it's a flat plane, why does it curve? Maria was gentle with him, reminding him he's standing on a round ball spinning madly in space. She held up her son's soccer ball and said, what looks flat isn't. Jorge accepted rather than understood her point.

Veronica likes Saturn. The rings are pretty. Jorge prefers Jupiter because he can see the moons orbiting the gas giant. Watching the planets is a matter of pride for him. Maria explained comet *Anduru* was too small to be seen by anything other than an observatory, but still he looks in case there's another one coming. This morning, Saturn is a pale yellow dot high in the west.

Jorge has been trawling in the southern *Bahia de Campeche* fishing grounds, eighty miles off the coast of Mexico. The run home has been smooth. The sea is like glass.

Life changed after the passage of *Anduru* over the Gulf. Even now, two years later, Mexico is still recovering. Entire cities have been abandoned. It's easier to build new infrastructure than it is to demolish buildings and repair power, water and sewage lines. People, though, are sentimental. It's difficult to move on even if there's no hope for renewal. Humans are nothing if not resourceful. The government may have abandoned ports like Vera Cruz, opting to relocate to *La Antigua* in the north and *Boca del Rio* in the south, but not everyone can wait on construction. Like Jorge, a lot of Mexicans are stubborn—but not in an ornery way. Persistent is a better term. The government might promise a new life further along the coast, but life is to be lived now—not in a decade. People need a roof over their heads, not sheets of canvas blowing with the wind. Promises are nice, but no one can live in a promise. No one can eat a promise. For better or worse, Jorge is committed to rebuilding Vera Cruz.

Seagulls squawk overhead. They drift on the breeze, looking for fish scraps. Occasionally, they land on the old trawler.

"Hey, sleepyhead."

"Huh?" Veronica says. Her eyelids flicker. She yawns, sitting up within the cabin of the fishing boat. She should have gone to sleep below

12

deck on one of the cots, but she prefers the plastic padded bench seats lining the wheelhouse so she can stay close to Jorge.

"Look," Jorge says, pointing at the clouds.

"So pretty."

The sea is calm. The diesel engine beneath the deck hums, pushing them on. The wake kicked up by the fishing boat sends waves racing across the slick surface.

Veronica wanders out onto the wooden deck of the boat, staring up into the sky.

"This is why I love the sea," Jorge says. "On this day, there is nowhere on Earth more beautiful—more peaceful. The Gulf is more stunning than any painting in the museums of Paris or New York."

Veronica nods. Jorge can see the wonder in her eyes. Being a ten-year-old orphan in Mexico, Paris might as well be the Neverland of Peter Pan, while New York is no more real than Alice's Wonderland. These are names thrown around by adults or fairytale cities on television. Jorge ruffles her hair. He'd love to take her to these mystical places one day. He'd love to see them for himself.

Jorge's been working on his nets for the past few hours, stringing them up on poles and repairing tears. He walks over and sits on one of the lids to the hold. With aging hands, he picks up a netting needle and continues weaving a thread back and forth. The more he does out here, the less there will be to labor over under the hot sun later today.

"Did we do well?" Veronica asks, stretching.

"We did well," Jorge says. "We have a good catch. We will feed many mouths today."

Veronica lifts the lid and peers into the darkness of the hold. Mounds of fish lie on top of each other in plastic baskets. Ice overflows around the edge, shifting with the slight rocking of the boat.

"Are you hungry?" Jorge asks, pulling an apple from his lunchbox. Maria always sends him out with too much to eat. She worries about him. She says he's too old to work the waters. Grandfathers should sit onshore, she says. For Jorge, the sea is life.

Pride keeps him going out to the fishing grounds. Maria has begged him to take some of the young men with him, but he'd rather they rebuilt Vera Cruz. The government might have moved on, but the young know. They see the future. As for him, he can handle the sea.

He hands Veronica an apple. It crunches as she sinks her teeth into the smooth skin.

For the next hour or so, they trundle along in silence, with just the hum of the diesel engine between them. Jorge works on his nets while Veronica sits in the wheelhouse, watching for other ships.

Eventually, she says, "We're approaching the harbor beacon."

"Aye, captain," Jorge says, returning to the wheelhouse. "Shall I take her in or will you do the honors?"

Veronica grins. "I need someone I can trust on the lookout."

"I can do that," Jorge says, smiling.

Veronica climbs up on the raised captain's chair and positions herself behind the wheel. Her feet dangle in the air. She rests one hand on the wheel and the other on the levers to her right. A quick glance at the dials in front of her and she's all business.

"Red, right, returning," she calls out, pulling gently on the throttle. "Passing to starboard. Reducing speed to ten knots."

"Aye captain," Jorge says, standing behind her in the doorway. He hoists his arm up on one of the joists supporting the roof of the wheelhouse. The wind catches his hair.

"Easy as she goes," Veronica says in perfect mimicry of him from days gone by. If anything, she's far more attentive than he is when at the wheel. Ten knots is a strict speed for her. Jorge normally comes in at anywhere under twenty. Whereas he'll lean on the wheel, she holds it with white knuckles. Jorge tends to come in too shallow, while Veronica keeps at least fifty feet separation from the various markers and buoys on approach.

She brings the trawler in toward the makeshift dock.

"Dropping to five knots," she says, easing back on the throttle and turning to follow the channel in toward land. "Fenders out. Ready on the ropes?"

"Fenders out. Ready on the ropes," Jorge replies, repeating her instruction back to her to show he's heard her. He tosses a couple of old tires over the side of the boat to act as bumpers against the dock.

"Three knots and we are in line," Veronica says. "Ready starboard?"

"Aye, captain."

Jorge stands on the gunwale with a rope in hand. Maria is waiting on the dock, but she doesn't look impressed. She's got her arms folded across her chest and a scowl on her face.

"Two knots," Veronica says, bringing the trawler to a halt. "And reverse. And full stop."

The boat barely bumps against the dock. Jorge steps off onto the wooden planks. Veronica shuts down the engine. Instead of exiting via the cabin door, she climbs out of the open side window and jumps onto the dock to help him with the ropes.

"Well done," he says as she joins him. They high-five.

"You can't keep doing this," Maria whispers to Jorge. "Not on a school day. She needs her sleep."

"She gets her sleep," Jorge insists, tying up the boat. "She sleeps better out there than she would in the orphanage."

Maria sighs. "If we are to adopt her, the government wants to know we can care for her. You can't just take her out fishing at night."

"We care for her," Jorge insists.

Veronica nods. "I'm cared for. I am."

"Don't tell anyone about this," Maria says to her. "No one. Do you understand?"

She nods.

"Nothing about the boat, okay? Not ever. They'll think it's dangerous. Too dangerous for a young child."

"Okay."

Vera Cruz was decimated by the wave that followed in the wake of

Anduru. The old city was swept away. Thousands of people died. The shoreline moved roughly two hundred yards inland following the tsunami.

Without government support, the rebuilding effort is slow. Padre Jesus is overseeing the construction of a new orphanage on the hill. Jorge and Maria live in a hut built out of debris cleared from the foreshore.

Jorge's original fishing boat was destroyed by the wave, but news of how he saved Padre Jesus and the orphans spread throughout Latin America. He became a folk hero. A retired fisherman from *La Ceiba* in Honduras gave him *The Santiago Apostol*, a forty-foot trawler. Since then, Jorge has been on a mission to feed as many people as he can each day.

Disaster aid still comes overland from *Xalapa*, but it's sporadic, with most of the effort going to the new developments. Only a handful of boats operate off the east coast of Mexico. Drinking water is plentiful but food is scarce. Schools are open. These days, they function more as a daycare than an educational institute. Helicopters fly overhead, ferrying in medical supplies. Even though the day has only just dawned, the sound of hammers and power saws can be heard as the reconstruction effort continues.

Most of what Jorge catches is given away. Maria works at a field hospital established by *Médecins Sans Frontières*. She talked the director into trading freshly smoked fish for diesel to power *The Santiago Apostol*.

Several locals help with preparing the catch for cooking. Like Jorge, they're volunteers. They begin unloading the catch onto carts and hauling it to the gutting station. Someone's already slicing fish open and emptying their entrails into the sea. Birds squawk, excited by the offal falling into the waves.

A car pulls up at the end of the dock. It's still got its headlights on, which is unusual given the sun is up. Someone's been driving for a long time. Given most of the roads are impassible, they had to have driven up from the south, taking the mountain route.

"Breakfast is ready," Maria says as they walk back home.

Two men make inquiries onshore, questioning one of the locals. Someone points at the three of them walking along the dock.

"Jorge? Jorge Rodríguez Mendez?" one of the men says in a distinct US accent.

Jorge eyes the man with suspicion, refusing to reply.

A friendly handshake is offered.

"Eric Brown, PBS."

"I pay my taxes," Jorge says in English. "I owe nothing to the US. Nothing!"

"Easy," Maria says, but Jorge is defiant.

"It was a long time ago. You cannot hound a man—"

"Papa," Maria says, resting her hand on his forearm. "PBS, not IRS."

Eric clarifies. "PBS is the US Public Broadcast Service. You might have seen some of our shows down here. Wonders of Mexico? Nova? SpaceTime with Dr. Matt O'Dowd?"

"Pati's Mexican Table," Maria says, nudging Jorge. "You've seen me watch Pati."

"Huh," Jorge says, unconvinced. He puts his arm around Veronica's shoulder, pulling her close. He's unduly protective.

"You're a hard man to reach," Eric says, being friendly. "We've been trying to get word to you for weeks."

Maria asks, "Where have you come from Mr. Brown?" She points at the car. "You've driven a long way to get here."

Thousands of bugs lie splattered across the car's grill. The plates aren't local.

"Vera Cruz is difficult to reach," Eric says. "We had to fly into Guatemala and drive up from there."

"You're very persistent, Mr. Brown."

"I am," he replies, apparently taking that as a compliment. Jorge, however, understands Maria's intent. As protective as he is of Veronica,

17

Maria is like a lioness. She's deeply suspicious. PBS sounds innocent enough, but Jorge finds it difficult to accept change as good. He'd rather one day was simply the repeat of another.

"Why have you come here?" Maria asks. That's what Jorge wants to know, but he doesn't say as much. He's happy for her to take the lead. Although Jorge speaks fluent English, for now, he plays dumb.

"PBS is working with NASA to sponsor a conference in Houston next year, examining the impact of *Anduru* on our world. We heard about your father—how he saved the orphans that night. We'd like to invite him to be a guest speaker. This is a chance for him to share his story with the world."

Maria has her hands on her hips. She's not convinced.

Eric gestures to the ruins around him. "Your father will be able to highlight the plight of the rebuilding effort here in Vera Cruz."

Jorge looks at Maria. Although he understands what's being said, he's struggling to grasp the implications. His initial reaction is this seems good, but he's unsure. He wants some reassurance. Besides, he's needed here. Someone has to fish the waters.

Maria says, "We don't have—"

"Flights and accommodation will be paid for," Eric says. "And expenses. Plus an honorarium. Your father will be our guest."

"No flights," Jorge says, shaking his finger. "No tin can for me."

"My father will not fly."

Eric says, "But he was evacuated in a helicopter, right?"

"And it terrified him for weeks afterward."

Eric addresses Jorge. "An airplane, a commercial flight, is entirely different—I promise."

"No. No. No."

Veronica tugs on Jorge's trousers, asking, "Can we go to Disneyland?"

Eric crouches before her, saying, "Oh, sorry. Disneyland is in LA. But I can get you a tour of the Johnson Space Center. You'd get to see rockets and astronauts."

"Like the ones that went to the Moon?" Jorge asks.

"Yes," Eric says, straightening up. "They all trained at JSC."

"Can we go?" Veronica asks, still tugging at his trousers. "Please can we go?"

"We have no passports," Jorge says.

Eric says, "We have plenty of time. The conference isn't for another seven months. Given the disruption caused by *Anduru,* the US Embassy in Mexico City has offered a waiver and issued you temporary visas. All you need is a driver's license or some other government-issued ID. We'll take care of the rest."

"Please, please, please," Veronica says, jumping up and down with excitement.

Jorge looks to Maria as though she were the parent. She smiles.

"By boat," Jorge says, raising a finger. "No plane. I will take *The Santiago Apostol* up the coast."

"Works for me," Eric says, offering Jorge a handshake. Reluctantly, the big man agrees.

SENATOR WILSON

"The technical issues have been resolved," a voice says through the speakers within the auditorium. "And we are live again in five, four, three..."

Kath is anxious. She wants to pee. She doesn't need to. She went to the bathroom before walking into the massive hall over an hour ago. It's just nerves, but her bladder disagrees. As one of the lead investigators into the journey of *Anduru* through the solar system, Dr. Kathleen McKenzie was called on to help prepare for this debate. She'd rather be back at NASA's JPL.

On stage, President Aston looks calm. It's an illusion. They've both seen the polling. They've both been briefed on the most likely talking points this evening. The alien spacecraft hasn't come up yet, but it will. Anxiety eats away at Kath's mind.

Senator Scott Wilson looks smug standing behind a Perspex lectern on stage opposite the President. Spotlights catch every carefully rehearsed facial expression. At 48, Wilson is a decade younger than the President. The senator's fit and trim, wearing a black three-piece suit, a heavily starched white business shirt and a brilliant red tie. With short grey hair on the sides of his head and wavy, dark hair on top, the senator's rockstar good looks and charismatic smile are magnetic.

President Aston, by comparison, looks worn and old. She's wearing a formal white dress along with white pearls, only the stage lighting does her no favors. Her skin is pale while her hair is wispy, almost sickly. Her outfit needs a splash of color to give it life. As for make-up, the senator's wearing more than she has had on for days. But for him, the blush daubed on his cheeks isn't gaudy. It plays well before the cameras, making him appear like an actor on a Broadway stage. To Kath's mind, he is.

Presidential debates ought to be more than fashion week in Milan. No one should care about appearances and yet everyone does. It's subliminal. Clothing may be a facade, but people read body language for intent. They read posture, temperament and styling as a measure of character. By themselves, these things are meaningless and yet they amplify the message being delivered by the candidates.

The floor manager points at the moderator. A red light glows above one of the cameras, indicating where he should direct his gaze.

"Welcome back to the final Presidential debate. We are one week out from the election and the eyes of the nation are upon us. The world is watching, waiting to see if President Aston will win a second term or if the firebrand senator from Texas has the momentum to snatch the White House. The final question of the night goes to you, Senator Wilson."

Long before the debate began, the senator knew he had public opinion on his side. The passage of *Anduru* over the Gulf of Mexico caused more than infrastructure damage and the loss of life, it eroded the President's political support. Everyone loves a war-time President. Once the war is over, though, it's time to shed dead weight. Senator Wilson offers the nation change. Whether that change is for the better remains to be seen, but the allure is there regardless.

After an hour and a half of fierce debate, Senator Wilson has President Aston on the ropes. Her stooped shoulders show she's been beaten. The President looks as if she's ready to head for the dressing room and start working on damage control with her campaign team. Senator Wilson, though, isn't finished with her. Not yet. There's a glimmer in his eyes, a slight smile on his lips. Is it anger? Cruelty? Spite?

The moderator says, "Two years ago, Comet *Anduru* skimmed the gas giants in our solar system. It used the dense clouds of Saturn and Jupiter to slow its approach to Earth. Here in the US, conspiracy theories were rife. Like comets during the Dark Ages, most people saw it as a harbinger of doom. The official line from the Aston administration was that the approaching alien spacecraft posed no threat to life on Earth. We now know that not to be the case. Senator Wilson, if you had been President at the time, what would you have done? How would you have handled this crisis?"

"First," the senator says. "I would have surrounded myself with competent advisors."

Ouch!

Kath shrinks a little in her seat. If this were a boxing match, Wilson would have just scored a hit with his lightning jab.

"Far from being hypothetical," he says, "this issue goes to the heart of my run for the presidency. We cannot afford another four years of Aston incompetence. We have to ask ourselves, what happens if another *Anduru*-class object approaches Earth?

"My opponent would have you believe we can deploy a series of autonomous nuclear weapons in orbit around Saturn to deflect the next vessel, but the concept is laughable. It's science fiction. Fantasy. At an estimated cost of eight trillion dollars, such a project dwarfs the entire US budget in any given year. Even with the support of our allies, such an undertaking is likely to exceed projections and timelines.

"How long do you think this will take to accomplish? A decade? Two? Plus another six years in transit just to get a spacecraft out that far? And the idea may not even work—that's the point that gets missed in all this.

"The President's guessing. She doesn't know. Ignorance is no way to set policy. What if the next *Anduru* uses Neptune and Uranus to slow instead of Saturn and Jupiter? What if those planets align better? We'll look pretty damn stupid if one of those things skates by our defenses.

No, I would back the Lunar Defense Perimeter Plan. It's a fraction of the cost, far easier to deploy and maintain, and it stands a higher chance of success."

The moderator says, "So you would back out of the UN Interstellar Defense Accords?"

"I would save us and our allies trillions of dollars."

The moderator brings the senator back to the question.

"But what would you have done eighteen months ago? Even with the benefit of hindsight, what could you have done differently?"

"We need answers," the senator says, yet again ignoring the question. "If I am elected President, I will declassify all the documents relating to *Anduru*. My opponent may label this as a national security issue, but I don't. I see it as a global security issue. Why are we hiding what we know?"

"We're not," President Aston blurts out, unable to contain herself any longer. The moderator raises a single finger, resting his other hand on the mute button, threatening to cut her off if there are any additional interruptions. She'll get her say in due course.

The senator is undeterred.

"We need a global response," he says, as if President Aston hasn't already been doing that. "My administration will establish an independent commission to examine our response to *Anduru*.

"In the US alone, forty-eight thousand people died with the passage of the alien seed pod. Families are hurting. They need closure. As I toured the southwest, I spoke to mothers bereaved of their children—and children left orphaned and homeless. Entire generations have been torn apart. They deserve answers. We all do.

"Make no mistake about my intention. If we find examples of criminal negligence or the failure to apply a duty of care in regards to *Anduru*, we will prosecute those involved."

"Those are harsh words," the moderator says, straying from his own question. "Do you have any reason to believe there has been criminal conduct?"

"I have questions," the senator replies. "I want to know why the US was left vulnerable to the approach of *Anduru*? We knew that damn thing was coming for months. Why did we fail to act? Why weren't we prepared for the passage of this exotic spacecraft over the Gulf of Mexico? Why weren't we warned ahead of time about the potential consequences? Why did we act so late?"

President Aston grips the lectern in front of her. White knuckles and pursed lips reveal her frustration, but she remains silent, waiting to respond to a debate question that will never actually be answered by the senator.

The senator seizes the moment. "I want to know what role Chinese foreign intelligence played in our decisions. Were our allies informed our actions were based on information originating from the Chinese Ministry of State Security?"

President Aston is flush with anger. Her cheeks go red. She grits her teeth. Veins appear on her neck, but she remains composed.

The moderator holds up his hand.

"Whoah. I'm going to stop you there, Senator. This is obviously new to me and our viewing audience. Ordinarily, I'd allow you to continue for your allotted time before giving the President the right of reply, but I'm going to allow President Aston to address this one point so it doesn't get lost." He faces her, asking, "Is this true? Were we acting on Chinese intelligence?"

President Aston hangs her head. It's slight, but it doesn't go unnoticed. She wasn't expecting this. Senator Wilson has blindsided her. She's not prepared for this level of disclosure.

"I—ah, I can't comment on matters of national security."

"You're the President," the moderator says, shrugging. "You can comment on anything you want. If it's classified, you can declassify it right here and now. You have that right."

"It's complicated," the President replies, and she's not wrong. Sitting in the audience, Kath has no idea how President Aston is going to respond without digging a deep hole for herself.

"It's not as simple as it seems," the President says, sipping on some water. "We were on the verge of the unknown. We needed help."

"From Chinese spies?" the senator asks.

The moderator is in shock. He lets the interjection go, probably because he's mortified by what he's hearing.

When the President doesn't respond, the senator says, "I have first-hand, corroborating testimony from those in the DC Metro Police and from sources inside the White House at the time. They told me about the CIA exfiltration of a Chinese spy involved in the attempted abduction of high-level staff within the administration."

The moderator's mouth falls open.

The camera crew doesn't miss it, broadcasting his look across the country.

That there's no denial from the President is damning.

Kath shifts in her seat. Oh, she remembers that night all too well.

The Chinese just wanted to talk. No one would listen. The Chinese ambassador had approached the State Department and been ignored. Chinese academics had reached out to their counterparts at NASA, but their requests were lost in the bureaucratic cogs of the machine. Letters were sent. Diplomatic entreaty was made. But everyone was so damn busy.

The Chinese were frustrated by the Americans. With an alien spaceship bearing down on the planet, there was no time for the usual channels. If they couldn't reach the US President, perhaps they could persuade her advisors. They thought it would be simple. The President's advisors were staying in a nearby hotel. The Chinese switched their regular driver with a deep-cover agent. He was instructed to feign getting lost. The plan was, he'd pull up somewhere out of sight and hand them a secure phone. Then they'd talk off-the-record. But the Chinese hadn't factored in the ire of the newly appointed Brigadier General Nolan Landis. Kath can still remember Nolan tearing up the upholstery and breaking the rear window of the car. The driver panicked and ran a red light and a police chase unfolded.

"It's true, isn't it?" the senator says, sensing the opening for a knockout blow. "Your national address was based on Chinese intelligence."

Kath grinds her teeth. The senator's making a gross oversimplification. Technically, he's correct, but he's glossed over dozens of other details and confused the timing. The attempted kidnapping and the national address were months apart. They were entirely separate events, but the President can't clarify that without going into layers of confusing detail.

President Aston swallows the lump rising in her throat.

Not a single camera misses the expression on her face.

The silence is painful.

In a whisper, she says, "We thought it was going to stop."

She looks down at the lectern. Tears well up in her eyes. Even the senator is silent as the President continues.

"We expected *Anduru* to come to a halt in orbit around Earth. We thought it would slow down. I guess we'd all seen too many dumb movies. Alien UFOs, right? They fly around like airplanes. Only they don't."

"So it's true?" the moderator asks.

The President says, "The Chinese figured it out. They'd done the math. They realized *Anduru* was coming in too fast. Venus was on the flight path beyond us. They knew *Anduru* couldn't stop in time on its first pass. They knew that, between Earth and Venus, there was enough aerobraking for *Anduru* to shed its phenomenal speed. They figured out it would loop around and come back to Earth a second time, later in our orbit of the Sun.

"You have to remember, this thing was still traveling at somewhere close to two hundred miles a second. Not an hour. A second. At that speed, it would cross the Continental US in under half a minute. That's New York to LA in less time than it takes to book a ticket online."

"And the Chinese told you this?" the moderator asks.

Kath is frustrated. She wants to blurt out from the audience, yelling, *It wasn't like that!* She wants everyone to understand it was a scientific insight, not a political point. The Chinese told Kath *where* to look. She ran her own calculations and informed the President. To say the Chinese told the President is a gross misrepresentation, but all nuance has been lost in the debate. Kath clenches her fists in her lap, hoping the President can recover from being battered by the fury of this storm.

"I was trying to save lives," the President replies.

"But you didn't," the senator says, sensing blood in the water. "You should have seen this long before it happened. Weeks before. There was time, wasn't there? There was plenty of time to prepare the southwest. You. You failed the American people."

Tears roll down the President's cheeks. Her lips quiver. She straightens her dress, trying to look composed, but she's not. What more can she say? For President Aston, this is no longer about politics or point-scoring in a televised debate. Tens of thousands of US citizens died on her watch. That's a burden she must bear for the rest of her life.

Kath is on the edge of her seat. Every muscle in her body goes tense.

President Aston raises her head high and proud. The silence within the auditorium is palpable. She raises her hand to say something even though no one's stopping her, but she thinks better of any more vacuous words.

The President drops her hand back to her side. With that, she turns and walks off stage. There's silence as she marches across the plush carpet. As soon as she disappears behind the curtain the studio audience explodes with voices yelling over each other.

Senator Wilson is speechless.

The moderator calls for calm, but no one can hear him. The audience is on its feet, screaming at the stage. Everyone is up. Everyone but Kath. She sits there with her head hung low, sobbing.

US PRESIDENTIAL ELECTION

A week has passed since the debate.

Kath is at a Washington DC hotel acting as the headquarters for President Aston's re-election campaign. Helium balloons adorn the stage with red, white and blue. Behind them, there's a massive wall screen. The plan is to release the balloons when the President walks on stage, with the background shifting to a montage of video clips from the past four years. As the night drags on, that's looking less likely.

Kath doesn't know anyone beyond Jim McGuire, the President's Chief of Staff. And she hasn't seen him in hours. Kath's sitting at a table near the front with a bunch of campaign donors and supporters. They all know who she is, but she knows nothing about them beyond their name tags and pleasantries. Where the hell is Nolan when she needs him? Being a general in the US Air Force, there was no way he was turning out for either side of politics. *Just come for a drink*, she said. *Fly halfway across the country for a drink?* he replied, laughing at her over the phone. *You flew halfway to the stars for an alien*, she said, only that joke fell flat. And here she is alone, smiling and making polite conversation with people that might as well be at a funeral.

"CNN has called Michigan, Indiana, and Pennsylvania for us," one of the men at the table says, staring down at his phone. His voice is flat. Even he doesn't believe what he's saying.

"Georgia's too close to call," the woman next to him says. "I think it's going to swing toward us."

Kath loves her confidence. She doesn't know. Both of these people are parroting online talking points. There's an underlying assumption that the pundits on TV are correct when, if anything, they're leading the count. Regardless of which news network these people follow, all the anchors want to be the first with a *Breaking Story!*

Kath's quiet, but she can see the woman's smartphone. 17% of the vote in Georgia has been counted. Given the vast differences between rural and suburban Georgia, it's impossible to draw any conclusions from such a small return, especially without knowing where those votes were counted. Where have those returns come from? The scientist in her wants to yell, *Stop extrapolating from incomplete data!* Damn it, Kath. That would not go down well.

"If she loses Arizona," someone else says and Kath knocks back her champagne, drinking the whole flute at once. Ah, if only she were sitting at home in LA. She'd play a proper drinking game with comments like these and be as drunk as a skunk before midnight.

Kath checks her phone. It's just after 11 PM. While everyone else is looking at election results, she sorts through her emails. Life doesn't stop.

A waiter walks between tables, offering late-night hors d'oeuvres on a silver platter. There's shrimp in edible phyllo pastry cups, bacon-encased roasted chestnuts and bruschetta, but it's the meatballs in chimichurri sauce that catch her eye. Toothpicks rise out of them. Kath's got her phone in her right hand. She goes to grab a toothpick with her left hand but she doesn't have enough dexterity.

"Sorry," she says, apologizing for holding up the waiter. He doesn't seem to mind but she feels as though she's an interruption, delaying everyone else from snacking. She puts down her phone and switches hands, grabbing one of the meatballs by a toothpick. The other guests at her table stare, unsure what's going on. Kath offers a brief smile but no explanation, biting into the meatball with a little too much fake enthusiasm to cover for being clumsy. "Mmmm."

Ever since her encounter with *Anduru* in deep space, out by one of the Lagrange points beside the Moon, she's worn gloves to hide her disfigured hands.

The Orion spacecraft she was in was badly damaged. Life-support failed. She and the crew suited up, prolonging the inevitable. As their power faded and their body heat was slowly lost, frostbite set in. They were rescued, but not before irreversible tissue damage had been done. Kath lost fingers and toes and almost lost the tip of her nose.

To this day, Kath has a scar where skin grafts were used to replace necrotic tissue on her face. She lost all four fingers on her left hand, but her surgeons were able to save the stubs leading to three of the knuckles. On her right hand, she kept her index finger but lost the others, leaving only partially flexible stubs. The geniuses at MIT, though, used 3D printing to build an exoskeleton that fits over the fleshy knobs, mimicking the motion of fingers. Wearing gloves allows her to hide the thin plastic frame from sight. She can't juggle, but she can pick up a glass of wine, so all is not lost. Her disfigured hands, though, leave her feeling self-conscious.

McGuire slips out a side door near the front of the stage. He follows the false wall within the ballroom toward the back. Kath sees him. As far as she's concerned, this is her cue. She's instantly on the move. Kath grabs her purse and excuses herself. She plots an intercept course and catches him in the corner.

"What's up?"

The look in McGuire's eyes is one of devastation and heartache.

Kath's a pragmatist. For her, there's a need for resolution. Either the President's won or she hasn't. Either way, let's get this over with. Kath's ready to head back to her hotel and get some sleep. On seeing McGuire, though, the prospect of a loss hits her at a deeper, more personal level. She might look at this as the mechanics of democracy playing out, but it's more than that. The skeptic in her considers politics as a glorified personality contest, but it's the implication of those politics that are important. Politics leads to policy, and that changes the shape of the country. Kath thought President Aston was a sure bet for

31

no other reason than she's worked with her and found her to be a woman of integrity. To Kath's mind, Wilson's a fake. If people can't see that, they're stupid. Only they're not. Besides, even if they were stupid, they still get a vote.

"She's calling him now," McGuire says, fighting back tears. "It's over."

"What?" Kath says in disbelief. "What about Michigan and Indiana? Georgia?"

"They've all gone to Wilson. The reporting you're seeing is delayed. We get counts slightly ahead of release. Once they counted Detroit, Michigan turned into a landslide against us. And as for Florida, well, Florida always was a swamp."

McGuire pushes on past a couple of reporters, making for the camera crew and the lighting team at the back of the room. Kath follows him. A sense of impending doom weighs on her. Kath's mind casts back to the debate. All the bluster. All the threats. All the vitriol and anger over *Anduru*. It's no longer hollow. Wilson is calling the shots now—or he will be by late January. As much as Kath would like to think she can appeal to reason, she knows President Aston was unique in that regard. That era is over.

McGuire talks with the production crew and then makes a phone call. "We're ready."

The lights dim. Silence descends on the ballroom.

The President walks out into the spotlights and, from around the room, people stand and applaud, only there's no cheering. Everyone knows. They may not want to admit it, they may still cling to hope beyond reason, but they know.

"Thank you," the President says, signaling for the audience to be seated. "Just moments ago, I called Senator Wilson to concede the race. At this point, it's clear to me Senator Wilson has won the US Presidential election. In a democracy like ours, there's nothing more important than the peaceful, orderly transfer of power, and that starts with the acceptance of electoral results. We, the people, have spoken. Through the ballot box, we have chosen new leadership—and I respect that. I called to be the first to congratulate him on becoming the 49th President of the United States of America."

The silence following those remarks is painful.

McGuire stands beside Kath in the control booth. He has his hand up, gripping his jaw. Clenched fingers cover his lips.

"I told President-elect Scott Joseph Wilson he has my full support during the transition to his administration. I have instructed my chief of staff and cabinet members to extend every courtesy to the incoming administration. Although this is not the outcome our party sought, we stand united as a country. We cannot let our political differences divide us."

President Aston reaches up and wipes away a single tear.

"Over the centuries, people all around the world have looked at our country from afar and wondered about our strength. From whence does it come? Does it arise from our military? Does it stem from our industrial capabilities? Our size? Or our technical innovation and ingenuity? I say our strength has always come from our unity. *One nation under God, indivisible, with liberty and justice for all.*

"Regardless of who is in the White House, we are one people. We may have our differences, but these are differences in policy, not passion. The outcome we seek is the same—*life, liberty, and the pursuit of happiness.* That's been the American dream for well over two hundred and fifty years, and it will continue to be the end we pursue for at least the next two hundred and fifty years.

"The Great Seal of the United States of America reads *E Pluribus Unum—Out of many, one.* America is at its best when we work together for a common goal, when we help each other, when we reach out as one.

"Your support over the past four years has been deeply appreciated. Your strength has been unwavering. Without you, I don't know that I would be standing here today. Our nation has faced challenges I could not have imagined when I stood before the Chief Justice at my inauguration, taking the Oath of Office. I don't know what the next four years hold, but I wish President-elect Wilson and his administration nothing but smooth seas and following winds. My

33

position is—if he succeeds, we all succeed.

"Thank you and goodnight."

The President bites her lower lip. Her eyes go watery. There's more she wants to say, but Kath can see she can't bring herself to continue.

President Aston's hands tremble. She nods, acknowledging the audience, and turns, walking off stage. Around the room, people sob.

Kath is numb. It's difficult to comprehend but, just like that, the world has changed. A storm is coming. She can feel it. A crowd mills around within the hall. They want something more, but nothing can change the outcome of the election.

"What now?" Kath asks, turning to McGuire.

He's brutal in his assessment of what's coming next.

"Get a lawyer. Get yourself a damn—good—lawyer."

MUSTANG

"We're now boarding group one passengers," a flight attendant says over a microphone to the travelers gathered at the airport gate. Roughly half of the people seated in front of the ceiling-to-floor glass windows get to their feet—far more than the number of seats being called. Kath understands. They're hedging their bets. By the time they trundle through the line, the announcement for the next section will have been called and they'll have worked their way to the front. Besides, if they get to the counter before then, the flight attendant is hardly going to send them back. She'll sigh and wave them through.

Kath fiddles with her gloves, making sure the 3D printed skeleton beneath the thin silk is set properly over the stubs of her fingers. Taking them off and putting them back on again after passing through airport security is always a pain. It's the looks she gets. Most passengers take off shoes and belts. Kath takes off her fingers. People try not to stare, but they can't help themselves. No one's mean. It's the novelty. Her hands are unusual. They're a spectacle. Something to behold. Only that leaves her feeling more and more self-conscious each time.

Rain lashes the glass. A storm is sweeping down from the north. The wind howls across the tarmac. Baggage handlers in florescent wet-weather gear brave the elements to load suitcases into the cargo hold. It's going to be a rough flight.

35

Group two is called.

Kath avoids the temptation to get up early.

A few minutes later groups three through five are called at the same time, which seems redundant to her. Why even bother with these additional groupings? Why not just say everyone else can come up?

Kath joins the line. She's seated in 44A by the window. If she's judged the flight correctly, she should be about five rows from the back of the plane, at the point the fuselage begins to taper toward the tail. The offset-seating there means there's a little more room. Oh, the seats are still about as practical as a sardine can, but the geometry of a tapering cylinder means a seat has to be pulled from the middle of the row to account for the narrowing space, and that means there's a bit more room between the armrest and the window on the sides of the plane. Like any good scientist, Kath has undertaken a thoughtful review of the seating plan and determined 44A is the optimum position for her. She's left-handed so it's easier to work on her laptop in that seat. Also, she can prop a pillow up and lean sideways to get a little more comfortable, leaning against the airframe.

When it comes to survivability in a crash, she has four exits within six seats in either direction. Being seated near the front of the plane might allow passengers to get off quicker at the gate, but that's low on her list of considerations. With a pair of noise-canceling headphones on and some tunes playing in her ear, an extra minute on the tarmac is meaningless. Statistically, those at the rear of a plane have more chance of walking away in a crash, so she'd rather wait to disembark. Besides, there's some aesthetic value in a window seat set well back from the wings. She'll get a great view of downtown Los Angeles and the Hollywood hills as they approach LAX. But the biggest consideration is space—that extra 2-3 inches to her left will be pure bliss. In the hyper-competitive world of air travel, an extra inch to stretch out in is bliss.

Kath gazes half-heartedly at her smartphone as she stands in line, shuffling forward. She's reading the news, most of which is old and regurgitated. The election was almost two weeks ago and yet it still dominates the headlines. One by one, passengers board. When her turn comes, she brings up the virtual ticket on her phone and a buff flight attendant in a tight shirt scans the code.

"Ms. McKenzie, can I get you to go to the service desk?"

"It's Dr. McKenzie, and sure—if it means an upgrade to first class?"

She smiles, but nothing more is offered in reply. The flight attendant deliberately ignores her playful comment, reaching out to scan the next ticket. Okay, that's a little rude. Whatever. Kath wheels her cabin baggage to the service desk. She's made traveling light a fine art and doesn't bother checking in bags. One Kath McKenzie, two bras, three pairs of socks, four pairs of underwear, five shirts, and a couple of skirts, and that's it. That and some gym gear. It means she has to do laundry one to two times a week, but that's no hardship for her.

"Hi," she says warmly to the flight attendant at the service desk beside the gate. "I'm Dr. Kathleen McKenzie. I'm on flight UX 577 to LA."

"Oh, yes. Ms. McKenzie. Just one moment."

Another flight attendant is talking to someone on the phone. "Yes, she's here... Okay. Understood."

Kath tries to hide her annoyance at the staff's insistence on ignoring her title as it was included on the booking and can be seen on her electronic ticket. Apparently, women aren't supposed to be doctors. Besides, the only real doctors deal with patients, not supernovae, right? She sighs.

Kath pulls her purse higher on her shoulder and leans on the counter.

"Can I ask what this is about?"

"Just one moment, Ms. McKenzie."

Before she realizes what's happening, two police officers flank her.

Guns make Kath nervous regardless of who's carrying them. It's the implication that death can be dispensed arbitrarily with the squeeze of a trigger. The officers are decked out in law enforcement equipment: thick black waist belts, stuffed pouches, handcuffs, tasers, pepper spray.

"Dr. McKenzie. Would you come with us please?"

Finally, she's being called *doctor*, but by someone she'd rather not meet. As for *would* and *please*, this isn't an invitation. Beyond those words lies the threat of force.

"There must be some mistake," Kath says, talking to the distinctly nervous flight attendant. "What is going on?"

"Please," the flight attendant says. "Don't make a scene."

For whose benefit? The airline and their staff? The other passengers? Or to avoid being strong-armed by the airport police?

"Where are you taking me?" Kath asks, addressing one of the officers.

"This way," he replies. He knows precisely where he's taking her. That he refuses to even name a location or an office is deliberate. It leaves her feeling powerless.

Kath is numb. It's the implication that unbearable pressure could be applied at any moment. Authority demands compliance. She has no say in this. No recourse. No right of appeal. None. She could run, but where? And why should she run? She hasn't done anything wrong. A taser in the back is hardly the kind of explanation she's after. Already, some of the passengers boarding the flight are taking photos. Far from being a celebrity, Kath is at least a public figure. As one of the lead investigators on *Anduru*, she was on television. They all know that—the passengers, the flight staff and the police.

The cops are foot soldiers. They're doing what they're told. For now, Kath's best strategy is to comply until she can reach out to someone in charge.

A hand presses against her lower back, urging her on. It's subtle but forceful. The other officer takes her cabin baggage from her. Against her better judgment, Kath walks away from the gate with them.

Once they're in the concourse, she asks, "What is all this about? I have a flight to catch."

She's stating the obvious, but it needs to be said. She blabbers on with, "I'm supposed to be in LA. It's Thanksgiving next week. I'm catching up with my grandma."

"You're not going anywhere, ma'am. You're on the *no-fly list*."

"What?" Kath comes to a halt, turning to face the officer. "That's ridiculous. There's been some kind of mistake."

The police officer raises a sheet of paper, reading from it. "Dr. Kathleen McKenzie, Apartment 2a, 522 Orange Grove Boulevard, Pasadena?"

"Yes."

"Born 17th January 1995?"

"Yes."

"No mistake."

Again, a firm hand settles in the small of her back.

"One phone call, right?" she says. "I get to make a call."

"You're not under arrest, ma'am. My instructions are to escort you from the terminal."

Kath reaches into her purse, pulls out her phone and scrolls through her contacts before pressing the call button. The phone rings. And rings. The call ends abruptly without going to a message service. Damn it, Jim. Pick up. Kath tries again.

After a few rings, a single word is spoken in haste.

"McGuire."

"Jim, it's Kath."

"Not a good time."

Tears roll down her cheeks. Kath is at a loss for words. Her lips quiver. She's never felt more intimidated in her life. She doesn't know who else she can call.

"They—They stopped me at the airport. I—I'm on the *no-fly list*."

There's silence on the line. In the background, there's an argument. President Aston is in a heated discussion with someone. There's shouting. A door is slammed.

In hushed tones, McGuire says, "Stay where you are. I'll call you back."

The officers escort Kath through airport security and out in front of the terminal. People stare. The circus is in town. Smartphones are held with cameras at the ready, longing for the latest five seconds of fame but Kath isn't going to do anything stupid.

"Do you need us to get you a cab?" the lead officer asks, finally dropping his hand from the center of her back.

"No. I'm fine."

Kath sits down on a concrete wall facing the road. She rests her feet on her suitcase. Birds flutter through the bushes behind her. Passengers continue to arrive, piling out of cabs and shuttle buses, gathering their luggage and heading inside. Airplanes roar into the sky every few minutes. The two police officers stand beside the automatic doors. Occasionally, they talk to someone using the radio microphones slung over their shoulders. They try to be discreet, but various passengers follow their gaze, noting Kath's the only person waiting outside the terminal.

Hours pass.

Night falls.

Kath's butt cheeks hurt. It's the rough concrete. She can't get comfortable. She needs to pee, but she can't go back into the terminal and pride demands she stays put until she hears from McGuire. Kath toys with her phone, flicking through Twitter and fighting the temptation to call him again. Clouds loom overhead. Thunder rumbles through the air, competing with the roar of departing flights. Rain continues to fall, but she's sheltered by the covered entrance extending out over the road.

Kath stares at her phone, willing it to ring.

20% battery remaining.

Come on, McGuire.

Her finger is poised over the touchscreen button. His name stares up at her from the screen. The call button is right there, but she doesn't press it. Jim won't forget her. If he's delayed in getting back to her, it's because all hell is breaking loose and he's fighting demons of his own. She knows that, and yet she still feels abandoned.

Kath almost drops her phone when it finally rings.

"Hello?" she says even though she can see the call has come from him.

"Kath, where are you?"

"Dulles."

He pauses. She knows him well enough to realize he's picking his words with care.

"I'm sorry you got caught up in all this."

"What's going on, Jim?"

"The President-elect is throwing his weight around."

"I don't understand? He isn't actually the President yet, right? Not until he's sworn in. He doesn't actually have any authority until after the inauguration."

"The term that's being thrown around here is *mandate*," McGuire says. "The transition team is bullish. They're making our lives hell. They're saying President Aston's a lame duck. They're accusing her of stonewalling them. They're demanding she makes all kinds of concessions. Basically, they can't wait until January 20th to seize power."

"But they have to," Kath says. "It's in the Constitution, right?"

Kath's not actually sure where that date comes from, but she knows that's when power transfers from one US President to another.

McGuire says, "The problem is, they're threatening to go public with their grievances. It's a case of—*do this the hard way, or we can do it the really hard way.* They've won, Kath. We're screwed. They get to set the agenda for the next four years and we're left licking our wounds."

"What about me?" Kath asks. She doesn't mean to sound selfish, but she wants to get home. She's been humiliated and it hurts.

"Can you get a car?"

41

"A car?" she says, almost dropping her phone. "You want me to drive across America?"

There's silence on the phone. Kath follows up with, "Why am I on the *no-fly list*, Jim? I haven't done anything wrong."

"I know. I know," McGuire replies. "Listen, I've spoken with Director Johnson at the FBI. I've asked him for clarification on your classification, but we have to tread lightly. The White House cannot be seen to interfere with a federal investigation during the transition period."

"A federal investigation?" Kath asks. "I haven't broken the law."

"You know that and I know that," McGuire says. "The problem is, facts don't matter in the wake of our election loss. It's all about public opinion. President-elect Wilson is happy to lose in court if he wins in the media. It's a question of timing. He wins today, making headline news and stirring up strife. He doesn't care if a case gets thrown out of court in a couple of months. By then, the damage is already done."

"Jesus," Kath says, running her gloved hand up through her hair. "But Director Johnson was appointed by President Aston, right? He can help."

"The FBI is like a sieve at the moment. There are leaks all over the place. The last thing the President needs right now is someone going public with an accusation of impropriety. Director Johnson has said he'll provide guidance on why the decision was made, but he won't reverse it. He can't. Not without stepping on toes. The middle management layer over there is auditioning for the new boss. They're not going to make waves for the sake of their careers."

"This is bullshit," Kath says.

"In a nutshell, yes. Look, I spoke to a few friends on Wall Street. I think I can get you on a private flight, but it can't be traced back to me. The government can't be seen to be providing you with any favors."

"Me?" Kath says, raising her eyebrows in alarm. "I'm the problem? How am I the problem?"

"These things are messy," McGuire says. "These guys love to

muddy the waters. They don't want black and white. They want a murky grey. Doubt is all they need to claim a scalp."

Kath hangs her head.

McGuire says, "This is just the start. They're going to come after us—all of us. Again. And again. And they ain't gonna play fair. You've got to be ready, Kath."

"But I haven't done anything wrong."

"I know. I know. It's not about what you have or haven't done. It's about power. Don't forget that. This isn't about right or wrong—it's about spite."

Kath is quiet. She's never been the target of such unbridled vitriol.

"Look," McGuire says. "Get a hotel for the night and I'll see what I can arrange with Bill Magnelli from EskaBall. He's crisscrossing the country all the time in his Learjet. I'm sure I can get you a seat. And, hey, it'll be a lot more enjoyable than a commercial flight."

The shuttle bus for a car rental company pulls up. Plastered on the side is a picture of a red Mustang convertible. The smooth lines, dark grille, chrome wheels and low-set body kit all scream of raw power. In Kath's mind, she can already hear the throaty roar of the engine. There's a woman in the driver's seat. The top is down. The wind is in her hair. That could be Kath. Damn it. It will be Kath.

"Thanks for the offer, but I think I'll drive."

"Really?" he asks.

"Oh, I think this might be fun."

"Okay," McGuire says. "Listen. If anything else comes up, if you hit any bumps in the road, I'm only ever a phone call away."

"Thanks," she says, grabbing her suitcase and boarding the bus.

COLORADO

"Landis."

"Hey, Nolan. How are you doing?"

"Kath?" Nolan says, getting to his feet and walking away from his desk. Behind him, both computer screens fall dark as the security switch in his seat automatically locks them. He walks out into the corridor at NORAD. "What's happening?"

"I—um—I'm in town. Just passing through. Thought you might like to grab lunch."

"You're in town? My town? Today? Like now?"

Kath laughs. "I'm on I-25 heading down from Denver. So. How about lunch with an old friend?"

"Um. Sure."

"Any good sushi down there?"

Nolan replies, "Ah, I don't know about raw fish this far inland, but there's a great burger bar in the Broadmoor Town Center."

"Broadmoor," Kath says. "M-double-O-R. Okay. Got it on Sat Nav. I'm twenty minutes away."

"Great," Nolan says, pleasantly surprised. "I'll see you there."

Something's wrong—horribly wrong. Nolan hasn't seen Kath

since they were awarded the Presidential Medal of Freedom. It's not that they've avoided each other so much as they've been locked in their own orbits. Kath was appointed as a director at JPL while the Air Force created a new division for Nolan. *Strategic Assessment* is an internal think tank looking at obscure threats. If it's already on someone else's radar, Nolan doesn't want to know about it.

Master Sergeant Jacinta Andrews reads the look on Nolan's face. She's worried. He may not have said anything but she's astute. A random phone call from an old friend like Kath is never social.

"Fancy a burger for lunch?" he says, grabbing his coat.

"Sure," is code for *whatever you need, boss.*

It's a fifteen-minute drive to the mall. As they're turning into the parking lot, a bright red Mustang convertible pulls alongside them. The top is down even though it's cold out. Kath's wearing dark aviator glasses and a smile a mile wide. Her hair is tossed, while her skin has a glow from being out in the sun and wind.

"Well, look at you," Nolan says, winding down his window. Kath simply smiles and pulls into an empty parking spot.

Jacinta greets Kath as she gets out of her car. "I've got to say, I'm liking the way NASA's spending its budget."

Kath laughs. "Oh, I wish."

After pleasantries have been exchanged, they order and take a seat in the restaurant. Rather than sitting outside, the three of them retreat into a secluded corner. Like most restaurants in the post-covid era, the burger bar has an open-air design, allowing the wind to swirl through, clearing the air. As it's autumn, the bar staff have portable gas heaters positioned nearby, sending radiant heat toward diners. The heaters are strategically placed and only turned on as needed. The bar has lots of lush green plants mounted in wooden sections, separating the eating area from the walkway outside. When winter sets in, they'll have to lower shutters to keep the plants from freezing, but for now, the ambient greenery is refreshing.

"So what's this about?" Nolan asks, knowing Kath all too well.

"I'm on the *no-fly list*."

If there's one thing Nolan loves about Kath, it's her ability to condense a complex subject into a succinct phrase. Normally, that relates to orbital mechanics or astrophysics, but she's just summarized the political machinations of Washington DC in six words. Jacinta's eyes go wide but she remains quiet. Kath grins in acknowledgment of her surprise.

"That bad, huh?" Nolan asks.

"Yep," she replies, sipping on some water. "I thought you should know."

Nolan nods. It's a slow, deliberate motion. Kath could have called him. She could have sent an email or a text message. That's normally how someone lets a friend know about things like this. Although she hasn't said as much, she's worried—and not just for herself. If she's driving from DC to LA, that's one helluva marathon effort. It's at least forty hours of driving time, but no one does it non-stop. Even with driver-assist technology helping on the freeway, it's an exhausting journey. And she's added at least five or six hours to her trip by diverting to Colorado Springs—regardless of whether she doubles back or drops down to Albuquerque.

"I take it they haven't come after you yet?" she asks.

"Military, you know. We're like pieces of furniture. They push us around wherever and whenever they want."

"So they're waiting to get into the command structure?"

"Probably."

"Listen," Kath says, leaning across the table and tapping one of the coasters. "This ain't over. We might be playing musical chairs with politicians down here, but that's nothing to *Anduru*. There will be another one out there. Hell, who am I kidding? One? There could be dozens on their way."

"I know."

Kath straightens her glass on the coaster, aligning it with the print of a sunflower.

"We've been running the numbers at JPL, looking to extrapolate from what we learned during the first pass, trying to predict future encounters."

"And?" Nolan says as their sodas arrive. Kath waits until they're alone before continuing.

"With only one interaction, there's no way to know for sure, but there are some reasonable assumptions we can draw."

A waiter comes over, delivering their food. Kath smiles politely and squirts some ketchup on the side of her plate. She munches on french fries as she talks. Nolan takes a bite of his burger. Jacinta doesn't move. Her eyes are glued on Kath, wanting to hear more.

"*Anduru* is what we'd classify as an invasive carrier. Normally, animals evolve in unison within a particular environment to form a distinct ecosystem. If antelopes get faster, lions have to adapt or they'll go extinct, so those cubs that have softer paws, better camouflage, and more explosive muscles to launch out of the long grass will keep pace with their faster prey. This tug-of-war between predators and prey forms a balance. It's sustainable. It might rock like a seesaw, but it's never grossly out of balance."

Nolan wipes some ketchup from his lip with a napkin, saying, "It's an arm's race."

"Exactly," Kath replies, twirling a french fry before devouring it. "On Earth, ecosystems are isolated from each other by oceans, deserts, mountain ranges, stuff like that. Within those ecosystems, there's a balance, but if those natural boundaries are crossed, a species that's in balance in one ecosystem can run out of control in another."

"You said *Anduru* was an invasive carrier," Jacinta says, still not having touched her food. "Can you explain that?"

"When Darwin sailed to the Galapagos, he was surprised to find land tortoises on the various islands there. Unlike turtles, they can't swim. Not for hundreds of miles. He wondered, how the hell did they get to the Galapagos? The answer is, they were carried out to sea by floodwaters. They spent weeks, possibly months clinging to anything that would float before ocean currents dragged them to the islands.

We're talking branches, matted vegetation, fallen logs, stuff like that."

"And that's *Anduru*?" Jacinta asks. "It's a raft?"

"Yes. Now, over on the mainland, adult tortoises have lots of predators—jaguar, puma, vultures, eagles."

"But not on the Galapagos," Nolan says.

"Uh-huh," Kath says, raising a finger in confirmation as she crunches on a fry. "So in the Galapagos, these guys are free to strip the islands of its vegetation. They grow to immense sizes there, up to 600 pounds."

Nolan says, "Because they have no natural predators."

"Exactly. On the mainland, their cousins struggle to reach half that weight."

"We are the Galapagos," Jacinta says.

"Yes. But when it comes to *Anduru,* it's the mode of transport that concerns me. The Galapagos were vulnerable because of the way ocean currents bring flotsam to the islands, but how often does that happen? Once every hundred years? Thousand years? Every ten thousand years? For the Galapagos, it's a low-probability random, chaotic event, but *Anduru...*"

Nolan nods. "*Anduru* was precise."

"Yes. *Anduru* was no accident."

Jacinta asks, "So how did it find us? How did it even reach us?"

Kath smiles from behind a disposable straw, slurping on her soda. "That's a good question. When it comes to the Galapagos, we can look at when the islands were formed and how ocean currents move. We can even set rafts afloat with GPS trackers and build models that refine our calculations."

"But *Anduru*?"

"When it comes to *Anduru,* we have a few ideas. First, life thrived here for 3.8 billion years without any encounters."

"That's a loooong time," Jacinta says.

"That's a very long time," Kath says. "It's *too* long a time. Given what we saw with the passage of *Anduru,* it's so long it's troubling."

"Why?" Jacinta asks.

"When it comes to science and the history of the cosmos, we see patterns. Everything repeats with a regular frequency. If we're curious about where stars are born or how planets form, all we have to do is look. Somewhere out there, everything is happening right now. Stars are going supernova. Black holes are colliding. Even within our own solar system, asteroids hit various planets all the time."

"But *Anduru?*" Nolan says.

"A one-off event is worrying. Things don't just happen once."

Jacinta says, "So you think there are more of these things inbound?"

"I think there *were* more of these things," Kath replies, switching the tense on her. "It's not simply a question of when will the next *Anduru* come, but has one come here before? "

"But this is the first one we've seen," Nolan says.

"We haven't been looking for long," Kath says.

Jacinta says, "If there were earlier encounters, wouldn't we have been overrun?"

"Not necessarily," Kath replies. "Think about how seeds fall from a tree. Some fall in the shade and can't take root. Others get eaten by birds or fall into streams and sink before they can germinate. Out of the thousands of seeds that fall, only a few drift in just the right way to land on fertile ground."

"So when it comes to past occurrences of *Anduru?*" Nolan asks.

"There could be near-misses," Kath says. "They could have hit on the wrong angle and formed a crater in the desert instead of skimming the atmosphere. They could overshoot us entirely or hit the Moon. There are lots of possibilities."

Jacinta says, "So we should be looking for past encounters?"

"Yes," Kath says. "I think we're more likely to find evidence of a past failure than spotting another one inbound."

"Interesting," Nolan says, eating a handful of fries. "So you think this has been happening for a while."

"It's more likely than *Anduru* being a one-off event."

"What attracted them?" Jacinta asks. "I mean, something drew them here, right? They ignored Venus and Mars."

"That's an interesting point," Kath says, sucking up the last of her diet coke. "3.8 billion years is an awfully long time. I doubt we've been constantly bombarded by these things as at least one of them would have stuck the landing by now. We need more data. We need a second point of comparison to be sure, but there may be something recent that's flagged Earth as ripe for harvest."

"Ripe?" Nolan asks.

"Jacinta's right," Kath says. "If these pods were distributed at random, they would have targeted Mars as well. If they were looking for basic bio-signatures in the atmosphere, they would have hit Earth two billion years ago during the Great Oxygenation Event."

"So what was it looking for?" Jacinta asks.

"I don't know," Kath says, finishing a bite of her burger. "But it's probably something recent. It could be radio waves. It could be pollution from the industrial revolution in the air. It could be nuclear isotopes. Whatever it was, it triggered a response. We're just not sure how many responses were triggered—and when."

"Are you expecting another one any time soon?" Nolan asks.

"Dunno," Kath replies. "In nature, various species have entirely different reproductive strategies. Some animals, like humans and elephants, have high-maintenance kids so they only have a few offspring. Cats and birds have a brief period in which they wean their young so they have larger clutches. Spiders and flies simply don't care so they have hundreds of offspring. Trees and plants will hit the thousands to tens of thousands of seeds. Basically, low cost results in bulk."

Nolan says. "So we're hoping they're more like us and less like a tree."

"That would be nice," Kath replies. "Given the difficulty of creating and launching these pods, I'm leaning toward rare rather than common."

"But not one," Nolan says. "You're thinking a few, but not thousands."

"Yes."

"Well, that's good news," he says.

Kath laughs. "Nothing about *Anduru* is good news."

"What about the Wilson defense plan?" Jacinta asks. "The lunar defense whatever he calls it?"

"Won't work," Kath says. "Any *Anduru*-class object will be moving too fast for us to engage. Even if we hit one of those things, we won't slow it down. If anything, we could deflect it into Earth or into some eccentric orbit that collides with Earth later."

"But if we hit it with a nuke?" Nolan says. "I mean, we destroyed the last one with a nuke."

"We got *inside* it," Kath says. "If we had to break through that outer shell, we'd still be floating around out there. Besides, anything that's inbound is going to be moving at hundreds of miles a second. Good luck setting up a rendezvous with that!"

"Okay," Nolan says, playing devil's advocate. "So we nuke it out by the Moon and deflect it, even slightly. Maybe it hits Earth. Maybe it doesn't. At least we stop it from hatching, right?"

Kath says, "As it is, *Anduru* is the equivalent of a biological weapon capable of taking out an entire planet. Nuke it out by the Moon and even if you destroy the biological material, you've still got hundreds of asteroid fragments inbound. About an hour later—just one hour after a successful hit—and you've got multiple impacts capable of taking out most of Europe and North America." She shakes her head, munching on a cold french fry as she adds, "Not a good plan."

"Yeah, that's not good," Jacinta says.

Kath raises an eyebrow. "And that's the best-case scenario for the lunar defense whatever."

"How long did it take *Anduru* to get here?" Nolan asks. "I mean, maybe they save their ammo. Maybe they'll only launch a second pod once they realize this one missed."

Jacinta asks, "If that's the case, when can we expect the next one?"

Kath shrugs. "I wish I knew. One data point isn't much to go on. And we saw it late. It was well inside our solar system even by the time the Russians picked it up."

Nolan sighs. "You want another coke?"

"No," Kath replies. "I need to get going. I've got a hotel booked in Santa Fe. I just wanted to catch up for a bit."

"For old time's sake," Nolan says, smiling.

Jacinta still hasn't touched her 7UP or her meal. "And you?" she asks Kath. "So you just drive everywhere now?"

"Hah, something like that." Kath leans over and pinches a cold french fry from Jacinta's plate, asking, "You're not hungry?"

"It's the end of the world, you know. It kinda ruins my appetite."

"You get used to it," Kath replies, smiling as she eats the fry.

Nolan says, "What about the shit-show down in Houston next year. Are you going?"

"The conference in March?" Kath replies. "If I'm not in prison. And you?"

"If they'll let me."

There's no mention of who *they* are. Nolan suspects he'll see her there regardless. It seems they're like north and south on a magnet, always being drawn together somehow. Kath gets to her feet, picking up her keys and swinging her bag over her shoulder. As they prepaid their meal before sitting down, they walk out into the carpark, thanking the staff as they leave. The sun is low on the horizon. A cool chill hangs in the air.

"And I'm sorry, okay," Kath says.

"For what?" Nolan asks.

"You know. If I get you in trouble for swinging by."

Nolan smiles. "I can look after myself."

"Oh," Kath replies. "Of that, I have no doubt."

She hits a button on her remote and the lights on her bright red Mustang flash as the doors unlock.

Jacinta calls out, "Take care of yourself, Kath."

"You too."

NORAD

Jacinta peppers Nolan with dozens of questions on the drive back to base. As they turn into the carpark, he says, "Did you notice what she didn't say?"

"No? What?" Jacinta asks, turning her head toward him in surprise.

"Anything about politics," he says. "Kath doesn't give a damn about taking sides. She'd rather not get caught up in it. She doesn't care. And she doesn't hold a grudge."

"No, she doesn't," Jacinta says as he brings the car to a halt and throws the shifter into park. They get out and walk toward the nondescript building where Nolan first had his crazy idea—that the Russians knew more than the Americans about an obscure comet that grazed Saturn. Back then, the world seemed like a much simpler place. Oh, sure, there was an alien coming to Earth. Most of the network pundits were running around like chickens with their heads lopped off, but for him, it was a straightforward problem. Analyze the risks. Consider the threats. Plan contingencies. Now, he doesn't know what to think.

The next *Anduru* could be approaching the Oort Cloud as he walks across the parking lot. Some previous *Anduru* might be still out there somewhere, having been deflected into an eccentric orbit. Like the booster stages of the Apollo program in the 60s, it might swing by Earth every couple of decades unnoticed. Or it might have crashed. It could have slammed into Earth a few centuries ago when barely anyone would have cared. What would a historical impact even look like today? What records would there be if it hit the Pacific before the age of European exploration? What if it struck high up on one of the Himalayan glaciers? Would it still be lying dormant beneath the ice, waiting until it slides down to the valley floor?

How far back should they be looking for abnormal atmospheric records? The 1800s? In Europe, there would be at least vague records as far back as the 1200s, but what about the rest of the planet? The Chinese were meticulous at keeping astronomical records, but the Polynesians relied on oral tradition. Tales of dragons flying through the air or islands being pulled from a raging sea are easily dismissed as folklore. Maybe there's more to them.

Nolan's lost in thought. He barely notices the two men in dark suits standing at the top of the stairs. They're wearing dark sunglasses even though they're in the shade and the sky's overcast.

"General Nolan?"

"Brigadier general," he says, correcting them out of habit.

Jacinta saw the two of them before he did. She slows her pace, recognizing their interest in Nolan. She comes up behind him, standing to one side. This is the reason Nolan takes her almost everywhere. She's sharp. People underestimate her. Not Nolan. If she's hanging back, it's with good reason.

"This doesn't concern you," one of the men says to Jacinta, nodding with his head for her to continue on inside.

"Fuck you," Nolan says, defending his research assistant. He holds his hand out, gesturing for her to stay put.

The silence that follows is awkward and that's fine with Nolan. Given these guys are civilians and not wearing any kind of ID, Nolan's got a fair idea whom he's dealing with. These chumps had to pass through two security checkpoints to get into this secure area. They

56

would have been issued with temporary security passes, but they think they're too damn important to wear them. Nolan can even see the outline of a pass in the older guy's trouser pocket. He's scrunched the lanyard cord in front of it, forming a distinct squiggle beneath the fine suit material.

If the incoming administration had the audacity to clip Kath's wings, it was only a matter of time before they flexed some muscle here. If anything, meeting Kath for lunch probably forced their hand. There's no sense in feigning pleasantries.

"Well," the lead suit says, taking his glasses off. He looks down at his shiny shoes for a moment, trying to wipe the grin from his face. "You don't disappoint."

He might struggle with eye contact, but Nolan doesn't. The brigadier general has his finger out, pointing at the guy's chest. He's on the verge of yelling as he hammers home his anger.

"You don't talk to a uniformed soldier like a bellhop. Show some goddamn respect."

"This is the way it's going to be, huh?" the younger man says, mimicking the older man and pulling off his glasses.

"State your purpose," Nolan says, ready for a fight.

Jacinta comes up beside him, but she's not looking at them, she's looking beyond them. She has one hand out, with her fingers spread wide, signaling to a couple of MPs stationed inside the building. She's telling them to hold where they are. They've seen the commotion and have come to the brigadier general's aid. One of them rests a hand on the door, with his other hand gripping his holstered sidearm. That doesn't go unnoticed by the two men in their fancy suits.

Nolan's a legend in the eyes of those that work on the base. The outside world might be hooked on conspiracy theories and slander, but the handful of senior officers that have read the classified report on *Anduru* have made it abundantly clear what they think. In their eyes, Nolan's a hero. And they haven't been shy about making their opinion known on the base. None of them agree with the President's decision to give Nolan a civilian medal rather than military honors. They understood the reasoning, but it doesn't mean they like it. If anything, his humility in not pressing for formal military recognition has only amplified their respect for him.

Nolan can see the realization in the eyes of the men standing opposite him. Coming here was a mistake. They should have nabbed him at home.

"We want to know where your loyalty resides," the older man says.

"My loyalty," Nolan asks, pointing at himself. "You're questioning *my* loyalty?"

"The President needs to know where your loyalty lies."

"President Aston knows precisely where my loyalty lies," Nolan says, goading them, knowing that's not what they mean. He's forcing them to spell it out.

"The President wants to know *he* has your support."

There it is—these guys are from the President-elect's transition team.

Nolan says, "You can be assured, I will continue to support and defend the Constitution of the United States."

Although his oath of office also includes the phrase, *against all enemies, foreign and domestic*, Nolan leaves that out. They know damn well what the oath says—and it's not about protecting people or positions. It's about the foundation of the country itself. But for all his bluster, Nolan's not trying to antagonize anyone by suggesting they could be a domestic threat. By coming here, they're sending him a message. He wants to ensure there's an equally clear response sent in reply. And he doesn't want to imply insubordination against a duly-elected official, even if they haven't taken office yet. It's enough for these assholes to know he's not playing games. Ambushing him on the steps of his office was a dog move. If anything, he's glad Jacinta's beside him as she's a witness of what's being said by both parties. And she's not dumb. She had her phone in her hand as they got out of the car. Now, she's got both hands behind her back, standing almost to attention.

58

Nolan's known her long enough to know she's keeping her phone out of sight for a reason. She must be recording the conversation.

A light rain falls, being blown by the wind. The grey clouds rolling over the mountains darken the sky. Thunder rumbles in the distance.

"We need you to keep us in the loop on *Anduru*."

Nolan smiles. These guys are fucking amateurs.

He says, "As private citizens, you're welcome to submit a Freedom of Information request with the Department of Defense. Be specific about the information you want. Any response will be carefully assessed in light of national security."

The older man with grey hair says, "The President—"

Nolan cuts him off. He steps forward, breaking into the guy's personal space and forcing him to step back. It takes all his restraint not to tap the man's chest. Nolan keeps his finger just beyond the man's deep red tie, barely a fraction of an inch from his starched white shirt.

"Let's get this straight," he says, towering over him. "The United States only ever has *one* President. Until noon on January 20th, that is President Elizabeth Aston. When Senator Wilson is sworn in, he will assume that office and take on that constitutional authority. Now, I get that you're part of the transition team. I get that you're keen to start moving on things, but you're going to need to be patient. The US military does not embrace your enthusiasm for bending the rules."

"Your work—"

Nolan lowers his hand, clenching his fist. "My work feeds directly into the daily briefing to the Joint Chiefs of Staff. If they think anything I've reported has any importance or bearing on national security, they'll include it in the President's Daily Briefing. My understanding is that briefing is being shared with President-elect Wilson. I'm sorry, gentleman, you're wasting your time here in Colorado."

"Stay away from NASA," the older man says, walking toward the steps. Nolan doesn't bite. He has no idea what the man means by that and he doesn't care. Nolan's not taking orders from anyone outside the chain of command.

The two men retreat down the stairs. The MPs walk outside, joining Jacinta and Nolan under the portico. No one says anything. They stand there watching, waiting for the men to get in their car and leave. Red taillights disappear into the rain.

"Everything okay, sir?" one of the MPs asks.

"All good, thanks."

Nolan and Jacinta go inside and take the broad staircase to their floor.

"You caught all that, right?" Nolan asks.

"Oh, hell yeah," Jacinta replies, holding up her phone. "What's the plan, boss?"

"Forget about those guys. Kath needs our help. From here on, we've got to look both ways. We've got to figure out if anything's coming at us—or if anything came and we missed it."

"Understood."

They turn at the top of the stairs and walk into the open-plan office. General Cooper is sitting on the edge of Nolan's desk, looking out over the carpark.

"You having fun?" he asks.

"Always."

General Cooper gets up, still looking at the gates and the blur of cars leaving the base in the rain. He carries himself with a sense of pride and purpose. Although he's only partially bald, Cooper keeps his head clean-shaven and smooth. He runs his hand up over the slight regrowth. If he could, Nolan's sure the general would shave several times a day just to keep that slick, smooth feeling beneath his hand. His only facial hair is a carefully groomed mustache and his pencil-thin eyebrows. With a heavily starched shirt and pressed trousers, General Cooper always looks impeccable.

"I'm getting some heat from the Pentagon," the general says, tapping the window and pointing in the direction of the main road.

"And?" Nolan asks.

"And you make a lot of people nervous, Brigadier General Nolan Landis."

"But not you," Nolan says, stepping up beside him and staring out into the gloom.

"Not me," Cooper replies. "All those ass-licking career officers climbing over each other up there. I don't know if they want to kill you or kiss you."

"So what do they want?" Nolan asks.

"They want to know everything. If you so much as scratch your ass, they want to be informed."

Jacinta tries not to smile at that comment.

"What did you tell them?" Nolan asks.

The general walks away, saying, "I told them to fuck off!"

For all the bluster, Nolan knows there's a day coming when he'll have to work with these assholes. Oh, it'll come down through the chain of command, but they'll petition the Secretary of Defense and instruct the Pentagon to allow them direct access to Nolan and his team. That's when the real games will begin.

GRAND
JURY

"And I shouldn't be worried by this?" Kath asks, sitting forward on the edge of the seat in her lawyer's office in Los Angeles.

It's February.

The last few months have flown by. The US election, Thanksgiving, Christmas, New Year's Day, the inauguration (which Kath deliberately avoided, refusing to watch it on TV), and her birthday have all rushed by in the blink of an eye. That's what happens when she buries herself in her work.

Kath's been so busy trying to formulate new ways to detect another *Anduru* she missed the holiday season. Oh, she went to her grandmother's for Thanksgiving and spent Christmas down in San Diego at her Mom's place, but beyond that, she's been poring over research papers. Rather than looking at existing astronomical surveys, she's trying to understand emerging ideas for new techniques to spot dark objects using the James Webb Space Telescope. Its sensitivity to infrared is a bonus. Kath's looking for anything that might give humanity an edge. To be forewarned is to be forearmed. If they can gain months' or even years' notice of an incoming threat, they can respond more effectively.

Then a letter arrived and it was as though life went from fast forward to pause.

The envelope alone was ominous. It had the US Department of Homeland Security logo on it and was made of thick material with a small plastic window inset into the envelope. There was a letter inside with her address lined up in the tiny window, but she knew it wasn't a bill. Homeland Security doesn't work like that. Besides, it was heavy. There were at least eight to ten folded pages. On opening the envelope, Kath saw a disruptive pattern printed on the inside to prevent anyone from viewing the letter before it was opened by holding it up to a bright light. Yep, this was not good news. Now, she's paying $720 an hour for legal advice. McGuire recommended these guys. Kath isn't going to second-guess him for the sake of saving her vacation money—not when the alternative is a vacation behind bars.

"No," Jonathan Masters says, leaning back in his chair.

The office reeks of money, which makes Kath uncomfortable. To one side, there's a plush couch with inset buttons pulling the shiny dark leather taut. Has anyone ever sat on it? If they did, they wouldn't make a dent. It's the kind of couch that's for show, not for comfort. The big armrests and deep back look as though they'd swallow her whole.

Behind the couch, there's a floor-to-ceiling bookshelf stretching the length of the room. Back at JPL, she has a shelf like this, only hers is messy. She has a computer printer hanging over the edge on one side. Piles of printed paper stacked in a mess on the other. Her books are shoved in no particular order, with no regard for size, shape, or color. Once she had an assistant that set up a structured filing system along with labeled folders, but like all good assistants, he got promoted and moved on. A half-assed categorization system mixed with her excitement-of-the-day approach to dumping things on the nearest clear shelf is chaos. A tornado could tear through her office and no one would ever know it by looking at her bookcase. Here, though, every book has been meticulously placed. The spines align. The books are grouped in sequence and by color. Damn, if any of these books are actually used for anything other than display, Jonathan would be able to find something quite quickly. For her, such a task borders on miraculous. Not only does she envy the bookcase, but it intimidates her into doing better back at JPL.

"It's an access play," Jonathan says. "By calling a grand jury and telling you about it, they're trying to intimidate you. It's a game. They want you to freak out and make a mistake."

"I don't understand," Kath replies, clutching her hands together as though she were back in grade school, sitting before the principal.

"They're hoping you do something dumb and make this easy for them. But think about it. By telling you there's a grand jury, they're admitting they don't have enough to prosecute you in open court. They're digging around. They're looking for dirt. What they really want is your records. That's why they're doing this. They think you may have something incriminating."

"But I don't."

"They think you do, although you may not even know it," he says, "Going through legal discovery won't help them understand *Anduru*. They're the government. They already have all those files. Oh, it'll be interesting for us. We'll look for any angles we can exploit, but they get no benefit from discovery other than access to your personal correspondence."

"My personal correspondence?" Kath asks absentmindedly. She's unsure what that phrase means in this context. "With Eugene?"

Kath doesn't understand how her partner comes into this.

"The terms of reference are limited to anything related to how the Aston administration handled the crisis."

Kath grimaces. That explanation isn't helping.

Jonathan says, "You don't have to reveal anything about the nature of your relationship with Eugene if it doesn't relate to *Anduru*."

"Well, it doesn't," she says. "What exactly do they mean when they say, *personal correspondence?*"

Jonathan picks up the sheet of paper he's been jotting notes on, holding it up for her to see. "Anything like this. Anything where you wrote down your thoughts. Anything outside of the official records on your government computer account."

"Hmmm," Kath says. Trying to remember passing details from two years ago is nigh on impossible, although she suspects that's the point. If she fails to produce something, it'll be spun as deliberate. Obstruction of justice is a crime in its own right.

"So if you sent an email about *Anduru* from a personal account, that would be personal correspondence. If you wrote a note on paper or called someone to talk about *Anduru,* that would also be personal correspondence."

"I drew lots of diagrams on whiteboards," she says.

"Did anyone take photos of them?"

"I don't know. Maybe?"

"We need to check. It may not be the diagrams themselves that are important but other notes written to the side. Basically, they're trying to piece together a jigsaw puzzle and they need to know they've got all the pieces."

Kath shrugs, saying, "I wrote on scraps of paper—a lot of paper."

"Where did that paper go?"

"Um. I can check with Jacinta. If something wasn't relevant or we learned more, I'd toss the old stuff in the bin."

"Whenever you work for the government," Jonathan says, slowing down his words and speaking with intentional clarity. "Throw—nothing—out."

Kath nods.

"This is important," he says. "From here, *nothing* goes in the waste paper basket, right?"

"Right," she says, feeling scolded.

"18 US Code section 2232 relates to the destruction of evidence. It's important you realize it carries a potential five-year jail term."

Kath swallows the lump rising in her throat as he continues.

"Also, under the code, you're forbidden to discuss the discovery process with foreign nationals. Do you understand what that means?"

Kath nods.

"From here on out, you need to be careful about what you say and to whom. We cannot afford any grey areas. If you take a call from someone in Europe or Asia, put it on speakerphone and drag someone else into your office as a witness. I don't care if you're talking about horoscopes or ordering Chinese takeout, you need proof you're *not* circumventing the grand jury. Don't give these guys any ammo to use against you."

"Ah," Kath says sheepishly, "When it comes to Chinese takeout..."

"What?" Jonathan asks. His voice is stern, but a little confused. He was being metaphorical, not literal.

Kath isn't sure how to explain the background behind the passage of *Anduru* across the Gulf of Mexico. At the time, everyone thought the alien object was a spaceship in the traditional sense of the word. The assumption was the UFO would pull some kind of high-tech, Hollywood-style, physics-defying maneuver to come to a halt. Kath was thinking warp drives or something. The reality is, Kath wasn't thinking, the Chinese were.

"You're going to have to explain," Jonathan says with his eyes narrowing.

"We weren't listening," Kath says. "We were so focused on how First Contact would unfold, who would talk to our extraterrestrial visitors and what we'd say, we stopped talking to each other."

"I don't understand," Jonathan says, leaning forward on his desk.

Most lawyers have computers on their desks, but not Jonathan. There's a leather desk blotter protecting the polished mahogany and an empty vase in one corner for decoration. No laptop. No screen. No keyboard or computer mouse. No desk phone. Jonathan brought the paper pad and pen he's using with him. Kath gets the impression this office is where contracts are signed, not where actual work is undertaken. Given she's a high-profile client, they're trying to impress her. Impress, though, is the wrong term. Perhaps intimidate would be better.

"Ah, I don't think it was deliberate," Kath says. "But with *Anduru* inbound, everyone was in shock. There was so much to do and the clock was running down to zero. The State Department, NASA, even our office—we were all so goddamn busy we weren't listening."

"To whom?" Jonathan asks.

"To the Chinese."

Jonathan leans back, getting a sense of what's coming. He purses his lips, holding them tight in front of clenched teeth.

"It's not their fault," Kath says, appealing with her hands out in front of her. "They couldn't get anyone's attention."

"Except yours?"

"They sent me some Chinese takeout."

Jonathan waves his hand back and forth. "Wait a minute. What do you mean *sent*? You don't *send* takeout. You *order* takeout."

"I was sitting at my desk," Kath says.

"In the White House?"

Jonathan wants detail so Kath gives it to him.

"Next door. In the Eisenhower Executive Office. Second floor. Back of the building. They call it the *Süd-Ost* corner. It was built in 1888 using classic European architecture. They used German terms back then."

Kath's rambling.

Jonathan is not impressed, but he is taking notes.

"*Süd-Ost* means southeast," she says, composing herself. "Ah, I was seated in the corner room, opposite the stairs. Desk 304. Overlooking the White House South Lawn."

Without looking up from his pad, he says, "And?"

"And I got a call from the front desk saying there was a delivery waiting for me at the West entrance."

"But you didn't order any food?"

"No."

It's obvious Jonathan is taking pains to remain composed. He places his pad on the desk, arranging the pen neatly on top, and breathes deeply, saying, "You're working in one of the most secure environments in the world, less than a hundred feet from the White House, and you accepted an unsolicited package?"

"Ah," Kath says, looking down at her feet. "When you put it like that..."

Right now, she feels more like a kid on their first day of school than the lead astrophysicist for NASA's Jet Propulsion Laboratory.

Jonathan clarifies, but whether that's for her benefit or his, she's not sure.

"And at that time, you were meeting with the President of the United States on an almost *daily* basis, right? And you accepted an unknown package from a foreign adversary?"

Kath cringes. She clenches her teeth together. Her lips pull back. The tendons in her neck go taut. Her eyes—she doesn't know what to do with her eyes. They dart back and forth, looking around the room. An awkward, "Yes," slips from her lips.

She grimaces. It's been two years and it's only now she realizes how foolish—how utterly stupid she was on that cold January day. She can still remember the snowflakes falling lazily from the grey sky.

"And what was in this takeout?"

"Ah, food," Kath says, trying to be helpful. "And a note."

"Did you tell anyone about this?" he asks.

"No," she says, rattling that word off a little too quickly. "Umm. I don't think so. Oh, I may have said something to Jacinta."

"Your research assistant?"

Kath nods, adding, "And the President."

"The President?" Jonathan says, almost leaping from his seat. "You told her? So she knew about this?"

"I don't know," Kath says, scrunching up her eyebrows and struggling to hold back tears. "I don't remember. I think so."

Jonathan is aghast. "You don't know?" He shakes his head, asking, "You're not sure whether you told the President of the United States you received unsolicited highly confidential information from a foreign adversary?"

"There was a lot going on," Kath says in her defense. "I mean, there was an alien spaceship hurtling toward Earth."

Jonathan says, "We're going to get eviscerated on the stand."

"I did what I thought was right," she says, but it doesn't sway Jonathan. He's still shaking his head.

He tears the page of notes from his pad and leans around the side of the desk, pushing it into a paper shredder. The mechanical engine starts automatically, pulling the page from his hand and turning it into confetti. Kath's got a shredder in her office, but hers produces thin strands of paper. This one mulches the paper. Jonathan pulls the next three pages from his pad as well, feeding each of them into the machine.

"Imprints," he says by way of explanation. "They can lift written text from imprints on subsequent pages."

Who the hell are *they?* The NSA? The FBI? Kath doesn't ask.

Where the hell was this guy when *Anduru* was on approach? She could have done with someone that had this kind of savvy. He's ensuring his notes can't be recovered from the slight indentation he made while writing. He taps his head, saying, "Let's just keep this conversation up here, okay? Just between us for now."

"Okay," Kath says, knowing she is way out of her league.

He leans forward, leaning his elbows on the desk. His fingers are outstretched and pressed together, being positioned in front of his face.

"Let's start again at the beginning," he says, sounding more like her shrink than her lawyer. "The delivery?"

"I got a call from the front desk," Kath says.

"So there's a written record of the delivery with security?"

"I guess so."

"We'll assume so," he says. "I won't openly ask for records from the Executive Office security group, but if they're included in discovery, I'll get an intern to go through and find the exact entry so we have the wording used."

Kath nods, realizing Jonathan is doing all he can to keep her out of jail. Before walking in here, she was naive. She's innocent. Or, so she thought. The innocent have nothing to fear, right? Now, she's not so sure. The most innocuous detail from that time could be turned against her and spun into whatever narrative suits the prosecution.

"Time is on our side," he says, apparently seeing the worry on her face. "You're not the only one that misses details after a couple of years. People tend to remember things that are notable. Passing interactions are easily overlooked. There's a good chance the security guard doesn't remember the specifics of what was said, and that will work in our favor."

"Okay," she says for no other reason than *okay* seems appropriate when conspiring to avoid jail time.

"And then?"

"I went down and collected the takeaways."

"In detail," Jonathan says.

"Oh, the security guard quizzed me about the meal. He pulled each of the items out of the bag. Opened the lid on the fried rice. Then he repacked the bag and gave it to me. And he told me not to order takeout again."

"Good. Good."

"I returned to my desk and rummaged through the meal. There was nothing there."

"Nothing?"

"No. It was takeout. Nothing more. Then we opened the fortune cookies."

"We?"

"Jacinta opened the first one."

"What did it say?"

"I don't remember the exact wording, but it was obviously not your standard fortune."

"Why?"

"Because it said something like, *It's not stopping.*"

"And that's what got your attention?" he asks, screwing up his lips. Kath's not surprised by his response. As far as secret messages go, it's innocent enough. It wouldn't mean anything to anyone other than her.

"Yes."

"You said *cookies.* How many cookies were there?" he asks.

"Two," she says. "The second said, *Look for love and you'll find its path.*"

"And that meant something to you?" he asks, narrowing his eyes.

"Yes. I knew immediately what they were telling me. We were watching the approach of *Anduru.* It was still pulling two hundred kilometers per second."

"That's fast, huh?"

"LA to Vegas in under two seconds," she says. "Oh, yeah, that's fast. It's so damn fast if *Anduru* hit Earth, with its size and speed it would have wiped out an entire continent."

"I can see why that would be a concern," Jonathan says, raising an eyebrow.

"*Look for love*—they were telling me to look for Venus. They'd figured it out. They'd done the math. They knew *Anduru* wasn't going to stop. At that speed, it couldn't. Like us, they'd seen it use the planets to slow down. When they ran the sums, they realized it could come to a halt by skimming through the atmosphere of both Earth and Venus."

"And you confirmed this?"

"Yes. In about ten minutes. Once I knew what we were dealing with, it was obvious. I could have kicked myself for not seeing it sooner. I double-checked my calcs and ran the idea by my scientific advisory team."

"And then?"

"And then I ran through the snow and sleet to get to the White House."

"I'm going to stop you there," Jonathan says. "Because this is where the prosecution is going to make its play for negligence."

"Negligence?" she asks, confused.

"That package could have been laced with anthrax, ricin, novichok, or any of a number of biological nerve agents. They *knew* you would rush to meet the President. If they had hostile intent, you would have been the delivery mechanism. If she was poisoned, the US response to the crisis would have been crippled."

"Oh," Kath says, sitting back in her seat and feeling stupid. She's a child caught up in an adult's strategy game.

Jonathan shakes his head in disbelief. Kath can see it in his eyes. He can't understand how she can be so smart and yet so utterly naive. He rubs the stubble growing on his chin as the day wears on.

"You went to the White House. Then what happened?"

"Umm, Jim McGuire, the President's Chief of Staff, took me to the reception area outside the Oval Office. He interrupted her meeting with NATO."

"So he believed you?" Jonathan asks. "He could see this was important. He felt he needed to interrupt the meeting?"

"Yes. Why? Is that important?" Kath asks.

"Oh, yes! It means someone else agreed with the assessment. Did he know it had come from the Chinese?"

"No."

"Did he look at your calculations? Did he understand the model?"

Kath says, "He trusted my judgment."

"And then you told the President?"

"Yes." Kath searches her memories. "I focused on what was about to happen. You have to understand, lives were going to be lost. There was no question about that. The only question was, how many?

73

Thousands? Tens of thousands? Hundreds of thousands? Every second we delayed made it harder to evacuate the region."

"But she knew this came from the Chinese?"

Kath shrugs.

"I'm not sure what I said to her. I was drawing diagrams on the back of printouts, double-checking my calculations by hand. It was manic in there."

"And you have these?" Jonathan asks. "Do you still have these sketches?"

"Me? No. They probably ended up in the trash."

"Oh, you really don't understand how the White House works, do you?" he says, grinning. "If it hasn't been shredded, if it's been scrunched up and tossed in the trash, it will be retrieved and examined."

"Really?"

"Really. And it'll be tagged, dated and filed. It'll be kept in a cardboard box somewhere for at least fifty years."

"Oh," she says.

"These are the kinds of things we need to look for during discovery. We'll be given access to all the records from that time. It'll be in there. You can be sure of that."

Kath screws up her lips a little, grimacing before asking the question that's been plaguing her mind.

"Am I guilty?"

"That's not for me to decide," Jonathan says. "Right and wrong in the eyes of the court is often a matter of perspective. The prosecution is going to paint this as a patsy-play, meaning they're going to say you were an unwitting accomplice to a foreign power."

"So, treason?" Kath asks, feeling as though she's falling down a rabbit hole.

"In a word, yes. But I think we can win this. You were in multiple discussions with scientists from around the world. You were encouraging scientific collaboration. We can demonstrate from your chat history that there were no political discussions, no policy discussions, no leaks, no threats to national security, no bribes offered, no blackmail coming into play. In short, you had no motive for treason."

"And the fortune cookies?" Kath asks.

"You were cut off from your peers in China," Jonathan says. "They spotted something in the data, something that was missed by both the Americans and the Europeans. They couldn't get through to you using the normal channels. We're going to tip our hand when we ask for State Department records of meeting requests from foreign embassies, but so be it. The Chinese knew they had to be creative to get your attention. They knew you were smart. They knew you just needed a hint, a clue. They realized if they could prod you in the right direction, you'd figure this out. But this was your calculation. Your team discussed this and agreed on it. The decision to take this to the President was yours."

Kath nods.

Jonathan says, "We need to shift the focus away from the loss of life and onto how many lives were saved. It could have been much worse. If you hadn't acted on that information, far more people would have died. We need to acknowledge the tragedy of those that were lost, but our focus—your focus on that particular day—was on how many lives could be saved."

"And you think they'll buy that?" Kath asks. "The judge? The prosecution? You think they'll believe that?"

"It doesn't matter what they believe," Jonathan says. "The only thing that matters is what the jury believes. Facts don't win cases. Emotions do. We need the jury to see this through your eyes. We want them to feel as though they were the ones that cracked open that cookie and decided to act. We want them to recognize the enormity of that realization weighing down on your shoulders. We need them to realize that any hesitation would have cost even more lives. If we can do that, we'll win."

HOUSTON

Time is an illusion. It only ever ticks by with the consistency of a metronome and yet weeks and months rush past as though in fast forward. For Angry Andy Anderson, the six months since the US Presidential election have been a blur. It's the lack of chaos. When shit is flying at him from every direction, time can't move fast enough. Smooth sailing, though, causes the calendar to disappear in the blink of an eye.

Andy's been invited to attend the NASA conference on *Anduru* in Houston, Texas. Back in Washington DC, a road trip sounded like a good idea. After driving through Virginia, Tennessee, Alabama, Mississippi and Louisiana, the idea doesn't seem that good at all. A smoke haze hangs over a distant city. The hum of his tires on the concrete road is his only companion. For a while, he listened to local radios, but now he's happy being alone with his thoughts. Andy's driving an old Buick. It's got the handling of a wet sock in a washing machine, but on the interstate, it's a smooth ride. The suspension glides over any bumps in the road.

Every couple of hours, he pulls over at a rest stop to relieve himself and stretch his legs. Louisiana is lush. Andy's not sure what he expected, but it's not all swamps. Thick, green woods reach up to within a few feet of the interstate. The edge of the road has been freshly mowed. It's not difficult to see how the grass could grow out of control.

Andy should have flown. Not only would it have been quicker, he would have saved money on a bunch of shitty roadside motels dotted over fifteen hundred miles of snow and ice clogging the roads. What should have taken two days dragged into four. He's already missed the opening day of the conference. The goddamn polar vortex dumped snow all along I-59. His weather app told him Texas escaped the storm, which is a relief. Already, the skies along the way are clearing.

Climate change is something Andy ridiculed on his show for years. Why? It was an easy target. Climate change was the puny kid at the back of the classroom. Everyone thought he was weird. It was easy to turn people against him in anger.

For Andy, the crazy thing about anger is it's righteous. Get someone angry about something, anything, and they'll double-down on why they're right and everyone else is wrong. *Not my freedoms*—that was the rallying cry. That's *always* the rallying cry. Whether it's true or not is another question. And as soon as freedom has been invoked, as soon as people think they're going to lose something, they come out swinging. That they've already lost clean water, lost their clean air, lost two dozen species to logging, lost the coastline to oil rigs and refineries—all of that is irrelevant. *It's my God-given constitutional right to drive a V8 pickup*—that was the line he used to joke about when discussing climate change on his podcast. It's not so funny anymore. Calling people snowflakes has been replaced with actual snowflakes reaching as far south as Corpus Christie in Texas back in January.

People are smart—and they know it. That's the problem, he thinks as the miles roll by. If they were stupid, it would be easy to correct things like climate change. There wouldn't be any opposition. It would be simple to put in place the fixes that are needed. But, nope, people are just smart enough and stubborn enough to become enraged by the slightest change in their lives. Inconvenience is the unforgivable sin. They don't stop to think about whether that change is for better or worse. It's a case of squealing—*Don't tread on me!* During COVID, this was particularly obvious. With a pandemic sweeping the world and vaccines readily available, freedom meant being stubborn even if it killed loved ones. Sitting there behind the wheel of his Buick, watching the mile markers drift past his side window, Andy shakes his head. Freedoms are an opportunity, not an excuse.

And as for Andy back then? Oh, he was a vulture sitting on the edge of the cliff, ready to swoop in and pick the carcass clean. He loved conspiracy theories. They were empowering. They gave him the illusion of knowledge—the illusion of control. In reality, they were a fool's paradise. Now, he feels ashamed. His initial response to that shame was to hide, but he knew that wouldn't solve anything, so he resolved to be part of the solution. He turned his podcast into a force for good.

No one's got a time machine. No one can undo the stupidity of the past, but they can set sail in a different direction. Andy's attending the NASA conference in Houston because he wants to help change attitudes.

He drives across the Sabine River into Texas. The scenery doesn't change much. He'd always imagined Texas as a dry desert, but this close to the coast, the towns are surrounded by thick woods.

He passes by another Holiday Inn, another McDonalds, another Best Buy, and yet another Toyota dealership. For all the diversity within the landscape over the past few days, some things remain the same mile after mile. A glance at his sat-nav and he realizes the smog he's seeing is from Beaumont. He's going to have to wait another hour or so for that fresh whiff of air pollution from Houston.

The road never ends. Andy shifts in his seat. He's itching to get out, but he's close. The road, though, is as flat as a pancake and has been for hours. For all he knows, he's caught on some infernal treadmill going nowhere. Then he sees it, buildings rising over the horizon. The billboard beside the interstate reads: *Welcome to Houston.*

Fifteen minutes later, Andy turns into the hotel parking lot and comes to a halt by the entrance. He opens his door and gets out, stretching his weary legs. His muscles are stiff.

"Can I get your bags?" a porter asks, rolling a cart over towards the trunk on his Buick.

"Sure," Andy replies, handing the guy ten bucks and popping the lid to the trunk.

"Who's that?" someone yells, but Andy pays them no attention, dragging a suitcase out and plonking it on the cart.

"Who the fuck?" someone else yells. "Is it one of them?"

"Can I park your car, sir?" another porter asks, offering him a plastic card in exchange for his keys.

"It's angry *fucking* Andy Anderson," a distant voice yells.

"Yes. Thanks," Andy says to the bellhop. He shoves a Lincoln and a few Washington's into the bellhop's hand along with the keys. Normally, he'd tip another ten dollars, but his wallet is empty. Andy's distracted, wondering where the nearest ATM is located.

"Annnn-deeeee," someone yells.

"Oh, hey," he says, turning away from the sliding doors of the hotel. He raises a friendly hand, pleasantly surprised a fan has recognized him.

A dark blur charges at him faster than he can react. Andy doesn't see who or what hits him. It's not even a fist. The guy jumps at the last moment, swinging his shoulder and slamming his forearm into the side of Andy's head, catching him above the jaw. The cartilage within his ear is compressed and torn. In a fraction of a second, it's already throbbing with pain.

Andy was relaxed, which makes the strike worse. He wasn't ready for the impact. His head lashes to one side. His knees buckle as his body crumples. He falls into the leaves of a palm tree growing out of a terracotta pot beside the entrance. The branches dig into his ribs.

"*You fucking asshole!*" is yelled inches from his already bleeding ear.

Andy's disoriented. The blood rushing through his head pulsates. In that instant, he has no idea where he is? Houston? Washington? Back in his hometown of Rome City, Indiana? All he knows is he's in pain. His instinctive reaction is to curl up on the marble tiles. He wants to protect himself, but he knows it's in vain.

Boots thunder into his ribs, kicking him against the pot. He's got his hands out, wanting to protect himself. He swats at the boots to no effect as they hammer his sternum. Through the tears flooding his eyes, he can barely see. There are several assailants. They're dressed in black, wearing dark sunglasses. Bandanas hide each nose and mouth from the ever-present security cameras looming over the hotel entrance.

One of the thugs goes to stomp on his head. A boot blots out the sun. Andy reaches out with his arms, trying to block the attack.

The boot never lands.

Security guards rush from within the hotel with nightsticks drawn. They're yelling, screaming at the crowd, but they're organized. They don't run madly into the fray swelling around him. Instead, they stamp their boots, forming a perimeter in front of him, forcing his attackers back. Nightsticks are swung through the air, but they don't connect. They're a threat. Their purpose is to back the attackers off without inflaming things further. One of the guards pulls a can of mace and sprays it into the crowd. A thin line of chemical foam cuts through the air, convincing the mob to retreat.

Andy wipes the blood from his lip, looking up at the crowd chanting, "Lies! Lies! Lies! No more lies!"

His attackers have already melted back into the surge of bodies jostling in the forecourt.

Hands grab him, reaching under his armpits. At first, his reaction is to fight against them, but they drag him back into the hotel. Two security guards haul Andy to his feet, pulling him away from the doors and over toward reception. Police come running from a side door. They're wearing black vests and an array of tactical gear: helmets, gloves, kneepads, and plastic body armor. These aren't officers out on patrol. They're from the riot squad. They've got their visors down. They were expecting trouble, but elsewhere in the hotel. The sound of their boots thumping echoes through the lobby. They join security, herding the crowd back away from the doors. Radios squawk with updates bouncing back and forth.

A news camera is stuck in Andy's face. He recognizes the make and model. It's an 8K portable, broadcast-quality, shoulder-mounted cinematic camera with a shotgun microphone and LED projection lighting. Andy knows the drill, only in the past, he's been the one on the other side of the lens. He reaches out with a bloody hand, pushing it away. His fingers leave red smudges on the glass. That'll look good on playback. Even though he's in pain and confused by what just happened, his mind is still in production mode.

"Are you okay, Mr. Anderson?" the hotel manager asks, waving for one of his staff to escort the camera crew away from them.

Andy's still taking stock of what occurred.

"I—I think so," he says, spitting blood from his mouth. A thick glob of red mucus hangs from his lips, staining his shirt.

Paramedics run up to him, pushing a gurney in front of them.

"We were expecting you a few days ago," the manager says. "Not today. We thought you'd pulled out of the conference."

"I—uh—bad weather," Andy says as one of the paramedics gets him to sit on the gurney.

"Just relax," the medic says. "I'm going to check you for signs of injury, okay?"

"Oh, sure." Granting permission seems strange, but somehow comforting. The paramedic reaches around Andy's head with gloved hands. He runs his fingers through Andy's hair, pressing firmly against his scalp, working methodically over his head.

"No obvious head trauma," he says. "Slight bruising above the left section of the temporal bone, consistent with a strike to the head, but not a fall to the concrete sidewalk. No damage to the parietal bone."

"Copy that," the other paramedic says, taking notes on a small computer tablet.

A flashlight is shone in Andy's eyes. A gloved hand pushes his head back slightly as the paramedic uses his thumb to hold the eyelid open and get a good look. Fuck, that's annoying. Andy fights him, trying to twist away, but the paramedic is persistent, checking the other eye.

"Mild concussion," he says for the benefit of his partner, who's opening a large plastic box filled with bandages and vials. "Equal dilation. No difference in hemisphere response."

"Any other injuries?" the other paramedic asks. She's short. The thought that dominates Andy's mind is—*Her boots are too big for her feet!* Her jumpsuit is baggy, hanging from her petite frame.

"Facial abrasions," the lead paramedic says, looking carefully at each of Andy's cheeks. "I'm going to unbutton your shirt, okay?"

It seems funny being asked, but Andy says, "Sure."

The male paramedic is precise, twisting each button in turn until he reaches Andy's waist. He reaches inside Andy's open shirt and presses his gloved fingers against each of Andy's ribs, working his way up. The medic's got fingers like steel rods. Andy's pretty damn sure this guy's prodding and poking would hurt regardless of any injury. He grimaces a few times but tolerates being treated like a rag doll.

"There's bruising from R4 to R6 on the left side, but no swelling—no fractures or breaks. The cartilage leading to the sternum is tender. We'll need x-rays to see if there's deep tissue damage, but I doubt it."

How does he know all this? Andy is astonished by how much the paramedic can determine from the press of his fingers and Andy's fleeting responses.

"And your jaw," the medic says, positioning himself directly in front of Andy. He puts his hands below Andy's ears, with his fingers touching along various parts of his jaw. "Can you give me a yawn? Nice and wide."

Andy does as he's told.

"Good. Good," the medic says, running his fingers along the side of Andy's face like a sculptor working with clay. "I'm going to check your teeth. Open up for me."

For Andy, this is a surreal moment of peace. It's a sensation he's never felt before. He's in pain. His chest hurts. Blood is oozing from his mouth, running down his chin and dripping onto his bare chest, but he's not bothered by the aches in his body. He's in good hands. He's trusting in the professionalism of a stranger, and with good reason. A mob attacked him. The system defended him—the system he once derided and ridiculed. Rocks strike the windows at the front of the lobby, marking but not breaking the glass. Even now, police are risking their lives to protect him and quell the violence outside.

The paramedic shines a light up inside Andy's mouth. He's deliberate but gentle, probing Andy's teeth and cheeks with his gloved fingers. He moves around, getting a good look at the back of Andy's mouth.

"Slight laceration on the inside of the left cheek," he says as the other paramedic continues typing details into the tablet.

The lead paramedic steps back, taking a good look at the way Andy's sitting on the gurney. "Okay, Mr. Anderson. You're a little battered and bruised, but I think you're going to be fine. We've got an ambulance around by the back entrance. We're going to take you to Hermann Memorial where a doctor will—"

"I'm fine," Andy says, getting to his feet and buttoning up his shirt.

"You really should come with us," the woman says, packing up the kit.

"Thank you, but I'm okay. Honest."

Andy walks forward, looking out of the windows at the angry crowd. They're chanting, raising placards to the sky and shouting, but at who? Where's the audience? No one's listening to them. Oh, there are a few cameras, but this protest seems horribly misplaced. There's no march from here to there. No leader driving them on. Nothing to picket. No stage to rally around. Their anger is misplaced.

No one notices him watching from behind the glass. This is the house he built. The irony of what just happened isn't lost on Andy. All his anger, all the spittle and desk-thumping during his online show over the years was to sell overpriced vitamins and spandex underwear for 'tactical comfort.' It was theater—for him, but not for them. And now he's standing on the other side of the great cultural divide. These are his people. They're the common folk he riled up. They've been worked into a frenzy, if not by him directly then by those he knows in the industry.

Andy's helpless. He's Dr. Frankenstein standing in the ruins of a medieval castle. Rain falls from a collapsed roof overhead. Lightning has brought the monster to life, but beyond that point, Dr. Frankenstein has no control over his creation. Dead hands grab a rack of test tubes, smashing them on the floor. Desks are overturned. Papers flutter through the air. The doctor steps back as rage destroys his laboratory. Yes, this is Andy. This is what he has wrought in American society. He's unleashed a monster.

Andy steps back from the window.

Ashamed once more.

THE PANEL

Kath walks on stage in the convention center at the back of the hotel. There are a dozen participants in the panel discussion. Four tables have been pushed end-to-end along the front of the platform. A dozen chairs have been lined up neatly behind pens and notepads. Pleated table skirts hide the chair legs from sight. The crowd gets to its feet. Kath waves and smiles. It takes her a moment to realize there's mixed sentiment. Some people are cheering, others are shouting in anger. Security guards stand at regular intervals along the sidewall, ready to intervene if there's any disruption. The doors at the back of the room are closed before all the seats can be filled, cutting off people outside in the hallway. Conference attendees argue with the ushers, demanding to be let in.

Spotlights hang from the steel rigging on the ceiling, illuminating the stage. Panel members enter from both sides. Kath's naive enough to think that's a matter of convenience, but then she spots Dr. Philip Monroe, President Wilson's scientific advisor and the lead investigator on the newly-formed *Anduru* Commission.

It's been months since the inauguration. Kath's had a number of terse emails from Monroe along with a rowdy zoom call. She didn't spot him on the list of invitees. It's all she can do to quell the anxiety rising within her chest. To be fair, there are twelve speakers in this afternoon's session but the program only listed five. He must have been a late inclusion. He probably muscled his way onto the panel, bumping someone else into the crowd.

The emcee invites both the panel members and the audience to be seated. He waffles on with vague pleasantries, noting that the hotel basement was flooded by the tsunami that followed the passage of *Anduru* over the Gulf of Mexico. He makes it sound worse than it was as Houston is easily thirty miles from the coast. The hotel was built on the edge of an industrial area south of the central business district. It backs onto a creek that's part of the Buffalo Bayou, a river system leading out into the bay. The flooding caused by *Anduru* coincided with a high tide that breached the riverbank. It was anything other than a Hollywood-esque style tsunami. New Orleans took a direct hit and was submerged by 30-foot waves. Houston was largely spared by Galveston Island, which had been evacuated.

"—I live in south Dickson. I spent a week mopping out my garage—"

But you still had a garage! Kath's not sure anyone's interested in his rendition of hardship when entire cities were sunk in Mexico. The Johnson Space Center was flooded and at least one building collapsed, but that was due more to erosion as the waters subsided rather than the wave alone. JSC was back up and running at full capacity within nine months.

"—privileged to have contributors from around the world at this discussion—"

Kath sits second from the left, on the far side of the stage, while Monroe is next to the emcee on the right—which is something she finds quietly appropriate. Besides, a bit of distance between them will hopefully keep the discussion civil.

Microphones have been placed on the joined tables at regular intervals, along with bottles of water. The elderly professor beside Kath leans forward. He turns the nearest microphone away from himself and toward her. Subtle. He grabs a couple of bottles and offers her one. She accepts, unscrews the top, and takes a quick sip as the emcee finishes outlining the discussion format.

"—will be followed by a question and answer session at the close of the—"

Monroe leans forward, speaking directly into his microphone, saying, "Are we going to stop *fucking* around now? We all know why we're here. We all know who we want to hear from, right?"

The emcee is flustered by the interruption. The swearing caught him off-guard.

All eyes turn to Kath, who's still holding her bottle near her lips. She raises her eyebrows. She's as shocked as everyone else at Monroe's outburst and his vulgar language. It's day three of the conference. So far, it's been constructive. Kath's attended seminars on astrobiology and triangulating deep space objects, as well as giving a talk on her spaceflight. Her lawyer gave her a list of *no-go* topics, such as any recollections of private conversations in the White House. She's stuck to the script, parroting public talking points while avoiding even friendly anecdotes of her time with President Aston.

Monroe stares down the tables, making eye contact with Kath. He's belligerent.

"I mean, we all know what happened. Let's talk about why. Let's do this. It's time to clear the air."

There's a smattering of applause from the front row.

The emcee says, "There's a proper format—"

"*Fuck the format!* I'm not here to play games. I'm here to talk to Dr. Mackenzie."

The other panel members have gone from feeling awkward to backing out of their chairs and shifting away from the table. They get to their feet. To Kath's surprise, they move around the stage, aligning themselves either with her or Monroe, leaving a gap in the middle. Kath is at one end of the long table, Monroe's at the other. The count is seven/three in favor of Monroe, with most of the scientists standing behind him and only a few of them remaining with her. Given all of their careers are on the line, she's amazed anyone's supporting her.

The emcee calls for calm as the crowd grows restless. He's an elderly scientist, balding on top with grey hair over his ears. He's flustered. He does his best to control the conversation.

Kath's heart races. She fiddles with her white silk gloves. It's a strange habit to develop, but having plastic fingertips induces an unusual tactile sensation in her hands. If she holds her hands in front of her and taps her fake fingers together, running them back and forth like a pianist, she can feel the motion reaching down into the amputated stubs of her fingers. The 3D-printed fingers extend her reach. When she gets nervous, tapping them together helps her relax. She breathes deeply, trying to calm herself.

Sitting before Monroe, the back of her hands ache. It's as if the mercury is dropping and a storm is rolling in. Kath straightens the fabric on her gloves, pulling them tight, fidgeting. She's trying to compose herself.

The emcee looks at Kath and then back at Monroe.

"W—What is it you want to discuss?" he asks.

Kath pushes her chair back but she resists the temptation to get up and storm off stage. She's been ambushed, but running didn't work for President Aston during the debate. It left her looking weak and opened her up to a barrage of attacks in the media. Besides, this guy's a Grade-A asshole. He wants her to feel intimidated. Kath's stubborn. Even if she comes out of this with the intellectual equivalent of a bloody nose, she won't give Monroe an easy win.

Monroe turns his chair on a slight angle, leans back on two of the four steel legs, and kicks his Texan cowboy boots up on the table with a thud. He crosses his legs, looking at home in the auditorium.

"The problem I have with Dr. Mackenzie is her approach is not scientific. All she's ever offered is her opinion. That's not how science works. It's been two years. Where are her peer-reviewed research papers into the prospect of a non-sentient Dark Forest? I'm sick of goddamn opinions, I want something that's testable, falsifiable. I want evidence for these *fucking* assertions!"

A couple of people at the back of the hall cheer in response.

"So, you think she was wrong in how she handled *Anduru*?" the emcee asks.

"I'm not saying that. I'm saying we don't know because nothing can be questioned. Raise a valid concern and she'll dismiss it as a fringe idea. She hides behind a lack of debate. That's not how science works. Science—good science—challenges all comers."

Kath stutters, "But I—"

Monroe cuts her off, speaking over the top of her.

"From day one, any dissent was dismissed as a conspiracy theory. I expect more rigor from someone with her academic experience. Science doesn't ignore ideas, it validates or refutes them. If we want to understand *Anduru* we need to be open-minded. We've got to question our assumptions."

"I've—I've never squashed any questions," Kath blurts out.

"Okay," Monroe says, removing his boots from the table. "Then I've got a question for you. Why did you panic and screw up our best and only chance at First Contact?"

"I didn't panic," Kath splutters. "We were attacked."

"Did it ever occur to you that they thought *you* were attacking *them*? I mean, you waltzed on in there with your probe, lowering it within their vessel. What the hell did you think was going to happen? What were you expecting? Were you playing Trick or Treat? Did you expect them to give you some goddamn Halloween candy?"

"I—"

Kath doubts herself. She's being goaded into a narrow response, but she's got to be careful. Her lawyer has warned her about the danger of unfiltered comments being used against her later in court. Everything she says has to be measured, but at the moment it's emotion that rules her heart, not logic. She wants to lash out. It takes all her resolve to pull back. Monroe, though, has no inhibitions.

"If someone busts into my house in the middle of the night, I'm gonna defend myself," he says. "I'm pulling out my Glock and protecting my family. Is it fair to say, they were protecting themselves?"

"Um—I don't think—"

"No, you didn't think, did you? You reacted. You panicked! And we lost the opportunity to learn something about an extraterrestrial species that can traverse the *goddamn* stars!"

"It wasn't like that," Kath protests.

"Oh, it wasn't?" Monroe asks, cracking the top on a bottle of water. "So what was it like? You were uninvited. You were trespassing. You *invaded* an alien spaceship. You lost a hundred million dollar probe. You almost lost the Orion. Tell me what really went on in between your ears, because I'll tell you what it looked like from down here on Earth. It looked a helluva lot like someone was out of their depth."

Kath tries to interject. Monroe's glossing over so many points she's unable to hit just one in reply.

"Fear is contagious," he says. "Before anyone could think about what had happened, before anyone could sit back and observe *Anduru,* before anyone could debate the next course of action, you ordered it to be destroyed. And they listened. They obeyed your call. That's what pisses me off most of all. There wasn't a single voice of dissent. Everyone was in lockstep.

"Tell me this, Dr. Mackenzie. What was the key finding in the Space Shuttle Challenger disaster during the 1980s?"

Monroe waves his hand back and forth as he speaks.

"And I'm not talking about technical details or the O-ring failure. You're not dumb. You know what I'm talking about. What was it that led to the destruction of that spacecraft and the loss of all seven lives?"

Kath hangs her head. She mumbles an answer, but the microphone barely picks up her voice.

"Louder," Monroe growls.

"Groupthink."

"And what is groupthink, Dr. Mackenzie?"

Kath sighs. She doesn't want to answer, but he's controlling the narrative. If she argues or tries to change tack, she's only going to look worse in the eyes of the public.

"It's the tendency for people to fall in line behind a decision made in a group setting."

"Without questioning it," Monroe says. "Without deliberating. Without debating the pros and cons."

"We'd lost contact with Earth," Kath says, feeling exasperated. "The Orion was crippled. We didn't know how much data had gotten through to Houston. We had to conduct a spacewalk to align the antenna. We didn't know how long the link would hold. I had to say something. I had to tell them what happened."

Monroe points at her, saying, "So you made the call. You made an executive decision even though you were a civilian—an unelected official representing the Aston administration. Your position on the crew was as a scientific observer. You weren't in charge. Captain Nikki Halstad was the NASA mission commander. Brigadier General Nolan Landis had overall operational command. But you overrode both of them."

"It wasn't like that," Kath protests.

"Do you know what I think?" Monroe asks. As tempting as it is to butt in, Kath remains silent. She's already lost ground. She's got to be strategic if she wants to regain the confidence of the audience. It's at that moment, she realizes this is being live-streamed to the internet. Most of the conference discussions have been broadcast online, but they're low-key. They would have gone unnoticed by the mainstream media. This, however, will be cherrypicked for drama. Kath tries to hide the sense of horror descending on her face at that realization.

"I think you're human," Monroe says. "You panicked. You overreacted. You made a mistake. It's typical, really. It's the story of our exploration writ large. Humans stumble across something new—and kill it!"

"No. No. No," Kath says, finally taking the metaphorical gloves off and throwing a few street punches for herself. "You can play Monday morning quarterback all you want. It doesn't change the facts. *Anduru* defied our expectations. We've all seen too many goddamn awful alien invasion movies. We've imagined UFOs blazing across the sky, firing their lasers. *Anduru* was a seed pod. We watched as it broke up. That's a process *it* initiated, not us. That act was part of its lifecycle."

"That's not entirely—"

"Now it's time for you to shut the *fuck* up," Kath says, matching his style and aggression. "You asked the question. You need to let me answer. Fair?"

"Fair," Monroe concedes. For all his bluster, Kath's read of him is that he's sincere in wanting to get to the bottom of the enigma. Like her, he's frustrated, but for different reasons. He wants answers.

Kath slows things down. In her experience, that's the best way to take the heat and emotion out of an argument.

"The problem is—we went into First Contact with incorrect assumptions and the wrong expectations. When we got up there, we found something very different from anything anyone had ever anticipated before. We had to be flexible. We couldn't afford to stick to the game plan. We had to be willing to learn—and fast. Damn fast.

"Back in the 1800s, no one knew where butterflies came from. Oh, they knew about caterpillars, but they assumed these were entirely different insect species. No one had watched a chrysalis hatch into a butterfly. The idea that caterpillars became butterflies was preposterous. The two insects—and they were thought of as two entirely separate species of insects—were so fundamentally different in size, shape, morphology, and habits. But now it seems obvious, right? To us, such a position is laughable, but that's where humanity was back then.

"What we're looking at when we see *Anduru* is a chrysalis. We would be fools to think we know what went into it or what would come out. We've seen just one point in the interstellar lifecycle of these things. We've seen how the seed spreads. We don't know how it's formed and, thankfully, we haven't seen how it would germinate in the fertile ground of Earth. It was enough to realize we were watching something in the process of metamorphosis."

Monroe is calm. He says, "And you're basing all this on one, brief interaction?"

94

Kath is equally calm. "*Anduru* mocks our preconceptions. We think we're so damn smart. We're convinced there's only one way into space. It seems obvious, right? After 3.8 billion years, it's only in the last hundred years that one exceptionally intelligent species has mastered the physics and engineering required to reach orbit, but *Anduru* puts lie to that assumption."

Monroe is quiet. He seems genuinely intrigued by her reasoning.

"Our lives are enhanced by technology," Kath says. "We're so reliant on our smartphones and computers, we're blind to other possibilities. If you can't speak Chinese, no problem. Google Translate will take care of that for you. Want to go to Paris? Jump on a plane and you can soar through the air with more comfort than our wildest fairytales ever imagined. Aladdin's magic carpet has got nothing on an A380. For us, technology is a panacea. It's a cure-all. But biology is far more adept at engineering than we are. Evolution still has a few tricks up its sleeve."

"How so?" Monroe asks.

"We think we're so clever achieving flight when birds have been migrating between continents for at least fifty million years."

Monroe nods. He likes that point.

Kath says, "We think we're smart, using electricity for energy, but our solar panels only ever reach 25% efficiency. Plant leaves convert 95% of the light they absorb into energy. That's a level of efficiency we can only dream of—and they do it in a million billionths of a second to avoid wasting energy as heat. And us? We take them for granted."

Kath points to the side of the stage. The Stars and Stripes hang from a flagpole. Next to the flag, there's a potted plant rounding out the stage decorations. Its green leaves are glossy, reflecting the stage lights.

"We think we're so damn smart we assumed *Anduru* must be the result of intelligence, but it wasn't. We think intelligence is the only real game in town. It's not.

"Consider quantum mechanics. We've only stumbled across this in the last hundred years, but we can only exploit it under laboratory conditions. And yet plants use quantum mechanics to achieve photosynthesis. They've been doing that unnoticed for hundreds of millions of years! I put it to you, we would be naive to think we're smarter than nature. Just because we can't imagine how *Anduru* formed as an interstellar seed doesn't mean it's impossible.

"We have a privileged position. We've emerged as the undisputed heavyweight champions of this world. We have eclipsed all opposition. Sharks, tigers, bacteria, smallpox—they're nothing in the face of our ingenuity.

"But privilege has blinded us to the evolutionary value of intelligence. It's not inevitable. It's not even desirable. Hell, bacteria have survived for *billions* of years without it. We look at intelligence as the pinnacle of evolution, a game-changer allowing us to reach into space, but this is a flawed assumption. Intelligence is just one of hundreds of evolutionary strategies. From a biological perspective, the best strategy is determined by one factor and one factor alone."

Monroe says, "The ability to reproduce."

"Yes," Kath says. "Evolution doesn't care for smarts. It cares about the next generation. Evolution is driven by whatever improves the odds of the next generation succeeding. If anything, our intelligence is an impediment to that. We're burning fossil fuels for this generation, not the next. We're cutting down the rainforests for ourselves, not our kids. Oh, we hide behind the stock market and our local supermarket, but we're all part of this, with each of us acting for ourselves alone. Our intelligence is actually kind of dumb."

"Bravo," Monroe says, offering fake applause with a golf clap. "Nice speech, but you're so focused on your own logic you're missing the obvious."

"What am I missing?" Kath asks.

"The laws of physics apply constraints. Yes, birds can fly, but they could never fly us around. We couldn't strap them to a wing and expect to get airborne. Oh, they might have evolved lighter bones and a faster metabolism, but there are limits on what they can accomplish—limits we can exceed using science and engineering."

"We're still limited by those same laws," Kath says, not seeing how this refutes her point.

"We are, but we can squeeze every last drop from them."

"Just like our solar panels, huh? At 25%? Don't flatter yourself," Kath replies. "We've done pretty well, but we're a long way from duplicating things natural selection has mastered with ease. Nature is the great innovator, the greatest inventor."

"Biology hasn't invented a computer," Monroe says,

"It went one better," Kath says, tapping the side of her head. "It invented a brain that could invent computers."

Monroe smiles. He's not stupid. He sits back in his chair, content to listen. He's not conceding anything by allowing her to elaborate. He smiles. If anything, he's setting her up. Kath gets the feeling he's working her like a boxer jabbing at the head and the ribs, forcing his opponent to block and defend. She's got to come back at him with an uppercut.

"For all our advances, the natural world around us is still well out in front of us. Take smell. Our noses can detect a single extra neutron in a molecule. That's something that's chemically indistinguishable—and yet we can do it with a single sniff. Our sense of smell uses quantum tunneling to distinguish between hydrogen isotopes—and it's been doing that for hundreds of millions of years, long before we arose as a species, long before we could develop a centrifuge to identify isotopes."

Monroe says, "Your point being?"

"My point being—humans are really good at hubris. Just because we planted a flag on the Moon, we think we're masters of the universe. We're just getting started. Even with all we've learned, there's more we don't know than we do. To ignore the threat posed by *Anduru* or to assume nature can't accomplish panspermia is not just foolish. It's arrogant. It's unbridled conceit."

"Assumptions, huh?" Monroe says, letting a slight smile escape from his lips. "We both think we're operating on too many assumptions. My problem with you is you're not actively testing your ideas. If you can't falsify a claim, how do you know it's right? If there's no way to challenge or disprove your ideas, you'll never see the flaws in them."

"Like?" Kath asks, affording him the same courtesy he did when she counteracted his claims. She can't have it all her way. She has to let him speak freely.

Monroe opens a folder and pulls out a bunch of papers, with several of them being stapled together. Even from where she is, Kath recognizes them as peer-reviewed scientific research papers. It's the format. He selects one. There's a title in bold text, but it's not too big. Immediately below that, there's a dense paragraph of italicized text—that'll be the list of authors. It's the abstract that gives it away. Although the page is split into two columns, there's a single, broad paragraph beneath the names. It's inset and spans both columns, grabbing the reader's visual attention, just as it should.

"Alejandra Traspas and Mark Burchell, et al, published a paper entitled *Tardigrade Survival Limits in High-Speed Impacts*. They've calculated the upper limit on the viability of microbes seeding Earth. At less than one kilometer per second, even hardy microbes like tardigrades are turned to mush."

Kath tries not to smile. Monroe is making a good point. It's perfectly valid, but little does he know, it's about to be an own-goal. If this were basketball, he'd be shooting a three-pointer at the wrong net. She waits patiently, ready to pounce.

"At five kilometers per second," he says, "single-celled amoebas and bacteria splat like bugs on a windshield. Dr. Mackenzie, would you mind telling the audience the average impact speed of an asteroid on approach to Earth?"

Kath clears her throat. "Roughly twenty kilometers per second, or about 12 miles a second."

"And that doesn't bother you?" Monroe asks. "You don't see that as a problem for your theory about *Anduru?* Doesn't that make it impossible for these so-called seeds to spread? How can they germinate if they're destroyed by the very process that brings them to Earth?"

Kath smiles. He thinks he's got her. She watches the expression on his face closely as she delivers her rebuttal.

"Ah, the et al. For those that don't know, that's a way of saying everyone else that contributed to the paper, right?"

Monroe squints at her.

Kath says, "From memory, there were around ten contributors to that paper. Do you mind?"

She waves her hand through the air, pointing her finger as though she were casting a spell with a wand at Hogwarts.

"Could you read through a few more of those names? Perhaps skip down to number seven or eight."

Monroe's face drops. He turns his head sideways as he scans the front page of the paper. He's on the verge of laughing. A wicked grin reaches his lips.

Kath presses her point forward. "Do you mind telling the audience what you can see on there, Dr. Monroe? Who else is listed as an author on that paper?"

He smiles. He's a goddamn sadist, or is it masochist? Kath's not sure of the term. Even though she's delivered a stunning counterblow, he's enjoying this. If it were her, she'd be mortified by such an oversight.

"Kathleen Mackenzie," he says, reading the name aloud. He nods his head toward her, conceding that point.

"It's a good question," Kath says. "How could any of the biological material on *Anduru* survive a fiery entry into Earth's atmosphere? The answer is, we don't know because we weren't prepared to sit around and wait to find out."

Monroe crosses his arms over his chest. It seems he's interested in listening.

Kath addresses the audience.

"Given we saw *Anduru* breaking up when it came to rest at a LaGrange point, it seems unlikely it would go through a process like the asteroid that formed Meteor Crater in Arizona. That monster was roughly the width of a football field. As Dr. Monroe suggests, it would have come in at around twenty kilometers per second, or about forty-five thousand miles an hour!

"The interesting point to note, though, is it didn't hit Earth with that size or speed. About half of its mass was vaporized as it blazed across the sky. Like a bullet fired into a swimming pool, it lost a lot of its momentum as it passed through our atmosphere. By the time it hit the desert, it was going half as fast. It still had enough energy to carve out a crater, though. It probably hit with around two megatons of TNT. That's well in the range of nuclear weapons. You wouldn't want to have been nearby when it hit."

"And *Anduru?*" Monroe asks.

"It's speculation," Kath says, willing to concede that point. "But we know that the sweet spot for meteorites surviving atmospheric entry is about the size of a car. Like the asteroid that hit Meteor Crater, something the size of an SUV will largely vaporize, but the section that does reach the ground will be about the size of an engine block—and importantly—it'll hit at around terminal velocity. It won't be going tens of thousands of miles an hour. It'll be going much slower. And at slower speeds, biological material can survive."

"At a cellular level, maybe," Monroe concedes. "But for something like the human body, terminal velocity is around 120 miles an hour. That's not survivable. Do you really think one of those creatures we saw inside *Anduru* could somehow be cocooned in a shell that survives atmospheric entry and then survives smacking into the planet at a hundred, two hundred, or even three hundred miles an hour?"

Kath has to be honest. "I don't know. The point is, there are other options. There are other possibilities beyond what we'd think of as a meteor impact. We know *Anduru* had the equivalent of an ablative shield. It had already used that to slow down before reaching Earth. I don't think the intent was to hit the ground at thousands of miles an hour."

Monroe is blunt. "Whether it's 40,000 miles an hour or 400 miles an hour—it's still dead on impact. It's going to be a goddamn bug on a windshield."

Kath is frustrated. She stammers. She's flustered. She doesn't have an answer for him. No one does because it didn't happen. She and the rest of the team that observed *Anduru* weren't prepared to wait to find out.

"M—Maybe they have some other mechanism—like a dandelion seed."

"Really?" Monroe asks, rolling his eyes. "And if it gets down here—to the bottom of our gravity well—how does it get back out into space again to infect other worlds?"

"I don't know," Kath says, "but it would be a mistake to assume it can't."

"Are they going to build rockets?"

"No. I don't know," Kath says, aware she's contradicting and repeating herself, but she's frustrated. "I don't think so. We assume there's only one way of getting into space—using rockets—but that's not the case."

"It's not?" Monroe asks, raising an eyebrow in surprise at that point.

"No," Kath says. "There's a company here in the US called SpinLaunch."

"Hah," he says, laughing. "What? Like a spinning wheel?"

"Yes."

"So they're building something like a catapult to fling someone over a medieval castle wall? Only the wall is our atmosphere? Are they going to build a trebuchet and *yeet* themselves into orbit?"

She shrugs. "Something like that, I guess. The point is, there are other ways to reach orbit. It would be a mistake to dismiss SpinLaunch just because they're solving the problem of escaping Earth's gravity in a different way."

"They're going to *yeet* themselves into space?" he says, still laughing at that point. "I'm sorry. I'm not laughing at you. It's just—the mind picture that creates, lol."

"You're focusing on what we don't know," Kath says. "Think about what we do know. We know *Anduru* could travel immense

101

distances through space. We know it was in the process of changing states when we rendezvoused with it. We know it's been successful before. It had to have been as it must have germinated on some other planet around some other star before heading here. We might not know the final steps in its lifecycle, but we know it has a lifecycle."

"I just can't see it," Monroe says. "Our gravity well is too steep."

"There are other possibilities," Kath says. "Earth might be a dead-end for them. They might prefer habitable moons with lower gravity. The point is, we can't take an Earth-centric view. We can't ignore other possibilities just because Earth is all we know."

Monroe says. "Do you really think an organic creature can reach Earth over such vast distances?"

"We're organic," Kath counters, shaking her head. "We made it into space."

"We used rockets and computers," Monroe says dryly.

Kath says, "Don't underestimate nature. The Arctic Tern flies ninety thousand kilometers each year, from pole to pole. They've been known to depart Japan and not make landfall until they reach New Zealand. That's across almost ten thousand kilometers of open ocean and yet they find the same breeding grounds year after year.

"Salmon will travel ten thousand kilometers through the ocean only to return to the same stream, thousands of kilometers up the Yukon River. As exceptional and remarkable as this seems to us, for them it's normal. They can sense the magnetic field of Earth, navigating via an internal compass.

"Our problem is we underestimate the precision in nature. Just because we get lost in the next suburb doesn't mean animals are as dumb. Birds make a mockery of us and our Google Maps. *Anduru* used some similar celestial equivalent. We may not know what, but we'll figure it out."

"And you believe all this?" Monroe asks.

"Believe?" Kath says, lowering her head and peering at him over her glasses. She's not sure if it's a slip of the tongue or a trap. "Beliefs are meaningless. You know that."

"You know what I mean," he says. "Do you really think living organisms can survive the heat of entry into the atmosphere?"

"It's possible," Kath says. "Plausible, at least. We even have a precedent for something like this here on Earth."

That gets another raised eyebrow from him.

"California's Giant Sequoia and the Eucalyptus trees of Australia both need fire to open their seeds. At first glance, such a concept seems preposterous. Why would trees evolve to be dependent on fire? Fire is destructive. Fires devastate the wilderness. The concept is entirely counterintuitive and yet it works. It's an evolutionary strategy, allowing the species to survive devastating forest fires. Individual trees may die, but their seeds open to reveal the next generation. In the same way, what seems absurd from our perspective could be perfectly normal for *Anduru*."

"But it's guesswork," Monroe says. "You're guessing."

"It's an educated guess," Kath replies.

"Science is not guesswork," Monroe says.

Kath grimaces. Regardless of all she's said, that's the kind of statement that tends to get picked up in a soundbite. Waffling on with longwinded explanations doesn't make for good TV. The media want something short, sharp and pointed. They're not going to replay her rambling points. They'll pick something punchy that cuts to the heart of the issue.

"I don't think we were as vulnerable as you think," Monroe says. "For me, this is tragic. Just stop for a moment. Think about what's been lost. We missed an opportunity to study life that evolved on another planet. If you hadn't panicked, we could have taken samples. We could have studied their biological processes at a cellular level."

Kath says, "But if one of those things got down here."

Monroe huffs. "If one of those things got down here, I'd deploy a squad of Marines or call in an airstrike. Do you seriously think they would have stood a chance against us? I mean, look at us. We've got thermonuclear bombs and rail guns. We could literally blow them off the face of the planet."

Kath says, "We're single-point sensitive. We have one home. We could not afford to expose Earth to harm."

"Pfft," Monroe says as spittle flies from his lips. "You said it yourself. Our true strength lies in our intelligence. Humans are pathetic when compared to a lion or a shark. None of us could take on a Grizzly or a cobra barehanded, but we don't need to. It's not muscles or claws that make us strong. It's not bite-strength or speed. It's our ability to come up with unique solutions.

"We've beaten all opposition by banding together. We've learned to leverage technology. At first, it was grabbing a fallen branch to protect ourselves. Then we sharpened straight bits of wood to become spears. Later, we added a stone head. Then we shot it from a bow. We smelted iron to form swords and armor. We fashioned cannons and guns, bombs and planes. Honestly, once we picked up that first stick, the natural order never stood a chance."

"And you think we could defeat these things in open battle?" Kath asks.

Monroe laughs. "Of course, we could."

ICE CREAM

Several days ago, Jorge anchored his aging trawler *The Santiago Apostol* in the lee of Smith Point on the edge of Galveston Bay, just outside of Houston. He and Veronica have been commuting back and forth to the NASA conference in the heart of Houston. Jorge prefers the ocean to some fancy yacht club. It's quieter. The gentle rocking of the waves is soothing to his soul.

"Can we get some ice cream?" Veronica asks.

"Not for dinner," Jorge says. "Maybe dessert."

Veronica giggles. "Not for dinner, silly."

There's a slight inflection in her voice. Jorge's not stupid. She's trying to downplay her fascination with American ice cream. For an orphan growing up in poverty in southern Mexico, this trip to Houston is a glimpse of fantasy land. If she had her way, she'd eat ice cream for breakfast, lunch and dinner.

Jorge smiles. Given there are twenty-three different flavors and Veronica's determined to have each one, that's the dessert menu for the week laid out. He may play the grumpy granddad, but Veronica knows she's got him wrapped around her little finger. He has to put up at least some token resistance or Maria will scold him when they return to Vera Cruz. As it is, she lectured him not to spoil the child.

They climb down from the old trawler into a longboat. Maria insisted Jorge take a second craft along with him. He pointed out that *The Santiago Apostol* would never be more than fifty miles from shore and well within radio contact, but Maria's the boss. Jorge regularly visits distant fishing grounds several hundred miles from the coast of Mexico, but Maria had her mind made up. Once, it was Jorge who set the rules. Now he listens. He doesn't mind, though. He knows she challenges him for one reason alone—she cares about her aging father.

Veronica grabs the rubber fuel line and pumps the bulb in her palm, priming the outboard motor as Jorge undoes the rope. Even though there are seventy years between them, they work seamlessly together.

Jorge should have taken up Eric Brown's offer to stay in the hotel. Veronica would have loved it. But he's an old man. He loves the sea.

Being anchored on the edge of a wildlife refuge allows them to see vast flocks of birds circling in the sky. The sunrises over the outer peninsula are spectacular. It's the same sun rising over the same ocean he's seen for decades, but from Texas, it's serene. Why get boxed up in a tiny hotel room when the freedom of the ocean calls? Besides, it's only a twenty minute boat ride to Clear Lake. From there, it's a short bus ride to the hotel. This afternoon, though, PBS is taking them on a tour of the space center.

"Are we going to see an astronaut?" Veronica asks, steering the longboat out into the channel.

"Maybe."

She guns the engine. The hull rises out of the water. The longboat skips over the waves.

The longboat is a rigid inflatable just over eighteen feet in length. It has an aluminum hull with inflated sides and was designed for ferrying scuba divers to nearby wrecks. It could easily carry ten people. With just two, it races across the bay. If anything, it's too light with only Jorge and Veronica on board.

The straps on a bunch of lifejackets flap around in the wind. They've been stowed in the center console along with a first aid kit, flare gun, fire extinguisher and several plastic containers full of freshwater. Maria wasn't taking any chances on her elderly father. She made him promise to wear the vests. '*If it's rough,*' he said. She shook her head, knowing it was pointless to argue. Jorge appreciates her concern, but she worries too much. He's in America. This is the land of everything. They have spaceships. What could go wrong?

Not many people would be confident with a ten-year-old at the helm, especially as container ships and tankers use the channel to sail into port, but Veronica is an old soul. Jorge hasn't had to teach as much as guide her. She knows when to ease off because the swell is becoming too rough and when to open the throttle to pass well clear of another vessel. Given she's short and sitting at the lowest point of the longboat, her judgment is as keen as his, perhaps even better. He's steered enough boats to know she's mindful of safety.

"Perhaps a little more throttle," he says for no other reason than he's supposed to be in charge and making decisions of some kind.

Veronica's hair whips behind her as she sits at the stern, steering with the outboard engine handle. She loves being on the water.

"What's the time?" she calls out over the wind rushing past.

"Three-thirty," Jorge replies.

"There's plenty of time. No rush," she says, leaving him wondering who's the responsible adult in this relationship.

After passing Blue Water Atoll on the edge of the shipping lane, Veronica eases off the throttle, coming into the gentle waters of a vast open bay. She follows the river leading beneath a busy road bridge and past the local marina. Without anything being said, she follows the wake rules, keeping the longboat under five knots.

Clear Lake is a shallow inlet with a bayou to the north. Alligators sunbathe on the grassy banks. They're small, being only four to five feet in length. Jorge eyes them warily. Veronica ignores them, watching their approach to the pier at the far end of the lake. Beyond that, NASA's parkway drive winds along the edge of the water. Johnson Space Center is visible across the open fields. The huge, boxy buildings rise up several stories, towering over the grasslands. Several of them don't have any windows at all, which confuses Jorge. He wonders about what lies within those walls.

Jorge stands in the longboat, watching as they approach the dock. He has a pike in hand. The steel tip is useful for fishing rope out of the water when mooring, while the eight-foot wooden shaft ensures it'll float if dropped in the sea.

"You won't need it," Veronica says dryly.

"Old habits," Jorge says, ready to use the pike to adjust their approach so the longboat turns parallel to the dock. Veronica, though, feathers the throttle. She turns the boat, switching the engine into reverse and bringing the boat to rest without so much as a bump against the rickety wooden platform.

Jorge stows the pike and steps off with a rope in hand. "Nice."

Veronica says, "I've got to work for that ice cream."

"Hah, yes, you do."

Jorge holds out his hand, wanting to be a gentleman and help her out of the boat. She accepts even though she doesn't need assistance. Veronica pockets the engine key, shoving it in her jacket. Of course, she does. Jorge just smiles. Between her and Maria, he's in good hands. Age might weary him, but her youth is invigorating.

Eric Brown from PBS is standing at the end of the pier beside a van with the NASA meatball logo on the side of it.

"Jorge," he calls out for the camera recording their meeting. "It's good to see you again. I enjoyed your speech yesterday at the conference. It was really interesting to hear your experience at the orphanage."

Jorge shakes his hand. He's unsure what to say in reply. The camera distracts him. He smiles, baring his yellow teeth.

"And you, young lady," Eric says. "I see you're the captain!"

"Aye, aye," Veronica says, offering a salute.

The driver opens the van door.

"This is Phil, our lead roving camera operator," Eric says,

introducing them to the man standing beside him. "Phil's going to escort you to JSC and get some b-roll for the documentary."

"Bee?" Jorge asks, confused.

"Um, it's an industry term. It means footage that gets sliced and diced. Something used in transition shots. Stuff like that."

Jorge nods. He has no idea what Eric means, but there are no actual bees involved, which is good. Jorge's allergic to bee stings.

"You're not coming with us?" Jorge asks.

"I've got to film an interview back at the hotel, but I wanted to see you again. Don't worry, you're in good hands. We've got shots planned by the neutral buoyancy tank and inside one of the early Orion mockups. You're gonna love it!"

"Thank you," Jorge says, shaking his hand again.

Jorge and Veronica climb into the van, followed by Phil, who sits opposite them with his camera rolling.

It's a three-minute drive to the Johnson Space Center, passing grassy fields and drainage ditches.

Phil says, "You guys are getting the VIP tour. The center closes to the public at five, but we've arranged for you to go behind the scenes and have dinner with an astronaut at seven tonight. Then at nine, we're connecting live with Tranquility Base. You'll get to watch that from the viewing area at the back of Mission Control."

"Cool," Veronica says, but she doesn't sound overly excited. Unlike kids in the US, she hasn't grown up with a staple diet of rocket launches and space movies. For her, it seems, it's a novelty. Jorge has no doubt she'll enjoy it once she sees astronauts bouncing around on the Moon, but it'll all be new to her.

"Do they have ice cream?" Jorge asks. Veronica nudges him with her elbow, grinning. She both did and did not want him to ask that.

"Oh, they have *space* ice cream in the gift shop."

Veronica's eyes light up. "Space ice cream? What is this *space ice cream?*"

Phil laughs. "It's freeze-dried."

They both look confused so he continues, saying, "It's not cold. It's a crunchy powder, kind of like a candy bar, but it tastes like ice cream."

Veronica screws up her face at the thought. "Astronauts eat warm, crunchy ice cream?"

"Yep."

Even Jorge's looking forward to trying space ice cream. He can't wait to tell Maria about something he hasn't even tasted yet.

Emergency vehicles race past their van. Their driver pulls over, letting the vehicles pass with ease. Sirens scream. Lights flash.

A police car flies down the road at high speed. A white EMS ambulance with a red stripe follows hard behind it. Several more police cars come around the corner. Another EMS ambulance follows the convoy, only this one is pulling a trailer. Behind the next police car, there's a fire engine. It's huge. The front bumper alone protrudes at least two feet, while the vehicle is easily forty feet long and bright red.

All the vehicles are shiny and new. Perhaps that's what's most surprising to Jorge. Their glossy paint and chrome fittings are stunning to behold.

More police cars arrive, followed by more EMS trucks and several more of the big, heavy fire engines.

"What's going on?" Jorge asks their driver as they wait on the side of the road.

"I don't know."

Shots are fired.

Even from within the confines of the van and at a distance of several hundred yards, the sound is terrifying. Their driver turns onto the grassy shoulder of the road, giving himself enough room to perform a U-turn. Another state trooper rushes past in a patrol car followed by a motorcycle cop.

There's a break in the emergency vehicles swarming into the space center, allowing their driver to swing the van onto the other side

110

of the road. Several other cars follow them, turning away from the center.

"What's happening?" Veronica asks, peering over the seat-back, trying to see further down the road.

"Active shooter," the driver says, but he's guessing. He has to be.

Several more gunshots ring out in the distance.

Why would anyone want to shoot someone at NASA?

Jorge doesn't understand guns. Oh, he knows the mechanics of how they work, but not the politics or the ideology associated with them. To him, it's strange to see anyone that doesn't work with guns in a professional capacity having any interest in them whatsoever. They're tools. He doesn't understand the obsession. Guns make sense for soldiers, police officers and security guards. Oh, he's heard the arguments about self-defense. He's also heard the shocking statistics about how often there are accidental shootings, suicides and murders from domestic violence. To his mind, these are heartbreaking. Jorge's a simple man. He doesn't care for complexities. He doesn't mind if people call him naive, he'd rather live in a world without guns. Sure, criminals could still get them, but even that would become rare. As for freedoms, he has all the freedom he needs.

Three additional fire engines rush past with lights flashing and sirens blazing.

"Why do they need the fire department for a shooter?" he asks the driver.

"Dunno, but I'll get you back to the dock."

The NASA publicity van rushes the other way, taking them to safety. Veronica pops her seatbelt and turns around on the bench seat. Jorge can't blame her. He does likewise. As they turn back onto the parkway leading to their boat, a police car is flipped in the air far behind them. They turn, seeing it land on its roof. The cabin of the vehicle is crushed along with its flashing lights.

Neither of them says anything. Even the driver is silent. Jorge's sure he saw the cop car flip in his rearview mirror as the driver keeps checking behind him. It's another minute before they pull up beside the pier on the western edge of Clear Lake.

"I—um—I'm sorry you couldn't get to go on your tour," the driver says, "Maybe tomorrow."

"Maybe," Jorge says, pulling on the door handle and climbing out of the van. For him, in this context, *maybe* is a hard *no*.

"Nice to meet you," Veronica says, shaking the hand of the cameraman.

The van drives off, leaving them standing on the side of the road. Out across the open fields, dozens of emergency vehicles span the length of the main road within the space center. The shooting has stopped, but that doesn't mean it won't start again. Jorge isn't sure how far a stray bullet can travel, but he hopes nothing comes their way. They're side-on to the whole tragedy so any gunfire should be directed along the road. If anything, they have the best view, which strikes him as profoundly sad. He wonders how many families will receive a knock on the door before sunset.

Veronica stands beside him, watching the grass sway in the breeze. "No ice cream, huh?"

"No. Not tonight," Jorge says. "Tomorrow. I promise."

They walk along the pier. The design is reminiscent of a crazy 'F' with lots of side walkways poking out into the lake from the main pier. Most of the dock is empty. A bunch of sailing boats have been tied up at the end of the pier. They're trainers. They're barely eight feet long with a single mast. They probably never leave the shelter of the lake.

Their longboat is docked just over halfway along the pier on one of the narrow walkways leading to the side.

Something's wrong. Jorge can feel it in the air. And it's not just the sound of distant sirens setting him on edge. The pier feels different. Water has splashed up on the wood, but other than that, it looks as it did when they arrived. It's the same and yet it's not. Jorge feels rather than thinks they're in danger.

"Look!" Veronica says, pointing at the murky water.

Blood swirls in eddies. The familiar scales of an alligator break the surface, but they move in an unnatural way. Instead of swaying from side to side or back and forth, a tail rolls diagonally. Rather than swimming, it's as though the reptile has been caught in a tumble dryer. Jorge puts his hand out, pulling Veronica back from the edge, wanting her to get behind him. The main pier is three feet above the surface so they're safe—or so he thinks.

Even though they're alone, Jorge can't escape the feeling they're being watched.

The dark scaly skin on the tail resolves into bright red flesh and crushed white bone. As the tail is five to six feet in length and as thick as a tree trunk, the alligator must have topped twelve to thirteen feet easily.

"What could do this?" Jorge asks, looking out across the water. "This lake is too shallow for a Great White. And too far from the open ocean."

"Maybe alligators fight," Veronica says.

"Maybe," Jorge replies, not convinced.

"What should we do?"

"Leave," Jorge says.

A severed alligator foot floats on the surface near the longboat. With its claws extended, it's bigger than his foot.

The water near the pier is still—and that worries him. Given the size of the alligator, he expected the water to be churned. Mud should be rising to the surface. It's as though the animal died without a fight.

"Get the engine started," Jorge says.

Veronica jogs along the rickety wooden boards. Jorge doesn't. He faces the shore, looking down the pier. He edges down the smaller, lower, side-walkway where their longboat is tied up, but he can't turn his back on the land. His eyes take in the distant flashing lights, the buildings, the grassy fields, the roadway, the riverbank leading into the lake and the dock. He's searching for someone—something.

"I can feel it," he mumbles, seeing a slight flicker in the sunlight before him. It's as though Maria's handed him a pair of polaroid glasses. The light doesn't distort so much as shift, drifting in shades.

Behind him, the outboard engine on the longboat splutters into life.

The wooden boards on the pier creak, but not in response to his motion.

Through gritted teeth, Jorge says. "I—see—you."

"See what?" Veronica asks, leaning out of the boat and undoing the ropes tying it to the dock.

Jorge squints, watching the way the light plays on the water, reflecting up at the pier. Birds soar overhead. Grass sways onshore, rocking with the breeze.

Veronica says, "There's nothing there."

Jorge can't bring himself to turn away from the empty pier.

Wooden slats sag near the shore.

"*El Diablo*," he whispers, desperate to catch a glimpse of something that seems real one moment and a dream the next. There's movement. The background blurs and then comes back into focus. "It is the *fantasma*—a ghost."

Jorge isn't superstitious. He's pragmatic. He only believes in what he can see—and from where he is right now, he can see the body of a dead alligator in the long grass at the edge of the water. Its severed tail bobs beside the dock. One of its feet rocks against the support struts of the pier. The alligator was sunbathing not more than twenty feet from the dock, but down close to the waterline. There's no bite mark as such on the back of the animal. It's as though it's been guillotined just behind its head, cutting through its scales and into its lungs. Blood soaks the grass, seeping down into the water.

Jorge's fingers tremble. An active shooter can't flip a police car. An alligator this size has no natural enemy. It could be shot between the eyes and even the largest bullet would struggle to penetrate its thick skull. No, something is wrong.

Veronica revs the outboard engine, but she hasn't slipped it in gear. She's warming it up for their journey back to *The Santiago Apostol.*

Jorge backs up next to the inflated side of the boat.

"Get in," she calls out, having seen the dead alligator on the bank.

"Not yet," he says. "I can't."

"Why?"

"We're being stalked."

Jorge crouches, keeping his eyes up, looking at the empty pier in front of him. He reaches into the boat, grabbing the pike.

The water beneath the pier trembles. Ripples resound from the pillars holding the planks above the lake. The wooden walkway shakes. Waves roll across the lake.

Jorge wields the pike like a lance. He jabs at the air, thrusting forward, aiming for the center of the walkway.

"Back, demon!"

"Papa, you're scaring me," Veronica says.

"Go," he calls out. "Don't look back."

"I'm not leaving you, Papa."

Behind him, the engine roars. Water swirls beside the pier. Mud is kicked up from the shallow bottom. The longboat turns through 180 degrees. It's now pointing at the middle of the vast lake. Veronica edges the boat back slightly, ensuring it's alongside him less than a foot from the pier.

"Come, Papa. Come."

Jorge waves the pike. The metal tip strikes something in mid-air, but what? He strikes again. The point at which he hits goes dull. It's as though the light has dimmed, but only in an area the size of his palm.

"You will not take us," Jorge says. He backs up, edging down the side-walkway. He wants to turn and run. He could throw the pike and jump for the boat, but the invisible creature would be on him. Given what this thing did to the alligator, he has no doubt this is a race he'll lose.

"Please," Jorge says to Veronica. "Go. I'm an old man. You. You have your whole life ahead of you."

A tiny voice says, "I'm not going, Papa. Not without you."

The creature advances. Although Jorge can't see it, he can see the way the wood bends under its weight. Several boards break, splintering beneath nothing at all.

Has he gone mad?

To anyone watching from shore, he's Don Quixote prancing before a windmill.

Teeth appear. It's as though a movie screen has split open, revealing a monster hiding behind the silky fabric. Reality has been fractured. The monster's teeth are jagged. They're densely packed, curling back into a dark throat. Unlike a lion with its orderly teeth and huge canines or a shark with its interlocking sharp teeth, these appear thin and long. They're needles—spikes. They crisscross each other, forming a chaotic mesh, but they're teeth, of that Jorge has no doubt. The mouth opens, revealing a dark throat.

The invisible creature lunges at him. Claws extend into the wood, appearing out of thin air. The tip of the pike is snapped like a matchstick, leaving half of the wooden shaft in his hands.

"Go!" Jorge yells, advancing on the creature. In the absence of any other strategy, he rushes it, yelling, hoping to bewilder it.

The mouth opens.

Jorge thrusts with the severed pole, jabbing inside the creature's mouth. This is it. This is how he dies. It's not how he imagined death. He's terrified, but he must protect Veronica. Jorge always imagined dying in his sleep. Is there any death as comforting as to close the eyes and not wake? He wanted to be with Maria and his grandsons. He wanted to die in Mexico, not on some rickety pier in Houston.

A fireball rushes past, singeing the hairs on his arm. It's come from behind him. A brilliant red light rushes through the air. Fumes billow into the sky. A plume of toxic, acrid smoke trails behind the flare as it strikes the inside of the creature's gaping mouth.

"Get away from him!" Veronica yells, reloading the flare gun with another thick round. She's standing beside the engine, but she's turned around facing him. Veronica pushes the shell into the barrel and locks the action in place. Maria has taught her well.

Veronica has swung the longboat around so it is floating near the end of this branch of the pier. As the boat's not tethered, it drifts a few feet from the support columns.

Veronica fires again, only the creature retreats, closing its mouth. Once again, it's invisible, but it's no longer hidden. Smoke drifts from where its teeth were moments ago, seeping from beneath its lips as it shakes its head.

The red flare cuts through the air.

It bounces off the animal's hide and ricochets into the sky.

Jorge tries to climb into the longboat, but he's rushing. He trips and falls over the inflated sidewall. He splits his lip on the steel floor, falling headfirst into the boat.

"Vero!" he yells, grabbing the center console as he scrambles to get to his feet.

Veronica throws the empty flare gun at thin air. Within a few feet, it bounces, spiraling to one side and landing in the water.

"Go. Go. Go!" he yells, grabbing a fire extinguisher and getting back to his feet.

Veronica turns the handle on the idling engine. The bow of the boat has drifted so it's facing the shore, preventing her from racing away across the lake. She twists the throttle and pulls away from the dock.

Jorge jerks the pin from the fire extinguisher. He sprays the wooden slates on the pier. Thick, white clouds of carbon dioxide billow through the air. He waves the nozzle around, forming a curtain between them and the creature. Through the haze, he can see the outline of an animal easily four or five times the size of the alligator.

Veronica opens up the throttle. Jorge lurches, being rocked off his feet by the acceleration of the longboat. He's still unloading the extinguisher. He collapses into the inflated side of the boat.

The fine white mist confuses the monster. It lunges, jumping for them. Its huge body soars through the air. Claws pass within inches of the sidewall of the boat, but the creature misses, landing with an almighty splash in the water.

Veronica guns the engine. The hull lifts out of the water. The longboat skims along the surface, skipping like a stone on the smooth lake. The dock disappears behind them. Within seconds, they're over a hundred yards from shore. Veronica doesn't look back. Jorge can't look away. He watches as the creature splashes in the shallows.

"W—What was that?" Veronica asks as they race toward the bay.

"I'm not sure," Jorge says. "All I know is—it's not of this world."

9/11

It's been twenty-four hours since Andy was attacked by protesters outside his hotel in Houston. He attended one of the conference sessions this morning, but the scratches on his cheeks and the bruising under his left eye attracted too many stares. If anything, he's probably being overly sensitive. Perhaps that's the most difficult lesson he's learned stepping back from conspiracy theories. The world revolves around the poles, not him. Oh, he never literally thought that was true, but he was raised on a diet of *me, Me, ME, MEEEE!* Now he's all too aware of how the world passes him by. Although, if anything, he would have liked a little less attention when he arrived at the hotel.

Andy flips open his laptop, setting it on the desk by the window. He's got the curtains open, flooding the hotel room with light. Behind him, a suitcase sits on the bed but the angle of the screen means it's out-of-shot. He positions himself so the print of a fossil sits over his shoulder.

"I'm okay," he says, starting a live stream on schedule. Four hundred thousand people are already watching the way the light catches the bruises on his face. He set up the video within half an hour of checking in yesterday, knowing there would be interest in the assault. Normally, Andy uses studio lighting and a touch of blush on his cheeks to make himself look alive. Not today.

His skin appears washed out and grey.

"Fucking cowards ambushed me by the entrance to the hotel."

Smartphone footage of what happened has already gone viral, forcing him to respond to accusations he somehow provoked the attack. He could have blended in imagery from the security cameras with his video, but that's going to be used as evidence in court. Besides, there's merit in going low-tech. Most of his videos are slick and professional. At times, they can come across a little too professional. It makes them appear staged. There's value in the odd gritty session. Speaking from the heart can be very effective.

"It's the revision that hurts most. People are already saying I threw the first punch. Hah! I was waving at them. I turned away from the crowd. I went to grab my camera from the trunk when I was hit from the side. I was sucker-punched, but facts don't matter. These people have an agenda to keep. I've got to be the bad guy so the narrative changes to make me the bad guy.

"See? This is the problem with the fringe. Something happens and it doesn't fit their narrative. So what do they do? They're not going to change. Hell, no. Why should they change their thinking? The solution is—change history.

"Those of us old farts that were around on 9/11 know what I'm talking about. We saw the planes. We saw them fly into the towers. Oh, the first was only just caught on the edge of a frame by someone filming downtown. The second, though. Everyone saw that one coming. We watched as the plane banked and—*wham!* Hundreds of people die in a goddamn fireball. And then we saw the cruel outline, the dark shadow, the ghost of the plane imprinted on the side of the building. Smoke poured out of a gash that had been a Boeing 767 moments before.

"But that wasn't the only target. They hit the Pentagon. And they wanted to take out the Capitol. Who can forget the courage of those on Flight 93? The sight of that aircraft hitting the field outside of Shanksville in Pennsylvania is something I'll never forget."

Andy lowers his head, dropping his eyes from the camera and looking down as he utters those last two words again, "Never—forget."

He grabs a can of soda, pops the tab and takes a swig.

"So what about you? Have you forgotten that day? Were you even alive then? Or did you watch the footage later? What do you remember? What did you think when you saw that plane hit the open field? Did it make you sick to your stomach? As a patriot, did it make you angry?"

He puts his soda down.

"Because it never happened. Oh, Flight 93 crashed all right, but no one saw it. It wasn't captured on camera and yet I know people that *swear* they saw footage of the crash.

"You see, this is the danger we face. History can be revised without anyone even noticing. Sometimes it's even well-meaning and sincere. We think we're smart. We *think* we remember. And this is what they use to draw us in. The fringe knows how to play us, folks. They know how to troll us."

He points at himself. "And I know this better than anyone. These are the tactics I used. Oh, the buildings fall on 9/11 and they ask—*but what don't we know?* They say—*you can't trust the government. It was a controlled demolition using thermite.* And just like that, a brand new, fancy, scary, bad word gets lips buzzing. *Thermite. Thermite. Thermite!* Everyone bullshits like they know what they're talking about. Hell, most of these assholes wouldn't know thermite from a turd floating in the toilet."

He shakes his head, trying not to laugh.

"They revise history. It's what they do. *Oh, Hitler. He wasn't that bad. There weren't six million Jews in those camps. Hitler was misunderstood. The real enemy was Stalin.*"

Andy snaps his fingers.

"And just like that, they belittle mass murder. They talk about it as though they were discussing player swaps in the NBA. But all this reveals their weakness. They can't exist *without* revising history. The past *must* be rewritten or they've got nothing. Not a goddamn thing! *The government was behind 9/11.* That's bullshit and you know it. That's an insult to everyone that died on that day. But, oh, no. Reality isn't good enough for these assholes. Reality must be rewritten.

"And now it's *Anduru*—and yet a lot of you saw that fucker with your own eyes! *Oh, it wasn't alien. It was an experimental spacecraft. Or it was the Russians. Or the Chinese.* It's everyone and anyone other than aliens. For a country that has seen a helluva lot of UFOs and had more than its fair share of abductions and anal probes, the rush to avoid the truth is baffling.

"And I'm getting it too. *Andy was never angry. He's a plant—a stooge. He's a deep-cover operative that went active.* Hah! Have you seen the shit I used to put out? Jesus H. Christ. I was worse than all of them and look at me now!

"Don't fall for it, my friends. Lies are like magnets, drawing us in. If you don't resist, you *will* get dragged in. If you're passive, you *will* lose. If you're not careful, you *will* be fooled. *Oh, but I'm too smart.* Really? There's nothing that blinds us more than our own ego. There's no drug, no shot of whiskey, no line of cocaine with more of a hit than our own pride."

Andy laughs.

"Believe me. I know."

He cracks the seal on a small bottle of rum from the minibar and pours it into the half-empty can of coke.

"Life is a *choose-your-own-adventure.* Just be careful which adventure you choose. Me? I choose reality."

Andy raises his soda, toasting his invisible audience. The real-time counter on his video has already passed a million hits. Not bad for a guy with a black eye and lousy lighting in a shitty hotel room.

"Later, my dudes and dudettes."

MER SOLEIL

Although the sound is muted on the television above the bar, Kath follows the subtitles from where she's seated alone in a booth near the toilets.

"In breaking news," a reporter says, standing in front of a massive NASA logo, "the Johnson Space Center has been thrown into lockdown following reports of multiple active shooters on the grounds. Details are sketchy, but the response from local law enforcement has been one of overwhelming force. Aerial footage shows almost a hundred units onsite, including state police, EMS and fire engines from three counties."

"Well, that's just fucking great," she mutters. "That's just what we need."

Kath knocks back a glass of white wine as though it were orange juice. She pours herself another, ignoring the TV. Curious, she picks up the bottle, taking a good look at the label: *Mer Soleil Silver Chardonnay* from Monterey in California. That's just below San Francisco. A blur of alcohol rushes through her system, touching softly at her brain cells, soothing her troubled soul. She can sense its effects in the heady feeling within her forehead. Ah, sweet nectar of the gods!

The bartender might have thought her selection of wine was

random or that she'd tried it before, but Kath was working entirely from her understanding of astronomy when making her selection. And what a fine choice it was!

"French," she mumbles, mulling over the words as she swirls the wine in her glass. Kath can't speak French, but she has an eye for astronomical terms in various languages. *Mer* is related to the Latin *Mare*, meaning sea or ocean. Most people know *Soleil* from the *Cirque du Soleil* troop. Not Kath. Like *Mer*, she knows the French word *Soleil* comes from the Latin *Sol* or Sun.

The silver sea of the Sun. Kath's not sure about that as a concept. She would have chosen the term *golden*. The golden sea of the Sun would be quite a nice description for the superheated plasma raging on the surface of the nearest star. She sips at her wine, thinking of a simpler time when all she cared about was complex equations.

There have been three Kathleen Mackenzies over the years.

The first was a child with the enthusiasm of a chipmunk. That launched her through her teens and into college with boundless energy. Kath loved the challenge of her studies and defended her dissertation with the wide-eyed excitement of someone that was destined to change the world.

Kathleen Mackenzie 2.0 had a Ph.D. and passion. It took barely six months at Cornell for that to be beaten out of her. She thought all the hard work was behind her now she held a doctorate, but far more lay ahead. Suddenly, science wasn't about ideas. It was about personalities and positions. It was about navigating the very social hierarchies and authoritarian structures that science abhors. Grants were a lifeline—when she could get them. Sexism was rife. Equality was a paragraph on an induction letter. Ageism was the great surprise. *You're too young. You need to hitch your wagon to this professor or that lab. Don't go leading a paper until you've built respect.* Kath felt her life draining away. She fought for her own sense of identity, and it was a fight—every time. Standing against institutions is like wading into a stream. It takes effort just to stand still, let alone walk on.

Then she got a phone call while in the bath. Getting out of the warm water and draping a towel around her became the origin story of Kathleen the Third. At the time, she was annoyed. Some jerk at NORAD wanted to drag her ass to Washington DC because she'd tweeted a few vague ideas about a comet that failed to break up on its approach to Saturn. *It's not aliens. It's never aliens.* That was the mantra. Holy Mary mother of God—*it's aliens!*

Kathleen the First and Second would barely recognize the woman she is today. Gone are the pleasantries. Oh, she tries to be civil, but life really is too short to pander to assholes. Her potty mouth gets her in trouble these days—as do her crazy ideas.

She knocks back her glass of wine.

"You're a difficult woman to find," a familiar voice says.

"Nolan!"

Without thinking about what she's doing, Kath jumps to her feet and hugs him. She bumps the table. Her glass topples sideways. Wine spills on a food menu.

"Oh, fuck," she says.

"It's okay," Jacinta says, grabbing a handful of napkins. She stands the glass up and wipes the spill away.

"Can we join you?" Nolan asks.

"Sure."

Kath plonks herself back down in her chair. She's past caring what anyone thinks of her.

"Corona?" Jacinta asks as Nolan sits opposite him.

"Yes. Thanks."

Jacinta heads over to the bar, leaving them in the corner booth.

"Ah," Kath says, pointing at Nolan. "I see we have another astronomically-motivated, refined drinking choice."

"Huh?" Nolan says, looking at her sideways.

"The corona reaches hundreds of miles above the surface of the sun," she says, tapping her bottle. "Above *Mer Soleil.*"

"It's a beer made in Mexico," Nolan says.

"Oh."

"It's nice with a twist of lime."

"Ah."

"Are you okay?" Nolan asks.

"No," is all Kath can say in reply. She feels devastated by the afternoon session and the debate with Monroe. Between that, being on the no-fly list and under investigation by the feds, she feels lousy.

"I didn't think you were going to make it," she says, trying to compose herself.

"Oh, I wouldn't have missed that afternoon session for the world."

"You saw that, huh?"

Nolan smiles.

"What did yah think?" Kath asks, pouring herself a fresh glass of wine.

"I thought you made some great points."

"I got my ass kicked," she says.

"Oh, I think you landed a few punches," Nolan replies.

"He's right, you know," Kath says, sipping her wine. "I panicked. I saw *Anduru*. I saw the sheer size of that thing and was afraid."

"I was there," he says. "Remember? I saw that damn thing up close too."

"But were you afraid?"

Nolan laughs. "Hell, yes. And I've been shot down by a SAM."

"Who's Sam and why did he shoot at you?" Kath asks becoming muddled in terms she doesn't immediately understand. The wine is going to her head.

"I was in a plane," Nolan says.

"Oh."

"SAM isn't a person. It's an acronym. It's a surface-to-air missile."

"Ooooh."

"I was in an F22 operating out of Kuwait. We were in support of freedom-of-navigation exercises in the Strait of Hormuz."

"Iraq," she says, snapping her fingers and correcting herself with, "Iran!"

Nolan smiles. "Bailing out of a crippled fighter spinning out of control as it plunges toward the ocean isn't nearly as scary as an alien crawling upside down within a cavern hundreds of thousands of miles from Earth. When that thing started pulling us in, I thought that was it. I was sure we were gone."

"Nikki, huh," Kath says, raising her glass and toasting the commander of the Orion mission to *Anduru*. Jacinta returns. She hands Nolan his beer and sits down next to him. She's got a glass of red wine.

"To Nikki," Nolan says, touching the neck of his bottle against the rim of Kath's wine glass.

"May her memory live on," Kath says.

"Wait?" Jacinta says, looking alarmed. "Nikki's dead? How? When did this happen?"

Kath smiles. "You don't have to be dead to be remembered. Only awesome."

Jacinta laughs, shaking her head. "Okay then." She tips her glass against Kath's and sips her wine.

"I'm not drunk," Kath says.

Nolan replies, "I never said you were."

"I might be slightly pickled, but I'm not drunk."

Jacinta and Nolan look at each other. Kath's unsure if it's because of her insistence on not being drunk or if there's something else they want to say. Either way, this is more than a social call. They didn't track her down to get sentimental about the old days.

"I should have been a doctor," Kath says, trying not to slur her words. "Well, I am a doctor. Just not that kind of doctor. I should have been that kind of doctor. You know, the kind that cuts you open."

"A surgeon," Nolan says.

"That's it—a sturgeon."

"A sturgeon's a fish," Jacinta says.

"Ah," Kath says, pouring herself some more wine. "I've never wanted to be a fish."

"Kath," Jacinta says, sounding way too serious.

"They make more money," Kath says. "Doctors. Not fish. But not a doctor of astrophysics. We make peanuts. I should have been a brain surgeon. Less stressful."

Nolan shakes his head, but he's got a grin on his face.

"Brachiopods," Kath says.

Neither Nolan nor Jacinta reply to that random outburst. They glance at each other and wait for Kath to continue.

"I should have told him about brachiopods."

"What are—no, why?" Jacinta asks.

"Things that can survive," Kath says, staring down into her empty glass before refilling it. "People think it's just cockroaches, you know."

Nolan purses his lips. It looks as though he's dying to say something, but he lets her speak.

"Scorpions too. Actually, most things with an exoskeleton or a shell will survive."

"Survive what?" Jacinta asks.

"A nuclear explosion. Or the kind of impact energies unleashed by a meteorite. Wasps can survive 300 times the lethal dose of radiation for humans! The point is—we're not a good metric for this stuff. We're lousy. We're big old soft bags of mush with tent poles keeping us propped up!"

Jacinta turns to Nolan saying, "I think I like Drunk Kath."

"Me too."

Kath raises a finger. "I'm not—"

"We know," Jacinta says.

"Listen," Nolan says, shifting his beer to one side and leaning close. "We found it."

"Found what?"

"*Anduru*. Another one."

"Fuck," Kath says, downing the rest of her drink in one hit. She leans forward, pressing her elbows on the table and burying her head in her hands.

"I'm sorry," Nolan says. "Bad timing. We can talk about this tomorrow."

"Oh, hell no," Kath says looking up at him. "You don't go ruining a girl's drinking session with a bomb like that and then get to run off." She slaps the table in front of her, adding, "Lay it on me, pal."

"Are you sure?" Jacinta asks.

"Sure. Let's see if Drunk Kath is better at handling this shit than Sober Kath."

"You were right," Nolan says.

Kath sits up straight, pressing her back against the leather seat in the booth. If only there was a sober pill. Her eyes narrow. Already, her mind is swinging back into its analytical mode. She was right? About what? She wants to ask, but she doesn't. It's his train of thought that's important, not hers. Kath tightens her lips, wanting to throw off her alcohol-induced lethargy.

Nolan explains. "We've been looking into deep space for these things. We've had everyone looking along the ecliptic."

Kath holds her hand up, wanting him to stop for a moment. She turns to Jacinta, saying, "That's the plane on which the planets orbit. Think of it as a racetrack with cars going around—only the cars are planets and asteroids and stuff."

Kath circles her hand, adding, "The only problem is it gets you looking in two dimensions. You've got to look up and down, not just sideways at the racetrack."

"Exactly," Nolan says. "We were looking for something approaching Earth—not something that had already approached Earth."

"Ooooh," Kath says, delighted by the idea. She still has her elbows on the table. Kath presses her fingers together, lost deep in thought. "So how do you look for something in the past?"

Nolan points at the ceiling. "That's the question. If something came close at some point in the past, where would it be now?"

"It could be anywhere," Kath says. Being at least slightly drunk, even by her own reckoning, her reactions are amplified. She throws her arms wide with those words. "I'd wager it's anywhere other than the ecliptic. If one of those fuckers approached us in the past and failed to make landfall, it probably got deflected."

She drops her hands to her side, letting them flop on the seat. "What did you find? How did you find it?"

Jacinta says, "We took the characteristics we saw in *Anduru* and started looking for similar historical events."

"And?"

"In 1908, an asteroid passed over Russia."

Kath snaps her fingers. "Ohhh, Tunguska."

"Yes," Jacinta says. "There's been a lot of conjecture, but no one's been able to settle on just what it was that flattened the forest. It could have been an air-burst bolide or a comet."

"But?" Kath says, pushing her wine glass to one side even though it's full.

"But there's no impact crater—no scattered debris."

Kath has a funny look on her face. It's almost childish. She turns her head sideways and looks up at the ceiling, saying, "It's almost like something passed through the atmosphere without breaking up. What could do that, I wonder?"

"We think it came in at a slightly steeper angle," Nolan says.

"And deflected out into space," Jacinta says.

"Why?" Kath asks with a brash look on her face.

Jacinta says, "At its closest approach, *Anduru* passed over several hundred kilometers of the Gulf."

"But?"

"But at Tunguska, the object only remained in contact with the atmosphere for about fifty kilometers."

"Oh, that's interesting," Kath says. She leans forward with her chin resting on her hands. "God, I wish I was sober."

Nolan laughs.

Jacinta says, "The shockwave at Tunguska flattened around eight hundred square miles of forest, but at an altitude of a hundred kilometers, that's still only a glancing blow."

"Interesting."

"It gets better," Nolan says. "If we assume it approached along the ecliptic—"

"Fair assumption," Kath says, interrupting him.

"—at a similar speed to our *Anduru*—"

Kath claps her hands together like a kid in elementary school. "We can calculate the angle of deflection!"

Jacinta looks at Nolan, saying, "Drunk Kath is sharper than sober Jacs," referring to herself.

Kath leans across the table and squeezes Jacinta's forearm, saying, "You want some of my wine? It's really good."

"I'm fine."

"So," Kath says, clapping her hands again. "The angle?"

Nolan says, "Relative to Earth's equator, we make it somewhere between 74 and 78 degrees, heading north."

Kath looks up at the ceiling.

Jacinta points at the ceiling, saying, "You know that's not north, right?"

"I know. I know," Kath says. Her mind feels sluggish and yet electrified. It's difficult to make the rapid-fire connections she's used to. She finds herself regretting the forty bucks she turned over for the whole bottle of wine.

"So it's going to be a yoyo," she says. "It wouldn't have lost enough speed to be captured by Earth's gravity, but it's probably within the Sun's gravity well. It's going to bounce back and forth across the ecliptic rather than moving with it. There will be points, though, where it comes back close to Earth."

"And we won't see it," Nolan says.

"Right," Kath says. "Because we're not looking for it. We're looking for asteroids and comets and *Andurus,* but only this way." She gestures with her hands, running them out wide. "And not this way." Kath points her fingers up and down.

"Exactly," Nolan says.

"But you found it?"

Nolan lowers his head, shaking it softly.

"Oh, no," Kath says. "Why do I get the feeling this is where things go bad?"

"NASA found it," Jacinta says.

"Before us," Nolan says. "Long before us. Eleven months before us."

"Well, that's good, right?" Kath says.

"Before the election," Jacinta says.

"Oh," Kath says, pausing for a moment. "Wait. What? Way back then?"

Nolan nods.

"Why didn't they tell us?" Kath asks, pointing in different directions with her hands.

"The election campaign was already underway," Jacinta says. "They didn't want to interfere with the politics surrounding *Anduru.* NASA couldn't be seen taking sides in the debate over what should or shouldn't have happened with *Anduru.*"

"And they weren't sure," Nolan says. "They needed to be sure. They couldn't risk upsetting either side of politics with a dud."

"But now they're sure?" Kath asks, confused.

"Oh, yeah. They're sure," Jacinta says. She turns to Nolan. "Are you going to tell her?"

"Tell me what?"

"You know about NASA's *Aquarius* mission, right?"

Kath says, "Ah, to return water-ice from Ceres and Juno?" She stops speaking. Her mouth falls open. "Oh. No. You're kidding, right?"

Nolan says, "The sample-return module splashed down in the Gulf two weeks ago."

"They didn't," Kath says. "Please tell me they weren't that dumb."

Jacinta says, "Initially, *Aquarius* was only going to conduct a flyby of this older *Anduru*-like object. They wanted to confirm what they'd seen. They re-tasked *Aquarius*, looping it beneath Mars on a slingshot trajectory. They needed to match the object's heading and speed without using too much fuel."

"But that takes time. You don't just re-task a mission overnight. When did this happen?"

"The week of the election," Nolan says.

"Fuck."

Kath's not normally this loose with her words, but she's intellectually battered and bruised and she's just a wee bit drunk. *Fuck* seems entirely appropriate given the circumstances so she has no regrets. Besides, it's succinct and she said it before. They're adults. They know.

"And they never told anyone?" she says.

"Not within the Aston administration. It was kept quiet."

"They had no choice," Jacinta says. "Can you imagine the stink if this got out to the press just days before the election?"

Nolan says, "They still weren't sure what they had in their sights. They had their suspicions, but the flight path was all wrong. They thought they'd picked up an extra-solar object captured by the Sun."

"They had," Kath says with her eyes going wide.

"When they realized what it was, they deployed the collection probe."

"When did they reach this thing?" Kath asks. "When did they deploy the probe?"

"On the 21st of January," Nolan says, hanging his head. "They waited until President Aston was out of office and President Wilson was in charge."

"They *fucking* knew," Kath says. "The transition team. They must have had someone feeding them information from within NASA."

"Oh, they knew, all right," Nolan says. "They warned me to stay away from NASA. At the time, it seemed bizarre, but now it makes sense. They didn't want me to figure it out and tell you."

"Fuck," Kath says. "Fuck those fucking fuckers!"

She leans forward, resting her forehead on the table. For a few seconds, she bounces there, bumping her head against the sticky surface, mumbling, "Fuck. Fuck. Fuck."

A wild thought hits her, striking like lightning. She sits bolt upright.

"Monroe knows," she mumbles. "He knows."

"My sources tell me he's going to announce it tomorrow at the close of the conference."

"That asshole," she says. "He debated me today and he knew. He was setting me up."

Jacinta says, "He wants you to look bad."

Kath laughs. "Well, that's not difficult."

"I'm sorry, Kath," Nolan says.

"Who else knows?" Kath asks. "Who was in the loop?"

"We're not sure," Jacinta says. "NASA's got a small internal team working on this. They've kept it quiet. I reached out to the Europeans and they were confused. They had no idea the mission was re-tasked. Maybe the Russians saw its course correction? Or the Chinese?"

"No," Kath says. "They don't monitor science missions. It's military space activity that gets them excited. Besides, no one's got a telescope sensitive enough to track something that size at thirty million miles. Hell, we can't even see the Apollo landing sites from here on Earth and they're only a quarter of a million miles away. We need a lunar satellite for that!"

Nolan says, "If the Chinese knew, they would have said something."

Kath nods. "Do you know what *Aquarius* got? Part of the outer shell or something more?"

"The artifact was split open," Nolan says, "Just like the one we saw. I don't know what they got, but the sample size was only about five to ten grams."

"A teaspoon's worth," Kath says. "That's not much, but it'll be enough. It'll allow him to leapfrog me. And I assume it's being held here in Houston—at JSC—at the Mars Sample Return Laboratory?"

Nolan nods.

Kath puts her elbows on the table and leans her head into her hands. She runs her fingers up through her hair.

"That fucking idiot," she mumbles. "He's gambling with our lives."

"It's in a BSL 4 facility," Jacinta says. "A bio-secure lab with double-door access, physical containment, positive-pressure suits, HEPA filters, effluent decontamination, one-way traffic only and a chemical rinse before exiting. It's like Fort Knox."

Kath reaches across the table and squeezes Jacinta's fingers. "Oh, my sweet, sweet summer child."

"What?" Jacinta asks.

"There's nowhere on Earth that's safe to examine that stuff."

"I don't get it. It's contained in a NASA cleanroom. It can't go anywhere."

Kath laughs.

"We should have kept this stuff in orbit. It's the only way to be sure there's no contamination."

"Why?" Jacinta asks.

"Our cleanrooms aren't clean. They have microbes found nowhere else on Earth. Oh, we're sure these bugs are out there somewhere, but we can't find them—except when we're putting together a spacecraft. And we've found them in other cleanrooms hundreds of miles apart—but nowhere in between. And these bugs are nasty. They eat bleach for breakfast!"

Nolan says, "Nothing's getting out of that room."

"I love your optimism," Kath says. "But we're not good with little tiny things. Smallpox and anthrax are the most carefully monitored, securely stored, biological contaminants on the planet—and yet we keep *fucking* up with them. Hell, a few years ago, someone stumbled upon a cardboard box in a storeroom that contained vials of live smallpox. It had been sitting there on a shelf for sixty years! Sixty goddamn years without a single person asking—*what the hell is this?* The building had changed departments several times over the decades. People had moved in and out of those labs and offices—and all without giving a second thought to the demon in the cupboard."

"Ooooh," Jacinta says.

"We got lucky," Kath says. "But the thing with luck is—sooner or later, it runs out."

Kath knocks back the last of her wine. She gets to her feet. She has an absent look on her face.

"Are you okay?" Jacinta asks.

"I'm fine," Kath replies, lying. She fakes a smile.

"Ah," Nolan says. "We were going to go and get something to eat. Do you want to join us?"

"No," Kath says. Her smile is forced. "Thank you. I—I think I'll go to my room. I'm going to crash."

"Are you sure?" Jacinta says, getting to her feet and giving Kath a hug.

"Yes."

SMOKE
DETECTOR

Kath wanders toward the elevators. Like most hotels of its 90's vintage, *The Fossil* is twenty-five stories of grandeur. Magnificent fossil replicas have been mounted at key points around the hotel like Greek sculptures. The rooms, though, are cookie-cutter copies of each other with cheap prints of fossilized crinoids and trilobites on the walls, but the walkways are like a museum. The hotel is comprised of four buildings joined together to form an open square between them. A glass roof stretches over the atrium. Birds fly through the trees. Water cascades over fake rocks, tumbling down the inside of the hotel into an artificial lake surrounded by cafes, restaurants and shops. Kath finds the sound pleasing to her ear. The greenery is easy on her eyes. A light mist hangs in the air, drifting onto the raised wooden walkway winding through the trees. For Kath, it's refreshing.

The wall cladding by the elevators in the lobby is made from sheets of ancient limestone. Although the panels are probably only a few inches thick, each one is ten feet wide and easily thirty feet high. Even though she's drunk, Kath can't help herself. Reasoning will be the death of her. Her fingers touch lightly at tiny fossils that formed in the limestone. Her mind kicks into overdrive.

Tens of thousands of ammonite shells have been entombed in the stone. The sheets of rock have been carefully separated, exposing the tightly curled shells. Most of the fossils are no bigger than a fingernail. They're overlaid on top of each other, leaving no room between them.

"Mass death," she mumbles to the elderly lady standing next to her. "Volcanic ash probably poisoned the water, killing them in a localized event."

The lady looks at her as though she's mad.

Kath doesn't care. She's drunk. "They settled on the bottom. Silt buried them. And then we dug them up!"

The woman looks away, trying to ignore her.

Kath taps the stone, reiterating her earlier point. "This is a mass grave."

Ah, Drunk Kath is so cheerful.

The doors to the elevator open and they walk in, waving their keycards to unlock their individual floors. Kath leans against the rail at the back of the elevator. A glass surround provides them with a spectacular view of the atrium as they race up a rail on the side of the building.

"Four hundred million years," Kath says, swaying in response to the motion of the elevator. It might be going straight but she's not. Kath struggles not to tumble sideways. "That's how long their legacy had been preserved until we dug them up."

"Are you okay?" the woman asks.

"I'd give them no more than two hundred years," Kath says, ignoring the woman's question. "Acids from our skin. Carbon dioxide and oxygen in the air. Humidity. They won't last. They lasted four hundred *million* years and they won't last much longer. Shame, really. Fascinating. Interesting. But ultimately futile. Such a waste."

The doors of the elevator open and the woman steps out, saying, "Good night."

"Is it?" Kath asks as the doors close. She speaks but only for the benefit of the chrome surrounds on the glass doors. "Is it night already? And if so, is it really good?"

Sitting in the atrium bar with Nolan and Jacinta, Kath couldn't tell what time it was. The panel discussion ended around three in the afternoon. How long was she sitting there in that booth drinking wine?

The bright lights within the hotel make the cycles of day and night meaningless. She looks up, wanting to see the skylight, but that makes her dizzy. It's not worth it to confirm a stranger's assessment of time. And as for good, well, that's entirely subjective.

"What's your criteria?" Kath asks the empty elevator. She yells, "How are you defining good?"

The doors open again and she steps out onto her floor.

"2231," she mumbles, fumbling in her purse for her keycard.

Kath's already holding her keycard between her thumb and her forefinger, but that doesn't register in her dull brain. She had it in her hand before she entered the elevator. She needed it to unlock her floor. Now, she peers past the card, looking for another card—one that doesn't exist. She's sure it's buried somewhere deep within her purse.

"Where the hell is it?" she says, transferring the keycard to her other hand. Kath pokes her gloved fingers into the various interior pockets looking for the card in her left hand. Her purse slips from her shoulder. Credit cards, cash, lipstick, tampons, and her smartphone spill across the carpet.

"Oh, fuck," she says, kneeling and gathering everything back into her purse.

"Ah, there you are," she says, seeing the card in her left hand. She cinches her purse strap high on her shoulder and continues on down the hallway.

One side of the hall is open. There's a low wall. Kath peers over at the trees so far below her in the atrium. The world seems to spin around her.

"Bad idea," she says, backing up against a nearby door.

"2231," she says, looking at the room numbers as she walks along the corridor.

Kath trips herself, kicking the back of her own shoe, but she doesn't fall. Her aversion to the curse that is high-heel shoes has saved her from a nasty fall. She may only be five foot six and forever looking up at everyone, but she's not self-conscious about her height. Sneakers and flat-soled shoes are all she ever wears, and today that habit has avoided her face-planting on the carpet.

"Ah, here it is," she says, waving her keycard over the black sensor above the chrome door handle to her room. The tiny red LED refuses to turn green.

"Come on," she says, swiping again and again. She tries the handle. The door's locked. Kath rattles the handle, getting annoyed. The prospect of marching back to reception to get a new keycard issued isn't appealing.

The door opens.

A middle-aged, balding man stands before her. His belly protrudes over his boxer shorts.

"Whaddayawant?" he growls in a mob-like accent that's originated from somewhere near Chicago. Kath wants to ask where he's from as she went to high school in South Bend.

"Um—you're. You're in my room."

Kath leans to one side, peering past him.

"Who is it, honey?" a woman calls out in a shrill voice. "Don't let her in! She could be a robber!"

The layout is wrong. Kath's confused. She's trying to process two things at once—the woman's insane assumption a crime is about to unfold and the fact the bathroom and bed have swapped sides within the room.

The man slams the door, yelling, "Wrong room, weirdo!"

Kath stands there for a moment, stunned by the speed with which events unfolded. She looks at the room number on the door: 2213.

"Ah," she says, stumbling further along the hallway. Even though she's sloshed, she takes the time to verbalize the room numbers, mumbling them to herself as she walks toward 2231. Her room is down a narrow corridor that peels off the main walkway.

Kath swipes her keycard and is delighted when the tiny red LED turns green.

"Yippee!"

She pushes the door open and points at the bathroom to her left and the bed, further along the narrow hallway, making sure it's there as well. That's enough confirmation for her.

The door closes behind her with a thud. The lock clicks and she's enclosed in darkness. Kath slips her keycard into the plastic holder by the door and the lights come on.

"Oh, too bright," she says, turning off the main light and turning on the side lamp beside her bed.

Kath picks up the TV remote, clutching it awkwardly in her quasi-mechanical hand. Her finger hovers over the *on* button but she doesn't press it.

There was something that interested her on the news earlier tonight. Kath watched something about NASA on the TV above the bar. What was that again? Her finger descends, resting on but not pushing the button.

Ah, it was an active shooter at JSC. But why? Why would anyone do that? Disgusted and feeling depressed by the notion, she tosses the remote on the chair. She doesn't want to know. As it is, it'll be all anyone in the space community will talk about for the next week. The prospect of being bombarded on social media by such heartache deters her from even opening her phone. She can wait. Besides, there's nothing she can do other than being horrified and hurt along with everyone else.

Kath peels off her clothes, tossing them on the floor. She drapes her bra over a chair back and slips on a singlet instead of pajamas.

She turns around beside the bed, throwing her arms out wide.

"It's a simple approach from Mackenzie," she says, roleplaying a sports commentator at the Olympics. "She's performing a backward dive with only a 5.5 degree of difficulty, but it's the execution that will carry her forward in this competition. We're expecting a flawless approach and a clean entry into the pool from this young woman."

Kath collapses backward on the bed. The duvet catches her. The mattress is soft.

"Ahhh... and there it is... And she gets a perfect score from the judges."

There's a tiny red LED on the ceiling, marking the location of the smoke detector. Kath stares at it, drifting off to sleep. Her eyes close only to spring open again at the sound of a loud chirp directly above her.

"Oh, fuck no," Kath says, knowing the silence is temporary. She sits up and leans against the headboard, looking up at the ceiling. "Come on you, bastard. Do that again. I dare ya!"

Kath's looking for confirmation it's going to continue. In her drunken stupor, she wants to be absolutely sure what's happening. Two minutes stretch into eternity. Just when she thinks it's not going to happen, there's a loud chirp.

She calls reception.

"Hello, this is Dr. Mackenzie in room 2231."

It was 2231, right? Not 2213. Kath checks the number scratched on the back of the cardboard sleeve her keycard came in.

A deep male voice replies, "How can I help you, Ms. Mackenzie."

"It's—" Kath refrains from correcting him and saying, *doctor*. "The fire alarm in my room."

"The smoke alarm," the concierge says, with no qualms about correcting her. Kath ignores the contradiction brewing in her mind.

"Yes, yes. It's beeping at me."

"Have you been smoking in your room?" the man asks.

"No," she replies, sounding offended.

"Have you been smoking in your bathroom?"

"No!" Kath says with more gusto than before.

"The alarm won't sound unless it's activated by smoke."

"I haven't been smoking," Kath insists. "I don't smoke."

"Okay," the man says. The line goes dead as he hangs up. And the smoke alarm sounds off again.

Chirp!

"Fuck," Kath says, dialing reception a second time. Her blood is boiling. She's ready to unleash unholy hell on the asshole that just hung up on her.

A soft, petite woman's voice says, "This is Samantha at the Front desk, how can I help?"

"Oh, I," Kath says, feeling her anger deflate. "I was just talking to someone down there about my smoke detector—a man. A big man. Deep, heavy voice. Do you know him?"

"There are no men on this evening," the woman says. "How may I help you?"

"There *was* a man," Kath says. "And I *was* speaking to him. And—"

Chirp!

Damn it! That wasn't two minutes,

The smoke alarm lets out its high-pitched shrill squeak yet again. Kath could swear it's getting louder and more frequent.

"What can I do for you?" the woman asks in a soft voice.

Kath sighs. "The smoke detector in my room keeps chirping."

"Have you been smoking in your room?"

Kath sags into the bed, staring at the ceiling with the phone held against her ear. Her muscles feel like jelly but she pushes on.

"I have not been smoking. Not in my room. Not in the hall. Not in my bathroom. Not by the door. Not in the cupboard. Not on the floor. I don't smoke here. I don't smoke there. I don't smoke anywhere, Sam-I-am!"

Kath waits, expecting the receptionist to respond with—*But would you? Could you?* It seems Dr. Seuss wasn't a favorite growing up as the concierge doesn't bite.

"I'm sorry," the woman says. "The detector will only sound off in response to smoke."

"It's beeping. Chirping. Screaming. Isn't there something like a battery you could change to make it stop?"

"There are no batteries in our smoke detectors. They're all wired together so that if one goes off they all go off. They have their own independent battery pack in the basement."

Chirp!

"There!" Kath says, getting excited. "Did you hear it? It just did it again."

"I'm sorry, ma'am. There's nothing I can do."

"Can you send maintenance to look at it?"

"I can log a request for you," the woman says.

"Great," Kath says, sitting up and feeling a burst of excitement at such a mundane response. "When will they get here?"

"Between ten and eleven tomorrow morning."

"Tomorrow? No, no, no. I need to sleep tonight. Can you get me another room?"

"I'm sorry, ma'am. All our rooms are full. We have a conference on this weekend."

"I know. I know," Kath snaps. "I know all about the conference. Can you please get me another room? I'll pay for an upgrade."

"I'm sorry, ma'am. We're full. Do you have EarPods or some travel earplugs you could use? Perhaps they'll help you sleep."

Kath sighs. Three *I'm sorry, ma'ams*, making it clear there's nothing to be done.

"I've raised a ticket for you," the receptionist says. "Your incident number is INC0101385. Do you want to repeat that back to me?"

"No, I don't. It's fine," Kath says, determined not to write down a meaningless ticket number when someone should be able to find her request using her name or room number.

"We'll have someone out to you in the morning."

"Thank you," Kath says, hanging up, although she's not sure what she's thankful for. It's phatic communion—wasted pleasantries.

Chirp!

"You little fucker," she yells, feeling her blood boil inside her.

In lieu of a screwdriver or a butterknife, Kath grabs a teaspoon from the kitchenette and climbs up on her bed, standing precariously on the edge of the mattress. The corner sags beneath her, threatening to dump her unceremoniously on the carpet. She digs at the side of the plastic mounting on the detector.

Tampering with a smoke detector is a Federal offense.

"I'm not tampering with it," Kath says to an inert sticker. "I'm fixing it!"

The casing comes away revealing a tiny circuit board, a bunch of wiring and an LED. There's no speaker as such. Instead, there are two wafer-thin metal plates the size of a quarter set on top of each other. As if to torment her, the alarm sounds again.

Chirp!

It's louder. It's definitely louder.

"Piezoelectric transducer—I have you now!"

Kath looks carefully at the design. There's a thin gap between the plates. She jumps down from her bed, folds up some toilet paper, climbs back on the mattress and uses the teaspoon to shove the paper into the gap. Her plastic fingertips struggle to hold onto the spoon, but she manages to wedge the paper in place.

Chirp!

"Not so feisty now, are you?" she says as the sound drops. Kath works a little more paper in, packing it tightly, and waits. And waits. And waits.

Kath collapses on the bed, staring up at the wires hanging from the ceiling. She closes her eyes, feeling content. Monroe may have bested her in the debate today, but she's been victorious. She's won the battle of the smoke detector. Kath decides she'll clean out the paper in the morning and let maintenance fix the damn thing. Hopefully, they won't notice a slight bulge in the thin plates.

Kath drifts off to sleep, but her slumber is restless. She dreams of distant alarms, boots pounding down the hallway, helicopters circling overhead, lights on the curtains and yelling from the next room.

At some point in the middle of the night, she mumbles, "We're in Houston, not Vegas. Now go to sleep, goddamn it!" Kath rolls over, pulling a spare pillow over her head, trying to drown out the noise. Eventually, there's silence and she falls into a deep sleep.

ΛLONE

Kath wakes with a jackhammer pounding inside her head and a bladder that's as taut as a balloon ready to burst.

"Ugh," she mumbles, getting to her feet and feeling her way to the bathroom. She hits a switch, expecting to be blinded by a flash of intense white light, but nothing happens. Kath's in too much of a hurry to care. After she's relieved herself, she washes her hands, splashes some water on her face, and wanders back into the narrow hall beside the wardrobe.

Her phone is plugged in. She picks it up and the battery reads almost empty.

"Damn."

She unlocks it, wanting to check emails and jump on Twitter for a quick dopamine fix. There's no cell signal and the wifi's down.

"Ah, probably for the best," she says, knowing Twitter would be a dumpster fire after her debate with Monroe. People from all sides of the discussion would be weighing in. She's not missing anything by avoiding that.

There are eight missed calls. All of them from last night. All of them are from either Nolan or Jacinta.

"Must have been one helluva good restaurant," Kath says, putting her phone back down. She jiggles the cable, assuming a broken wire has robbed the battery of charge.

"Coffee," she says. "I need caffeine. Lots of it."

Kath shakes the kettle, feeling how much water is left after having a few cups of coffee yesterday. She hits the switch on the base. She's expecting a soft glow and a slight hum as it heats the water, but there's nothing. Kath grabs a few of the tiny single-serve bags of instant coffee and tears them open, dumping them into a mug. After the third, she adds a packet of sugar. Leaning down, she opens the fridge to grab some creamer. No light.

"What the hell?" she grumbles, hoping her DIY alarm solution hasn't caused a short that's taken out the power in her room. She checks the keycard holder by the door. Her keycard is still in place but there's no power. She pulls it out and reinserts it a couple of times, hoping for a rush of electricity to surge along the copper wiring.

"I do not need this," she says, wandering over to the window and pulling open the curtains. The blackout curtains are heavy. She throws them open and peers through the outer lace curtains. "What the hell?"

Kath pulls the lace curtains open as well.

Although *The Fossil* is located near downtown Houston, on the south side of the city, Kath's room faces west across the industrial area, toward the suburbs. She might work for NASA but that doesn't guarantee her a view of NASA's Johnson Space Center, even if it is just a bunch of buildings hidden by distant trees. For that, she'd need to be in the south tower. The west tower has the cheapest rooms so that's what got booked by some nameless government travel agent hellbent on saving a few bucks.

Smoke rises from burning buildings in the distance. Fires happen, but dozens of uncontrolled blazes don't break out randomly across a city. Each fire releases a plume of black smoke reminiscent of burning oil rigs in the Middle East. The air is thick with smoke, giving it a bluish tinge. The sun appears as a smudge in the sky.

It's then Kath notices something she hasn't heard in several days—silence. There's no hum of the air conditioning, no voices outside in the hall, no footsteps passing by her door, no cars down on the street. The LED on the smoke alarm is flashing in a pattern—three long, three short.

"What is going on?" she asks herself.

In a daze, Kath wanders to the door and peers into the hallway. There's no one there. She steps out onto the plush carpet, looking both ways for someone—anyone. The door to her room swings shut behind her. She doesn't think anything of that motion until it's almost closed. Suddenly, her heart races. Panic washes over her.

"Fuck," she swears, rushing at the door.

Too late. Kath pushes hard against the steel, but it's to no avail. Deep within the hollow surface, she feels the lock click in place.

Ka-thunk!

"No. No. Noooo! Please."

In that instant, Kath's idle curiosity is replaced with abject terror. She's locked herself out of her room. It's pointless and she knows it, but she pounds on the door. For her, this is a nightmare scenario. No keycard. No purse. No smartphone. No ID. No clothing beyond what she slept in.

Kath's wearing a skimpy pair of underwear and a thin singlet with the image of Winnie the Pooh sticking his paw in a jar of honey.

"Oh, no."

Her hands immediately cross in front of her crotch, wondering who's going to pop out of the next room and see her looking disheveled and exposed.

"Great! This is just fucking great," she says, backing up against the wall and trying to disappear. If she could, she'd shrink into oblivion. At the very least, any wannabe paparazzi with a smartphone will only get a photo of her in side-profile. Her hair must look a mess. She ruffles her long locks in vain.

Reluctantly, Kath concedes her dignity is gone. Once these photos circulate on the internet, her reputation will be left in tatters. Reputation? Who is she kidding? What a joke. Given all she's struggled

149

with over the past few years, it's heartbreaking to think the public's going to fixate on *Hangover Kath* rather than *Science Kath*. No one's taking any photos, but she can't help herself. Her mind is unraveling at the thought of being caught in the corridor, unable to escape. She's horrified to think this as-yet-untaken photo will define her legacy. It'll be the image people call to mind whenever her name comes up.

What's worse is she's not wearing her gloves or the exoskeleton on her hands. Her missing fingers and scarred hands are no longer hidden from sight. It shouldn't matter but it does. Everyone she's ever met since the life-support failure on the Orion has told her it doesn't matter—and yet they still stare at the disfigured stubs she has for fingers. Oh, it's not always obvious. Sometimes it's a sneak peek but it always leaves her feeling like a leper. Appearances shouldn't matter says a society obsessed with Instagram posts and the supposed beauty of youth.

Why does she care? She wants to tell herself she doesn't, but that's a lie. It's the humiliation. It's the lack of any semblance of control. She's vulnerable. Helpless. Exposed.

Her shoulders sag.

Kath's room isn't on the main concourse so she doesn't get the luxury of a view over the atrium. She's a short walk from the central core of the hotel, but that means she's staying in a dead-end. Perhaps that's why it's so quiet. Maybe most of the conference attendees have already checked out. They probably left their baggage with the concierge before heading to the closing session.

What time is it? From the way the light comes in through the overhead windows in the atrium at the end of the hall, it's got to be at least ten in the morning—if not later. Kath's late, but she's not going anywhere. Everyone will be in the main conference hall listening to the summation and closing arguments. Monroe will be gloating about having retrieved organic material from another seedpod. Kath's supposed to be backstage. Perhaps it's best she isn't there. Either way, Monroe was always going to have fun at her expense—yet again.

Kath pounds on the door next to hers.

"Hello? Is there anyone there?"

No answer. She rushes to the next door, wrapping her knuckles on the steel.

"Hello? I need to call reception. Can I use your phone?"

No one replies.

She's manic, slapping her bare hand on yet another door.

"I've been locked out of my room. Please. I just need to call down to the lobby."

It's then she notices the red flashing light over the fire exit at the end of the hall. It's pulsating with the same rhythm as the smoke alarm in her room.

Ahead of her, there's a T-shaped intersection. Two of the three converging hallways look out over the atrium. She creeps toward the main hall, keeping to one side, trying to hide from view.

The walkway is empty.

A quick glance across the open area within the atrium allows her to see the walkways on several other floors above and below hers. There's no movement anywhere.

Kath peers over the edge of the railing. The cafes and walkways below are empty. Dark stains mark a few of the paths. As much as she wants to think someone dragged a sack of flour through spilled paint she suspects that's blood. The color, though, is dark, almost crimson, but that could be due to the shadows.

Tree branches shake. They move in sequence, tracing the path of something big that's hidden from sight. Whatever it is, it's meandering through the fake forest, keeping to the shadows.

"What the hell?" she whispers, stepping back from the edge.

Kath's a mess. Her mind is like a construction zone at the height of summer. Jackhammers attack the concrete as big trucks roll by. People yell to be heard over the noise. Horns sound. And all of this is occurring in the absolute silence of her mind. She rubs her temples, wanting to shake her headache.

"Damn it. I can't think straight."

There's a dead rat lying on the floor by the ice machine. Its back leg twitches. Okay, not dead. Dying. Blood drips from its mouth onto the carpet. A red fuzz covers its eyes and nose, hiding them from view.

Goosebumps break out on Kath's skin, but not from the cold. Her body is responding to the realization something's horribly wrong. All her worries melt away. She's no longer concerned about her lack of clothing. Even her headache seems to fade into insignificance. Her bare feet tread lightly on the carpet. She has no intention of banging on any more goddamn doors. Making noise and attracting attention seems like a bad idea—a very bad idea.

Although it's tempting to be alarmed by the *Jurassic Park* scene playing out beneath her in the atrium, it's the fuzz on the rat that worries her.

"Not good," she whispers. "So very definitely, absolutely not good. Monroe, what have you done?"

Against her better judgment, Kath takes off her singlet, pulling it up over her head. She bundles it together and wraps it around her face, covering her nose and mouth and using it as a mask. Those 3D printed extensions for her hands would come in damn useful right about now. As it is, she struggles to tie a knot with the stubs of her fingers. The dexterity she once took for granted is but a dream.

Rather than leaving the material hanging like a bandana, allowing airflow from beneath, Kath bunches it up like a gag and ties it tight behind her head. It's difficult to breathe through the layers, but that's the point. If there's an airborne pathogen, she wants no part of that in her lungs. In the absence of an N95 mask, this is going to have to do.

At that moment, Kath becomes acutely aware of someone watching her from further along the corridor looking out over the atrium. Before she turns, she senses a pair of eyes staring at her. Someone's standing there, blocking the walkway. Their shadow falls on the carpet.

Kath turns slowly.

A boy of maybe six or seven is standing beside a partially open door. He's in shock, that much is obvious from his dilated pupils. If he was freaked out before, he's got to be on the verge of hysteria now, seeing a strange woman standing before him topless in a pair of lace panties with a shirt wrapped around her face. All he can see is the panic in her eyes.

"I know this doesn't look good," Kath says in a muffled voice. She has her hands out in front of her, appealing for calm. As much as she wants to withdraw her arms and cover her breasts, she's worried the boy's going to scream. If anything, he seems more shocked by the scars lining her palms and the stubs where once there were fingers. Even though the accident happened years ago, the tender skin on her palms and the scars on her hands have a ruddy, pink tinge. It's as though she's still recovering from surgery. He's probably never seen anyone with this level of disfigurement and yet here she is—reaching for him. To him, she must be a monster.

"Please," she says, stepping slowly toward him. The boy's eyes drop. He stares at his shoes for a few seconds. Kath edges closer.

Without saying anything, he reaches up over his head and pulls off his t-shirt. He copies her, covering his mouth with the shirt and pulling the ends behind his head. He can't quite manage to tie a knot.

"Here, let me help you," she says, kneeling before him. He turns around, allowing her to tie off the shirt. Kath can't quite get it into a knot, but she gets enough folds to hold it in place.

"There," she says, gently turning him back toward her. "Biosafety first, right?"

He nods as though he knows what she means. That he's copying her tells her something important. He's lost. He's seeking help. He craves an adult to lead him through this nightmare, which begs the question, where are his parents?

"Do you know what happened?" she asks.

He doesn't blink.

"Do you know where everyone is?"

153

Tears well up in the boy's eyes.

"No. Of course, you don't. You're a child. You're scared. Hey, it's okay."

Kath kneels before him. Gently, she wraps her hands around his chest and holds him tight.

"It's all right," she says. "Everything's going to be all right."

That's a lie, but it's all she's got. She's lying both to him and herself. Somehow, lies make her feel better.

"What's your name?" she asks, leaning back and looking deep into his dark brown eyes. Tears roll down his cheeks.

"I'm Kath," she says, smiling, not that he can see her lips. "Crazy nude lady, huh? You must think I'm mad. I'm not. I'm a doctor—a scientist."

She gets up, taking his hand.

"Is this your room?" she asks, walking forward. A boot holds the door ajar, but it hasn't been placed there to stop the door from closing. It's fallen there. Someone's collapsed facedown inside the room.

The boy stops, pulling his hand away from hers, refusing to go any closer.

"You wait here," she says, letting go of his fingers. "I'll be back. I promise."

Hotel rooms are a dead end, right? So that's not a lie. She's telling him the truth. If she goes in there, she has to come out again, right? Kath shudders. If not her, then something is coming out of the darkness.

Kath pushes the door open. It creaks on its hinges. A middle-aged man lies on his stomach in the hallway with his head twisted to one side. His arms have sprawled awkwardly on the carpet. It's clear he made no effort to catch himself when he fell. There's a carry-on bag sitting beside the door. It's a child's backpack colored pink with flowers. Kath uses it to prop open the door, allowing natural light from the atrium to spill inside.

Kath steps around the dead man, taking care to avoid touching

154

him. It's irrational. He's not going to attack her. And yet she cannot bear to brush up against his jeans.

The kid is traumatized. He came from this room. This has to be his father. Crawling past his dead dad to reach her in the hallway when he heard her must have broken his heart. He had to have heard Kath slamming on the doors further down the corridor. That must have been what drew him out of the room. He's been hiding in here but where? And from what?

The man has a phone in his back pocket. The indent in his jeans is unmistakable. Kath grabs a trashcan from beside the minibar fridge. The thin plastic bag contains a crushed Coke can and a candy wrapper, but it's what lies beneath them that interests her. She pulls out the bag, scrunches it up, and leaves it lying to one side.

"Come on, housekeeping," she mutters. "Don't let me down."

At the bottom of the now-empty trashcan, there's a small roll of transparent plastic bags—spare bags stored for a maid in a hurry, allowing her to change out one bag with another in seconds.

"Yes!"

Kath pulls them out and unrolls a couple of garbage liners, slipping them over her hands and using the bags as impromptu gloves.

"Hygiene first," she mumbles to herself from behind her makeshift mask. "We follow best-practice in this lab."

She puts the garbage can back, saying, "You've got to love housekeepers."

Kath pulls the man's smartphone from his back pocket without touching him or the phone directly.

She's down on one knee beside the dead body. As soon as she turns the phone over in her hand, the internal motion detector causes the screen to spring into life. The lock screen is a photo of a couple at the beach with two children, one of whom is standing behind her in the hallway. Sorry, kid. Kath consoles herself with the realization that, as heartbreaking as it is, the young boy already knows what's happened. All she's done is confirm her suspicions. At the very least, she should be able to identify him and reunite him with his Mom—assuming she escaped *The Fossil*.

Looking at the battery symbol, the phone has about 75% charge. There's no signal though, not that she was expecting one given what she's seen so far. Kath hits the flashlight button on the lock screen. A brilliant white light illuminates the room. It's focused immediately in front of her. Slowly, Kath pans around, taking everything in. This room is exactly the same as hers, right down to the placement of the twin queen-size beds. Light ripples over toothbrushes and shaving cream in the bathroom, an empty shower cubicle and then back out into the room. To her relief, there's nothing hidden in the darkness.

Kath inches forward. She's in no hurry to stand up. Staying low gives her a better perspective. She shines the light beneath the beds. She's not sure what she's looking for—hopefully, nothing, but her heart races nonetheless.

The beds are made. That's an important detail to note. It tells her that whatever took place last night happened early in the evening. At a guess, she crashed around 6 pm. Someone as young as this kid is going to be put to bed around seven or eight. The phone is showing 10:52 am so it's been almost fifteen hours since all this went down. Whatever's happening here at *The Fossil*, Kath is way behind the play.

Several suitcases have been set standing next to each other in the narrow gap between the beds. Okay, so Mom took the daughter on the lock screen and headed down to whatever evacuation was taking place. Dad and the boy stayed behind. The damn fool didn't want to leave his luggage. What was so goddamn important? Nothing. Nothing is ever as important as people think.

Kath's mind casts back to a review she read on air travel safety. In an emergency, flight attendants estimate 90% of passengers take some kind of baggage with them off the plane. It's stupid, but it's human. It's tragically predictable. It's not selfish so much as narrow-minded. No one would intentionally kill themselves or any of their fellow passengers by taking a stupid bag with them, but selfishness leads to unintended fuck-ups. Kath can't fault the man. She would have grabbed her laptop—

like the damn thing isn't already backed up to the cloud and insured for its replacement value. Hell, it's not even hers. It belongs to NASA. Humans are dumb—and she means that in the nicest possible way—and she includes herself in that assessment.

Kath continues scanning the room. The curtains are drawn, but they're ruffled on the far side. There's a towel on the carpet by the curtains. It's not difficult to see this is where the kid hid from whatever went down. Those curtains probably saved him—not just from sight, but from anything in the air. The poor little guy would have spent the night in utter terror. It's no wonder he's not talking. But what was he hiding from? Whatever it was, it's gone—she hopes.

There's a backpack on the desk. The zip is open. Kath is about to get to her feet, satisfied there's nothing threatening within the room when a shadow crosses the door behind her. She freezes. With a deft touch, she turns off the flashlight. There's rustling. Something's creeping up on her, moving closer to her, looming over her. Kath's heart is beating so hard it's about to burst through her ribs.

She turns.

The kid is standing behind her. He's got his hands up in front of him. His fingers wiggle within small, transparent garbage bags.

Kath breathes. She wants to tell him not to do that again, but she can't fault the poor kid. He's standing with one foot on either side of the leg of his dead father.

"So you're a scientist too, huh?" she says from behind her scrunched-up singlet. If he's smiling, she can't tell, but there aren't any more tears. She's alive. That seems to give him hope. It appears he wants to be part of the team. Kath turns the flashlight back on.

Like the rat, the dead father has what looks like fungus growing over his face. Kath takes a towel from the bathroom and drapes it over his head. It's as much to hide his death as it is to avoid stirring spores into the air. She's slow, trying to show both him and his son a modicum of respect. Death is the cruelest aspect of life. Dignity is a poor substitute for life, but it at least gives the kid some closure.

Kath steps past the fallen man, being careful not to bump his body. She shines the light on the name tags attached to each of the three suitcases.

Phil Watson

Jenny Watson

Jimmy and Lily Watson

"James," she says softly, although she's not sure why she used the formal version of his name. The result, though, is instant. Jimmy looks at her as though he's seen a ghost. "I mean, Jimmy. We're going to get out of here, Jimmy. I'm going to get you back to your Mom, okay?"

Jimmy nods.

It's a lie, but he doesn't know that. Kath's already figured it out. If they're near the epicenter of some kind of interstellar biological contamination that's escaped the lab, they are well and truly fucked. It seems the samples NASA brought back from the *Anduru*-class object that skimmed Tunguska well over a hundred years ago were still viable. They're probably not a virus in the terrestrial sense of the word, but it would be impossible to tell for sure without an electron scanning microscope. The damn thing seems to be spreading like one.

They're going to die. Both of them. Kath doesn't have the heart to tell that to the kid. Up until this point, he's lived in a world of movie heroes overcoming all odds. How could she explain the need for sacrifice? How can she explain that they *need* to die to contain the spread? If they don't, everyone else dies? She can't even convince herself of that even though she understands what's going to happen next. The government is going to have to scorch the earth. Nothing within the contaminated zone will be allowed to leave. The chance of someone escaping with an undetected infection is just too great. If earthly viruses like *varicella-zoster* can cause chickenpox in kids and then lie dormant for fifty years before manifesting as shingles when those same kids reach old age, there is no way in hell anyone is getting out of this region alive.

Kath says, "I'm cold. I'm going to try on some of your Mom's clothes. Is that okay?"

Jimmy nods. She's not cold, but that nod has told her two things. He's compliant and he can't tell when she's lying. Kath pushes him a little further, wanting to better understand his mental state.

"Do you think she'd mind?"

Jimmy shakes his head. Okay, so he has a clear notion of his mother's kindness. Whether he's right or not is impossible to tell, but he thinks his Mom would give Kath some of her clothes. Most women would. Most of them would understand the embarrassment of being caught topless in public—not that men don't do the same thing all the time without anyone second-guessing them. Even for those women that like to push the boundaries of modesty, being accidentally exposed is very different from making a deliberate statement.

Jimmy looks up at Kath, watching her every move. He needs a strong, confident adult. With his father lying dead behind him, he needs a surrogate to help him through the pain of the moment. Regardless of what may come, Kath is determined to be there for him.

Kath pulls one of the suitcases onto the bed and pops it open. She rummages around, using the light on the smartphone to sort between skirts and dresses.

"Ah," she says, pulling out a t-shirt and shorts. "Mom likes going to the gym, doesn't she?"

Jimmy nods.

Kath's comment might have sounded casual, but it's calculated. She's going to talk about his mom a lot over the coming hours to help Jimmy keep his mind off his dead dad.

"Your mom is about my size. Perfect."

Kath slips on some shorts. They're baggy so she pulls the drawstring to tighten them. To slip on the white shirt with a red *Nike* symbol, she has to bite on her makeshift mask, keeping it in place. Kath holds her singlet with her teeth as she pulls the shirt over her head. Then she tightens her mask again. The chances are she hasn't stirred up anything from within the bag, but the act of dumping the case on the bed probably caused an invisible dust plume of sorts. Hopefully, the pathogen isn't airborne for hours. Given the air conditioning hasn't been running since the power failed, this extraterrestrial bug or whatever it is probably didn't make it this far within the room as the air is so still.

Kath checks the size of a pair of tennis shoes, holding them up against her feet.

"Your mom and I have the same size feet. I bet your mom is pretty cool."

Again, Jimmy nods. Kath pulls on some socks and then the shoes, all the while working with her stubby fingers inside plastic bags.

"That's better. Much better," she says.

A pair of reading glasses have been tossed on the table. Kath tries them on. The prescription is stronger than hers, but they allow her to read small-print. She won't be able to wear these for long without straining her eyes, but if she needs to read any fine print, they'll be invaluable. She slips them into her pocket.

Kath opens a bag of toiletries, dumping them on the bed beside her. There are a pair of nail clippers. That's the closest she's going to get to scissors in the hotel. She slips them into her other pocket, knowing they'll come useful at some point.

A bunch of pillboxes and elongated cardboard drug packets scatter on the duvet alongside a hairbrush. The Watsons must have been in the midst of packing as the toothbrushes and toothpaste are still in the bathroom. There's a shaving mirror in the bag, though. One side is convex, giving her a rather intimate view of her eyebrows in the dull light. She turns it over and the other side is a regular mirror.

"This could come in handy for signaling a helicopter," she says, putting it to one side.

Kath puts anything useful on the table beside the backpack.

"Looks like Mom enjoyed a bit of glam," she says, picking up several different types of nail polish along with a plastic bottle of nail polish remover. "They're not going to let these things on a plane. You guys must have driven here, huh? Where are you from? Texas?

Oklahoma? New Mexico?"

Kath sorts through the pills, mumbling, "Ah, God bless America and our love of prescription drugs!"

She squints to make out the labels, using the glasses to read the instructions and ingredients. She sorts through the pills and picks out packets that are of interest to her.

Kath pops a couple of ibuprofen out of their blister packs and slips them under her mask. She crunches on the tablets rather than trying to swallow them without water. They taste horrible, but she's aware she may get a placebo kick out of that—the worse a medicine tastes, the better it performs in trials, regardless of actual efficacy. She needs to get rid of her pounding hangover so she can think straight.

There's glucophage and levothyroxine. According to the labels, they're used to treat diabetes and thyroid disease, but there are no custom labels stuck on the bottles—no indication about who they're for.

"These are some strong drugs," Kath says, confused as to why Jimmy's mom would leave these behind. Perhaps the family was downstairs when the evacuation was called. Maybe they were already packed, ready to leave the next day. The evacuation was announced and everyone crammed into the lobby. Dad headed back to the room for his medication. Mom took their daughter with her to the evac point. From there, things must have become chaotic for him to have died here, stranding Jimmy in the room. In typical fashion, some evac coordinator probably told her they were on the next bus or something.

"Do you take any of these?"

Jimmy shakes his head.

Kath keeps reading the labels. Something about these pills isn't quite right. She turns them over in her hand and then it strikes her.

"Is your mom a doctor?"

Jimmy nods.

That explains the lack of personalized labels. Self-medicating is never advisable, but cutting corners to save a few bucks isn't a crime. She must know someone in the dispensary.

There's warfarin as well as a few other non-steroid anti-inflammatory drugs. Jimmy's dad was overweight. Perhaps he had a heart condition.

Child-proof plastic medicine bottles are difficult for Kath to open with her mangled hands. She dumps the pills she doesn't want on the duvet and keeps the empty plastic pill bottles. They're small and could come in handy.

Kath pockets a packet of Tylenol and turns her attention to the backpack.

She finds an open packet of cigarettes and a lighter. She keeps them out of sight in the bag. She doesn't want to ask Jimmy if his dad smoked. Finding them is confirmation enough. Jimmy needs to be thinking about his mom, not his dad. With some sleight of hand, she pockets the lighter. If dad smoked and had a heart condition, that might have contributed to his demise—along with whatever the hell is in the air.

It takes her a few seconds to poke around with the flashlight in one hand before she spots a wallet beneath a beach towel and a bottle of sun cream. So they weren't here for the conference. It seems they spent their time down by the swimming pool. To be fair, the outdoor pool at *The Fossil* is impressive. The term '*pool*' is an understatement. Although it's on the roof of the entrance and sprawls out over the hotel's shopping precinct, the pool area has been landscaped to look like an oasis. There are fake fossils of various dinosaurs placed around a vast, sandy beach leading down into the crystal clear waters of the pool. Palm trees provide shade. There are slides for the kids and lifeguards to let Mom and Dad relax—if only a little.

Kath rummages through the wallet. She finds a driver's license for Arizona. There's a date of birth.

"Yes," she mutters. Kath writes it down on a pad of paper provided with the room. She swipes up on the phone, wanting to unlock it. The keypad comes up.

Enter Passcode

"Okay, Phil," Kath says. "Come on. Don't let me down."

Six potential digits come up as blank spots on the phone. She enters his date of birth using month, day, and two digits for the year.

The phone opens.

"All right!" she says a little too loud and with too much enthusiasm for Jimmy. He shrinks back. "It's okay. This is good. Well, it's not good from a security best-practices perspective, but it's good for us. Your Dad was predictable—in a good way. Hmm, we still don't have any signal, but we can record things. We can show others what we've seen."

Kath holds up a scrap of paper with the date of birth, showing it to Jimmy. "This is really good."

It takes a bit of effort, but she tucks the paper into the back of the phone case, saying, "Regardless of what happens, anyone that picks up this phone will be able to learn about what happened here."

The significance of unlocking the phone is lost on Jimmy, but for Kath, it's a point of professional pride. She activates the video and pans around the room with the phone light on, catching Jimmy and returning to herself, speaking as she films.

"This is Dr. Kathleen Mackenzie. I found Jimmy Watson in the hallway and retrieved his father's phone from room 2217. We're going to collect supplies and make our way to the roof to signal for help. I'll document what we find along the way.

"At this point, I have no idea what's happening, but as you can see from my face covering, I'm concerned about airborne contaminants. I've observed what could be microbial mats or fungal growth around the face of dead creatures. This appears to be limited to the eyes, nose, and mouth. I have no way of knowing if there's a causal morbidity link or if this is simply some kind of correlation post-mortem. I'll continue making observations for as long as I can."

Kath pushes the stop button. There's a sense of resignation in the motion of her hand. The words 'for as long as I can' resonate in her mind. Someone's going to find this phone. Eventually. They're going to see the passcode. They'll charge the battery, unlock the phone and watch the various videos she records over the next few hours. For them, the videos will be a record of what unfolded within the abandoned hotel. Hopefully, the contents of the video will help them piece together what has happened in Houston, but she'll be dead. There's an awful sense of contradiction in the act of pushing the phone into her pocket. That particular moment feels both bitter and triumphant. For now, she's alive. She's captured her reasoning and thinking for others to see, but she knows it'll be watched in memoriam. Anyone that reviews her videos will do so with a tinge of regret. For her, though, this is a win. She's made progress.

A few minutes ago, she was functionally helpless and naked. Now she has resources—possibilities. To those that inhabit the future, though, seeing her recording will be a tragic testimony of loss.

GENERATION
OF VIPERS

Greenspoint is fifteen miles north of Houston. Several freeways converge there, forming a beltway on the outskirts of the city.

The streets around the freeway are blocked with traffic fleeing for the countryside, but there's nowhere to go. The freeways are jammed. State police try diverting northbound traffic onto the southbound lanes, but that causes even more confusion with a crash further along the freeway. Emergency vehicles are brought to a standstill by the gridlock. Their blue and red lights are ignored by those fleeing the carnage in Houston.

Andy is on foot. The buses sent to evacuate the hotel have been caught like icebergs in pack ice. It only takes a handful of fender benders to bring the freeway to a grinding halt. Most of the passengers have stayed on or near the bus as it sits idling on the side of the freeway with its a/c running, burning through its diesel for nothing more than comfort. Fuck that shit. It's the end of the goddamn world, but god forbid anyone should get sweaty.

Andy's angry.

"Sheeple," he mutters, hauling his backpack high on his shoulder as he walks along the edge of the freeway. As much as he may try to rationalize his behavior, he knows his efforts are futile. Walking is no substitute for driving. Even if the cars and trucks around him are only edging forward a few feet every couple of minutes, they'll still outpace him once the accidents are cleared. He might walk a hundred yards for their ten, but they'll race away when the road opens back up. Even so, he's restless. He needs to walk. Watching one boot after another crunch on the loose gravel at the side of the road helps clear his mind.

"The apocalypse has come and all we care about is the dumb shit we bought online," he mumbles, seeing an SUV with junk piled up in the back. Fishing rods and rolled-up yoga mats are visible through the windows. They've been shoved hard against the glass by sleeping bags and tents pushed in behind them.

Even when the camera isn't rolling, Andy provides commentary. This footage isn't going to be broadcast anywhere beyond his own skull, but he can't help himself. Talking is thinking out loud.

"Look! Some genius has decided he can bug out with his camping gear and save his family that way. Oh, like no one else has thought of that! He's in for a shock when everyone descends on whatever shit hole fishing spot he thinks is safe and secluded.

"Surviving off-grid is a fucking myth. Have you ever noticed how dependent those living *off* the grid are on all the shit we build *on* the grid? They're idiots! The only people they're fooling are themselves."

He walks on, talking to himself, much to the amusement of those sitting in their cars. Andy kicks at the loose stones on the shoulder of the freeway. He might not be going anywhere fast, but he's going somewhere. Those chumps in their cars are like lemmings lined up for the cliff.

"Anyone living in the suburbs is kidding themselves if they think they can just bug out and live off the land. Humans are too damn soft. We've domesticated ourselves. Hell, when the polar vortex hit Texas last year, it was those living off-grid that suffered the most. So much for survivalists. Me? I think there's all our plans and preparation and training and tough talk—and then there's the bitter fucking reality of screwing around in the woods."

Andy leans forward, working his backpack higher.

"We're all carrying too much shit," he says, regretting not taking his own advice and traveling light. He's carrying broadcast equipment, charged battery packs, cameras, and a portable data uplink router. He used this kit to perform a couple of YouTube shows on the drive down from DC.

He stumbles along the offramp, grabbing at the straps going over his shoulders.

"My Precious!"

As humorous as his mimicry of Gollum might be, it's not as far from the truth as he'd like.

Andy's resigned to being stuck in Houston.

"Hope is a disease. Hope blinds people to reality," he mumbles as his mind rambles idly through various concepts. It'll take everyone else far too long to realize they're not going anywhere. And by then, it'll be too late. They'll be out of fuel and at the back of the line for whatever evacuation the military eventually organizes. Not Andy. He can see what's coming. Any time people move *en masse*, it's always a cluster fuck. Always. The trick is not getting fucked by the chaos.

Weeds brush against his jeans. The flattened, almost mummified remains of a dead raccoon lie beneath the guardrail. Its leathery skin and crushed skull are a somber reminder of the fleeting nature of life.

Army helicopters fly low overhead, ferrying in supplies from Houston's George W. Bush International Airport. It's a civilian airport. It's just a few minutes away by car—if any of them could fucking move! Someone's decided to set up a command center in Greenspoint. As it's on the outskirts of Houston, it makes sense in terms of logistics.

Andy mumbles, "Bullets and bombs might win battles, but it's logistics that wins wars."

From the vantage point of the raised freeway, Andy saw several rows of khaki-colored tents set up in a mall parking lot. Helicopters land on the football field of a high school opposite the mall. The strip of road in between is clear of vehicles. That's got to be the only road within fifty miles that's not clogged with cars. It doesn't take a genius to realize this

167

place has become a military staging post. Civilians might be fleeing north. The army is about to head south.

Andy walks past a young couple in a convertible. They've got the top down, but not because of the unseasonably warm weather. Like everyone else, their backseat is packed with boxes and suitcases. They couldn't close the roof if they tried.

"Hey," the woman calls out. "Are you with the media?"

It's the tripod strapped to the side of his pack that gives it away. He nods. Technically, Andy's a YouTuber. He's not with the news, but he's media, in his mind at least.

"Have you seen them?"

Andy comes to a halt. He shouldn't. He should keep going and make contact with the military. Andy's got his eye on those empty helicopters returning to the airport for more goods. If he can weasel his way onboard one of those, he might be able to wrangle a flight out of Houston. Pride gets the better of him. Bragging will give him a dopamine hit and that'll make the pack seem a little lighter.

"Oh, yeah," he says. "I've seen them."

"So they're real?" the guy says. "This isn't some kind of dumb stunt? You know, like a conspiracy theory?"

The woman says, "I heard it was a joke."

"And yet you're here—sitting in traffic," Andy says.

"I heard they could fly," she says.

Andy sighs. Something he's struggled to explain to the likes of Dr. Kathleen Mackenzie and Brigadier General Nolan Landis is the fine line between misinformation and disinformation. Oh, the definitions are simple enough. Misinformation is *mis*taken—it's right there in the word itself. To his mind, disinformation is deliberate. It's cause and effect. They're both information, though, and that's the problem. Humans are information processing machines. Garbage in, garbage out. Someone is targeted with disinformation and they enthusiastically disseminate misinformation. The real issue is intent. Disinformation is malicious. There's a determined effort to mislead. Misinformation is inadvertent.

It's ill-informed but well-meaning, and that's what makes it so damn hard to counter. If someone lies to his face, Andy has no problem calling them a fucking asshole. If someone's sincere but misled, it's almost impossible to convince them otherwise. Pride demands they latch on to their misinformation and they burrow into his skin like a tick on a hot summer's day, refusing to relent. He's got to deflect before these guys become entrenched in their position.

"No, no, no," Andy says.

"How do you know?" the woman asks.

"I was at *The Fossil*," Andy says, boasting. He knows that's enough to win him some brownie points. Now he has to dissuade her of her misinformation. "They were on the ground. There was nothing in the air."

"And you got out?" the man asks.

Andy gestures to himself as though the answer is obvious. He adds, "It was bad but not as bad as they made out on TV. We had about an hour's notice before the damn things turned up. There's a bus depot next door. They loaded us up and shipped us out."

"Cool."

Andy can't hide the look of disgust on his face. Trying to sleep through the night in a bus that's crawling along at one or two miles an hour while knowing you're being chased by something from another planet is anything but cool. There's some kind of alien invasion or infection or whatever unfolding and they think that's cool? It takes a determined effort not to get angry. The young man doesn't mean anything by it. You want cool? Cool your jets, Andy.

Andy slows things down, asking, "Did you see the one that flipped a police car? They caught that on video."

They both nod.

"Okay, we were about three hundred yards further up the road when that happened. We were turning onto the freeway. I saw it dragging the cop out of the car."

"Damn," the man says. His eyes go wide.

"Is it true they can change shape?" the woman asks.

Andy is surprised by how quickly dis/misinformation is spreading. It hasn't been twenty-four hours and already the facts are being embellished. Flying? Shape-shifting? What's next?

It can't be disinformation—not yet. There hasn't been enough time for the usual antagonists to get involved and start trolling the American public like carnival barkers at a sideshow. *'Step right up. Step right up!'* says the man in the top hat and tails with the black cane and charming smile. *'For just the price of your sanity, you too can know the hidden secrets of this world...'*

Oh, the Redditors and the 4Chan dude-bros along with the Russians and the Chinese will eventually catch on and realize they can fuck with people's heads, but for now, this isn't another *'stolen'* election or a bunch of vaccine lies. This is good old-fashioned misinformation, as in, missing any valid, useful information.

"Not shape," Andy says. "Color. They're like a chameleon. You see one of these things and it's grey. You blink and it's gone, only it ain't. Look closely and it's still there—but you can't see it until it moves."

"I heard they can turn into things, like trees or a bus. They said they can morph into different things."

"No, it's like camo in the forest. Its skin turns into a bunch of colors. The one that flipped the cop car crouched by the bushes in the median strip, and—damn—I couldn't see it no more. It looked like green leaves and shadows and concrete and shit. And then it crept forward, breaking the illusion."

Although he's grumpy as hell, Andy's enjoying talking to the couple.

Andy's angry. He's always angry. He's got to be careful it doesn't show as people take him the wrong way. These two, though, make him feel smart. It's nice to feel important, but that's all he's got. He's out of alien encounter stories. From here on, it's all bullshit—and it sounds like they've already been fed a bunch of lies about these things.

The man says, "On the news, they were saying they came down

170

here in UFOs. They said NASA's been hiding them in a secret base beneath Antarctica."

Andy asks them, "Does this place look like Antarctica to you?"

The irony of refuting a conspiracy theory isn't lost on Andy. It brings a smile to his lips to know he can stay on task and not jump to a bunch of wild guesses. There was a time he would have been fanning these flames.

The woman says, "My brother told me there have been attacks in LA and New York."

"Really?" Andy says, doing his best to sound skeptical. Hearsay isn't evidence.

"They're fast, though, right?" the woman asks, picking up on his doubts. "If you blink, they're on you." She snaps her fingers. "Just like that."

"Well, they've still got to cover the ground in between," Andy says. "They're aliens, not magicians."

The two of them look to him for more information, but Andy's distracted by the helicopters passing overhead.

"Anyway, you guys stay safe, okay?"

"Wait," the woman says. "You're leaving?"

Andy's already walking on along the sidewalk. He turns, saying, "No point in staying."

"Where are you going?"

And just like that, Andy's got a couple of new best friends. What do they expect of him? Answers? Guidance? He's no guru. What's the old saying? Put out a saucer of milk just once and the neighbor's cat is yours for life. There's anguish in their eyes. They're stuck in their car with a bunch of ultimately meaningless possessions, but those dumb things are an anchor holding them back.

The pickup in front of them inches forward roughly ten feet. They almost rear-end the flatbed in their race to catch up to Andy.

"Get out of town," Andy says, stopping as they pull up beside him.

"Any way you can. This shit is only going to get worse."

"And you?" the woman asks as though she cares about him as anyone other than a stranger on the roadside.

Andy reaches back and pats the side of his pack, tapping his hand against the tripod. Talking to this young couple has helped settle his mind.

"Me?" he says. "I'm going back. Someone's got to show the world what's really happening here."

With that he turns and walks on, picking up the pace. It's strange, but Andy got off the bus out of a desire for self-preservation. The bus stopped moving, but he was compelled to keep going, even if only on foot. Back then, he couldn't put enough distance between himself and those damn things. Having seen the uncertainty in this couple's eyes, though, and the misinformation forming like fog over a lake, he knows what's about to unfold. It's not the aliens that scare him. Humanity always wins, right? If there's one thing Hollywood has drummed into the American psyche, it's that the good guys always come through in the end. No, it's what happens after the fight that bothers Andy. What happens once the war is over? What will happen to people like these two young, gullible folk in their VW soft-top convertible?

Andy crosses the road beneath the freeway, cutting between stationary cars in various lanes. Drivers stare at him as though he's defying some taboo. He heads down a side street toward the mall. Two Hummers have been parked across the road, cutting off access. Beyond them, a police car sits idle with its lights flashing. There's no cop, just an abandoned car with red and blue lights quietly flickering, slowly drawing down charge from the batteries. Such a waste.

"Stop right there," a soldier says as Andy approaches.

"National Guard, right?" Andy says, reaching around and unzipping the side pouch on his backpack. He keeps his movements slow, not wanting to spook the guy. Andy reaches in and pulls out a camera that's barely the size of a packet of cigarettes. He presses the red record button and checks a few settings. Although he's looking down at the camera, he's aware the soldier is nervous. "This is Angry Andy

Anderson reporting live from Houston, Texas."

"Who are you talking to?" the soldier asks.

Andy smiles. The military is predictable. Obedience is all that's understood. Soldiers live in a polarized world of good and bad, allies and enemies. All sense of nuance is lost. They expect compliance or hostility. When Andy offers neither, it makes the soldier feel unsettled. Another soldier jogs over in support. These guys have been posted on the back entrance to the mall with one simple command—*keep the public out*. But at what cost? Are they really going to shoot a civilian with a camera?

Andy clips the camera on the strap running across his chest, holding the two shoulder straps on his backpack in place.

"Smile," he says, looking up at the soldier.

"You—You can't do that," the soldier says, pointing at the black lens of the camera.

"Why?" Andy asks. "It's a free country. I know my rights."

The other soldier says, "You're in a restricted area. You need to leave."

"That," Andy says, pointing behind the nineteen-year-old, skinny private, "That isn't a restricted area. It's a fucking parking lot for some shitty old shopping mall."

"You need to get out of here."

Andy ignores him, pointing at his chest and saying, "And this is a camera. At the moment, it's broadcasting via satellite to my relay server in Washington DC and from there to the Internet. You boys are being live-streamed to a couple of million people wanting to know what the hell is happening here in Houston. What would you like to tell them?"

The second soldier reaches out, trying to pull the camera from Andy's chest. Gloved fingers snatch at the air. Andy's too quick. He steps back, staying out of reach.

"You really have no idea how this plays out, do you?" he says. "You've just caused interest to spike. Now, even more people are watching. Go on. Grab the camera. Break it. Bust it under your combat boots. What do you think that's going to accomplish? Do you really think that'll make everything go away?"

He points at the gas station behind him on the corner, saying, "All I'll do is retreat back there and set up with the telephoto lens on my main camera. And you damn fools will have ten million people watching you, asking questions, wanting to know what the hell you're hiding in there!"

"We're not hiding anything," the first soldier says.

It takes all of Andy's willpower not to grin. They've already lost. They just don't know it yet. The first rule of engaging with the media—any media—is don't engage at all. He's got them right where he wants them. Andy knows they don't have anything in those tents, but the suggestion there *might* be something to hide runs quickly to suspicion and they know that. They're nervous, which doesn't help either as it lends credence to the idea they're concealing something.

"You shouldn't be here," the bullish soldier says, which is a concession from him. He's no longer telling Andy to leave or trying to grab his camera. Andy has the upper hand and he intends to use that as leverage.

"Is General Landis here?" Andy asks, wanting to see past the various tents and military vehicles in the parking lot. His question gets a nervous response from them, with both soldiers speaking at once.

"No."

"Well, that wasn't convincing," Andy says, laughing. These two chumps are the best thing that could have happened to him. Although he can't see his social media counter, he knows how viral live streams work. Viewers will be messaging each other, telling their friends to jump online, posting on social media about the stream, etc. They'll grab a proverbial bucket of popcorn and sit back, wanting to see how all this is going to unfold. He can almost read the tweets from here—*fucking Angry Andy Anderson is at it again! #alienlivestream*

"You need to evacuate with the others," the younger soldier says, but he's backed up next to his Hummer. He's no longer as strident as he once was. He's defaulting to a standard response. He wants to turn

Andy away, but he's not confident.

Andy holds his hands out, gesturing around him and asking the question, "Where? How? You can see the main road, right? You can see those cars down there. They ain't going nowhere."

The soldier avoids eye contact with him.

"Listen," Andy says. "I'm an old friend of Nolan's. Take me to see Brigadier General Nolan Landis. Tell him, Andy Anderson has something for him."

"I'm sorry, sir. I can't do that."

Sir is an improvement in their ad hoc relationship.

Andy spots someone he recognizes walking briskly between tents in the distance. A woman. What's her name? She was Nolan's assistant. She was there when Nolan and Kath broadcast from his garage in DC back in what seems like another lifetime. She stood beside his busted garage door with her arms folded across her chest, listening to the discussion as they debunked the initial approach of *Anduru* over the Gulf of Mexico.

"Hey," Andy calls out, waving his hands. She turns, looking at him from a distance of easily forty yards. "It's me! Andy!"

"Sir," the soldier says, holding his hand out and appealing for him to stay put.

"Jacinta," Andy yells, remembering her name. "I need to see Nolan. It's important!"

The woman marches over. She's wearing fatigues and combat boots with a sidearm on her hip. She has her hair up in a bun and a cap pulled down over her brow.

"What's going on?" she asks the two soldiers as she approaches.

"He says he knows the brigadier general."

Jacinta looks at Andy, trying to place him.

"It's me," Andy says, pointing at himself. "Angry Andy Anderson. You came to my garage studio. You and Nolan and Kath. Just before *Anduru* struck."

"What can I do for you, Mr. Anderson?" Jacinta asks, standing well back from both him and the soldiers guarding the street.

"I need to talk to Nolan."

"Why?"

"I need to tell him."

"Tell him what?" she asks.

"It's complicated."

"What is there you want to say to him that you can't say to me?"

"The problem is bigger than you think," Andy says, spitballing. He's searching for the right words. "You're thinking about this too small. It's more than just those things back there. You're dealing with a generation of vipers out here. You've got to be careful. You can't just focus on what *has* happened. You've got to be thinking about what happens next."

Jacinta looks both ways. It's as though she's trying to throw off her own doubts. Her lips tighten. She doesn't want to bring him within the impromptu base, that's obvious from the grimace on her face.

"With me," she barks, and the soldier in front of Andy steps to one side.

Andy rushes forward to join her before she changes her mind. She turns, walking off into the parking lot. With the weight of his backpack, he struggles to keep up.

"Don't fuck with me, Andy."

"Have you guys found Kath?" he asks. "She was there, right? She was staying at *The Fossil.*"

"No, we haven't found her."

A truck drives past with soldiers in it. A helicopter hovers near the mall entrance, lowering a portable generator suspended by steel chains. The pilot sets it down while being careful to stay well clear of the lampposts in the parking lot.

"What did you mean by *what happens next*?" Jacinta asks as they walk up to an open tent. Officers move between tables, whiteboards, and TVs mounted on stands. They're focused, talking intently with each other.

"Nothing's changed," Andy replies. "This is *An˘—fucking—duru* all over again. Only this time it's worse."

"Wait here," Jacinta says, leaving him standing beside a guard outside the tent. Andy looks up at the tall soldier. This isn't some random joe posted on babysitting duties out on the perimeter. The muscle-bound soldier in front of Andy isn't going to take shit from anyone. If anything, he'd love Andy to do something stupid. That would give him an excuse to fuck him up real bad. Andy steps back a little, holding his hands out slightly so as to reinforce that he's unarmed. He's trying to avoid any appearance of hostility.

"What the hell is this all about?" Brigadier General Nolan Landis says, marching out of the tent to confront Andy. He looks every bit as formidable and invincible as he did when his boots crushed the broken glass inside Andy's garage. Back then, Andy was intimidated. Now, he's absolutely terrified.

"I—ah."

"Are you recording this?" Nolan says, pointing at the camera on Andy's chest.

"Broadcasting," Andy replies. He's not being pedantic. He wants Nolan to realize this is going out live.

"Jesus Christ, Andy. I don't have time for your bullshit!"

"Hear me out," Andy says. "You're fighting a war on two fronts but you don't know it."

Nolan sets his hands on his hips. He looks as though he could kill Andy in the blink of an eye. Jacinta walks up beside Nolan. Her right hand rests on her holstered sidearm. Subtle. Real subtle.

"This is *Anduru* all over again," Andy says. "Only this time, they're here."

Anger lines Nolan's face, only this isn't the fake anger Andy uses in his show. Nolan's nostrils flare. He's a volcano about to explode.

"I know. I know," Andy says with his hands flying around, making

177

wild gestures. "It's tempting to think it's different this time, but it's not. It's the same. You're facing the same goddamn fight as before. Don't you see? You can't just win the war. You have to win hearts and minds."

"What the devil are you talking about?"

"Back when this thing first appeared, you came to me because you needed me to reach people—those people that wouldn't listen to you. Nothing has changed. Not a goddamn thing!"

Nolan is impatient, but he seems to realize Andy's got a genuine point—one he's missed.

The brigadier general says, "I don't see how we need a podcast this time around, Andy."

Nolan's not demeaning him. Andy can see that in his eyes. He's genuinely confused as to why Andy is here. He wants to understand what's so important to Andy that he'd risk crashing a military base.

"Are you a religious man, general?"

"I go to church on Sundays."

Andy isn't surprised by the way Nolan couches his reply. He's also not surprised Nolan won't say which church. He didn't expect he would. The man has too much class to slip in a little proselytizing for one brand or another. He seems content to answer Andy's question, at least in an abstract sense.

"Consider this," Andy says. "Isaiah 5:20—*they called evil good, and good evil; they put darkness for light, and light for darkness; they substitute bitter for sweet, and sweet for bitter.*"

"Role reversal," Nolan says, scratching at the stubble on his chin. "Rewriting the facts."

"Rewriting history," Andy says. He has immense respect for the brigadier general. Nolan's staring down the barrel of an alien invasion but he has the presence of mind to stop and consider the insane perspective of a crackpot he's only met on a handful of occasions.

"It's always been this way," Andy says, pointing north, away from the city. "You're dealing with a generation of vipers. Not here. Not in Houston. Out there. All across America. All around the world.

Regardless of what happens here, they will call the good evil and the evil good."

Nolan tightens his lips. His eyes narrow as he listens.

"I was assaulted when I turned up at the conference. Me! I was sucker-punched as I got out of my car. And for what? For speaking the truth about *Anduru*. Nobody wants the truth. They want to confirm their beliefs—only reality doesn't work that way.

"We can't help ourselves. It's in our nature. We embellish. We exaggerate. Hell, I doubt most people even realize when they've wandered away from reality. Think about it. Kennedy being shot. Armstrong walking on the Moon. The World Trade Center falling after being hit by fully-laden 767s. Votes being cast in US elections. Vaccines that can halt a goddamn pandemic. These things should be indisputable, but *fuck!* We're nothing if not ornery. Our rallying cry is— *don't tell me what to think, goddamn it!*"

Nolan nods, but he doesn't say anything.

"*Anduru's* already being rewritten. What do you think they're going to say about this particular cluster fuck in a year's time? In a decade? You don't think this is going to be spun like a Catherine wheel on the 4th of July?"

Nolan is unmoved.

Andy says, "Wait until the deep fakes hit. They're probably already working on them, coming up with AI-generated videos to screw with the public. Hell, we've been dealing with deep fakes since Roswell and the alien autopsies. A plastic mask and a bit of fake blood is all that's needed to convince some people."

Nolan's blunt. "What do you want, Andy?"

Anyone else would misread the brigadier general as stonewalling them, but Andy understands. Nolan's pragmatic. He got where he is by seeing the big picture. He's playing chess, moving pieces around the board. He's not contesting Andy's point, he's asking where it leads. He's avoiding the weeds, just like Andy knew he would.

Andy says, "Send me in with your troops. Let me broadcast this shit show live to the world."

Nolan smiles. "You're an idiot. You know that, right?"

"Oh, I know," Andy says, grinning. "It's kind of my brand."

"It's going to be a one-way street."

"Life's a one-way street."

Nolan sighs. "I'm going to cop flak for sending a civilian in there with a camera."

"I thought you liked it hot and spicy. Besides, you'll get some good intel from on the ground."

Nolan pauses. He reaches up and rubs the back of his head.

Jacinta says, "This isn't a good idea."

"This is a very bad idea," Nolan replies, turning to look at her. "Which is precisely why he's the only one that could pull it off. All right, Andy. Come with me."

THE FOSSIL

Kath rummages through the mini-bar fridge, loading up the backpack with plastic water bottles, cans of soda and tiny bottles of alcohol.

"You know how your Mom said not to touch the minibar," Kath says. Jimmy nods. "Well, forget that. We're taking all of it with us."

She dumps packets of cashew nuts, potato chips and an assortment of candy bars into the bag. Jimmy's eyes never leave her hands.

"What's your favorite?" Kath asks, aware Jimmy hasn't uttered a single word since they met in the hallway. "Kit Kat? Reece's Pieces? Snickers?"

Jimmy's quiet.

"My favorite is Peanut M&Ms, but don't worry. I'll share them with you."

Jimmy's sitting on the edge of the bed closest to the door. His eyes cast down at the fallen body of his father lying on the floor in the darkness. The towel covering his father's face does little to hide the heartbreak of what happened.

"I'm so sorry," Kath says, feeling she has to recognize his grief if she wants to help him through the moment. She rests her hand affectionately on his shoulder. "I know you're scared. I—I'm confused. I'm still trying to figure all this out myself. It's okay to be scared. It's okay to be sad. You and me. We're going to stick together, okay? I'm not going to leave you. I promise."

Jimmy nods. A single tear rolls down his cheek.

"I need your help," Kath says. "I need to find something we can use to attract the attention of aircraft. It needs to be big but lightweight. We've got to be able to carry it up to the roof. Like a big square piece of cloth. Something white. Something that people can see from a distance—from a long way away."

Jimmy's eyes dart around. He looks at her, then the other bed, then back to her again as she sits next to him. His eyes go wide. It's as though he's saying, *you're sitting on the edge of it*, but Kath already knows that. She wants him to come up with a solution. She's trying to get him to speak. He looks back at her with a slightly worried look on his face, making as though the answer is obvious. Kath holds her nerve. She's trying to get him to engage with her.

Jimmy leans over and lifts the duvet, revealing the white bedsheet tucked into the mattress.

"A bed sheet," Kath says, trying to sound surprised. "Yes, that'll work."

For a scientist, he's probably thinking she's pretty dumb, but she's distracted him from the loss of his father so that's a win.

"Help me pull it off," she says, walking to the head of the bed. They roll back the duvet and pull the upper sheet free, folding it loosely.

"Now those shoes," she says, pointing at the open suitcases on the other bed.

Jimmy retrieves them one by one.

"I need four shoes," Kath says, taking the first shoe from him. Jimmy's got a confused look on his face, but that's precisely what Kath intends. She needs him to think.

Kath uses the nail clippers to cut a hole in one corner of the sheet. She feeds the laces of the shoe through and then ties them in a knot.

"It's going to be windy up on the roof," she says, cutting another hole and continuing to add shoes. "We'll use the shoes to anchor the sheet. We can shove rocks and bricks and other stuff in the shoes to weigh them down. Then we can spread out the sheet without it blowing away."

Jimmy turns his head sideways, looking at her confused.

"Then we'll use some rocks to spell SOS on the sheet. Anyone flying overhead will see that and know we need help."

Jimmy nods. He likes this idea.

"Can you get me the toilet paper from the bathroom?"

Jimmy turns, heading toward the door. Kath's comment, though, is carefully calculated. She's getting him to walk past the towel covering his father's head, corralling him toward the corridor.

"If you look under the sink, you should find spare rolls."

When Jimmy emerges from the bathroom, Kath is right there, holding the backpack low so he can shove them in.

"Okay, let's go," she says, stepping through the open doorway. She's got the sheet with the shoes draped over her shoulder.

Jimmy doesn't hesitate. He doesn't look back. He trusts her. It breaks her heart to realize that as she thinks they're going to die. All she can do is distract him from the inevitable.

Kath wears the pack on her front instead of over her back. She has no idea what they're going to run into but she wants quick access to—what? The *Mars Bar*? The toilet paper? The macadamia nuts? It's dumb, but she feels better with the illusion of being prepared for the unknown. Lies are a placebo, even when told to oneself.

Kath rearranges a few of the items, pushing the plastic water bottles to the bottom and keeping things like the mirror handy. As tempting as it is to shove the bedsheet in there, the four shoes won't fit. It's annoying having them bouncing against her shin on one side and her calf muscle on the other as the sheet drapes over her shoulder, but it's the best she can do. If she runs into any other adults in the hotel, they're going to think she's mad. Jimmy, though, doesn't seem to care

183

what she looks like. His tiny fingers reach out, taking her hand.

"You okay?" she asks.

Dumb question.

Really dumb question, Kath.

The boy's father is dead. He hid behind the curtain for six to eight hours, perhaps longer. Damn, it must have been a long, scary night. Now, he's trusting a stranger. No, Kath. He's not okay.

"Listen," she says, turning and kneeling before him. She adjusts his makeshift face mask, but not because she needs to. She's trying to show she cares. "I know this is hard. You're doing great."

Jimmy nods. There's a reason kids are called dependents—and it's not economic. He squeezes the stubs of her disfigured fingers. He's looking for something to hold on to emotionally, but Kath's afraid about what's to come. She's not a parent. She's clumsy. She has no idea how to handle children of any age. Back in the hotel room, she made a promise she can't keep. Oh, she'll try, but it's bravado at best. Perhaps naive is a better description.

What happens if he panics and bolts down the corridor? Or worse, what if she needs to run and he's frozen in fear. Either reaction could cost both of them their lives.

What if something happens to her?

What if she can't keep her promise?

What if he needs to go on alone?

"I'm going to do everything I can for you, okay?" she says, looking deep into his puppy dog eyes. "If anything happens to me—go to the roof. Go up. Don't go down. When you get up there stack three piles of rocks on the helipad. Three. Okay? They'll see three piles of rocks."

He nods.

Kath's making shit up. She's clutching at thin air, trying to give him hope. It's a lie. The chances of him being spotted are slim to none, but at least he'll be busy doing something instead of waiting around to die. Her heart sinks. If she's dead, regardless of what happens next, he won't be far behind her.

"Everything's a weapon," she says, kneeling on the carpet.

Kath berates herself. This is not the kind of positive pep-talk she thinks it is, but she's got to say something. If anything, she's convincing herself to go on unarmed.

"We don't have claws like a tiger. We don't have big sharp teeth like a lion. We're not as fast as a cheetah or as agile as a monkey. So how did we survive for so long? We used the things around us."

Kath pulls out a roll of toilet paper. She's trying to make light of their situation while also teaching him something.

"See this? Toilet paper isn't going to hurt anyone. That's silly, right? But it can distract them. Throw it one way and you go another."

She puts the toilet paper back and pulls out his mother's hairspray.

"This stuff is great on hair, but it's lousy on the eyes. It stings. If someone gets too close, spray this at their face and run."

Kath shoves it back into the pack and pulls out a few small plastic bottles.

"Shampoo and conditioner might not seem useful, but you can tip them out on the concrete. If anyone comes racing along they'll slip and fall. If that's on the stairs, they could tumble down to the lower floor."

What is this? *Home Alone*? And who is this *someone* or *anyone* you're speaking of, Kath? She has no idea what's stalking through the atrium down among the trees, but it's not human.

She puts the plastic bottles back and pulls out a drinking glass.

"You can throw this. It might not seem like much, but it could buy you time to get through the next door."

Jimmy nods.

She holds up a tiny bottle of vodka from the minibar.

"Get a scratch on your arm and you can rinse it with this. It'll sting, but it'll stop it from becoming infected."

Kath puts it back and zips up the bag.

"See? We don't need knives or guns. We need smarts."

She gets back to her feet. He seems happy enough, but she's not. All she's done is talk herself out of her so-called preparation because it's so damn feeble.

There's an abandoned housekeeping cart by the elevators on the far side of the hotel.

Loud noises drift through the air, coming from the atrium, only this isn't the hustle and bustle of the guests. Branches snap. Leaves are crushed. Rocks break and fall.

"Shhh," she whispers, but Jimmy didn't say anything. He walks along beside her, brushing up against her leg.

Kath stays away from the edge of the walkway. As tempting as it is to peer over the low concrete wall from the relative safety of the 22nd floor, she resists. The logical, scientific part of her mind is curious. Emotionally, though, she doesn't want to know. For now, emotion wins.

They creep between rooms, retreating into the slightly recessed entranceways. Even though the doors are locked, there's a sense of safety in being out of the line of sight. It's an illusion. Any human staring down the corridor would easily pick them out. Kath's bulky pack on her front sticks out even when she flattens herself against the door. She's not fooling anyone. Not even herself.

Kath isn't sure what she's expecting. Her mind is playing games with her. The layout of the floor is that of a hollow square with the atrium in the middle. On each corner, there's a narrow side corridor reaching to the cheap rooms on the wings. There's nowhere to hide. Oh, she might obscure herself from the view of anyone further along the hallway, but to anyone watching from any of the other three sides of the square, her motion is comical. She might as well be trying to hide a giraffe in short grass. Regardless, moving in short bursts and ducking back into locked doorways feels safe. As emotions are in the driver's seat, feelings are important. Kath likes to pride herself on being coldly logical, but Mr. Spock is a work of fiction. No one is emotionless. No one should be devoid of emotions. Besides, emotions aren't the enemy of logic, they're the complement.

"Okay," she says under her breath, speaking as much for herself as for Jimmy. "Before we hit the stairs, I want to look in that cart. There could be things we need."

Things we need? That's just marvelous, Kath. *Things?* Could you be any more vague or obscure? Scientist Kath berates amateur survivalist Kath but she can't shake the feeling they're horribly exposed and alone. Kath feels as though she needs something more. What she should do is head straight for the roof. *Do not pass Go! Do not collect two hundred!* Although she knows that's the right thing to do, something's wrong. It seems emotional Kath isn't ready to follow rational Kath just yet.

There's a banging noise somewhere nearby, just a few floors below them. A steel door swings erratically in gale-force winds that do not exist within the closed confines of the atrium. The random, clanging metal is unnerving.

"Not good," she says, creeping past the elevators. Jimmy squeezes her hand tight. "You hear that too, huh?"

As suddenly as it started, the noise stops. Kath stands still. As bad as the clanging was, the silence is terrifying. Kath knew roughly where the noise was coming from and that gave her some confidence. Now, whatever made that racket has fallen quiet. Where has it gone? Whatever it was, it had to be big to make so much noise with such ease—and that scares her.

As the doors on the elevator shaft are made from glass and the shaft backs onto the atrium, Kath can see through to the inside of the hotel. She peers past the cables and black support beams, down onto the floors below them, looking at the other side of the atrium. At a guess, she's seeing the eighteenth floor and up. Shadows move in the distance. A tail flickers. Whatever's down there, it's long but not tall. It doesn't protrude above the edge of the low concrete wall on that floor. Like an alligator, it races along on all fours, scurrying across the carpet. The shimmer of dark, scaly skin catches the light as the creature's back arches.

Kath is equal parts fascinated and terrified. There's something alive down there. It's the way the creature moves that gives it away. It winds its way around the side corridor, avoiding the doors.

Jimmy tugs on her hand, drawing her toward the fire escape.

"What are you doing?" she asks the creature, ignoring Jimmy and staring through the glass at the lower floors. "Why are you up this high? What do you want?"

Jimmy leans back, tugging on her arm. What he wants is clear. He pulls her toward the stairwell.

Want—that's the key. Whatever these creatures are, regardless of how they got here, a few of them have remained in the hotel for a reason. Every animal on Earth is driven by impulse, be that for food, sex, instinct, companionship, or the need to mark territory, something drives their actions. And all of this has one goal—reproduction.

Kath is curious. How do these creatures fit into the overall lifecycle of *Anduru?*

All the grandeur in nature—the call of the lyrebird, the song of the thrush, the ripple of colors on the side of a cuttlefish, the brilliance of a peacock's feathers, a whale's lament, the antlers of deer and even the intelligence of humans—it all has one evolutionary goal: the survival of the species. When it comes to these intruders, though, they're part of a larger ecosystem that results in disseminating seedpods between stars— but how? Are these things an isolated threat? Or is there a bigger danger looming? The fungal-like spores she's seen on various dead things worry her.

Kath feels sick. She thinks she knows. She hopes she's wrong.

Jimmy moans, jerking at her arm, desperate to flee.

The banging starts again, but it's louder now, closer. The noise comes from right beneath them on the floor below them. Vibrations reverberate through the concrete. There's strength there but it's on a different scale to humans. Perhaps the march of elephants would be similar, but it's well beyond what most terrestrial creatures could accomplish.

Jimmy's lips quiver. He's afraid.

"We can't leave. Not yet," Kath whispers, crouching before him. "I have to know what they're doing—and why."

She lets go of Jimmy's hand and rummages around on the housekeeping cart. There's a first aid kit with a shoulder strap. Kath hoists it over her arm without looking inside. It should be fully stocked. Even if it isn't, it'll have a wide variety of simple medical items: bandages, gauze pads, tape and hopefully more painkillers.

"What else?" she mumbles, checking the layers beneath the cart. Verbalizing what she sees helps her think about the options before her. "Soap. Towels. Sheets. Garbage bags. Air freshener. More toilet paper."

Kath pauses, holding up two aerosol cans. The can of lavender feels almost empty, but the frangipani can is full. She looks at Jimmy, whispering, "Well, if either of us farts, at least we've got options."

Jimmy doesn't laugh. He edges toward the fire escape, but he's torn. She can see it in his eyes. He dances between the rail on the cart and the door handle a few feet away, unsure whether he should stay.

"It's okay," she whispers. "Head for the roof. I'll meet you up there."

Tears well up in his eyes. She said she wouldn't leave him but she's pushing him away. He must think she's mad. He stands still. Anguish lines his face. A crazy adult is better than no adult at all. After a few seconds, he rushes to her side.

"You should go," she says, speaking softly. "Get up top. I can't leave. Not yet. These things have killed a lot of people. We need to learn something about them. I—I'm a scientist. I must know."

Kath unzips the first aid kit and retrieves the tape. The roll is half empty. Although she can't get a good grip with her fingers, the tape can be torn using her teeth. She wraps it tightly around a roll of toilet paper, binding the loose leaves together. Kath rests the roll on the cart and douses the top half of it with nail polish remover. The tape prevents the fluid from seeping into the lower half of the roll. This allows her to pinch it from below, with her thumb and her one good finger between the inner cardboard roll and the outer paper.

She says, "Let's see how these things react to fire."

Kath flicks the lighter. A tiny flame appears. She doesn't need to touch the toilet paper. It bursts into flames as the lighter approaches. A wave of heat washes over her face. Yellow flames dance above a blue flicker.

As they're standing beside the elevators in the middle of the floor, they can see down onto the sides of the next few floors. Kath grabs the toilet paper roll and pulls her hand back over her head. She never was any good at baseball. Flames lick the white paint on the ceiling, scorching the sheetrock. She leans over the sidewall and hurls the roll of toilet paper through the air. Flames spiral through the atrium as the roll soars between floors. It hits the wall on the lower floor and bounces on the carpet. The tape burns through, allowing the roll to unravel for a few feet, leaving a trail of flames in the corridor.

Kath fumbles with the smartphone, hits the camera button and starts recording. She rests it in her left palm and uses her thumb and her finger to zoom in.

"I knew it," she says softly.

To her horror, the roll isn't lying on the carpet. It's roughly a foot off the floor, resting on some kind of transparent gelatinous mass running the length of the corridor. The flame burns the jelly-like substance, turning it black. Soot allows her to see undulations in the shape. There are mounds of the stuff set at regular intervals. In the eerie light, she can see small creatures wiggling within the gel. They're agitated by the flames. They're cooking under the heat of the burning toilet paper roll. Parts of the gelatinous structure catch fire.

For the sake of the video, she whispers, "They're using the hotel as a nest."

Kath stops the recording and slips the phone back into her pocket. She reaches out, taking Jimmy's hand.

"Time to go, little guy."

Somewhere several floors beneath them, concrete breaks and crumbles. Bricks fall through the atrium, crashing into the fake lake below. From where she's standing, Kath can't see over the edge and she really doesn't want to. She peers through the glass doors of the elevator.

There's a shimmer, four or five floors down. Something's clinging to the concrete. It's climbing between floors. Claws reach out, puncturing the low walls on the various walkways, but she can't make out the shape of the animal. Its body seems to extend from the hotel. It's as though she's peering through water or looking at a reflection in a crazy mirror at the county fair. Her eyes don't seem to focus properly. There's a fuzzy outline. She can see the distorted shape of the trees and walkways below.

The animal is in motion, leaping between floors, tearing chunks of concrete out in the process. If anything, it's the falling bricks that give her a sense of its location.

Jimmy clings to her leg. His arms are up around her thigh. She couldn't run if she wanted to. The fire escape is easily fifteen feet away. The housekeeping cart might provide some cover, but it's been pushed hard against the wall. She can't get behind it without moving it and that's going to take time—time she doesn't have.

Kath grabs Jimmy raising him up on her hip, but it's too late. Although her back is to the atrium and she's rushing toward the fire escape, she knows she's not going to make it. She's carrying too much shit—the backpack, Jimmy, the sheet hanging over her shoulder. It all slows her down. Even if she could get the door open with him on her hip and her horribly dysfunctional hands, that monster would simply tear through the door.

There's nowhere to run.

Nowhere to hide.

Kath comes to a halt, standing still in the corridor. Her bladder loosens. Urine dampens her crotch. Options. She needs options. There are none, but her mind refuses to believe that. Bricks tumble from the wall behind her.

Kath does the only thing she can. She steps back, sinking toward the crumbling wall separating them from the atrium. To her left, the glass within the elevator shaft breaks. Sheets of reinforced glass come loose and plunge down the atrium. Glass panes catch on the steel frame, shattering into millions of pieces. They shower the trees and lake with tiny fragments of safety glass.

Jimmy must be able to see the creature behind her. He's on her hip. He's facing back toward the atrium. His fingers dig into her skin, but Kath's committed to staying put. Every other course of action is futile against an animal that can tear through concrete.

She leans back, falling on her ass and pushing up against the cinderblocks. Her shoulder hits the low, atrium wall. Her butt slumps to the carpet. She has her knees up. Tears stream from her eyes.

With Jimmy beside her, she struggles with the smartphone, working it out of her shorts. She tries to start the recording again. If she's going to die, it'll be while capturing data others can use. Kath has no idea what's in focus or where the lens is pointing, but she directs the phone over her shoulder and above her head. She's shaking. She can only hope someone will find this one day and realize what happened here.

With her other hand, she buries Jimmy's head into her neck and shoulder. He shouldn't have to see this. No one should have to watch their own grisly end. Kath pulls her knees in tight against the backpack, squishing it against her chest. She's trying to make herself as small as possible.

Claws pierce the low wall beside her, exposing the brickwork. They puncture the cinder blocks and concrete with ease. The creature hauls itself up. Kath can't help herself. A whimper escapes her lips.

She looks up.

The alien is staring straight ahead, or at least she thinks it is. The animal's talon-like claws have pierced the concrete on either side of her head. She pushes Jimmy's head into her soft neck. She's desperate to avoid him screaming.

Teeth appear. Given the size of the creature, they're long and thin. There are no canine teeth or incisors as she'd expect on a terrestrial predator. These look like knitting needles. They're a sickly yellow in color. They seem to drift in the air above her as she peers up at the monster. The rest of the creature's skin is invisible, allowing her to see the roof above. The teeth disappear as the monster closes its mouth.

If she squints, Kath can make out overlapping scales. They distort the light that seems to pass through the alien. It's as though a bunch of smooth, finely polished lenses have been set up, distorting the view of the ceiling beyond the alien. The animal relaxes. For a moment its body is a deep burgundy color, then a pale grey, and then invisible once again.

Kath is astonished by what she's seeing. A moment ago, she felt as though she couldn't see anything at all, just the ceiling above her. Then the vast body of a scaled creature appeared. She blinks and it's gone—only it isn't. It's still there. It's adopted some kind of active camouflage.

She has her hand up, with the camera on the phone poised inches from the scales. The stubs of her fingers twitch. She ignores Jimmy's quiet sobbing, reaching up with what remains of her other hand. She wants to touch this creature from another world. She won't, but her hand gives her a sense of size. Each scale is roughly the size and shape of a silver dollar coin. Knowing this, she can catch the subtle ripples in the alien's armor-plating.

Regardless of what happens to them, this footage is invaluable. Kath doubts anyone else has been this close to one of these things and lived. If she can get this video out, it could help others understand what they're up against. They need to know how these things can be detected and defeated.

As seen up close, the image of the ceiling is slightly cloudy. Blurry. The creature's camouflage isn't perfect. From a distance, it's indistinguishable from the background, but there is some distortion. In the same way a fishing pole distorts when the tip is stuck into the water, changing its apparent angle, the alien isn't entirely transparent as such. It warps the light around it, bending and twisting it but not perfectly replicating it.

How is this possible? At a technological level, the sophistication of such a system would be absurd. Biologically, it would require light-sensitive cells within the scales that transfer their readings to a nervous system that links to the opposing scales on the other side of the animal.

If someone were watching from above, they'd see a distorted image of her and Jimmy. It's reminiscent of an octopus changing color and suddenly blending in with corals and rocks on the ocean floor. The camouflage isn't perfect, but it's damn good. When seen square on, as she is now, it is utterly convincing. If she looks to the sides of the creature's head, though, where its scales turn to follow the contours of the body, there's a shimmer. The view along that edge is distorted, revealing the animal's dimensions. Kath is careful to catch these distinctions in her video.

The alien's head moves from side to side. It's looking for her. She wants to whisper, 'Binocular vision,' as commentary on the video as the animal's motion is reminiscent of a big cat hunting its prey, but she can barely breathe, let alone speak. Besides, speaking would be spectacularly dumb right now. Its primary sense must be sight. If it was relying on smell, it would realize how close they are.

Goo drips on her shoulder. Thankfully, it doesn't land on Jimmy as it would freak him out. As it is, he's shaking like a leaf in the wind. He's still got his head buried into her shoulder. Kath has her neck craned back, watching the alien with a sense of awe tinged with fear. Thick mucus slides down her neck. Most of it lands on the bedsheet/sign she has hung over her left shoulder. It oozes onto the shoes she's tied to the ends of the sheet. The smell is pungent. Kath detects ammonia. Her skin tingles. Whether that's from a chemical burn forming or just the sheer terror she feels is impossible to tell. Her breathing is shallow.

The head protrudes and then retreats. The creature withdraws its claws from the wall. It doesn't leave, though, that much is obvious from the lack of sound. It's smart. It's hiding. It knows she's up here somewhere. It's setting a trap, waiting for her to move and expose herself.

Kath's heart is on the verge of beating out of her chest. She sits there, trying not to hyperventilate. By reversing the camera on the smartphone, she can look at the screen and see her pale face along with the globs of saliva on her shoulder. The white sheet has been stained by the goo. She mouths the word '*ammonia*' a couple of times, hoping someone will eventually see this footage and understand what she's saying.

Kath has always been a pragmatist. Her mother says she's fatalistic. What her mom describes as pessimism, Kath calls realism. At heart, she's an optimist, albeit one that can't willfully ignore the odds. Like Jimmy, her body is trembling, but not because of the cold. Her mind may say they're going to make it out of this, but her body isn't fooled by any more lies. When she stops to think of their chances, she knows her efforts are futile. It's not just that the hotel has been overrun with these things, Kath is being hunted. The creature is toying with her, tempting her to make a run for it, wanting her to show herself.

A tear rolls down her cheek.

PRESIDENT
WILSON

Andy has to rush to keep up with Nolan as they march across the parking lot—and that's the way Nolan likes it. He leads from the front. There's no better way to drive that home than forcing others to keep up. It's the length of his stride. Nolan's not swinging his legs that much faster, but his legs stretch wide. Jacinta can keep pace with him, but Andy has to jog to keep up.

Jacinta strides beside Nolan, saying, "We've established checkpoints at most of the major intersections on I-610 beltway along with Routes 6 and 8 further out."

"Force strength?" he asks, still looking forward and marching toward a military tent in the parking lot.

Jacinta says, "Recon only. In some cases, just a spotter."

"Standing orders are to observe and not engage," Nolan says. "We need eyes out there, not bodies."

"Understood," she replies, tapping on a handheld computer tablet. The screen is surrounded by thick, vulcanized rubber. The cover is scratched and torn. It looks as though it's been run over by a tank.

"I want them to fall back when approached. Keep these things in range, but do not fire upon them. We need intel. We need to know where they are, what they're doing, where they're going, and in what numbers."

"Got it," Jacinta says, peeling away from them as they walk into the command tent.

Poor Andy doesn't know what he's got himself into, but Nolan's confident there's learning even in these passing comments.

Nolan's curious about who has tapped into Andy's live feed. It won't just be American civilians. Hell, the CIA will be apoplectic. Someone from Langley will already be on the phone to the Pentagon demanding answers. The pencil heads there will contact NORAD. General Cooper will shrug. His position tends to be—if Nolan's pissing someone off within the chain of command then he's doing his job just fine. Cooper knows Nolan well enough to run interference for him. As for the rest of the world, the British will think Nolan's mad allowing Andy to tag along. The Chinese will appreciate the heads up. They'll be worried about the possibility of a breakout eventually reaching them. The Russians will think Nolan's playing an angle. They won't believe it's unscripted. Convincing President Wilson won't be easy, but Nolan can see merit in flooding the airwaves with accurate information instead of conjecture. Besides, he loves a challenge.

Dr. Monroe stands before a hastily erected screen with a disposable cup of coffee in hand. He smiles. It seems, even in the midst of an alien invasion, there's always time for a little caffeine.

The room on the other end of the camera feed is all too familiar. It's been years since Nolan has been in there but he recognizes the chairs and the distinct, polished meeting room table. President Wilson is seated at the far end of the Situation Room. He's flanked by various generals and admirals in uniform. A bunch of other people in suits and business attire have squeezed into the room behind the President. The wooden panels on the walls look old, but that's precisely how they're supposed to appear. The Situation Room is the most sophisticated command and control center in the world and, as such, it needs to seem understated to avoid giving away trade secrets.

Nolan walks up beside Monroe, stepping into the camera frame. Andy hangs back.

"Oh, no you don't," Nolan says, reaching out and grabbing Andy by the loose fabric on his shoulder. He drags him in beside them.

"What's he doing here?" Monroe asks.

"He's my plus one," Nolan says without cracking a smile.

"It's your funeral."

Within the Situation Room, someone walks up to the camera, getting so uncomfortably close their nose appears outlandishly large. They adjust the position of the camera, looking deep into the cold, electronic eye.

"We're ready when you are," Monroe says. The man adjusting the camera touches at an earpiece, making it apparent he's the only one that can hear them at this point.

"Just waiting for the discussion about the troop withdrawal from the Middle East to wind down... ah, okay, we're ready for you now. Patching you in."

"Good to see you, Nolan," the President says, addressing him casually instead of using his formal, military title. When it comes to President Wilson, nothing is casual. Every word is calculated and spoken for effect. Nolan has no doubt he's being played, but that's okay, he's brought his own chess piece to this particular game.

The President asks, "Where's Major-General Dedrick of the Texas National Guard?"

Nolan tries not to smile. It seems the President can go with formal titles when he wants to, especially when they outrank Nolan. It's unusual for Nolan to be the subject of the President's power-plays, and he's not quite sure why. The reason will become clear soon enough, of that, Nolan's sure.

"We're still awaiting his arrival," Nolan says, standing almost to attention.

"And in the meantime?"

"I've been coordinating the initial response, sir."

"You're not actually in the established chain-of-command, though, right?"

"That's correct, sir."

"You're not even in the same branch of service?"

"No, sir. Most of our current, on-site assets are from the National Guard. I've flown in senior staff from NORAD and from the Army Depot in Corpus Cristi to help coordinate our response."

President Wilson punches the man next to him on the shoulder. "God, I love this guy. You told me he was an asshole. He's nothing of the sort. He's a doer. A go-getter. We need more men like this guy."

The man he punched is four-star General Gus 'Grizzly' Andrews, the acting head of the Joint Chiefs of Staff. Nolan is careful not to respond. He doesn't want to give anything away in his facial expression. He's known Grizzly for over a decade. There's no way in hell Grizzly called him an asshole. It's not his style. If anything, such a term is too obscure for the four-star general. If Grizzly's chewing someone's ass out they'll get a string of expletives, not just one.

Even though the President is only in his first year, he's already developed a reputation for setting staff against each other. It seems he likes to watch them fight. Nolan has no doubt these comments are designed to inflame tension. For that matter, so is the flattery. Jealousy is as effective a weapon as resentment. Grizzly, though, will see through it, of that Nolan's sure.

Nolan keeps his eyes square on the camera. He doesn't look at his own image to the bottom right. He doesn't want to give the President the satisfaction of knowing he's getting under his skin. Even Dr. Monroe is quiet. He might be the President's scientific advisor, but he knows well enough to measure his words.

"And who's this?" the President asks in a relaxed tone. That he hasn't asked for an update but is curious about Nolan's guest is telling. Pecking orders are important in President Wilson's myopic world. If Elizabeth Aston was still in office, she'd trust Nolan. She'd want an update. She'd be worried about the possibility of the alien menace breaking through their hastily established lines.

"This is a civilian. Mr. Andrew Anderson," Nolan says, teasing the President by giving him Andy's formal name, which is an utterly useless piece of information without any additional context. The President obviously wants to know who Andy is from a practical perspective, and why Nolan's brought him into a classified discussion. Nolan will get there but in his own sweet ass time.

"He's a YouTuber," Monroe blurts out. Someone's no good at playing chicken.

"A what-er?" the President asks.

Nolan says, "Andrew runs a popular channel on the social media video site YouTube."

"I know what YouTube is," the President snaps, even though seconds before he sought clarification. Nolan is a bastard. He knows precisely how hard to push the President. Jacinta's warned him he's playing with fire, but Nolan doesn't care. He values his honor above his career. Besides, he'll make a helluva lot more money in the private sector once he retires from the military. And right now, the President needs him. If he didn't, he would have pulled him out of Houston on the first return flight.

Nolan reaches over and taps the camera on Andy's chest, saying, "He's broadcasting live—right now. On YouTube."

"He's what?" the President yells, exploding out of his seat. His chair shoots back into one of his aides. The poor man winces on being hit by the chair back. It's all Nolan can do not to smile with delight. He clenches his jaw, refusing to reveal so much as a glimpse of what he's thinking.

President Wilson leans forward with clenched fists pressed hard against the table. "You brought a civilian to a secure meeting with the President of the United States of America and the Joint Chiefs of Staff? Without asking? Without telling anyone?"

"That's correct, sir," Nolan says, still not giving anything away in his facial expression. For him, this is like hunting grouse in the heavily wooded countryside of southern Colorado. It's all about timing and placement. If you've only got one shot, you've got to make it count.

"What the hell were you thinking?" the President demands.

Dr. Monroe has turned away from the camera. He's facing Nolan. It seems he too is astonished by Nolan's brash move. Andy is pale. If he could, Nolan has no doubt he'd shrink into oblivion. For Nolan, it's refreshing to have Andy beside him as it's allowed him to ambush the President, stealing his thunder. Asymmetrical warfare is all about the element of surprise. It's nice to see President Wilson on the defensive. Now it's time for some well-placed reverse psychology.

"With respect, Mr. President. We made a mistake with *Anduru*. During the previous administration, we had numerous meetings like this one, discussing the threat and our potential response, but we never went public with them. Oh, we discussed the points raised in press briefings, but the American public never got to see the decision-making process for themselves."

Although he's still standing in front of his chair, the President's tone drops. He mumbles, "So the public never trusted the decision-making process."

"Exactly, sir."

The President bangs his hand on the table saying, "Well, we're avoiding those kinds of mistakes in this administration."

"Yes, sir."

"What's the plan, general?"

Still, there's no curiosity, no request for updates, no concern about soldiers in the field. More to the point, the President doesn't have any questions about what these things are and how they escaped. All he wants to know about is *the plan*. To Nolan, plans are meaningless devoid of context, but okay.

Nolan had hoped to turn the spotlight on Monroe, but that was before Andy waltzed into the impromptu army base. As it is, Nolan's managing-up, trying to steer the President. The last thing he wants is this dip-shit in Washington giving him nonsensical orders that get people killed.

"We're running a three-pronged strategy, sir.

"First, we need to evacuate civilians. Not just for their safety, but to clear what we anticipate will become a battlefield. This will simplify our engagement. With over two million people on the move from the Greater Houston area, we have a significant challenge on the roads. Colonel Masters from the Texas National Guard is coordinating with state and local police, along with EMS and Fire Departments to relocate the population to Hempstead in the west and Conroe to the north.

"Second, we need to understand the movement and spread of these creatures. We have recon units stationed at key intersections within Houston and aerial assets overhead. At this point, they're moving to the northwest. Why is unclear."

"And third?" the President asks, becoming impatient with too much detail.

Nolan pauses. This is the moment he's been dreading.

"Third is combat deployment. I'm reluctant to engage these things with military assets until we have established logistics in place. We need supply chains to ensure the movement of soldiers, equipment, fuel, munitions and medical support. At the moment, we have insufficient force for anything beyond recon."

"We need to strike," the President says, shaking his fist in the air. "I want to hit them—and hit them hard! We need to show these things— no one messes with the United States of America!"

"Sir," Nolan says, taking a deep breath. For the President, this might be a game, but for Nolan, it's about lives. He's not going to send his troops into harm's way without coordinated ground and air support. "We don't know how they will react. At the moment, we have them contained in a limited geographic area. That's to our advantage. I've got heavy armor being flown in from Fort Bragg and M1-Abrams coming overland from Fort Sam in San Antonio. We're establishing an air presence, but we need time to build up local munitions and fuel depots so we can undertake a sustained campaign."

"This is America," the President says with disdain dripping from his words. "We have the home ground advantage. I will *not* allow us to take a backward step."

"Yes, sir," Nolan says, struggling to compress the complex logistic and military planning being undertaken in the various tents within the parking lot. There's danger in oversimplifying strategy. Any misunderstanding is potentially worse than any enemy they meet in the field. With a loose cannon for a President, Nolan's got to thread the needle. He needs to act as a buffer between the President and the military planners he's assembled. He's got to placate the President while ensuring his troops stand a chance. Battles are won with discipline, not bravado. Rushing into the unknown has never been an effective military strategy.

"I want boots on the ground," the President says, pounding his fist on the table. "I want us marching in there, kicking ass and taking names!"

Nolan's tempted to point out that the Houston business district is fifteen miles south of them. That's a day's march for fully-laden Marines—if he had any on-site. They need vehicles. And vehicles need fuel. They could helo in troops, but the noise would negate any element of surprise. If anything, it might draw in the creatures before their squads have time to establish defensive positions and conduct scouting.

Nolan clears his throat. "We're mobilizing soldiers from the Joint-Reserve in Fort Worth and Fort Hood. We're setting up a staging post fifteen miles north at Spring Creek."

"Good. Good. Send them in," the President says, waving his hand toward the screen.

"They need armor in support, sir. And the roads are clogged."

"Don't wait," the President says, ignoring Nolan's comment. "We've got civilians in there. We need to protect them. Send in the troops. Now! Send in what you've got. And when more arrive, send them in. Is that understood, general?"

"Yes, sir."

"And him," the President says, pointing at the image of the three men on the screen. "Send him in with them."

"Yes, sir," Andy says before Nolan can respond.

"That is all," the President says. And with that, the screen goes black.

It strikes Nolan as profound that someone was sitting there waiting for those three words, itching to cut them off without the possibility of any further discussion. The President knows precisely what he's doing. Introducing Andy has changed the equation, but not enough. At least it'll take the President and his advisors some time to realize they came off as brash and irresponsible. Oh, they'll spin it in their favor, but Nolan's pleased the meeting was broadcast to the public. Regardless of what happens next, there's no doubt about what he's dealing with in the chain of command.

"Have fun," Monroe says, needling Nolan.

Damn, Monroe got off light. He sulks away without saying anything else. At some point, the attention has to turn on him and the lab breach, and when it does, Nolan wants front row seats to the fireworks.

Nolan rests his hand on Andy's shoulder, saying, "Looks like you got your death wish."

THE ROOF

Kath doesn't know what to do.

Tears stream down her cheeks. It's all she can do not to sob, but any noise is going to attract the alien stalking her.

Kath's sitting in a hotel corridor next to an open-air atrium well over twenty stories above the ground. Broken cinderblocks lie scattered on the carpet in front of her, having been crushed by a creature that evolved around some other star.

It's been ten minutes. Or has it been several hours? Hell, it could have been ten seconds. Time has lost all meaning. All she knows is the damn thing hasn't moved. It's still there, just below the ledge, clinging to the side of the hotel, waiting for her to make a break for safety.

Kath lifts the smartphone with her trembling hands. She wants to add the phrase, *Ambush predator* to the commentary, but that would be a mistake. Instead, she mouths the words.

Like a tiger in the rainforests of Asia, the creature uses camouflage to hide its approach. She'd like to think it will show up in infrared as humans do, but given the scales manipulate light, there's no reason to think they're limited to visual light. These damn things are probably invisible to all but radar.

Kath stops the recording and slips the phone into her pocket. As

207

Jimmy's clinging to one side of her and the bedsheet's draped over her other shoulder, she's got to work with her hand to bury the phone. She doesn't want it to fall out.

Kath's tempted to abandon the phone, wondering if that's the best way for it to be found. They're going to die, of that, she has no doubt. They're trapped. There is no escape. But what will happen to the phone? Perhaps she should slide it across the carpet away from her to help ensure its survival.

Where's Monroe and his squad of goddamn Marines? He was so damn sure humanity would prevail. As much as she despises his hubris, she'd love nothing more than to see him come charging in with a bunch of highly trained soldiers by his side. This is the one time in her life she'd be quite happy to be rescued as a damsel in distress.

The goo on her shoulder is cold. It oozes down the back of her neck.

Under her breath, she mumbles, "Think, Kath."

Quietly, she unzips the pack seated in front of her and rummages through toilet paper, plastic water bottles, candy bars and shampoo. She takes care not to knock the tiny glass bottles of alcohol against the cans of soda.

"What are you looking for," she whispers, berating herself. "A bazooka?"

The housekeeping cart is less than ten feet away, while the fire escape is just beyond that. She could crawl. Would she make it?

Kath would stand a better chance alone. She could shed the pack, leaving the first aid kit and the bedsheet, but Jimmy? Could she really abandon him? Besides, there's no way to know if she'd make it more than a few feet before that damn thing pounced on her. No, she can't do that to him. There's got to be another way.

As best she understands it, she was beneath the creature as it straddled the wall. That allowed her and Jimmy to escape its sight. Regardless of the senses it uses, it seems confident it can hang out of view and launch into action at the slightest movement. That's got to imply hearing of some sort. If its reaction was based on sight, it could be in the infrared spectrum. The concrete wall is too thick for heat to penetrate. Ironically, that makes the two of them invisible to this seemingly invisible creature. Regardless, as soon as she breaks cover, it's going to pounce.

Kath's not going to make it to the door, but she has to try.

She slips the bedsheet off her shoulder. The four knotted shoes rock sideways on the carpet as she pushes them clear. Beneath her, rocks fall as the creature flexes its claws. It's aware of even that subtle motion, but it's waiting for the best time to strike. Its reaction speed seems to be similar to terrestrial animals, with a slight, sub-second delay. Kath makes a mental note to add that to her video blog. If she gets out of here, these are the kind of details she needs to tell others.

Kath slips one arm out of the backpack, but she can't free the other while Jimmy is clinging to her. Gently, she raises his head, holding a finger to her lips to keep him quiet. She wriggles free of the backpack straps.

Claws scratch at the concrete behind her, touching lightly at it. Although she can't see the creature, she imagines it has multiple points of contact and is using one arm to probe the wall. It's trying to make sense of where she is but seems confused. It knows where it was when it mounted the wall, but where is she? There's the intelligence of a hunter at work. The animal assumes she isn't right there in front of it because that's where it sat, leaning over the wall. It hasn't realized she was directly beneath it. To it, that doesn't seem possible. All of these points give her insights into the nature of these creatures. The alien seems to have the cunning of a bear or a lion. And importantly, it can be confused.

Jimmy is on his knees beside her. He's in no state to run anywhere. She's going to have to haul him up on her hip and that is going to slow her down. She needs a diversion. She considers throwing the toilet paper rolls. A flutter of paper unraveling as it soars through the air might confuse the alien. Or perhaps one of the soda cans? If she cracks the tab, she might get enough fizz to propel the can onward as it bounces. That might replicate the motion of something that's alive.

It might fool it.

It probably won't.

This thing had enough intelligence to realize where she was based on how she threw the burning roll of toilet paper. It's not going to fall for anything she throws. All that's going to do is confirm her location. This time, however, it won't be fooled by her crouching behind the wall.

Kath is resigned to her fate. She's not getting out of this alive, but Jimmy can. She can provide him with a chance at least. After all, this monster can only eat them one at a time.

She leans forward, drawing Jimmy's hair back. It breaks her heart, but she shoves the phone in his hand. She pulls her makeshift face mask down, whispering in his ear, "Get ready to run. When I stand up, you run and you don't look back, okay?"

He nods.

"Get to the roof. Get to the helipad." Tears stream down her cheeks. "Wait there. Someone will see you. I promise."

It's not a promise she can make, but she has to give him hope. If someone gets that phone, she tells herself it'll be worth the cost of her life. It won't, but she has to believe her death won't be pointless.

Kath adjusts her scrunched-up singlet back over her mouth. Why? At the moment, sharp teeth are far more of a concern than alien microbes. Honestly, nothing matters anymore and yet she has to believe she's going to escape even if she knows it's impossible. She whispers, "Give them the phone."

Kath swallows the lump in her throat. She sits back, cupping her hands around his tender face.

"Ready?"

Jimmy's lips quiver. He's not ready for anything.

She nods, letting him know it's time.

Kath gets to her feet. She grabs the bedsheet in one hand and the backpack in the other. Anything that might distract the creature a moment longer gives Jimmy a little more time.

"Go," she yells.

Jimmy shrinks in place.

The creature, though, doesn't hesitate. In a fraction of a second, it leaps up, grabbing at the crumbling wall. Dark claws sink into the cinder blocks just inches from Jimmy's shoulder. Concrete crumbles as it perches on the wall, surveying the corridor.

Kath staggers backward, bumping into the housekeeping cart.

"What are you waiting for?" Kath yells, throwing her arms wide. She's holding the backpack in one hand and the sheet in the other. She can't quite get a good grip on the backpack. The shoulder strap runs over her palm. The stubs of her fingers wrap around the edge of the material as the pack jiggles around.

The invisible monster surveys her from its perch on the wall. She can see a slight shimmer as its head turns.

In that instant, Kath's aware she's following a classic terrestrial behavior. Like a cat arching its back and raising its fur, she's bluffing. She's trying to look bigger than she is. She hunches her shoulders forward, holding her arms out like the wings of a crane, trying to unsettle the monster. But the only one that's frightened by her behavior is Jimmy. He shrinks back against the wall beside the creature.

"Run," she yells.

The monster sees him. Its transparent head turns. Light glistens off its scales, revealing the faint outline of a broad, flat head. Teeth appear. There are thousands of them lined up in rows.

"Oh, no you don't," Kath yells, hurling her backpack at the invisible animal.

In less than a heartbeat, the pack is crushed. Broken bottles and bits of fabric fall from the animal's lips.

"The fire escape, Jimmy. Run!"

Kath dances sideways, drawing the animal's attention away from Jimmy, giving him the opportunity to escape. The poor kid is frozen in fear.

A large padded paw steps down onto the carpet from the wall. Claws retract. Part of the concrete wall collapses as the alien steps into the corridor. Although it's difficult to judge its size, based on the shimmer surrounding its shape, Kath would guess it's roughly five times the size of a fully-grown alligator—and ten times as mean and angry.

Kath steps back. She's careful. No sudden moves. Her shoes glide across the carpet. It's sizing her up. It's still trying to figure out where she came from and how she originally outsmarted it.

Jimmy's behind the creature. Its massive, transparent tail knocks him into the low wall overlooking the atrium. He scrambles to avoid the gap where the wall has collapsed.

"Go," Kath whispers.

Jimmy looks at her. He's looking for her to do something. He needs to run, but he can't. He needs her.

The creature is so broad it knocks the housekeeping cart into one of the hotel doors. It's unnerving not seeing anything distinct, just a slight shimmer of light shove the cart to one side.

All Kath's got is the bedsheet. Four shoes bump into each other, spinning around their laces.

"Come on, you asshole," she says, crouching and making herself smaller. If she's going to die, it's not going to be without a fight.

She holds the sheet with both hands, facing down the alien like a bullfighter.

With her singlet still wrapped around her face, she yells, "You want me? Come and get me!"

She waves the sheet like a cape, only it's white, not red. Colors don't matter to a bull. What about this thing?

Claws appear, sinking into the carpet. The alien is readying itself to pounce.

Kath throws the blanket out in front of her. She leaps to one side, slamming her body into the narrow opening in front of a hotel room. Her shoulder hits the door as the creature launches itself at her.

The shoes attached to the sheet fan out as they tumble at the end of their laces. The sheet spreads, ballooning as it catches the air, filling the corridor. The alien lunges. Its head is caught in the sheet. It thrusts forward, tangling itself in the white bedsheet.

Kath flattens herself against the door to the nearest room.

The animal's confused. Its body, once entirely transparent, flashes white, blending in with the sheet. It shakes its head, trying to lose the sheet, but that only causes the shoes to fly around and bump into each other. That motion seems to confuse it even more.

Kath runs for Jimmy.

A white tail swings through the air, collecting the housekeeping cart and crushing it against the sheetrock wall. Kath ducks, sliding in toward Jimmy like a baseball player heading into home plate. The tail whips back, missing her. Her singlet slips down from around her face to around her neck.

She grabs Jimmy and heads for the door.

Behind her, the monster turns. It's still as white as the bedsheet, giving her a good look at its body shape. Eight legs. Eight goddamn legs and a head like a massive salamander. It's heard her or felt her as she darted past. The damn thing knows where she is, but it's clumsy in the confined space of the corridor. Its tail scrapes across the inner wall, hitting several doors, adding to the confusion.

Kath has Jimmy on her hip.

Rather than panicking and throwing open the fire door, she uses the precious few seconds the bedsheet has brought her to slip quietly through into the stairwell. The alien shakes its head. Its mouth snaps at the sheet, but these two actions are contradictory. One seeks to fling the sheet from its head, the other keeps it in place. The sneakers swing wildly through the air, banging into doors and walls and adding to the mayhem.

Kath eases the door shut, only it's set on a hydraulic piston. Try as she may, it closes slowly. Even though it's an emergency exit, someone's engineered the door not to slam so as to avoid waking guests in the nearby rooms.

Great. That's just fucking great!

It's all she can do not to freak out.

Kath pushes on the door, willing it to shut quicker but it eases closed. Through the thin glass, she can see the creature flickering in color, changing from white to transparent. It's got the sheet off its head.

The door closes to within a fraction of an inch.

Outside in the corridor, silence descends. The alien disappears from sight. It's holding still, trying to locate her. Whereas seconds ago, Kath was desperate to close the door, now she wants to slow it down. She's dreading the thunk of the lock clicking in place. She rests the toe of her shoe in the narrow gap, preventing it from closing the last quarter of an inch. As soon as that monster hears the lock or feels the clunk resound through the floor, it's going to be on top of them again.

Jimmy stands beside her. His eyes are as big as saucers. Tears leave streaks down his cheeks. He's terrified. He holds up the torn remains of the backpack. Everything's gone. The pockets have been ripped open. The main pouch is covered in goo while the padded shoulder straps have been wrenched from their clips.

Kath reaches for it. She can't quite grab it without leaving the door.

Jimmy holds it out for her. He must think she's mad. She is.

She feeds what's left of the padded straps into the thin gap in the door, preventing the lock from engaging. The door's all but closed. Claws scrape at the carpet beyond the fire door. Thick pads support the weight of the creature, allowing it to move in silence as it stalks its prey. Through the small, reinforced safety glass window in the fire door, Kath can see the outline of padded feet flattening the carpet.

She holds her finger to her lips and creeps away from the door.

Kath stays close to the wall within the stairwell, minimizing her visibility from the main corridor. She picks up Jimmy. The poor boy is pale. His pants are soaked with urine, but that's okay, so are hers. She holds him tight, as much for herself as for him. Quietly, they climb the stairs. Jimmy reaches up, straightening the t-shirt she's using as a face mask. The knot has come loose so he holds it in place with his tiny fingers, melting her heart.

After several turns in the stairs, they arrive at the roof.

"Yes."

Kath feels overwhelmed with a sense of relief.

Just minutes ago, she thought she was going to die. Now, there's hope. She reaches out, grabbing the brushed metal doorknob.

The door is locked.

"You have got to be fucking kidding me," Kath says, suddenly feeling embarrassed with Jimmy right there on her hip.

"No, no, no," she says, leaning against the cold steel door and sliding down onto her ass. "Please."

They're stuck in a dead-end. If one of those things gets up here, there's nowhere to go. The thought of going down twenty-five flights of stairs and risking those creatures on the ground is heartbreaking. With all the two of them have been through, it feels cruel to be stopped by a locked door.

Jimmy hangs his head.

Kath's impromptu mask slides down around her neck, hanging over her chest like a loose bandana. She could fix it back in place, but she doesn't care. Nothing matters. All her plans have come to naught. Her vision of reaching the roof and signaling for help is gone. She no longer has the bedsheet to act as the backing for an SOS. Without the mirror, she has no way of signaling distant aircraft.

Even if she could get on the roof, what's the point? At a distance of just a mile, they'd be all but invisible to flight crews. The chances of being found now are zero. Correction: found alive. Kath reserves the luxury of thinking humans will win this encounter. The analytical side of her brain may have doubts, but emotionally she has to believe they'll prevail.

Jimmy hands her the phone.

"Thanks, buddy."

She hangs her head. Kath would cry if she could, but she has no tears left.

Soft fingers touch her shoulder. They rub back and forth on her shirt, providing comfort.

"Hey," she says, looking up into Jimmy's eyes. He's lowered his mask/shirt as well. His lips are downturned. Kath tries to put on a brave face, but he must see it in her eyes—the sense of utter defeat. "I—I'm sorry."

Jimmy wraps his hands around her neck. She pats him tenderly on his back. After all he's been through, he's still holding on to hope. Kath can't lie to him or herself anymore. Mentally, she's at the end of the road.

It takes a few minutes, but, deep down, Kath can't give up. It's irrational and she knows it, but she feels compelled to get to her feet. She's got to keep trying—for Jimmy's sake. His world has been destroyed. His father is dead. He's got nothing but her. She can't stand the thought of breaking his heart again. As much as she may want to quit, she owes him her best. It's irrational as she knows they're probably both contaminated with alien microbes, but it's the emotional side of her thinking that holds sway.

"Okay," Kath says, sniffing. She wipes the snot running from her nose, composing herself. "We're locked in. That's not good. What options do we have?"

Kath's not expecting Jimmy to reply. She's talking herself into action. She looks around. On the wall, there are the usual obligatory signs about safety. There's lots of fine print no one ever reads. A big red sticker in the shape of an old-fashioned camera warns her the door is under constant surveillance.

"If only," she says, looking up at a dark Perspex dome covering a camera in the far corner.

No one's watching.

Even if there was someone alive in the security room, there's no power anyway.

216

"Huh," she says to herself as the spark of a meager thought lights up within the recesses of her mind. "If I was on the hotel admin staff and someone needed access to the roof, would I really leave the key on the ground floor?"

She ruffles Jimmy's hair.

"Can you imagine that? Perhaps you're up on the 15th floor chasing the cleaners about a dirty room and someone calls you over the radio. They want you to head up the stairwell to let the maintenance crew onto the roof so they can wash the atrium windows. Are you really going to traipse all the way down to the ground floor for a key? Oh, you might carry a key on you, but what if you're sick? What if someone needs access outside of normal hours? No, you've got to keep that key handy. You've got to ensure it's accessible."

Kath feels a rush of excitement. She reaches up above the doorframe, running her fingers along the thick metal edge of the fire door, searching for a key. Nothing.

"Or what if the a/c goes down and an electrician needs to get up here in a rush? Or some rich jerk is flying in on a helicopter and hospitality has to greet them? The door's got to be kept locked, but you also need easy access to the roof. What if there's an emergency—like this? Are you really going to leave the key downstairs? I think you're going to hide a key up here somewhere. You don't want a bunch of stupid teens finding it, but you need other people to be able to find it when needed. Where would you put the key?"

There's a small metal box on the wall. Kath opens it. A bunch of fuses and junction points are lined up in neat rows, but there's no key.

"You might even have to send someone else up to escort the window cleaners if you're busy. You want the key to be accessible to them. It needs to be hidden but easily found. You've got to be able to describe where it is to someone over the radio."

Kath runs the stubs of her fingers under the junction box, feeling for anything unusual.

"Ah," she says, feeling a small container attached to the underside. It's magnetic. She pulls it off and opens it. A smile breaks out on her face as she holds up the key. Jimmy claps with excitement. He's clearly enjoyed hearing her talk herself through this.

Kath unlocks the door and steps out into the bright sunlight. The sense of relief is overwhelming. In reality, they haven't made it anywhere of significance. They're standing on top of an alien nest. They're all but invisible to the rest of the world and yet it feels as though they're victorious. They've won!

The wind whips across the rooftop. It's a welcome relief as they won't have to wear their makeshift masks. Kath had all but given up anyway. A raised metal walkway carries them over a boulder field covering the flat roof. Why did they haul large rocks up here? Is it something to do with heat insulation? It can't be for aesthetics. Large stainless steel crates house the industrial air conditioning units cooling the hotel.

The door closes behind them. It's unlocked. If they need to seek shelter inside, they can. Kath gets her first good look outside. Standing on the raised walkway, she turns through 360 degrees, taking in the whole of Houston.

"See that?" she says, pointing and directing Jimmy's gaze to the north. "That's not good."

Several office buildings back onto a park. Of itself, that's not unusual, but vines are growing over the windows, reaching up toward the roof.

"That's really not good. Nothing on Earth grows that fast. Not even bamboo."

It's difficult to tell at a distance, but she thinks she can see several other buildings with greenery creeping up the walls. There's a nature strip beside the onramp for the freeway less than a block from the hotel. The bushes there are green and lush. To her alarm, though, they're spreading onto the road, covering half a lane.

"I don't like what I'm seeing, Jimmy."

The four buildings that make up the hotel form a square with the pyramid-like windows over the atrium rising to a point in the middle.

Steel beams support the glass, forming a symmetrical lattice.

"Wait here," Kath says, dropping down from the walkway onto the pebbles and rocks. She creeps to the edge and peers into the hotel. The top floors are empty, but there's movement about five stories down. Kath cups her hands around her eyes, wanting to peer into the shadows. Hundreds of creatures swarm over the facia within the atrium. At a guess, they're no bigger than a dog, but they haven't started hiding their bodies yet, probably because there's no immediate threat.

Kath swallows the lump in her throat. She goes to turn around when Jimmy cups his hands over his eyes, mimicking her as he stares through the glass.

"We've got to stop them, Jimmy."

Jimmy looks at her and nods.

"We can't let those things escape."

Kath picks up a rock, looking thoughtfully at it. Jimmy walks beside her back to the raised walkway, only he's struggling on the uneven rocks. Kath drops her rock and lifts him onto her hip. She hoists him back onto the walkway and climbs up beside him.

Military helicopters circle easily five miles north of them. It's frustrating. They're so close, but she has no way of signaling for help. High in the sky, she makes out the shape of a small aircraft with wide wings.

"There's a drone up there," she says, pointing.

If she had a flare gun, she could get someone's attention. As it is, the military is looking for a needle in a haystack without knowing there's a needle there to start with. She sighs. No one's looking for them. The motion of those helicopters probably indicates the leading edge of the alien advance. The idea of survivors this far behind the lines wouldn't occur to anyone. Oh, they would have looked for a while. They would have held out hope, but when no one emerged for hours, they would have gone on to help others. The battle for Houston has passed the two of them by.

Kath follows the raised walkway to a helipad on the far corner of the hotel. She and Jimmy climb the steps. The surface is old and worn. The gigantic **H** marking the landing zone has faded over the decades. The rocks on the roof are grey, while the helipad has been bleached white.

"I need rocks," Kath says. She steps down and gathers up a bunch of rocks, carrying them in a pouch she forms by stretching her t-shirt in front of her. "Can you help me?"

Jimmy nods. Over the next hour, they ferry rocks from the roof to several points on the helipad. Kath dumps them in various piles. Jimmy staggers after her with sweat dripping from his brow. The sun is sitting low on the horizon by the time they finish.

Kath sits Jimmy on the edge of the stairs, thanking him.

"You've been wonderful," she says. She leaves him there as she begins arranging the rocks, forming letters on the helipad. It's a long shot, but if there's any kind of artificial intelligence being used to analyze the drone imagery, it'll pick up on a distinct change like this. Photo analysis will miss the movement of people, but it'll detect changes in shapes. Kath only hopes someone's watching.

She shoves the rocks and pebbles around, moving them with her hands and occasionally her shoes. Then she stands back to examine her handiwork. Originally, she was going to write SOS, but she can't bring herself to form those letters.

Kath turns her back on the message spelled out by the rocks and walks back to join Jimmy on the stairs leading down to the roof. She hopes the lengthening shadows make her words more distinct. She doesn't have the heart to tell Jimmy what she's written. From his perspective, it's upside down and spread out wide. If he has figured it out, he doesn't say anything.

A cool breeze blows in from the bay, causing him to shiver.

Kath sits down next to him. She puts her hand around his shoulder, warming him. She can't bring herself to say everything's going to be all right. It's not. Behind her, there are three words she hopes will prevent a disaster.

FIRE
BOMB
ME

They're going to die on this rooftop. There's no escape. She's known that since she saw the dead rat outside her room. Bunching up a t-shirt over her mouth was futile, at best. The odds are, they're infected with whatever killed that goddamn rat.

At least, this way, it'll be quick.

THE
NUCLEAR
OPTION

"I want a goddamn update on that munitions depot," Nolan yells at a sergeant sitting at a table with a laptop open in front of him. Nolan's barely a foot from the man's ear. He leans down beside him, but he could be screaming at him from the other end of a football field and still be heard with utter clarity. "I want every thermobaric bomb on the east coast—in Texas—before sunset! Is—that—under—stood?"

"Yes, sir," the soldier replies, sitting bolt upright.

Nolan's rage subsides, but the passion in his voice is still there. "No excuses. No delays. Feed me armament!"

"Yes, sir. Understood, sir," another soldier says, keeping his head down as he taps on a keyboard.

"People are dying out there. Minutes cost lives. Make it happen!"

"Understood."

Nolan's frustrated. War is about avoiding chaos. Command and control are necessities, not buzzwords. At the moment, everything is arrayed against him. He can't get the support he needs. The US is used to building up to engagements. It's the weekend. Recalling troops and aircrew on a Sunday is a nightmare. It only takes one person to be late and a C130 already laden with supplies is grounded, awaiting a pilot. Then there's the unfolding civilian disaster. People are getting angry.

People with guns—lots of guns. Nolan's had to divert soldiers to support state troopers in quelling fights. It's the only way to keep vehicles moving north.

To his shock, while he was on the south side of the mall, a bunch of medics set up a field hospital to the north. They've pulled in doctors, nurses and medical supplies from a convoy fleeing the Lyndon B. Johnson Memorial Hospital to the south. With the roads clogged, they were stuck. Here, at least, they can tend to their patients and provide support for those on the road. Nolan can't fault them for using their initiative and doubling up with the military. It makes sense. He also can't ignore their requests for aid. They've busted open several mall stores to gain access to practical supplies like running water and electricity, but diverting troops to help them establish a field hospital further dilutes his resources.

The President has put him in an impossible situation. He can't turn his back on civilian needs and yet he's been instructed to prosecute a war. With what? Against what? Hell, the only descriptions he's heard are nonsensical. Creatures that can blend into the background. One survivor says they're the size of an elephant. Another says they're like wild hogs. Most of his recon units are either dead or have lost contact with the advancing horde.

Jacinta rushes up to him.

"General Cooper's exercising Title 49 provisions. He's commandeered a bunch of civilian aircraft from United and American Airlines. He's setting up an airbridge between here and Oklahoma City. Fly in with troops and supplies. Fly out with civilians."

"Finally," Nolan says. "Some good news."

"At the moment, it's fifteen aircraft, but he's working with the airlines to increase that to over a hundred within the next few hours. If it's in the sky, he's diverting it, using Oklahoma as a staging post."

Nolan breathes deeply, calming his mind. "We've got to start thinking about displacement camps on the outskirts of San Antonio, Austin and Fort Worth. We're going to need them sooner rather than later. Get Eamon to reach out to the Red Cross and

Médecins Sans Frontières. Tell them to be thinking large-scale, something akin to a hurricane evacuation. We are about to swamp those cities. They need to be ready."

"On it, boss," Jacinta says.

He blinks and she's gone. Nolan doesn't know what he'd do without Jacinta. She's like a thoroughbred racehorse. He might be *The Boss*, being a thinly-veiled reference to his love of Bruce Springsteen, but she's the powerhouse. Somehow, she turns his fleeting ideas into reality. He has no doubt she's saving hundreds of thousands of lives.

Andy fidgets in the subsequent silence. He's nervous. Nolan's so busy gathering his thoughts he forgot the firebrand YouTuber was shadowing him with a camera running. The yelling was probably over the top even for the fabled Angry Andy Anderson.

"We're still broadcasting, huh?" Nolan says, facing him.

"Oh, yeah."

Nolan leans down, getting close to the camera. He waves to whatever audience is watching, saying, "I should have been a drill sergeant, huh?"

"You missed your calling," Andy says, smiling.

"Have you served?"

"No, sir," Andy replies.

"So you've never seen combat?"

"No," Andy says as they march out onto the street separating the mall from the local high school. A helicopter flies overhead, carrying a howitzer slung beneath its belly. It lowers it onto the football field.

"Well, you are in for a treat," Nolan says. "You'll be going in with special forces—the US Rangers."

Easily a hundred soldiers dressed in camouflage mill around on the road. Their backpacks are stuffed with ammo and equipment. Nolan marches up to the commanding captain. She's got a map of Houston spread out on the hood of a Humvee.

"Sir," she says, saluting as Nolan approaches.

Nolan returns her salute. "What have you got for me, captain?"

"Sir, our first flight has three rifle platoons. That's twelve squads. Just under a hundred and twenty soldiers, but we are not in company strength. We lack the normal command structure."

"That's not good," Nolan says. He does not want to sacrifice troops like pawns on a chessboard.

The captain, though, seems undeterred. She's not making excuses for their disarray. "What are our orders, sir?"

Nolan hesitates. He's sending these troops into the unknown. Most if not all of them will die. He can't pass the buck. It would be easy to point on the map and leave the captain to disseminate the orders. He's got to be honest with them. Nolan has no doubt POTUS is watching the live feed along with most of the senior planners in the Pentagon. He climbs up on the hood of the Humvee. The captain anticipates what's coming.

"All right, Rangers," she bellows. "Stand to attention!"

The soldiers get to their feet, forming up into their squads, surrounded by their gear.

"At ease," Nolan yells over the noise of another helicopter passing overhead. "Listen up. I need you to know what I know. I'm sending you into the dark. We are facing an enemy unlike anything ever seen on Earth before."

An eerie silence descends. Not only does he have the attention of the Rangers, but several other units also stop what they're doing to listen. For a moment, the skies are clear. Helicopters are still flying, but they're heading back to the airport.

Andy stands to one side, directing his camera up at Nolan as his voice bellows through the air.

"I will not bullshit you. I will not blow smoke up your ass. The reality is—we are not ready for battle. We are still moving chess pieces around the board. The problem is—we're out of time. We have to hold the airport. If we lose the ability to land troops and supplies, we lose this battle. If we lose this battle, we could lose the war. Do you understand?"

"Hoo-rah," the Rangers yell in response.

"We have reports of creatures advancing through Homestead to the south and Green's Bayou to the east. The roads are blocked. You'll have limited support. You may end up on foot. These things are practically invisible. They're like lions, sharks, tigers. They're ruthless, merciless."

He points in the direction of the helicopters disappearing over the buildings. "If they make it to the airport, they could shut us down in a matter of minutes. We need logistics to survive.

"I am sending you in understrength with no air support. You will have the ability to call in artillery fire, but it will be fleeting and is not guaranteed.

"I will not order you to march to your death. I'm asking you for your help. I need you to do the impossible. You've got to buy us time to bring in heavy armor. What say you?"

With one voice, the soldiers yell, "Rangers lead from the front!"

Nolan nods, fighting back tears. He climbs down from the vehicle. His boots thud on the concrete as he jumps from the brush guard at the front.

The captain is a woman in her twenties. She's thin and slight of build.

Nolan asks her, "What do you need to coordinate your action?"

"With respect, sir. I'll go in with my troops."

"Understood," he says, nodding in respect of her decision. Nolan introduces Andy. "I'd like you to take a civilian observer with you."

"A civilian, sir?" the captain says, taking a good look at unshaven Andy in his grubby clothes.

Nolan taps the camera on Andy's chest. "He's broadcasting live. Everyone's watching."

"Everyone?" the captain asks. "Is that a good idea, sir?"

"It's an idea, captain," Nolan says, granting her skepticism with at least partial acknowledgment. "It's what we need—both now and into the future. We lack visibility. We need to know what's going on back there."

"I understand, sir."

Nolan turns to Andy, saying, "I'll leave you with Captain Winters. Good luck."

"Thank you," Andy says, shaking his hand.

"All right," the captain says to Andy. "Let's get you kitted up."

Nolan walks away. He doesn't look back. He's got to move on. There's too much that needs to be done. Too many people are relying on him. He doesn't have the luxury of doubt. Second guesses will plague him for years to come. The faces of those he addressed will haunt his dreams. For now, he consoles himself. He's making the best decision he can with limited information.

If it were up to Nolan, he would hold back his troops in reserve. He'd use the interstate as a firebreak and dig in along the freeway. Three lanes on either side would give his soldiers multiple clear lines of fire. Also, there's little to no cover for the creatures. Traditional wisdom is, defenders have the advantage. They could lay concertina wire and claymores. They'd be able to put up one helluva fight, but POTUS rejected the idea, even when Nolan contacted him through his chief of staff, wanting a backchannel. Oh, Nolan could refuse to send in the Rangers. He could resign. But what would that accomplish? If he did that, chaos would ensue and more lives would be lost. As it is, he's sidestepped the President, keeping his troops close. Defending the airport is a legitimate strategic decision. Sending them downtown would be suicide. At the very least, he's given them a chance. He only hopes their deaths won't be in vain.

"Where are my goddamn Bradleys?" he snaps at a subordinate. "What's the ETA on those M1-Abrams from Fort Bragg?"

For an Air Force general, Nolan's doing his best to think like a grunt. Oh, for the luxury of an F-18 cockpit. Life was much simpler at 35,000 feet staring down an infrared bombsight. Hell, it was even easier when special forces would light up the target for him with a laser.

"We need to talk," Monroe says, cornering Nolan as he grabs a cup of coffee. Someone's liberated an old filtered coffee machine from one of the admin offices in the mall. An extension cord winds back to somewhere someone's tapped into electrical power. The coffee's stale. It's been sitting on the element for hours and has a distinctly burnt taste. It's perfect for an old hand like him.

Nolan's been dreading the need to work with Monroe. So far, the action has been an evacuation in one direction, logistics in the other. In that regard, it's been predictable. Slow, but manageable. Nolan's nervous about how combat is going to change that dynamic. He'd rather have an armored division at hand and saturated skies. Apache attack helicopters are on their way, but they need to be transported in the back of C130s.

The two of them step back outside as a light rain falls.

Monroe says, "The President is asking about the nuclear option."

That gets Nolan's heart to skip a beat. He walks away from the tent out into an empty portion of the parking lot, well away from anyone else.

"What have you told him?"

"I said it was an option of last resort."

Nolan nods at that point. It's precisely what he would have said.

Monroe continues. "The President is concerned we may wait too long."

"Rushing in is a mistake," Nolan says. "We need to move in strength to avoid breakouts. Right now, we've got them bottled up. They're in one place. They don't feel threatened so they're not scattering. From their perspective, they're dominant. I'd like them to keep thinking that. I want them to feel secure. I don't want them to see the sledgehammer before it hits. Once our heavy armor starts rolling, we'll be able to take the initiative but we need time to prepare. It's been less than 24 goddamn hours since the shit hit the fan and about 12 hours since we realized just how bad it's getting out there."

Monroe asks, "Do you see nuclear weapons playing a role in

containment?"

Nolan is careful with his words. He does not like the idea of unleashing a nuclear bomb on a US city, particularly while civilians are still on the move. And if nukes are going to be used, he doesn't want to be sitting in the front row.

"No. I think nuclear weapons would be a mistake. They're blunt. We need precision. Also, we have no way of knowing if they'll be effective. They'll introduce more chaos, which will make military operations more difficult. And they'll deny us access to the battlefield. That could lead to a breakout of alien survivors."

Monroe nods. Nolan has no doubt he's under specific instructions from the President to drill Nolan on his strategy. The rug could be pulled out from under Nolan in a heartbeat. Hell, he's an OF-6 one-star general. Although it sounds impressive, brigadier generals are a dime a dozen in the Pentagon. It's the three and four-star generals that carry clout.

Monroe speaks with deliberation. "For now, my recommendation to the President will be to continue with the defense of the airport."

"Thank you," Nolan says, knowing how fragile his position is.

Jacinta comes running up to them in the rain. She's oblivious to the machinations of their discussion. She has no way of knowing they were discussing the possibility of destroying Houston in a blinding flash of light.

"We've found her!"

"Who?" Nolan asks.

"Kath! Dr. Kathleen McKenzie."

"What? Where?" Monroe asks.

"She's on the roof of the hotel. Somehow, she survived. She's up on the helipad. I've dispatched a Blackhawk to get her."

Nolan is confused. "How do you know it's her?"

"She wrote a message on the roof."

"What message?"

"She said, *firebomb me!*"

Nolan laughs. "That's Kath, all right."

SAFE

Kath is tired.

It's late afternoon. The sun sits low on the horizon. The wind blows her hair around. She tucks the loose strands into the collar of her shirt, but erratic gusts pull them loose. She's looking for a military airplane somewhere in the distance, wondering how quick the end will be. Will she have time to react? Or will her life simply blink out of existence? She hopes it's the latter.

Jimmy points north. He still hasn't spoken, but that's okay. He's dealing with the stress of all that's happened in his own way. Kath hasn't let go of him for over an hour now. At first, it was to keep him warm. Then, as the winds built up, it was to keep them both warm. Now, it's for emotional comfort.

A helicopter flies low over the city. That's not unusual. They've seen dozens of military helicopters dotted over distant buildings. This one's different. It's heading straight for them.

"No, no, no," she mutters, getting to her feet.

As the helicopter gets close, it banks, circling the hotel before approaching and setting down.

Kath swings her arms over her head. She's not signaling for them to land. She's trying to wave them away.

"Leave us," she yells, but her voice is drowned out by the deafening thump of the rotor blades. A loadmaster stands in the open doorway. He's got one arm up, holding onto a handle on the roof, the other rests on a bright red first aid kit. The support strap on the kit wraps diagonally across his chest. He's wearing a white helmet with a dark sun visor pulled down over his face, hiding his eyes. A microphone sits in front of his lips. He's talking calmly to someone somewhere. She's frantic, yelling, "Don't land!"

Kath runs to the middle of the helipad. She crosses her arms over her head, trying to visually warn them off. The Blackhawk descends regardless. The hurricane-like winds scatter the rocks and pebbles spread out over the helipad, sending them tumbling across the platform and destroying her message.

"You don't understand," she yells, shielding her face from the wind and dust kicked up by the rotor blades. Her t-shirt is buffeted by the winds. The fabric flaps madly against her skin.

The loadmaster jumps before the wheels touch down. He crouches as his boots take the impact of his landing. He keeps his head low as he runs in toward her. Kath's hair swirls around her, blinding her. Frayed, split ends whip before her eyes. The grit kicked up by the whirling blades makes it impossible to see anything other than a blur.

The loadmaster runs past her. He grabs Jimmy, lifting him up and seating him on his hip. Kath catches the flash of jungle camo out of the corner of her eye as he returns.

"We're infected," she yells. Regardless of whether he hears her, he reaches over her shoulder, grabbing her back and bundling her toward the open helicopter. The Blackhawk shifts sideways. Its wheels skid across the helipad. It's barely touched down. The craft rocks with a wind gust sweeping over the roof.

Before she knows what's happening, Kath's standing in front of the cargo hold. The floor of the helicopter is at chest height. The loadmaster dumps Jimmy on the deck. Then he crouches, pinning her legs together and hoisting her inside while she's still arguing with him.

Within seconds, he jumps up beside her, pulling her away from the door. Kath yells at him as he yells at her. He grabs a pair of headphones, handing them to her. A thick, tightly coiled cord connects the headset to a jack on the roof.

Kath feels overwhelmed. She's conflicted. Logic says she and Jimmy carry a high risk of spreading extraterrestrial microbial contaminants. Her emotions, though, ask whether that really matters in the larger scheme of things? How far has this stuff already spread? Would her sacrifice mean anything? Her heart demands she accept being rescued. If she were in a control room somewhere, watching all this play out on a video screen, she'd tell the military to leave the poor saps. She'd tell them it was the kindest thing they could do. She'd rationalize it by saying a quick death is better than a lingering, painful demise. But it's her on the other end of that analysis—and that hurts.

Kath slips the headphones on as the Blackhawk lifts into the air.

"Please," she blabbers. "You need to destroy this building."

"We've got an F-16 up there ready and waiting," the pilot says, turning to face her. "Armed with thousand-pound JDAMs."

"Is it a fuel bomb?" she asks. "You can't just drop bombs. You have to incinerate these things. You've got to burn them."

"Burn them?" the pilot says, hovering thirty feet above the helipad. "Hang on. I'm going to patch you through to command."

Kath holds onto the roof of the helicopter, looking out over the hotel. Even though she only has one good finger and thumb on her right hand, she's built up strength in them over the past year and can hold on tight. She backs her left shoulder into the wedge of the far door, giving her two good points of contact as the Blackhawk hovers. What seemed impossible moments ago has come to pass. They've been rescued. As good as that feels, Kath's not fooled. The danger doesn't come from those glistening creatures with their massive claws. It's whatever got into the lungs of that rat.

The loadmaster straps Jimmy into one of the jump seats.

"Kath," a familiar voice says over the radio and her heart sinks.

"Nolan?"

"Hey, don't worry. You're safe now. Everything's going to be okay. We've got you. We'll get you back here and do a full debrief."

"You don't understand," Kath says, blabbering. Emotionally, she's exhausted. She thought she was going to die down there on the roof. Her mind is unraveling. "We can't escape. None of us can."

"What do you mean?" Nolan asks.

"Forget everything you've seen in Hollywood," Kath yells into her microphone. "Those things—as terrifying as they are—they're not the real threat."

"Say again," Nolan replies. "Repeat your last."

"You've got to see the big picture," Kath says. "Where did they come from? How did they develop so fast? The invasion is happening at a microscopic level. You've got to burn them. You can't bomb them. You'll spread the infection on the wind."

"Infection?"

Kath sobs. "We're infected. We were down there too long. We can't leave. The risk is too great."

"Jesus, Kath. What are you saying?"

It seems the pilot has been listening in. He talks over the top of them, saying, "Ah—Awaiting confirmation. Are we heading back to the airport?"

"Negative. Negative," Kath says, trying to use military terminology to drive home her point. "We need to go into isolation."

"Kath, we don't have—"

"Look," she yells, pointing at the atrium in the center of the hotel. Glass panes shatter. Steel beams fall from the pyramid-like structure. Dozens of creatures scramble out onto the roof. It's impossible to see more than a blur. Rocks and gravel are scattered by invisible legs. The railing on the steel walkway is crushed. Metal twists and crumples under the weight of animals no one can see. There's a flicker in her field of view, like an old-fashioned film skipping a frame, allowing a glimpse of these creatures as their camouflage adapts.

The loadmaster is standing in front of Kath. He mutters, "What the?"

His silhouette partially blocks her view. She shifts to one side, wanting to see clearly.

"Get us out of here!" she yells.

"Copy that," the pilot says, pulling on his flight controls. The Blackhawk peels away from the rooftop, but the creatures are fast. By Kath's reckoning, there are at least ten to twenty of them tearing up the gravel. Their camouflage distorts as they move. Claws dig into the helipad, ripping up the concrete.

"Go. Go. Go," she yells.

The helicopter turns away from the edge of the hotel. The view down the side of the building is terrifying. Dark glass windows stretch toward the parking lot so far below. The palm trees outside the entrance look like twigs from this height.

A shudder reverberates through the Blackhawk. The helicopter rocks violently to one side, tipping back toward the hotel as it sags under a sudden increase in weight. The engines whine.

Kath's legs swing out from under her. She's got a firm grip on the rail above her, but her feet dangle in the air. She struggles to get hold of a support rail with her left hand. One of her disfigured fingers extends to the second knuckle, while the others only reach the first, but she's determined not to let go, cupping her hand around the railing.

Somehow, the loadmaster keeps his footing. He pushes against the ceiling, defying gravity, staring down at the parking lot below them. Jimmy's arms and legs are flung outward. His seatbelt holds him in place. His eyes, though, speak of a familiar terror. Kath feels it too. Claws puncture the fuselage near the copilot. The front door is ripped off its hinges. It plunges to the concrete hundreds of feet below them.

"Mayday. Mayday," the pilot cries as the Blackhawk begins to spin off-axis.

"Shoot it," Kath yells into her headset.

"Shoot what?" the loadmaster replies, pulling out his sidearm. "There's nothing there!"

Another set of claws digs into the deck of the Blackhawk just inches to his left. Although Kath can't see the animal, she knows what's happening. The creature is straddling the side of the helicopter, hanging onto the cockpit with one paw inside the cargo area. The Blackhawk rocks erratically as the creature tries to board the craft, swinging its transparent body around beneath the wheels.

"It's there—right there. Shoot in front of you!"

The helicopter twists through the air. The pilot wrestles with the controls. The engine strains under the load. The hotel flashes past. Rotor blades threaten to tear into the windows and metal cladding. Even in their reflection, there's no sign of the creature beyond the flicker of a faint outline. It looks as though they're spiraling out of control due to a mechanical failure.

"Do it," Kath yells.

The loadmaster points his gun in front of his boots, but he doesn't fire. He can't see a target. He searches, pointing his gun in different directions.

Kath screams, "Fire!"

She points at the massive set of claws visible beside his leg, but she's behind him. He can't see her arm. From his perspective, those claws extend beyond his legs. The alien has reached in past him in its effort to mount the chopper.

The helicopter spins. It takes all of Kath's might not to be flung from the open side of the Blackhawk. She jams her shoe into a gap between one of the racks at the rear of the helicopter and the fuselage, gaining some leverage. Kath starts to speak when the loadmaster's first aid kit is torn open. Bandages and plastic wrappings swirl through the air, being caught in the downdraft.

The pilot gains control of the aircraft. He drives the Blackhawk higher, moving away from the hotel. The cabin sags to one side. The engines scream in anger.

Kath blinks and the upper torso of the loadmaster is gone. His death is so sudden it doesn't seem real. Blood sprays through the air, splashing across the inside of the cabin. His dismembered legs topple forward, falling from the aircraft. A faint red smudge highlights the face of the massive creature. Thousands of tiny spots of blood make its outline apparent. The alien is bigger than she thought. It's so large its jaw can barely fit through the open doorway. Thousands of tightly packed, jagged teeth appear, stretching several meters in length.

Claws reach for her, slicing through the air.

"Roll the chopper!" Kath yells, trying to back up but with nowhere to go. Her boots balance on the edge of the cabin behind her. There's an empty feeling beneath her heels. She's hanging over the fuselage of the Blackhawk. Her hands grip the rail on the roof for dear life.

"We can't fly upside-down," the pilot yells in reply.

The head of the alien sways. With a blood-soaked paw, it reaches for Jimmy.

She yells, "Do it!"

"We'll crash."

"We have to shake this thing," Kath says, kicking at a paw the size of a basketball.

"We'll die!"

"We'll die either way," Kath replies. "At least we die fighting!"

It's risky letting go of the railing but Kath has to do something to protect Jimmy. She reaches in and releases the ties on a cargo net at the back of the Blackhawk. Supplies tumble into the hold, confusing the creature. Kath has no idea what she's grabbing. She hurls heavy metal boxes at the alien. It's a futile, feeble effort, but it distracts the monster.

A muscular paw reaches for her. Claws cut through the air, slicing open the front of her t-shirt. She shrinks from them, pulling her stomach in and arching her back behind her. Kath leans out of the Blackhawk as it rocks. The wind whips past, catching her body. She's outside the helicopter. She can see the fuselage. Only her feeble hands and the tips of her shoes are still inside the cargo area.

"Goddamn it," she yells. "Flip us over!"

The helicopter lurches in response to the creature's shifting weight. Red lights flash on the control panel above the pilot. The twin-engine turbines generate four thousand horsepower, driving them on. Four rotors thrash at the air. At the crazy angle it's on, the Blackhawk struggles to gain any more height. The suburbs of southern Houston rush by a thousand feet below them. It's all Kath can do not to be sick.

"Now!" she yells as the helicopter pitches.

The pilot doesn't reply. Instead, he pulls hard on the yoke, dragging it to one side as he guns the engine. The Blackhawk twists, turning on its side. Kath holds on to the door on the far side of the cargo bay. Her legs swing down beneath her, hanging just inches from the open mouth of the creature. Teeth snap at her shoes. The monster sways below the helicopter as it flies sideways, turning in a wide arc.

"More," she yells. "Further! Keep going."

The Blackhawk falls from the sky. It wasn't designed to fly on its side, let alone beyond 90 degrees. The pilot struggles with the controls. The slope of the horizon twists, rolling over the top of the cockpit windows. The airframe shakes. The roofs of homes and garages whiz past. The helicopter plummets. Buildings seem to rush up from the ground, racing in toward them. The rotor blades spin at three hundred revolutions a minute, cutting through the air. Even though they're whipping by five times a second, they can't keep the aircraft aloft at such an extreme angle. In that moment, the Blackhawk has the aerodynamic profile of a brick. Still, the pilot turns, reaching through 120 degrees. The helicopter careens to one side as it falls.

Gravity draws the tail and legs of the creature into the rotor blades. Brilliant blue/black blood explodes from the rear of the alien, spraying the side of the helicopter with sticky goo. The Blackhawk shakes violently as the rotors shave chunks of flesh from the monster, revealing its immense size. The animal loses its grip, falling away from the Blackhawk. Large swaths of the alien clip the rotors. They slice through its body as it plunges to the freeway. Dark blood sprays across the concrete road. Splatter hits the median strip.

"And back," Kath yells.

If only it were that easy. The twin turboshaft engines scream in agony. Power surges and fades. Black smoke billows from the exhaust. Far from leveling out, the pilot overcompensates. The horizon swings past. The helicopter shudders, shaking under the stress of flying with damaged rotors. Kath holds on, not wanting to be thrown from the aircraft several hundred feet above the streets of suburban Houston.

"We are going down," the pilot says, wrestling with the controls. "Mayday. Mayday. Mayday. This is Alpha-Foxtrot One-Zero declaring an emergency. Losing flight controls. Heading for water. South by southeast. We are going down. We are going down!"

CAPTAIN WINTERS

Captain Winters is in her late twenties. She has short, dark hair and eyes that could melt a glacier. Winters cinches the straps on Andy's tactical vest, pulling the bulletproof ceramic plates tight against his chest.

"Is this really necessary?" he asks. "I mean, they don't have guns, right?"

"Worse," she says. "Claws the size of kitchen knives. Trust me. You don't want one of those punching through your ribcage."

Andy's cosplayed as a soldier at gun shows, but he's never worn actual tactical gear. It's heavy. The rags he sold on his online show were more stylish than the Ranger uniform they've decked him out in. His stuff looked good on a mannequin, but this is different. There's purpose in the material. The boots are old, but they're more rugged than anything he's ever worn. The trousers are slightly baggy, but he can sense how that avoids restricting his movement. There's a blank piece of velcro on his chest plate. Normally, this would hold a soldier's surname. To everyone around him, he has no name. If he falls out there, he'll die without any sense of identity.

There's a mount for night-vision goggles on his helmet, allowing him to attach his camera. He syncs his smartwatch so it acts as a monitor, allowing him to see what's being broadcast.

Captain Winters looks down at his scruffy backpack and the various pieces of equipment he's laid out on the edge of the garden bed beside the mall.

"Choose carefully," she says. "Our priority is ammo then water. Everything else is a luxury."

"I need those battery packs," Andy says, pointing. "And the uplink. Beyond that, just a spare camera."

Andy's helmet is resting on the edge of a garden bed, catching their every move and streaming it to an internet satellite service and on to his studio back in Washington. Once color correction and image stabilization routines have automatically massaged the feed, it goes up on his YouTube channel.

"You won't be transmitting shit if you collapse from dehydration," she says, dumping a water canteen in front of him.

"We're in the 'burbs, though, right? There should be running water."

"Assume nothing," the captain says. "You'll live longer." She adds a 9mm Beretta in a holster along with a bunch of ammo clips to his gear. "Do you know how to use one of these?"

"Yes," Andy says, swallowing a lump in his throat.

Captain Winters isn't convinced. "This is only for use as a last resort. Understand? You don't draw unless we're being overrun."

Andy nods.

"Keep the safety on and the barrel pointing in a safe direction at all times—or it won't be the goddamn aliens you'll have to worry about. Are we clear?"

"We're clear."

With that, Andy dons his helmet. He checks his smartwatch. As there's a slight delay, he can see the interaction between the two of them still playing out on the screen. *Likes* and *hearts* stream up the side of the screen, signaling the audience's approval of the captain's attitude. From the comments, it's clear they liked seeing Andy being berated by the captain. It seems he's not the only one that can get angry.

Captain Winters shows Andy a map of northern Houston, laying it out on the hood of the Humvee.

"We've been tasked with the eastern flank. Our area of operation is below the toll road and east of I69."

"There's a golf course," Andy says, surprised to see that featured on the map.

"And a helluva lot of forest," the captain says. "My objective is to hold the bayou. See this section? It's a creek used for flood mitigation. The banks are clear of trees, giving us roughly fifty meters visibility in front and several hundred meters either way along the creek. If we can get there, we can hold the whole line."

"But to get there?" Andy asks, feeling there's a catch.

She taps the map. "We have to get through this industrial area here—and then through the suburb of Fall Creek."

"And?"

"And there are already reports coming in of activity in those streets."

"That's not good," he says.

"All news is old news," the captain says. "If we're hearing about it now, it's already history. My fear is these things have already crossed the bayou."

"So what are we going to do?" Andy asks.

"What Rangers always do—fight like hell!"

She folds up the map and they climb onto the running board on the Humvee. Captain Winters stands beside the open window on the driver's side, talking to the corporal behind the wheel. The Humvee is already packed with troops. A gunner swivels a 50 caliber machine gun from the roof turret.

"Let's ride!" the captain yells, punching forward with a gloved fist.

The Ranger behind Andy reaches around him. He grabs a strap from Andy's vest and clips him onto the railing running along the roof.

"Stay safe, bud," he says, patting him on the shoulder.

Six humvees pull out into the avenue. They drive against the flow of traffic. They're all overloaded with troops hanging onto rails. Andy looks down at the road racing by just inches below his boots, knowing the camera will catch that shot. He looks up and leans out. The wind whips past but he's got a good view.

Andy's wearing a headset beneath his helmet. A tiny microphone wraps around in front of his lips, allowing him to provide commentary. He holds up his hand, shielding the mic from the wind.

"This is it," he whispers for his online viewers. "We're going to war."

The freeway is clogged with traffic. The convoy follows a service road running parallel to the toll road. At several points, the service road comes to an end in industrial areas, forcing the convoy to wind its way through side streets. The Humvees mount the footpath to get around traffic jams. They crush fences, driving through backyards to make their own roads.

Several helicopters fly overhead. Although they could outpace the Humvees, they don't. They're spotters, watching over the convoy, alerting them to detours and looking for creatures.

A broad, flat concrete drainage ditch allows them to cross beneath the freeway interchange. Once the convoy's on the other side, the Humvees split up, taking different avenues as they head south.

In the distance, burning cars block the street. Flames leap from spare tires stacked near a crumbling brick wall.

"What the hell?" Winters yells over the sound of the wind.

The captain has command of several platoons, but now she's isolated from the other squads and their Humvees. In Andy's opinion, she should have stayed back at the command center. That would allow her to coordinate all three platoons effectively rather than just the squads in this one Humvee. Being this close to the action doesn't seem wise. Winters should direct her twelve squads like chess pieces, moving them around the board as needed. Andy wants to ask her about her strategy, but he's aware he's already an unwanted distraction. Perhaps there's something more for him to learn from her.

Winters barks commands through the window of the Humvee as it comes to a halt.

"Three Alpha. You're in reserve. Hang back with the H and cover us with the fifty. Six Charlie, advance on the western flank. Two Alpha, you're with me on the east."

There's no bravado. No *hoo-rahs* or calls of any kind. The soldiers are quiet. They peel away from the vehicle with their M4A1 assault rifles pointing forward. Andy's fascinated by their professionalism. Each squad moves in short bursts. Two soldiers at a time work their way forward, never jogging more than twenty feet before dropping behind cover. As soon as they're down, the soldiers behind them are on the move. The squad rolls forward, covering the hundred yards between the Humvee and the barricade in less than a minute.

Captain Winters follows twenty meters behind the advancing troops with a private beside her. He's carrying a machine gun. Andy recognizes it as a Squad Automatic Weapon. He once bragged that the M249 SAW was the easiest way to chop down a tree, but in reality, he's only ever seen one in action on YouTube. The SAW is belt-fed from a pouch slung beneath the action. At a guess, it carries at least a hundred rounds. Andy stays on the other side of the captain, matching the position of the squad gunner. His earpieces are noise-canceling, but he has doubts about their effectiveness to the sharp crack of gunfire.

"What have we got?" Winters asks, speaking into the radio microphone by her lips. Andy can't hear the reply.

"Box them in," she says, crouching beside a cinder block wall. "I want eyes on all sides. Don't fire unless fired upon."

"What's happening?" Andy asks, struggling to catch his breath.

"We've got a bunch of civilians holed up ahead. Five guys drinking on the front lawn. They're armed. AR-15s. Shotguns. Various sidearms."

"What? Why?" Andy asks. To him, that is the dumbest thing in

247

the world to do in the middle of an alien invasion.

"Dunno. I guess they figure they can defend their home against these things. Six Charlie is reporting several women and a bunch of children inside the house. The good news is there's no sign of contact this far north. Our 42nd platoon has advanced another mile south of us. They're reporting unusual structural damage. Collapsed roofs. Crushed trees. They're forming a defensive line, but are yet to engage."

"What are we going to do about these guys?" Andy asks, pointing at the burning cars.

"We need to get them out of here before shit goes down."

Captain Winters speaks into her radio mic. "Connors, you've got point. Identify yourself and start a dialogue. Everyone else: action-imminent."

One of the soldiers near the burning tires shoulders his rifle. He stands, raising his arms, holding his hands near his helmet. It's the classic *I'm-no-threat* position.

With a loud voice, he yells, "United States Army on approach! I'm Corporal James Connors, 75th Ranger Regiment. 3rd Battalion. Recon Company. Two Alpha Squad. I need to speak to whoever's in charge."

No one's in charge. Oh, there'll be some big swinging dick in there with an ego the size of the Statue of Liberty, but all he's in charge of is the beer. The others will bow to his brilliance. Andy knows these guys— not personally. He's met enough of them at gun shows to imagine the kind of pigheaded stupidity it takes to dig in like this.

Andy's close enough to hear Winters whisper into her radio, "Cover fire ready. Six Charlie, confirm targets and hold."

Those beyond the burning cars might be under the impression a single soldier is walking forward without a weapon raised, but Winters has crosshairs on everyone in there. The captain darts sideways, wanting to improve her line of sight. Andy stays close by her side.

"What do you want, soldier boy?" a gruff middle-aged man with a beer gut says, getting to his feet. He leaves his AR-15 leaning against his chair, but he's got a holstered pistol on his hip. His use of the term *boy* is demeaning.

Connors calls out in a loud voice, "Houston is under martial law. There's a general evacuation in place. I need you and your people to leave this area as we are expecting hostilities."

"Jeezus H. Crisp," the man says, slurring his words and swaying under the influence of alcohol. "The fucking feds are here!"

"US Army, sir," Connors says, lowering his hands slightly so they're in line with his shoulders. He's not surrendering. He's appealing for calm. "We're here for your protection."

"Mah protection?" the man says, turning sideways so he can face his buddies still drinking beer. "Can you believe this shit?"

Winters creeps closer, using an abandoned car to come up level with the smoldering tires. Connors hasn't walked beyond them. He's kept his distance.

He calls to those inside the makeshift compound. "I need you and your family to fall back beyond the toll road. From there, we'll evacuate you north."

"I ain't going nowhere," the man grumbles.

"We don't have time for this," Winters whispers, looking at Andy.

"Where's your commanding officer, son?" the man calls out.

Connors says, "If you'd like to remove your sidearm, I'll take you to her."

"Her?" he yells. "A fucking woman? You're taking orders from a girl?"

Connors replies without hesitation. "Captain Winters is an outstanding leader, sir."

"Shit! It's all fucking lies. They're giving the guns to the goddamn women. What the fuck next? We're gonna be singing *Kumbaya* with the aliens."

To Andy's surprise, Winters stands. She's seen something through the gaps in the barricade. Andy follows but doesn't look where she's going. Instead, he peers through the old tractor tires.

249

Two women stand on the wooden porch of a rundown house next to *Lou's Garage*. The backyard is full of rusting cars. Several have been stacked on top of each other, crushing the roofs. Most of the cars have been stripped of their wheels, engines, windows and seats. It's a junkyard. In front of the women, there are several kids—none of them over the age of five.

Winters flips the cover off her holster but she doesn't draw her Beretta. She steps out beside Connors. Andy joins her. The soldier with the SAW stays out of sight. He rests the barrel of his machine gun in a gap between two smoldering tires, aiming at the men seated on the lawn.

The Humvee rolls quietly down the road, reducing the distance between it and the burning vehicles while staying out of sight.

"Oh, is this her? Is this the pretty little thing giving all the orders? How're you doing, darling?"

Winters says, "The President has ordered the evacuation of Houston. I need you and your family to leave immediately. You're endangering not only yourselves but our operation."

"Your operation?" the man says, laughing. "Listen, doll face. I don't give a *fuck* about you and your precious boy scouts. I know mah rights. You got no right being here."

"Under the declaration of martial law, I have every right," Winters says, resting her hand on the Beretta mounted on her hip. "If you want to debate this in court, I'll gladly appear in Dallas, Austin or San Antonio, but Houston is closed for business. You need to leave."

Andy's aware he's broadcasting this confrontation live. He takes the time to pan with his head, sweeping over the scene, allowing everyone to see the layout.

There's a rundown liquor store directly across from the garage. A bunch of old cars have been pushed across the road, blocking access from both directions. Most of them don't have tires. There's a gap of about fifty yards between the rows of cars, with the home and the garage in the middle. A forklift has been abandoned next to a tow truck. Men sit in lawn chairs, watching the commotion as if it were a reality TV show. They've gathered around an old wooden table that's been dumped half on the grass, half on the sidewalk. Empty cans lie on the lawn. Liquor bottles sit on the table along with open bags of corn chips. The women standing back in the shade look terrified. One of them has a dark black ring around her left eye.

"Hey, hey," one of the men seated at the table calls out. "Look. It's Angry *fucking* Andy Anderson." He waves a smartphone around, adding, "I'm watching him right now. This is us! He's right there, recording all this!"

"No shit," one of the other men says, grabbing the man's arm and looking at the screen.

"Oh, it's delayed by a few seconds, but it's him all right."

"What happened to you, dude?" the other man yells. "You sold out. You used to be cool, but now you're with these chumps? There ain't no goddamn aliens out there. It's the government, yah know. They're taking our freedoms. They're violating our rights."

Andy's quiet. Now is not the time to debate a drunk.

"Ah, fuck you," the man at the table says, knocking back the last of his drink.

The middle-aged man with the beer gut grins, eyeing Winters. "You shouldn't have come here, sugar."

"We're following orders," Winters says. "You are delaying a military action. I'm not going to ask you again. Get your shit together and leave."

The man brags, smiling as he says, "Sweetie, I'm okay. I ain't going nowhere. I don't need your protection."

"What's your name?"

"George."

Winters is blunt. "You need to follow my directions, George."

"Oh, really," he says, pulling a Glock from his holster.

"Don't," Winters yells. She crouches slightly, holding her left hand out in front of her. The fingers on her right hand grip the Beretta in its holster, but it remains seated on her hip.

"Don't?" he asks, ignoring her and holding up his gun proudly. "You don't get to tell me what to do, missy."

"Put the gun down."

"Or what? Are you going to shoot me, babe?"

George might have sunk a few beers, but being an asshole is clearly a choice he embraces with glee. He waves his gun around loosely, pointing it up into the sky and then to one side.

He yells at her.

"I asked you a question, bitch! You gonna—"

George never finishes his sentence.

Andy is stunned by how quickly the next fraction of a second unfolds.

Winters is a blur. As soon as the Glock is pointed at her, she drops to one knee, drawing her Beretta in a single, swift action. With both arms out in front of her, steadying her aim, she fires.

The crack of thunder breaks beside Andy, causing him to flinch. A hundred and sixty-two decibels of unbridled chemical violence is unleashed in a fraction of a second. A tiny red dot appears on the man's brow. It's slightly off-center. His head lashes back. Blood, bone and brains spray out across the grass as his body crumples. The Glock falls from his dead fingers.

Andy blinks. He can't help it. Such a reflex is instinctive. When his eyes open, there are Rangers everywhere. They're inside the row of burning cars, on the low porch beside the house and out in front of the liquor store with their rifles raised. Several of them surround the men on the lawn, making sure no one is dumb enough to reach for another firearm.

Captain Winters walks over to the dead man and kicks the Glock well clear of his fingers. She looks up at the other men and says, "Does anyone else have any questions?"

There's a chorus of muttering. "No, no, no."

She holsters her sidearm. The Rangers secure the weapons and get the men to their feet. The soldiers march them toward the gap in the tires.

Winters walks over to the women on the porch. "I'm sorry. I hoped it wouldn't come to this."

They nod. They don't seem overly upset or surprised by what happened. Perhaps they're in shock. Andy's still trying to process what just occurred. It seemed as though a storm was brewing, but when the end came, it escalated in a heartbeat.

"His name is Art," the woman with the black eye says. "Arthur James Menzies. He goes by Art—not George. Never George."

Winters nods. Lies have a way of compounding. As it was, the whole drunk routine seemed to be laid on a bit thick. It was convenient. It was all a game to him. He needled her, wanting to see how far he could push a woman in command. Well, he fucked around and found out.

"Listen carefully to me," the captain says, taking the woman by the shoulder. "Your lives depend on getting north of that toll road. Do you understand me?"

The older woman nods. The two women grab their kids, resting them on their hips.

"Connors," the captain says, "Get these civilians in the Humvee and escort them to the toll road. From there, they'll have to continue on foot."

"Understood."

Connors leads them away.

The captain continues barking orders. "Mahatma, get that tow truck running. I want the road cleared so we can bring the Humvee through. Smith, make sure the house is empty. Check the garage as well. The rest of you—eyes outward. Watch for any threats on approach."

Winters steps down from the porch.

"Are you okay?" she asks Andy. "You look pale."

"I—ah. It's just."

"It's a lot to process," she says, briefly looking down at her boots.

"I mean. How? What did—w—why?"

"We are not here to play games," the captain says. "We're in combat. We don't have the time or luxury to play kindergarten cop with these people."

"No. No. Of course not," Andy says. "It's just. Don't you wonder?"

"Wonder what?" she asks, pointing at the corpse on the lawn. Blood and brains have oozed out on the grass. "Whether that asshole was going to squeeze the trigger? There was no way in hell that was going to happen—whether by accident or by design. This isn't a *fucking* Star Wars reboot. I was *not* going to let goddamn *Greedo* here fire first."

"I get it," Andy says. "Forget about aliens. Sometimes, we're our own worst enemy... It's just—"

"It's not fair," the captain says. "It's war. We don't play fair in war. We win. We survive. When George, or Art, or whoever the fuck he is pulled out that gun, he was living on borrowed time. When he pointed it at me, the clock struck twelve."

Andy hesitates. He feels there's more to be said. "But?"

"But nothing," Winters says, setting her hands on her hips.

"All this is on video," Andy says, pointing out the obvious. "It's being broadcast live."

"Good." Winters looks up at the camera mounted on his helmet, saying, "If you're in the Houston area, you need to evacuate now. If you run into US Rangers, they will help you evacuate. Do not—under any circumstances—seek to impede the mission of the US Rangers. Evacuate now! Don't wait. Get yourself north of the Sam Houston toll road."

She pats Andy on the shoulder, looking him in the eye as she says, "There! Is that better?"

Andy's hands are shaking. "Aren't you worried about being court-martialed?"

"Court marshaled?" Winters says, laughing. "You think we're getting out of here alive?"

254

She walks on past him, adding, "Oh, you're adorable."

CLEAR
LAKE

"Brace! Brace! Brace," the pilot yells as the Blackhawk plummets from the sky. The rotors vibrate as they spin. The fuselage shakes.

Grassy fields whip by beneath the helicopter, being visible through the open doors. Jimmy is strapped into a jump seat. He has his hands out, reaching for Kath, but she can't go to him. She wants to, but some primal sense of survival keeps her at bay. As impossible as it seems, she's trying to weigh her options. A concrete freeway passes a couple of hundred feet below them. Houses. Garages. A side street. Then there's more grass and finally a dark, murky lake. Alligators flee from the banks, taking to the water at the sound of the military helicopter racing overhead.

Kath says, "I'm sorry," but Jimmy can't hear her over the whine of the engines screaming around them. She backs away from him. A shudder comes through the airframe as the helicopter struggles to maintain its altitude.

Kath is a lousy judge of distance. In her mind, they're a few feet above the surface of the lake. She jumps, wanting to be clear of the Blackhawk when it hits. Unlike Jimmy, her body is not restrained. Even if she had all her fingers, there's no way she could hold on during a crash. The idea of being thrown into the mangled steel fuselage on impact is not appealing. Worse still is the prospect of being thrown clear only to be clipped by the rotors. Her only chance lies in bailing out.

The wind roars past, tossing her hair around.

Sunlight reflects off the lake.

Kath jumps.

She crosses her arms over her chest and bends her knees slightly, plunging feet first. For what seems like an eternity, she hangs in the air. She's falling. She knows she is from the way the air rushes up around her, but the lake never seems to get any closer. She's still got some sideways momentum from the chopper, so she plummets on an angle, heading out toward deeper water. Fractions of a second seem like hours. When she finally hits, the water feels like concrete. The shudder that resounds through her legs is like nothing she's ever felt before. It's as though she's been shot out of a cannon into a wall. Rather than sinking into the lake, her body cartwheels across the surface, colliding with the waves. Just when she thinks she's landed on a sandbank, she sinks into the depths.

Everything hurts—her arms, her legs, her hands, her feet, her hips, her head. Water swells around her. Bubbles hint at the surface somewhere above her in the darkness. She kicks, breaking through the gloom.

Waves lap at her face.

Air has never smelt so fresh or alive.

Salt spray cascades through the air, falling back to the water. Waves race across the surface. The tail boom of the Blackhawk protrudes from the lake along with a single, sagging rotor. Kath swings her arms over her head, shifting her body into a freestyle swimming position only to feel her shoulder muscle tear. Pain surges down her arm.

"Ah, fuck," she splutters, spitting water from her mouth.

She turns, lying on her back, and kicks with her feet. Kath pulls against the weeds and pushes through the water. Blood trails behind her, coming from a cut on the side of her head. Are alligators like sharks? Can they smell blood in the water?

Kath hasn't given any thought to how far she is from shore. For now, it's all she can do to make for the downed helicopter. She's got to get to Jimmy. She owes him that much at least.

An eerie calm descends on the lake. The only noise Kath can hear is the splashing of her own flailing limbs.

Kath turns, craning her neck and looking for survivors. She thrashes the water, driving her legs hard, desperate to reach the helicopter. There's a lot of splashing but not much forward momentum. She pauses, peering around, hoping to see someone made it from the wreckage. There's no one else. An oil slick spreads on the surface. She pushes on. Her lungs are burning under the exertion. Kath gets close to the submerged Blackhawk and pulls herself alongside the tail boom.

She takes a deep breath and dives into the murky gloom. With her left arm trailing behind her, she feels her way with her right hand. She gets hold of the open edge of the cargo cabin with her thumb and her forefinger. The Blackhawk is sitting in fifteen to twenty feet of water. Kath can't see her hands at the end of her blurry arms let alone Jimmy or the aircrew.

Bubbles slip from her lips. Knives stab at her shoulder. There's no one or nothing there beside her, but in the darkness, using that torn muscle is excruciating. It feels as though some invisible monster has sunk its teeth into her shoulder. Regardless, she pulls herself on, working hand over hand along the airframe. Although her injured arm feels as though it's on fire, she needs both hands. The stubs at the end of her stunted fingers grab at the cold metal.

In the darkness, Kath touches the steel frame of a seat and then a shoe—a small running shoe. She works her hands up over a tiny leg, feeling for the five-point harness. In the murky water, she can't see anything beyond a muddy haze. Feel is her only sense. Her mangled hand rolls over the harness, understanding how the clips link together, searching for a release. There! She squeezes. The straps pop open.

Carbon dioxide builds in her bloodstream. Her chest tightens. Her lungs scream for air. Kath has to surface. She has no choice, but she can't. She has to check the cockpit. Her limp left arm holds onto the scruff of Jimmy's shirt. He bobs around lifeless behind her.

Kath knows the reflex to breathe is a lie. The overwhelming desire she feels to suck in anything, even if it's water is an illusion. She's okay. Her body violently disagrees and her throat constricts, but Kath understands the mammalian dive reflex. She's never needed it before, but her ex-boyfriend was a free diver. He was always talking about how he'd push through the urge to breathe. He even had her try it one Sunday afternoon in an Olympic-size swimming pool. Kath lasted all of a minute. He stayed on the bottom for six. Above all, she has to relax. She's got to fight the impulse to panic. Once she's on the other side of the urge, she knows her spleen will release its store of oxygen-rich blood and it'll be as though she's taken another breath.

Every cell in her body screams for oxygen, but Kath knows she can't surface. If she does, she won't come back down. Even if she were to try, her body would betray her much sooner the second time. She's got to be strong and push through the barrier in her mind. In theory, it's easy. In practice, it's torture.

Her thumb and finger touch the helmet of the copilot. It's shattered. Hair brushes against her wrist. Fragments of bone and mush slide over her skin. He's dead. He must have hit the control panel or the window frame on impact.

Kath swivels, reaching for the pilot. He's out of his seat and facing backward. The stubs of her fingers run over his arms. He's floating upside down against the cockpit ceiling, but he's not caught. He must have had enough time to free himself, but not enough to clear the Blackhawk as water flooded in.

Kath grabs his vest, anchoring her hand in the middle of his chest by pushing her wrist beneath one of the straps. She swings upside down, pushing her feet against the roof of the submerged chopper. To get him out, she has to pull him down. Spasms strike at her leg muscles, but she can't give up. Kath drags both him and Jimmy through the cargo hold and out into the lake.

Her lungs are desperate for air. Sparkles of light glisten before her eyes. She's losing consciousness. She's on the verge of blacking out.

Something brushes against her. Thick scales run across the back of her head, sweeping her hair along behind them. Muscles flex. Claws push off her shoulder. A long tail scrapes against her, whipping past as it plows through the murky water.

Above her, there's a dull light. Somewhere up there is the surface. She kicks, dragging Jimmy and the pilot with her. They're heavy. They weigh her down. She drives with her legs, fighting to break through to the surface of the lake. Every muscle fiber in her body screams in agony, begging for oxygen.

A tail whips past again, brushing against her bare arms. Twenty feet of water feels like two hundred. Long thin strands of light pierce the gloom. Sunlight teases her.

She reaches the surface, gasping for air. Oil sticks to her hair. Thick goo hangs from her lips, but she can breathe. Spasms ripple through her body, but she keeps her grip on Jimmy and the pilot. Hauling them toward the surface causes her to slip back beneath the waves. She's less than ten feet from the tail boom of the Blackhawk. If she can make it there, she can pull herself up.

Who is she kidding? With her hands? No way.

They're dead.

Both of them.

Even if she could reach the tail boom, there's not enough room to drag them out of the water, let alone to administer CPR.

Black eyes peer at her from beside the rotor blade as it emerges from the water. Scales are visible, breaking the surface. An alligator stares her down. Kath feels her heart race.

A shadow passes over the sun behind her. Before she knows what's happening, she's being hauled backward into a boat. Some enormously powerful man has leaned over the sidewall of an inflatable boat. He's reached into the water and grabbed her under her armpits. Somehow, he drags her into the boat. She's still got hold of Jimmy and the pilot.

"The soldier," the stranger says to someone nearby. "Grab him."

Kath coughs. She splutters, spitting oily water from her mouth.

A girl of not more than ten leans over the sidewall of the boat. With both hands, she grabs the pilot. She doesn't make much headway, but she prevents him from slipping back into the depths.

The alligator circles. It stays well clear of the splash of water as Kath and Jimmy are pulled from the lake. Kath finds herself lying on her back looking up at the clear blue sky, wondering what just happened. Jimmy's body lies limp by her legs. An elderly man steps over her. He grabs the pilot and hauls him into the boat.

"Get us out of here," he says to the young girl. To Kath's surprise, the girl grabs the handle of the outboard engine. How does she know what she's doing?

The old man drags the pilot up, dumping him half on the center console. His back hits with a thud. Water drips from his lips.

"The boy," the old man says, pointing. He begins stripping the pilot, exposing his chest. Once he's got bare skin and can see how much he's compressing, he begins CPR.

"Yes, yes," Kath says, realizing there will be plenty of time for questions later. She lays Jimmy on his side and uses her one, good finger to clear weeds from his mouth. Water drains out onto the steel deck. She checks for a pulse and rolls him on his back. Kath blows into his lungs, inflating them. Then she begins CPR. Within a few thrusts, Jimmy moans, clutching at his chest.

"Hey, there buddy," she says, kneeling beside him and smiling. Water drips from her hair. "It's okay. You're okay. I've got you."

Jimmy throws his arms around her neck. He buries his head into her shoulder. Kath lifts him up and sits with him on the inflated side of the boat.

The longboat passes under a road bridge and out into the bay. The girl at the helm offers Kath a slight wave and a smile, but she keeps her focus on the boat. Now they're clear of the lake, she backs off the throttle.

The old man works on the pilot.

"Come on. Come on," he mutters, driving hard against the pilot's chest and occasionally offering two quick breaths. Slowly, color comes back to the pilot's face. He blinks.

The old man sits back, exhausted. He rests one hand on the pilot's shoulder and the other on the side of the boat.

"Easy, my friend," he says in a distinctly Mexican accent. "You are safe now."

The pilot clutches his chest. His ribs are bruised, but not from the crash. The old man was making damn sure blood was pumping around his body and now it rushes to where his ribs are throbbing. The old man may not have been as clinical as a doctor, but the pilot's alive.

The pilot slumps into the footwell of the boat beside the old man's legs. He taps them with feeble arms. "Thank you."

"It is okay. We are here to help."

"How did you?" Kath asks, barely able to speak those words.

"We saw your helicopter," the old man says. "We saw you fighting one of those things in the air. The ghosts."

"You've seen them?"

"We too have fought with them," he says.

"Who are you?" the pilot asks, pulling off his helmet and dumping it on the aluminum hull.

"I am Jorge Rodrigo and this is my daughter, Veronica."

Kath looks at them. There's got to be sixty or seventy years between them, but—whatever.

"She is my ward," he says, clarifying the confusion on her worried brow. "She is an orphan."

"But not anymore," Veronica says with the wind in her hair.

"Now, she is my daughter and I am very proud of her. We have been ferrying survivors to the far shore. It is safe over there."

"You," Kath says, pointing at him. "You're the fisherman from Vera Cruz. You spoke at the conference."

"Yes, I am," Jorge says, bursting with pride.

Veronica says, "We saw *Anduru*—the demon in the sky. It flew over us."

Kath shakes her head in disbelief. "I sat and listened to your tale. Extraordinary."

For her, the passage of *Anduru* over the Gulf of Mexico two years ago was little more than a smudge on a computer screen. Tens of thousands of people died that night. Jorge and Veronica are the first people she's met who actually witnessed the event firsthand. She has dozens of questions for them, but there are more pressing matters.

"Where are you taking us?" the helicopter pilot asks.

"*The Santiago Apostol,*" Jorge says. "It is safe. We are at anchor on the other side of the bay. In the lee of Smith Point."

Veronica opens up the throttle on the boat and the bow lifts out of the water. Salt spray fills the air, but for Kath, it's joyous. They're alive. They're mobile. More importantly, they're safe. Even Jimmy seems to relax. Her shoulder aches, but even that is welcome. She made it.

The water within the bay is calm. Seagulls fly overhead.

"Do you have a radio?" Kath asks.

"There's a radio here," Jorge says, pointing at a control panel beside Veronica. "But it is short-range. I have a maritime radio on *The Santiago Apostol.*"

"Good. Good," Kath says, shouting over the roar of the engine and the wind howling past.

As tempting as it is to move over next to the pilot and talk strategy, she's aware the boat needs to be balanced so she stays opposite him. For the next twenty minutes, she's content just to have survived.

THAT
ΛSSHOLE

There's something about the way the longboat skims across the water that sets Kath's heart at ease. Perhaps it's the gentle rap of waves tapping against the aluminum hull. It could be the soft, almost trampoline-like feeling of the inflated sides of the boat cushioning the ride, or the wind whipping past, catching her hair, or the warmth of the sun on her back. The drone of the outboard motor is soothing, forming a kind of white noise.

Then it strikes her.

For the first time in months, Kath hasn't had to be anywhere or do anything. All expectation is gone. She's a passenger. She can look up at the seagulls riding on the wind and not feel as though there's a clock ticking and she needs to get back to work.

Salt spray kicks up from the hull, landing on her cheeks, but she doesn't care. It feels invigorating rather than annoying. Damn, it's only now she realizes she's been so busy doing *stuff* that life itself has passed her by. Maybe it's surviving a near-death experience that's unlocked this feeling. Adrenaline can only sustain someone for so long. And yet, the sensation she has isn't one of feeling deflated. It's not as though she's coming down from a high. Far from it, she's relaxed.

She's safe.

Veronica brings the longboat in a sweeping arc toward the rear of an old trawler. Waves ripple outward, washing over rocks on the nearby shore. Jorge ties the boat to the stern and helps them climb up onto the trawler.

Once they're on board, he hands around some towels, saying, "We have fish, freshwater, coffee, tea."

"A bathroom?" Kath asks, rubbing her hair dry. She drapes the towel over her shoulders, wrapping it around her like a shawl.

"Inside the cabin. On the right."

Kath excuses herself, leaving them to talk. As she closes the door, she spies Veronica talking to Jimmy. The young girl is excited. She holds his hands. He seems relieved and, for the first time, happy.

Once Kath's finished and has washed her hands, she rejoins the others on deck. Jorge is buttering slices of bread. Jimmy slathers peanut butter and jelly on each piece as it's handed to him. Veronica is at the end of the line, assembling the sandwiches. Kath's on the verge of blurting out the need for proper hygiene and isolation to stop spreading a potentially fatal extraterrestrial microbe, but she stops herself. They're human. All of them—including her. There's something primal about sharing food, something soothing. Half an hour ago, they were fighting an alien creature hanging from the airframe of a Blackhawk. Then they almost drowned in that goddamn lake. Alligators were circling, looking for an easy meal. But they're not dead. They're alive. And that's cause for celebration. For once, the scientist within her turns a blind eye.

"We thought you might be hungry," the pilot says, handing Kath a sandwich. His right arm is in a sling. Kath's not sure if he's broken it or sprained his shoulder, but he moves gingerly. Her shoulder is stiff and sore but feels better than it did twenty feet beneath the waves.

"Thank you," she says, biting into the soft white bread.

"America has the *best* bread," Jorge says with all the enthusiasm life has to offer. "So soft."

He could have been pulling corpses from that lake barely twenty minutes ago, but all of that is gone now. He's excited, effervescing with life.

"Good, huh?"

"It's pretty good," Kath says, talking with her mouth full. "Listen, I need to—"

"Yes. Yes. The radio," Jorge says, leading her into the wheelhouse. He picks up an old handset, turns a few knobs and speaks into the microphone. "US Coast Guard. US Coast Guard, this is *The Santiago Apostol* out of Vera Cruz, Mexico, currently at anchor in Galveston Bay. Do you read me? Over."

There's silence for a few seconds. Kath feels deflated. To her, it seems as though they're all that's left of humanity. Jorge, though, is upbeat. He smiles.

"Ah," he says, hearing something cryptic in the radio static. He points at the old speaker as the reply comes through.

"*Santiago Apostol,* this is the US Coast Guard. This channel is restricted to emergency use only at the current time. Please stay off the channel unless you are declaring an emergency."

Jorge hands her the microphone, saying, "Don't forget to let go of the button or you won't hear their reply."

"Got it," Kath says, smiling. She doesn't mind a refresher. The old man rests his hand briefly on her shoulder. The strength in his arm is quietly reassuring. His fingers are calloused and weathered, and yet they're tender. He pats her shoulder softly and leaves her sitting by the radio.

"US Coast Guard. This is Dr. Kathleen Mackenzie onboard *The Santiago Apostol.* I need to speak to Brigadier General Nolan Landis."

She lets go of the transmit button and waits for the reply.

"*Santiago Apostol.* You are transmitting on an open channel—on the emergency maritime civilian radio band. We don't operate a switchboard. Over."

Kath's not angry. She's not impatient. She's focused.

"US Coast Guard. Listen carefully to the names. I'm Dr. Kathleen Mackenzie of NASA's JPL Astrophysics Laboratory. I need to speak to

Brigadier General Nolan Landis of NORAD. I know this isn't a phone. I know it's an insecure channel. None of that matters. You need to make this happen or a helluva lot of people are going to die. Over."

A different voice replies.

"*Santiago Apostol*. This is the US Coast Guard. Please remain on the channel. This may take some time. Over."

"Copy that," Kath says.

Jorge slides the door open. He's holding a cup of coffee.

"Sugar?" he asks.

Kath's tempted to ask for some, but the prospect of a caffeine hit alone is overwhelming. She reaches out, taking the mug from him. Cream swirls on the surface.

"Oh, this is perfect. Thank you."

She sips at the coffee, warming her aching palms against the cup. The pilot pokes his head in the door.

"Did you get hold of anyone?"

"Yes. The Coast Guard is trying to reach Nolan."

"He'll be pleased to hear we're alive."

"He'll be surprised," she says.

"Maybe," the pilot says, turning his head slightly as he adds, "Maybe not."

Kath smiles. Several minutes pass, but Kath is content. She's warm, she's dry, she's had something to eat and she's got a strong cup of coffee in her hands. What more could she want?

The radio crackles.

"Priority call. Priority call. All other stations please stay off the channel. This is Forward Base Greenbriar calling *The Santiago Apostol*. Come in. Over."

Kath puts down her coffee. The days of holding two things at once are gone for her. She enjoyed warming her hands, but now it's time to focus. She picks up the radio transmitter and speaks clearly.

"Greenbriar. This is Dr. Kathleen Mackenzie on the *Santiago*

Apostol. Go ahead."

"*Santiago Apostol.* Greenbriar. I have Brigadier General Nolan Landis. Patching you through. Please hold."

Kath's hands tremble with excitement. She fights back tears. Out of eight billion people on the planet, there are only a handful she trusts. Top of that list is Nolan. Finally, they can talk.

A familiar voice says, "Kath?"

There are no formalities or fancy titles. There's no caveat about being on a public channel. Who gives a fuck anyway? The more open their conversation the better.

"Nolan," she says, holding the handset beside her lips. "It's so good to hear your voice."

"It's damn good to hear yours again. And you're safe? They tell me you're safe. They said you made it out of the city, that you're on a boat?"

"It's one helluva story," Kath says, "but I'm fine."

"Good. Good."

"Where is he?" Kath asks. "Please tell me that asshole made it out of there alive."

"Monroe?" Nolan asks. Even with the rough crackle of the radio, Kath can hear the subtleties in his voice. Nolan was on the verge of laughing in reply. "He's standing here beside me. He can hear you."

"Good," Kath says. "And the President?"

"In the Situation Room," Nolan says. "Listening to us. We're on a conference line. They can hear you over the speaker."

"Don't let that asshole drop a nuke," she says, being deliberately vague as to which asshole she's referring to.

"Kath, the creatures are spreading north to northwest. We're fighting along a front extending at least eighteen miles. I've got heavy armor on the move, but we're losing light. I'm worried about the ground we'll lose overnight."

"You can't bomb them," Kath says. "No nukes. No cluster bombs.

269

No high explosives. Nothing like that. You have to burn them!"

"You're going to need to explain," Nolan says.

"You think you're fighting these creatures. You're not. They're a distraction, nothing more."

"They're killing people, Kath."

"I know. I know. Lord, do I know. But the real battle is happening at a microbial level. I've seen fungal-like growths on dead animals and on people within the hotel. I've seen accelerated plant growth throughout the city. Drop a nuke and you'll kill these creatures, but it'll be like throwing gasoline on a fire. You'll spread this crap everywhere.

"Nukes push a wall of air out in front of them before sucking it back into a mushroom cloud. The fallout would spread across several states. It's not the radiation you need to worry about. If this stuff gets beyond Houston, we'll never contain it."

Kath releases the transmit button and waits for a reply, but it's not just Nolan she's talking to. Beyond him lies the authority of the President, his advisors and his senior military leadership. Convincing Nolan isn't enough. She has to reach them without being able to talk to them directly. It's frustrating. She wishes she could hear their reasoning, their arguments, their counterpoints and concerns and priorities.

After almost a minute, Nolan says, "Kath. We're trying to stop an invasion here. The consensus among the Joint Chiefs is to throw everything we've got at these things—and that means bombs—a lot of bombs."

"You've got this all wrong," she says into her microphone. "This isn't an invasion, it's an infection. As scary as those aliens are, it's what's happening at the microscopic level that scares me—and I've been toe to toe with several of these creatures.

"You've got to ring-fence the city. Start out wide and work in, burning everything! You've got to raze Houston to the ground. Nothing gets out. No one and nothing."

She releases the transmit button, wiping her eyes with the back of her hand.

"Kath."

"You've got to isolate those that have come in contact with this stuff. You can't let them move around the country."

"We're talking about *millions* of displaced people," Nolan says.

"I know, but we've got to keep this contained. I'm worried about how this stuff is interacting with our ecosystem. You can't focus solely on those creatures. That would be a mistake. You'll win the battle but not the war."

"We're juggling a lot of things here," Nolan says. "We've got to get the balance right."

Kath ignores him. "Use napalm, incendiary bombs. Hell, drop jet fuel if you want, but you've got to burn every square inch of this city."

"Jesus, Kath."

"I'm sorry. It's the only way. This war isn't about bullets and bombs. It's being waged on an entirely different scale. When it comes to the harbor, you need to flood it with oil. Set up containment floats offshore. Flood the bay with petroleum. Oil floats. It'll form a barrier. It'll sit on top of the water and insulate marine life. Then... set it alight. You've got to burn everything. I—I only hope we're not too late."

There's silence on the radio. Kath has no doubt it's not for lack of questions or controversy. She hopes her comments spur a rethink. The command group needs to change its strategy.

A crazy, random thought hits her head as she waits. Kath squeezes the transmit button and blurts out, "Paintball."

"Say again your last," Nolan replies.

"Arm your troops with paintball guns. They're small. Lightweight. And they can carry hundreds of rounds. Thousands if you stuff your pockets with pellets."

"I don't understand."

"You can't hit what you can't see," Kath says, trying to rein in her mind as it races along at a million miles an hour. "But if you clip one of those creatures with a paintball, all of a sudden you have a target."

Nolan transmits. "Got it. Jacinta?" In the background, Kath hears another friendly voice call out, "On it."

"Can you put Monroe on?" Kath asks.

"That asshole?" Nolan replies, ribbing her. "Sure."

Kath waits for what feels like forever.

"Monroe here."

"What did you bring back?"

"Almost nothing," he says. "Grams. Not kilograms. I—I don't understand. I don't know how they got out or how they got so big."

"But you knew about them?" Kath asks. "These creatures?"

With each click of the microphone, her rage grows.

"No. They told me there was cellular division, but nothing like this. The sample was kept in a level 4 biosafe laboratory. Nothing could get out."

"But something did," Kath says. "And it's not just these things. I'm seeing vegetation spreading over buildings. That doesn't happen overnight—not on Earth."

"We've seen that too," Monroe says, speaking slowly. "Variations in foliage."

"You've got to get the President to see the bigger picture," she says. "This isn't some dumb Hollywood script playing out before us. This isn't confined to just a few nasty aliens running around the city scaring people."

"I know, I know," Monroe says. "We're using satellites, overhead flights and drones to track these creatures. We're picking up massive growth in vegetation across the city. Trees. Lawns. Parks. They're overgrown. It's like they've turned into a jungle."

"You need to burn it," Kath replies. "All of it."

"I know. But I don't understand—how is this happening?"

"They have aggressive metabolisms," she says. "The creatures in the hotel were second or third generation. They're going to overrun us with their sheer numbers. That's their strategy. That's how they win. Buildings are convenient, empty shells. They give them cover. They allow them to hide while they gestate. You've got to burn this place to the ground, starting with *The Fossil*."

Monroe asks, "How are we ending up with so much growth? Is it hijacking terrestrial cells?"

Kath doesn't respond. She doesn't know and doesn't want to guess.

Sitting there in the wheelhouse of the aging trawler, rocking with the waves, she's a world away from everyone. Blue skies open out above her. Seagulls squawk as they fight each other for scraps. White clouds drift across the sky. Long shadows stretch across the water. Life out on the bay is serene. It's difficult to believe what's unfolding just a few miles from here.

Kath sits there with the microphone in her lap for a few seconds, thinking deeply. Even though it seems obvious, she knows they need to learn more before settling on a hypothesis. She's aware there's a danger of cascading assumptions leading to bad decisions and she does not want to encourage that. Besides, she's more curious about the original source of the contamination.

"What did you learn about the samples at a cellular level? What does the data reveal?"

Monroe stutters. "I—I don't know."

Kath can't believe what she's hearing. Monroe doesn't know? How is that possible? He's the only one in a position to know. Anger boils within her. Even though she's only got one finger and a thumb on her right hand, along with a bunch of stubs extending from her palm, Kath is on the verge of crushing the old plastic microphone. She calms herself, breathing deeply before she keys the microphone to speak again.

"What do you mean, you don't know? You must have someone poring over the data even as we speak."

"No. It's all in the MSR lab."

"But the Mars Sample Return lab has backups, right? They store their data offsite, right? You've got data in the cloud, right?"

"No. Not for this," Monroe says. "It was deemed classified—a national security risk. Backups were taken, but they were stored on site. We kept the lab isolated from the net. Nothing was sent online. I—"

"You moron!" Kath yells into the microphone, talking over the top of him. She's not sure how the radio broadcast works. She knows she cut him off but did he hear her outburst or did he just keep talking?

"We were worried about leaks. We couldn't take the risk of data dissemination."

Kath grits her teeth. She closes her eyes for a moment and speaks with slow deliberation. "Sharing—data—is—good—science."

Jorge, Veronica, Jimmy and the pilot have all gathered around the open door to the wheelhouse. Kath's not sure how long they've been listening. When Monroe doesn't speak, she continues, venting her frustration.

"You risked bringing those things to Earth, but you couldn't risk anyone knowing about them? Even though that knowledge could help us defeat them?"

Kath releases the microphone button. It's not really a question. It's a statement outlining what she sees as utter stupidity.

She hopes her short, sharp transmissions convey the gravity of the problem. "You've left our entire biosphere vulnerable to compromise."

"Can you quantify the risk?" Nolan asks over the radio. It's telling that Monroe is silent. "I need to make a threat assessment."

Nolan is pragmatic, but he's thinking like a general, not a scientist. He wants details she can't provide.

"It's not that simple," she says. "There are too many unknowns."

"Work with me, Kath," Nolan says, which is a not-so-subtle rebuke of her attitude toward Monroe. As much as that riles her, he's right. This isn't about point-scoring. She's no longer in a debate. If they can't work together, everyone loses.

Nolan seems to sense her hesitation over the radio waves. "I need to understand. You're telling me not to use three-quarters of my arsenal, I have to understand why. It's not that I doubt you, it's that this slows down our response—and that could be disastrous."

Kath slows herself down. She breathes deeply, steeling herself before squeezing the button, saying, "We're witnessing a clash between biospheres. Historically, on Earth, this has only ever been one-sided. When Europeans landed in the Americas, they unwittingly brought with them diseases that wiped out tens of millions of people. The West wasn't won by cowboys and cavalry, it was smallpox that cleared the land."

"And that's what's happening here?" Nolan asks.

"That's what *could* happen here," Kath says, qualifying her comments. "That's the danger. We're far more fragile than we think. We all have DNA, right?"

"Right?" Nolan says, although his reply is clipped and the word barely makes it through. He held down his transmit button for barely a fraction of a second. Kath can almost hear it rebound away from his fingers. As for her, she's trying to distill a cohesive, plausible argument from the scattered fragments of information she has available to her. She's taking potshots in an attempt to avoid an ecological disaster if the alien biome spreads on Earth. It might sound as though she's talking to Nolan, but she's addressing everyone else that's listening in. She needs the President and his advisors to grasp the weight of the situation.

"DNA is flimsy. It's easily corrupted by chemicals absorbed through the skin or by things as simple as too much sunlight—and both of those lead to the kind of cellular malfunctions we call cancer. DNA is not as robust as we would like to think.

"DNA determines how your body functions. It allows the cells in your body to differentiate into eyes and arms, hands and feet, the heart, lungs and brain. Put that all together, and that's you, right?"

"Right."

"Not quite. Only about 2% of your DNA codes for genes."

"I'm not sure I follow," Nolan says.

Kath is blunt. "Most of your DNA—98% of your DNA—has nothing to do with the genes that make you human. Oh, and you have four times as much viral DNA as gene-coding DNA. Four times!

"Our cells are like a sieve. They interact with our environment in ways we barely understand. Not only are you the descendent of everyone that came before you—your DNA holds code snippets of the various retroviruses they suffered and survived. Humans are a walking library of their ancestors' medical history. The portion that makes us who we actually are is stupidly small."

The reply that comes over the radio waves is one word spoken in a heartbeat. Kath's not even sure who said it. She thinks it was Nolan but it could have been Monroe.

"And?"

"And we're exposing our DNA to an unknown extraterrestrial pathogen. The results might not even be apparent to us. We could corrupt our genetic line with irreversible damage—damage that hinders our physical or intellectual capabilities for generations to come. We have no idea what the impact will be, but we can already see there's at least some interaction with the fungal-like growth coming from corpses. We need to understand what's happening at a cellular level."

All eyes on board *The Santiago Apostol* are on her. Kath composes herself. As much as she doesn't want to go back into Houston, she knows what needs to be done.

"Nolan. I need to get into that lab."

The response is nigh on instantaneous.

"I'll have a SEAL team to you by dawn."

"And a laptop with a satellite uplink and a damn good battery. Oh, and a sample collection kit."

"Understood," Nolan says, and with that, the radio conversation comes to an end.

Jimmy has tears in his eyes. Veronica has her arm around his shoulder, comforting him. The Blackhawk pilot is looking down at his boots. Jorge has a furrowed brow. The prospect of heading back into

Houston has everyone on edge.

"Hey," Kath says. "It's okay."

She holds her arms out. Jimmy rushes over and hugs her. He still hasn't said anything to Kath, but she's seen him talking with Veronica. Perhaps he feels more comfortable talking to someone around the same age.

Kath wipes his tears away, saying, "It's going to be okay. You'll be safe here with Jorge. I need to do this. We need answers. Do you understand?"

Jimmy nods.

All she's offered him is half-truths, but that's all she's got. That's all she's ever had.

THE SUBURBS

"We're pushing south toward the bayou," Andy says, speaking for an audience reaching into the hundreds of millions according to the counter on his smartwatch. He can't actually see the leading digit as it's scrolled off the screen. He's never had this kind of reach. A handful of pixels make him think that number's a two.

"We've cleared the industrial area and have moved into the affluent suburb of Fall Creek. The streets here are a maze. No grid layout. Nothing runs north to south. Every street is a detour. The Rangers are sweeping the homes on either side."

Andy's standing on the sideboard of the Humvee with Captain Winters in front of him. The vehicle rolls slowly down the road. The soldier on the machine gun is nervous. He swivels, checking all approaches.

"The gunfire you can hear is from the squads in Oak Knoll to our southwest. They've had sustained contact for the past hour. The army has sent a Bradley Fighting Vehicle in support of the action there."

Rangers jog quietly across the grass on either side of the Humvee. They crouch slightly as they run with their rifles pointing in front of them. Such a sight is incongruous with the carefully manicured lawns, well-kept gardens and lavish homes in suburban Houston. Soldiers help each other to clear the various brick walls separating properties. Fire hydrants and topiary form a stark contrast to camouflage clothing and combat boots.

"We're stretched too thin. I understand what Command is doing in Oak Knoll, but I don't like it. The army's determined to hit hard where it can, but it leaves the rest of us horribly exposed. We've got one fully-automatic fifty-caliber machine gun, but it's mounted on a Humvee that's sorely lacking in armor."

Captain Winters ignores his commentary. She points, directing the driver inside the vehicle to pull up at the next intersection. Four roads join at the corner of a park. A thin smattering of trees leads down to a lake. There's a pier. Ducks swim on the dark water. Long shadows stretch from the forest across the open grass.

"We're losing light," Andy says in commentary. "No one thought to bring night-vision goggles—not that they'd necessarily work against these things. We just don't know what will work against these creatures... I didn't see any goggles at the staging point so there was probably nothing to bring."

An explosion rocks the ground. A fireball rises over the houses and trees to the east. Like the contrast between lightning and thunder, the sound of the blast is delayed by a few seconds. It rumbles overhead, scaring the birds.

Winters turns back toward him saying, "Third Battalion has deployed to Eagle's Creek. They've got multiple contacts and have had to call in artillery fire."

The glowing fireball is replaced with black smoke drifting in the breeze.

"That's good, right?" Andy says. "If we run into one of these aliens, we can call in a strike as well."

"Dunno," Winters says. "It's a bit like shooting a fly with a Glock. If it remains still long enough it'll work, but it's overkill. Chances are, the damn thing won't be there when the shell lands. If anything, explosions like that will make them more wary of us—more cunning."

Andy's nervous.

"They're close," Winters says. "I can smell them."

She turns back to the driver, talking with those inside the Humvee.

Andy whispers. "The worst part of our advance is the suspense. Everyone's on edge. We've had reports of at least one creature making it to the airport. No one here is going to let that—"

The Humvee comes to an abrupt halt. Andy doesn't have a good grip. He lurches forward and grabs at the roof of the vehicle to steady himself. Winters points. The house on the opposite corner has a damaged roof. Dozens of tiles have come loose, exposing the wooden framework beneath. If anything, it looks like storm damage but there are no nearby trees. Something heavy hit that roof. The way the tiles have shifted, it appears as though something has slid down onto the lawn.

Winters says, "Defensive positions in support of the Humvee."

The Rangers fall back from their line, forming a circle thirty feet out from the vehicle, facing in all directions. Winters is on the radio, seeking confirmation on the size and shape of the aliens. Andy provides more commentary.

"We've heard conflicting reports about the advance. Some troops describe a reptile-like creature several times the size of an alligator. Others say they never saw anything until they were attacked. Back at the hotel, I saw one of these things and it was like looking at a mirage on a hot day."

"Goddamn paintball?" Winters says, talking to the driver. "Are you *fucking* kidding me? That's what they recommend? That's the best *fucking* advice they can give us? What is this? A game? Jesus! We're so screwed."

"What?" Andy asks, wanting some clarification for his viewers.

"Not now," Winters says with a raised hand. She's got her back to him, looking out across the intersection between them and the house. A concrete block wall falls, collapsing into the street. Dust billows but nothing comes through the gap in the fence. Bricks tumble onto the concrete. The gunner lines himself up, pointing the fifty-caliber at the hole. A tree inside the yard sways. Leaves and branches rock as if in response to a storm bearing down on them, but there's little to no wind.

Winters points, signaling for a couple of her troops to advance on the fallen wall. They creep forward, using low-lying shrubs and bushes for cover. All eyes are on them. Andy uses the zoom on his smartwatch to cut in tight with his camera, framing the troops as they step over the shattered bricks. Thin black barrels point the way.

Gunfire breaks out.

Ducks lift off the lake, rising high into the air. The way the crack echos between buildings makes it impossible to determine the direction, but it's not the soldiers by the wall that are firing. There's screaming. Andy's confused. He widens the angle, taking in four soldiers instead of two. They've turned around. They're firing back past the Humvee. They're aiming at something on the other side of the vehicle.

The gunner swings around and opens up with the fifty-caliber machine gun. The Humvee shakes with each outgoing round. Empty shells rain down around Andy, bouncing off his helmet and shoulders. The engine roars. The Humvee turns, mounting the curb.

Captain Winters drops to the sidewalk, yelling commands in the heat of battle. She slips a grenade into the M203 slung beneath her combat rifle. Andy reaches for the clip securing him to the Humvee, wanting to follow her. Before his gloved fingers can flick the catch open, he feels a tremor rumble through the chassis.

The rifle fire is chaotic. Bullets rip through the air. Even with ear protection, the noise is overwhelming.

Before he realizes what's happening, the Humvee is lifted off the ground. The wheels on the far side of the vehicle leave the concrete. Metal groans. The gunner has stopped firing. Blood drips from the roof. A hand hangs over the edge.

Andy unclips his harness. His instinct is to jump clear of the vehicle, but all four wheels are now off the ground. The thin strip of grass between the road and the sidewalk drifts beneath him. Rather than jump, he drops, falling flat to the grass. In that instant, the Humvee is thrown to one side. The vehicle spins, tumbling over him. The front tire clips the side of his helmet as he falls. The Humvee crashes into a grassy slope. It rolls, crushing a nature strip and comes to rest against a sapling.

To Andy's amazement, the other side of the road is empty. The soldiers are firing on a patch of grass leading down toward the lake. Bullets ricochet off the concrete. Bark splinters off trees.

Winters stands where the Humvee was moments ago. She levels her rifle and fires the grenade launcher. Andy's expecting the round to sail through the air for hundreds of yards. They're opposite the park. There are trees in the distance along with a picnic area and playground, including swings and a child's slide. An open field stretches around the lake. A gravel path winds over the grassy mounds and hillocks. It must be used as a walking/running track.

The grenade travels no more than fifty feet. It explodes in a flash of light, hitting something in midair. The concussion wave rattles his bones. As the smoke clears, Andy sees a creature lying on the grass. It's writhing in agony. Winters and the other Rangers close in from three sides, firing short bursts at its head. They march rather than run, moving and firing methodically.

Andy gets to his feet. His camera points wherever he looks, which is at the black marks on the concrete, the shell casings by the curb, and the upturned grass turf. He jogs over, adjusting the noise-canceling headphones he's wearing. If it wasn't for them, he'd be deaf. As it is, he feels pretty damn close, yelling into his mic as he speaks to his viewers.

"They got one. The Rangers have brought one of these things down. It attacked us, but they got it."

His commentary is hardly deserving of a Pulitzer but it's the best he can do as adrenaline surges through his veins.

He comes to a halt twenty feet away. Winters signals for the others to cease fire. She walks forward to inspect the dead creature, prodding its leathery scales with the barrel of her rifle.

"Eyes out," she yells. "Defensive posture. There are more of these things out there."

She turns to her lieutenant and points back at the road. "Mahatma. See if you can right the Humvee. I need to know if it's still operational."

Several soldiers have been injured. They limp or hold bloodied arms. A medic tends to them. Not everyone was so lucky. Body bags are rolled out on the grass and unzipped. Those that have fallen were brutally mangled. A severed leg lies beside a dead soldier. He bled out in seconds.

Andy walks over to join Winters. He makes sure he gets a good, long shot of the animal. The alien stretches twenty-five feet in length. Each of its overlapping scales is the size of a bread plate. Now that it's visible, its body sags, allowing gaps to appear in its armor. A crown of thorny horns adorns its head. They're small, barely a few inches in height.

"We lost three good soldiers," the captain says, kicking the carcass.

The head moves. Winters pulls her M4 hard into her shoulder, ready to fire at point-blank range. A clawed paw twitches, clutching at the grass.

Winters fires, emptying a clip from her rifle into the creature's skull. Bullets slam into the scales, leaving tiny blue dots where they struggle to pierce the thick skin and bone. She aims for the gaps in the armored plates. Blue blood sprays across her boots. She's close—too damn close for Andy's liking. The captain is right on top of the alien, standing less than a foot from its mangled teeth. Although it's in its death throes, the creature musters the strength to lash out at her. A massive paw swats her rifle. Sharp claws cut through plastic and steel, tearing the M4 from her hands. The butt of her rifle rakes across her face. Blood drips from her mouth.

Winters pulls out her side-arm and sets her boot on the animal's head. She fires three more times into the creature's skull, Yelling as she does so. "This is for Andrews... Induru... and Edwards..."

The head of the creature slumps to one side. Its body goes limp, rocking slightly with each shot. The captain spits blood at the alien.

"That's a *fuck you* from the people of Earth!" she says. Her rifle lies on the grass, bent and twisted into scrap. The alien swatted it like a matchstick.

Winters stares down along the barrel of her Beretta, ready to shoot again. To Andy's mind, her stance is madness. If rifle fire barely scratched this thing, what's a side-arm going to do? Captain Winters has no fear. Having her boot planted on the creature's head allows her to feel any movement. She rocks her foot back and forth, trying to provoke a response.

"Is it?"

"Dead?" Winters says. "Yes."

"Eight legs," Andy mumbles, providing commentary for the video footage he's capturing. "There's no fur. Look at that flexible spine. And that tail. I can't see a neck as such. Its head is no wider than its body. If anything, this creature looks like a mutant weasel or a mongoose."

"Are you finished playing David Attenborough?" Winters asks as he crouches, getting a good look at the blue blood oozing from the corpse.

"I never even saw it attack," he says. "How the hell did it hide in plain sight?"

"It's like a chameleon," she says. She kicks it again, making sure it's dead, only this isn't a slight shove. Winters takes out her frustration on the carcass. She kicks it with the force of a soccer player taking a shot at goal. Nothing. "The damn thing just blends into the background."

"Nasty."

Winters picks up her rifle and looks at its newly acquired L-shape. She tosses it aside in disgust. The captain moves between the squad commanders, talking with each of them. Andy shadows her. Mahatma uses a winch on the Humvee to pull it over, anchoring the cable around a lamppost. The vehicle rocks back onto its wheels. Oil and fuel seep out on the ground.

"Axle's broken," he says. "She's not going anywhere."

"What can you salvage?"

"The fifty-cal is gone. That thing snapped the barrel like a twig. We've got plenty of ammo, but we're not going anywhere in this thing."

"Have you still got that shotgun?" the captain asks.

Mahatma looks confused by the captain's seemingly random request. "Sure," he says, reaching inside the back of the vehicle. He pulls out a shotgun they commandeered from the roadblock. "What are you thinking?"

"I'm thinking aliens aren't going to respect our embedded reporter," she says, handing the shotgun to Andy along with a box of shells.

"Will this even work?" he asks.

"It'll fire," the captain says. "How well it'll work is hard to tell. We unloaded on that creature but we barely scratched it. I don't know if we missed or if our bullets were glancing off the damn thing. It wasn't until I was square on that I saw rounds punch through its armor."

Mahatma says, "We got lucky with that grenade."

"We did."

There's a strap on the gun. Andy pushes a few shells into the breach and shoulders the shotgun. He shoves what's left of the box of shells into his vest pockets.

"Okay, listen up," Captain Winters says, calling out so everyone can hear her. "Command is dispatching a Bradley for our wounded. Until it gets here, we're going to set up in that house on the corner. From the porch, we'll get three clear lines of sight on anything approaching the intersection. These fuckers are difficult to spot until they're right on top of you, so I want you to form up into teams of two— gunner and spotter. Stay sharp. I want overlapping fields of fire."

The soldiers go about their work quietly. There's a lot of pointing and talking, but no one is freaked out at the prospect of being stuck on the front line without backup. Mahatma seems to sense something is bothering the captain. He talks quietly with her as they walk. Andy stays close enough to hear the conversation.

"All good, boss?"

"Depends on how you define good."

Mahatma wants some clarification. "When can we expect that Bradley?"

"No time soon."

They walk up the driveway toward the house.

The two-story home is set on a raised embankment, giving them a good view of the disabled Humvee and the dead alien in the park. Ducks return to the lake, skidding across the water as they come in to land. Andy was sure the gunfire would have scared them off, but they seem content the danger has passed. Andy's not so sure.

"So much for the *dumb-as-fuck* animals Chambers told us about," Winters says to Mahatma, her second-in-command. "From the reports I'm getting, these things have executed a pincer movement on the airport. They faked us out. They feigned a southern approach. They knew we'd concentrate our forces here. They sent a few creatures at us, but their main thrust went east and west before circling north."

"They've gone around us?" Mahatma says.

"Yep. Leaving us several miles behind the front line."

"And the airport?" Andy asks, alarmed by what he's hearing.

Winters holds her hand to her ear, cupping her fingers. The implication is clear. The explosions and gunfire they can hear in the distance are coming from there. A battle is unfolding north of them.

"So the Bradley?" Mahatma asks.

"We'll get one in the morning," Winters says. "If there are any left."

"If there are any of us left," he says.

"It's going to be a long night."

Andy hangs his head. "Fuck."

"Hey," Winters says, reaching out for him. "Are you still transmitting?"

"Oh, yeah," he says, showing her the screen on his smartwatch.

Winters addresses the camera on his helmet. She grins, saying, "Hi, Mom!"

And with that, she walks away.

Mahatma breaks a window to gain access to the house. The wounded soldiers are dragged into the living room.

Winters opens a set of screen doors leading to the front yard. The Rangers use lawn furniture, a barbecue, and a wooden table to set up impromptu hunting stands behind the brick walls surrounding the property. This allows them to look out across the intersection and, hopefully, affords them some protection.

"What are they talking about?" Winters asks, glancing down at Andy's watch.

"Oh, it's difficult to read," he says raising the tiny screen and letting her see the miniature comments scrolling by. "The text is small. It changes too fast. I need to set up aggregate comments, but at the moment they're debating the third amendment."

"The *third* amendment?" she asks, confused. Winters screws up her face. "What's that?"

"It forbids quartering soldiers in a home without the owner's consent."

Winters laughs, shaking her head. "Un—*fucking*—believable!"

"Yeah, I know, right?"

She shakes her head. "Social media is a cesspool."

"You're telling me?" Andy says. "I used to make a living splitting hairs like this online. The mantra was—if you can turn a molehill into a mountain, you'll make money."

"You're the fake news guy, right?" Mahatma says.

"I was."

"And now?"

"It makes me sick."

Shadows crowd the house. Streetlights come on. Birds soar overhead, looking for somewhere to roost.

"Do you ever wonder?" Winters asks. "I mean, why are we like this? Why do we quibble over dumb shit?"

"We have the attention span of goldfish," Andy says. "We're like a raven with a piece of shiny metal. Honestly, most of the time, it's entertainment. It amuses us. For a while, at least. And then we get angry."

"And when we're angry?" Winters asks.

"We become armchair quarterbacks. Arguing online is a way of being involved without actually—you know—being involved. It's just like football. It doesn't matter that the game is on TV. We'll yell as though the ref can hear us anyway."

"And that's social media, huh?" the captain says.

"That's social media. It's the most goddamn anti-social thing we've ever created. Publishing a tweet is like shouting random nonsense at a bus driving past on the freeway."

Winters leans against the door jamb, looking out across the lawn at the intersection. With all they've been through and all that is to come, it seems this is a chance for her to decompress and think about something else.

"And trolls?"

"It's sport to them," Andy says. "They toy with people like a cat plays with a mouse. The problem is—most people don't realize it's a game. Flat Earthers started out as a joke on Reddit. Oh, there were a few kooks around, but they were nobodies. 4Chan and Reddit, though, fanned the flames for the lolz and regular Joes took the bait."

"Huh?"

"That's the thing that bugs me," Andy says. "Lies take on a life of their own."

"Do you want to know what's really mental?" Winters asks him.

"What?"

"That we're debating reality TV and social media on a live feed." She laughs, shaking her head as she adds, "Oh, the irony."

∃AIT

Kath wakes in the middle of the night to the hum of a rough, old engine running somewhere at the back of the trawler. The wooden hull shakes with the gentle rhythm, lulling her back to sleep. Waves lap at the side of the vessel. The sound is soothing to her aching body.

Wait.

They're in motion.

They're supposed to be at anchor.

Kath's eyes explode with life. She sits bolt upright within the cramped confines of the cabin below deck.

Outside, a chain runs over the hull, dropping into the sea. The anchor is being lowered. The engine falls to an idle.

"What the hell?" she says, throwing her heavy blanket to one side.

The cabin is narrow. The ceiling is low, even for her. There's a kitchenette and galley along with bunk beds. Ropes lie coiled on the floor. The smell of diesel hangs in the air along with the stench of dead fish. Jimmy and the Blackhawk pilot are both asleep.

Kath gets up. She steps over buoys and life jackets, working her way toward the stairs. The rough, worn planks form more of a ladder than a staircase. Without fingers, it's difficult for her to pull herself up.

She ducks through the hatch, climbing onto the deck.

Veronica's in the wheelhouse. She has her hand on the throttle. She cuts the engine and silence descends.

Jorge stands on the bow, looking at the darkened shoreline. Fires burn in the distance.

"What's going on?" she asks, working her way along the narrow walkway beside the wheelhouse toward the bow.

"You should sleep," the old man says. "Tomorrow is going to be a long day."

"Where are we?" she asks, ignoring him.

Jorge points. "Trinity Bay. That's the Kemah Waterfront."

"That's a rollercoaster!" Veronica says, leaning out of an open window and pointing at the foreshore. "I've been on it. It's fun."

Kath stares at the chaotic framework of wooden trusses and the insanely tight curves of the distant track. Nothing makes sense. She's still waking.

Kath asks, "Why are we here?"

She's not entirely sure where here is as the terms *Trinity Bay* and *Kemah* are meaningless to her.

Jorge explains, or he thinks he's explaining. From Kath's perspective, he confuses the issue even more. She finds his comment alarming rather than calming.

"We're anchored by the entrance to Clear Lake, near where we found you."

Kath grabs at her head in disbelief. "But why? Why would you do this?"

To her, this is the last place in the world she wants to be.

"Your general—"

"Nolan?"

"He called. On the radio. There's been a problem."

Kath's mind immediately switches into overdrive. She's a control freak. Oh, she doesn't think she is, but anyone that works with her

292

does—and her Mom isn't afraid to tell her to let go and trust others. As much as she wants to, she can't.

"What problem? Why didn't you wake me?"

"The general said we should let you sleep."

Jorge is calm. He has the demeanor of a grandfather but the physique of a bodybuilder. He's skilled and capable, of that, she has no doubt. He might not have a Ph.D. in astrophysics, but he's not dumb. For all her smarts, Kath still invariably puts Ikea furniture together the wrong way. When she gets to the end of the wordless instructions something's upside down or back to front—and there are *always* spare pieces left over. Always. On reaching the end of the cryptic diagrams, she finds herself with screws and nuts and small bits of laminated wood from some earlier, critical step. Jorge, though, looks as though he doesn't need instructions. He's got the kind of practical intelligence that intuitively understands how everything fits together.

"He said to tell you, no bombs. The hotel is burning. He said that would mean something to you."

Kath's mother was right. She needs to trust others. Hell, this guy survived a direct encounter with *Anduru* passing over the Gulf of Mexico. Not only did he survive the pressure wave, he also survived the tsunami that followed—and all without any warning whatsoever. That damn thing killed tens of thousands of people but he and this little girl survived. Then today, he dragged Kath and the others out of the lake. He's clearly capable of making good decisions under pressure. Take a deep breath, Kath, and trust this guy.

"Okay," she says, sighing.

Kath sits back on the gunwale running along the side of the deck. Her heart rate lowers.

Jorge seems to sense the machinations of her tortured mind.

"We are a team," he says, resting his hand on her shoulder. Kath hates being touched by strangers, but Jorge elicits no reaction from her. It's as though she's being comforted by a lifelong friend. "We work together."

"We make a good team," Veronica says, bubbling with enthusiasm.

"You do," Kath says, quickly correcting herself with, "We do."

Jorge says, "The airport was taken."

Kath avoids the temptation to ask for clarification. What does he mean *taken*? The problem is, that would be Micromanagement Kath rudely interrupting him. Science Kath knows he's relaying information. If he knew more, he'd tell her. To butt in would be to break his train of thought. Let him speak, Kath.

"They lost a lot of equipment. Planes. Bombs. Fuel. Their biological warfare suits. The general, he wanted to delay your mission. He said it would take time to get replacements, but I knew. I'd heard you speak on the radio. I understood your passion. This is too important to delay, no?"

Kath is astonished by this humble Mexican fisherman. His perception is up there with any scientist in her research group.

"So what did you say?" Kath asks, genuinely fascinated by him.

Jorge points at his chest, saying, "I said, no delay. We stick to the plan. I told him, I will organize the suits for your protection."

Kath shakes her head in disbelief. She's baffled by his confidence. She doesn't want to ask how. She wants to believe him even though she knows there's no way in hell he can source a bunch of hermetically-sealed, positive-pressure lab suits with HEPA filters in the middle of an alien-infested, burning city. Kath smiles. She's looking forward to hearing his solution to something she considers an intractable problem. She has no doubt he's solved this.

Jorge hands her a pair of binoculars, pointing at the waterway leading to the marina. The dull outline of a sign is visible above one of the buildings.

"The dive shop?" she asks, peering through the binoculars, confused.

"Scuba," he says as though he's uttering a magic incantation. "I was in there on Friday. They have everything. Full-face masks, wetsuits, gloves, boots, hoods, air tanks."

Kath is floored by his resourcefulness. "You're a genius!"

And she means it.

Genius is not a word Kath uses lightly. Normally, in a situation like this, she'd feel stressed and anxious. With Jorge, she feels composed.

Scuba gear may not be hazmat compliant but it sure beats a t-shirt wrapped around her face. Veronica smiles. It's clear to see she loves the old man.

"And Nolan knows?" Kath asks.

"He liked the idea," Jorge says.

"I bet he did," Kath replies, grinning at the thought of her old friend conspiring with Jorge to keep the mission on track.

Jorge walks across the deck. "You should rest. I'll go ashore and bring the gear back."

"Oh, no," Kath says. "There is no way I'm letting an eighty-year-old man go into a city overrun with alien monsters. You can't go in there alone."

"But you are no different. You have no gun," Jorge says, climbing down into the longboat. "You have no weapons either. It is better if I go alone. Less noise. Less risk. If anything happens—"

"Hell, no," Kath says. "We stick together. Besides, the greatest weapon we have isn't bullets or bombs, it's smarts. The only way we'll win this war is by working together."

Jorge nods. He offers her his hand, helping her down into the longboat. She accepts, grabbing his huge, calloused fingers with her forefinger and thumb.

Veronica leans over the gunwale, peering at them as Jorge unties the boat.

"You're in charge until I get back," he says, which elicits a salute from her.

The Santiago Apostol is at anchor roughly a quarter of a mile offshore. Jorge starts the outboard on the longboat and heads in toward the dive shop. He guides the boat into the channel leading to the marina and cuts the engine when they're fifty feet from shore, allowing them to drift in on the waves.

EMS vehicles and police cars line the bridge beyond the marina. Their blue and red lights flash, but there's no movement. It's eerie seeing cars abandoned with their doors open. Kath hates to think about what happened to the paramedics and police that turned up here. As the marina is only three miles from the space center, it would have been one of the first places overrun. The confusion must have been overwhelming. Now, those empty vehicles stand as tombstones to the dead.

The boat glides in, being carried on by the current. With a deft touch, Jorge brings the longboat alongside several dive boats ready to take tourists to the wrecks off the coast of Galveston Island. Kath reaches out, steadying herself as Jorge noses the longboat into a gap. She jumps up onto the pier with a rope in her hand. She may not be able to tie off the boat, but she can wind the rope around a bollard. Jorge joins her and works his magic with the rope, weaving it back and forth.

"Come," he whispers, leading her up the gangway to the shore.

Air tanks sit in a rack next to the entrance.

"How do we know if they're full?" Kath asks.

"If they're heavy, they're full," Jorge replies.

Kath lifts one. It feels pretty damn heavy to her. She tries another one and it feels even heavier. She feels as though she's trying to lift a compact car by the bumper. "This one's good."

There's a trolley beside the door. Kath wheels it over and starts shifting full tanks prepped for the next dive onto the metal tray. She's careful to keep her noise down.

Jorge pulls on the crossbar on the door. It opens outward with ease. "I'll get a dive gauge so we can check the pressure."

Kath thought they'd have to break a glass window to get inside. It's a relief not to bust in as the noise might attract attention. The owners must have fled pretty damn quick not to lock up.

Jorge returns with a bunch of wetsuits draped over his arm and a gauge console in his hand. He hangs the black suits over the cart and then attaches the gauge to one of the tanks.

"Two hundred bar."

"That's good, right?" Kath asks. She knows Earth's atmosphere is one bar at sea level, while Venus has a crushing 90 bars of atmospheric pressure. She has no idea what's normal for a scuba tank. Two hundred sounds excessive. It's certainly not empty.

"Should be good for about an hour," Jorge says. "It's around a thousand breaths."

"A thousand breaths?" she says, surprised by the notion. Kath doubts *breaths* are an internationally accepted unit of measure. Anyway, how many breaths does someone take in a minute? Or an hour? What about the difference in lung capacity between a man and a woman? Are a thousand breaths for him twelve hundred for her? And what about when they're lugging these tanks around on their backs? They're going to be breathing deeper than they would when swimming. Will that reduce the number of effective breaths? A thousand seems like a lot but under physical exertion, she's sure she could burn through them quickly. Is she supposed to count her breaths?

Kath struggles to slow her mind down. These are questions they can discuss on the boat. Jorge seems to sense her anguish as he adds, "Maybe more."

That doesn't help. Kath desperately wants to know how many more. She resists the temptation to ask for clarification.

Kath doesn't do generalizations. She likes precision, but for now, *a thousand or more vague breaths over an undetermined period of time* will have to do.

Jorge leaves the gauge with her and disappears back into the store. Kath's tempted to remind him he's a big burly guy with all his fingers. He could handle these tanks with much more grace than she can, but he's also older. Besides, he knows what he's looking for in there. Kath would wander around in a daze. Jorge comes back out with a plastic crate full of gloves and boots, masks and other equipment she doesn't recognize.

"Are we borrowing or stealing?" he asks.

"Liberating," Kath replies in a whisper.

Jorge puts the crate down next to the cart. He holds up a small black box with bright yellow stickers on it. "Look what I found. Underwater radios. There are six of them so someone's going to miss out, but this is good."

"How many do we need?"

"The general said he was sending a team of eight."

"Okay, I've got ten cylinders," she says.

"Let's grab a few more," Jorge says. He grabs two at once, lifting them and carrying them under his arms, holding them against his hips as he heads down the dock to the longboat.

Kath is flabbergasted by his strength.

She mutters, "Must be empty."

"What?"

"Nothing."

Kath struggles to push the cart. Once she hits the ramp, it's all she can do not to be dragged down out of control behind it. She has visions of herself plunging over the edge of the dock into the water—still holding onto the trolley. Jorge steadies the cart as she reaches the bottom of the ramp and turns onto the pier. He handles the tanks with ease, taking each one from her and stacking them around the boat. He distributes the weight evenly.

Jorge turns the cart upside down and puts it in the boat as well. It's bulky, hanging over the edge of the inflated sides with its four wheels sticking up in the air, but there's still plenty of room at the front and the rear of the boat. Kath has to think about it. Why is he taking the cart? Huh. They're not going to swim to NASA's JSC. Jorge's giving them some options to make the load easier to carry on land. He's got an impressive amount of foresight.

He turns to her and says, "We need two more wetsuits, two more full-face masks and some gloves."

"How many gloves?"

"A few."

Kath shrugs, walking up the ramp behind him. Her desire for precision evaporated under the weight of those goddamn air tanks. Besides, there's a kind of freedom in not caring. Less is a problem. So long as they have more, it won't matter. She likes his relaxed thinking.

Once they're inside the darkened store, Jorge loads up another plastic crate, stuffing it with what Kath can only think of as *scuba stuff*. She's happy to trust his judgment.

A scream pierces the silence.

It's sharp, coming out of nowhere. Someone's in pain. They cry into the night in agony.

Jorge and Kath freeze. The two of them peer out of the storefront window toward the bridge. A paramedic is lying on the offramp. His legs have been severed mid-thigh. He uses his hands to pull himself down toward the marina. Dark black straps mark where he's applied tourniquets to his own legs. Blood stains the concrete behind him, forming a dark trail on the road.

Kath steps toward the door. She has her hand out, ready to grab the handle. Jorge reaches out in front of her. He plants his huge hand in the center of her chest, holding her back. With his other hand, he holds a finger to his lips. Jorge moves toward the display window but remains behind the mannequins in their black wetsuits.

There's a flicker of color on the offramp near the medic. At first, it's difficult to distinguish from the red and blue emergency lights still cycling on failing batteries. They're no longer striking and bright, but they still cast shadows.

A tail appears, whipping through the air. For a second, the body of the creature is visible. Dark scales ripple as muscles flex. The alien cycles through shades of grey before disappearing from sight. Its head appears briefly. It nudges the paramedic, knocking him back into the guard rail. With that, it's gone—only it isn't. Kath knows it's still there, weaving between the abandoned vehicles.

She whispers, "I don't understand."

Jorge points, moving his finger in an arc tracing the line of the bridge. Dozens of emergency vehicles form a traffic jam of their own. He mumbles, "Bait."

Kath feels her skin go cold. Goosebumps rise on her arms. He's right. These things drew the police into a trap and wiped them out. There are claw marks beneath the bridge, revealing how they straddled the underside of the overpass, hanging there, waiting to ambush first responders.

The alien appears again, it's further away, but still twisting and turning, coiling itself and then fading from sight. Claws sink into the concrete barrier at the point the offramp leaves the bridge. The alien has abandoned the paramedic—for now.

"We can't leave him," Kath whispers.

Jorge looks back over his shoulder at the dock and then returns to the window. He seems genuinely torn. He peers on an angle, looking at the curve of the bridge as it passes overhead. The marina and the dive shop are on a small island at the mouth of the river. Bridge footings rise out of the narrow strip of grass and rock.

"In Mexico," he says. "We have a saying—it's not the scorpion you see that strikes!"

He moves his head around, looking through the bridge pylons, over at the yachts in the marina, and then up at the overpass.

"See," Jorge says, pointing across his body at the far corner of the bridge. "There's more than one."

Kath can't see anything. She squints. Stars move. A creature was there, moments ago, but now it's gone. Although she didn't get a good look at it, the way it moved makes it apparent it's bigger than the creature on the offramp.

"They must have heard our engine out on the water," Jorge says, "but they couldn't pinpoint the sound. This poor man. They've prodded and poked him, wanting him to call out to us."

"The terror he must feel," Kath says, seeing him crawling over the rough concrete, trying to reach the bottom of the offramp. "We've got to do something."

Jorge holds up a speargun. It's as long as a rifle, but it's still no match for one of these things—and it only holds a single shot.

"Oh, no," she says, shaking her head softly. "That won't be enough to kill it. I've seen these things. They—"

"I don't need to kill it," Jorge says, setting the gun against his hip and pulling the thick band back, locking it in place. He sets a barbed spear in the cradle. "Smarts, remember? That's how we beat them. Together."

"Wait," Kath says, reaching out and taking his forearm.

"Veronica," he says. "If anything—you'll care for her, right?"

"Jorge," Kath whispers. She wants to hold him back but she's unable to grab him with the stubs on her feeble hands.

The elderly man slips out through the front door. He closes it quietly behind him. From where Jorge is, standing under the eves of the building, he's hidden in shadow. The moon sits high in the sky. He peers around the corner, looking for something that's practically invisible.

Kath's heart pounds within her throat. Her hands shake. She watches from behind the mannequins. The injured paramedic is at least fifty feet away. He's reached the bottom of the offramp, but his strength is failing. His arms stretch out across the curb at the side of the road. His fingers clutch at loose gravel. He's struggling to pull himself on.

Kath is manic. Where the hell are those aliens? What is Jorge thinking taking on two of the damn things? What if there are more? He's got one shot. That's all. But at which one? What can he hope to do with a single shot?

Jorge creeps forward into the moonlight. He darts into the shadows of a palm tree set in an ornate, four-foot-high, ceramic garden pot. Several palms line the front of the store, acting as ram guards to prevent someone from driving a pickup through the front window and stealing scuba gear. Jorge creeps over to the next one, working his way toward a van parked in front of the next store.

Kath scans the bridge, the parking lot, the marina and the offramp, desperate to spot at least one of these creatures—not that she can warn him. It breaks her heart to think she may see one of these animals stalking him and be unable to help. She could grab another speargun, but with her crippled hands, she could never pull back the band. The display stand by the counter has fishing knives, but even if it was unlocked, she could barely hold one. Besides, what is she going to do with a knife?

Think, Kath. Think.

She can't. She's paralyzed with fear. For the first time since the loss of her fingers to frostbite, she feels utterly helpless. Back in the hotel, she held onto the chance of escape, however slim it may have been. Loading up the backpack with items that might come in handy gave her a false sense of hope. Standing here in the shadows, she feels naked.

Kath loses sight of Jorge as he creeps behind the van. She leans forward, wanting to get a good look out of the display window. In particular, she wants to see the length of the bridge. She's convinced that's where the aliens will be. It's a natural vantage point. From there, they can see the whole southern end of the island.

The glass in front of her distorts. The terra-cotta pots seem to sway as they sit on the concrete not more than ten feet from her. The various trunks of the palm trees bend before her eyes. The sidewalk wavers as though the sun is bearing down on it in the middle of a hot summer's day. Kath's confused. Claws tap at the concrete.

It's there!

It's right fucking there, just inches from the glass!

Kath steps back, shocked by how the alien was able to get so close without her seeing anything out of the ordinary. It's circling out wide, looping around the wounded paramedic at a distance. The damn thing is hunting for them. Its invisible back reaches four feet in height, distorting the light as it trails away, leaving her looking at the trunk of the palm trees yet again.

Kath can barely breathe.

Where the hell is Jorge?

He doesn't stand a chance out there alone.

What is she going to tell young Veronica?

A police car lies on its side near the bottom of the overpass. From the way its roof has crumpled, it was thrown from the bridge. Jorge kneels beside it. Kath wants to shout at him, to scream for him to run, but warning him is hopeless. All she'll do is expose both of them to these monsters.

Jorge edges forward with the speargun out in front of him. An oil slick has formed on the concrete, seeping from the engine. The paramedic sees him. He immediately starts crawling toward the old man but Jorge holds up a clenched fist and he stops. Jorge points at a drainage ditch behind the paramedic and mouths something, speaking without making a sound. The paramedic nods. The wounded man straightens his arms and pushes off the concrete road, dragging his bloody legs toward the edge of the road. The only logical reason Kath can think of for the paramedic's motion is to distract the creatures and draw them away. Jorge doesn't want the paramedic to give away his location.

Jorge's at the base of the offramp. He leans around the crushed cop car, aiming his speargun up the ramp. What is he looking for? What can he see?

He fires.

The spear arcs through the air, curving as it flies upward, sailing toward an ambulance at the top of the ramp. Moonlight glistens off the polished chrome shaft as it cuts through the night. What has he seen up there? Is he hoping to wound one of the aliens? Will the spear pierce its hide or bounce off?

The thin shaft reflects the light around it, passing in and out of the shadows. Its motion is obvious and in stark contrast to the still of the night.

The spear pierces the driver's side window on the ambulance. It plunges clear through the glass and into the headrest. The safety glass shatters into a million pieces with a burst of noise. Tiny fragments rain down onto the bridge.

The aliens converge, rushing at the ambulance. In an instant, the roof is crushed by the weight of one of the invisible creatures. The flashing lights bend and break, dying as massive teeth tear them apart. The side of the vehicle is peeled open by sharp claws.

Jorge breaks cover. He crouches as he runs, staying low. The paramedic reaches for him. Jorge hoists him up over his shoulder, clutching his aging arms around the man's waist. Within a fraction of a second, he's dropped into the drainage ditch.

On seeing that, Kath understands. It's an open storm drain. The ditch leads down to the river. Jorge's using it to double back without the need to return to the front door. From there, he can move in the shadows, remaining out of sight. She grabs the crate with the extra gear and slips out the back of the shop.

The night air is cool down by the dock. Behind her, metal crunches. Plastic panels are ripped open. But all that noise is coming from well over a hundred yards away up on the bridge. Kath rushes down the ramp and onto the pier. She takes pains not to make noise and avoids stepping into the moonlight, keeping to the darkness around her. Invisibility is a game two can play.

Kath knows precisely where Jorge's going to emerge from the ditch as she saw it when they first approached. She unties the longboat and pushes it away from the dock, jumping onboard at the last moment.

Kath dares not start the engine. The boat turns, drifting with the current. There's a paddle stowed along one side. Kath clambers over the cart. She pries a few air tanks away to reach the paddle, but she works it out from beside the hull. She kneels at the bow, dipping the paddle in the water and pulling herself along. With her mangled hands, she has to pin the paddle against her chest to get some leverage. She shifts her weight, rearranging how she's seated so she can work with the paddle. Her feet dangle over the inflated bow like alligator bait. She doesn't care.

Jorge wades into the water, barely making a ripple. Behind him, glass breaks. One of those things has smashed its way into the dive shop. It takes all of Kath's strength to pull the paddle through the water. The longboat inches forward. With her legs gripping the fat sides of the inflated bow, she flexes from her waist, dipping the paddle into the river and pushing the boat along.

Jorge walks out into the channel. Blood drips from the paramedic's severed legs. Within a few feet, the water is up to Jorge's chest. He lifts the man high above his head. Kath steers the boat over toward them. The paramedic grabs for the inflated sides of the boat. He pulls himself onboard without a word and collapses against the center console.

Jorge hauls himself up out of the river, rocking the boat as he swings his legs over the side. Water drips from his clothes. The boat drifts toward shore. Kath pushes off the rocks with the paddle, desperate to keep them in the channel.

Once Jorge's in the boat, she surrenders the paddle to him and shifts back to help the paramedic. No one speaks. Back on shore, a chainlink fence surrounding the empty lot beside the strip mall is crushed. Something clambers over it in the dark. Rocks tumble into the water by the marina. The aliens are tearing apart the foreshore looking for them. It seems they don't like being outsmarted.

Jorge whispers, "Stay low."

Kath sinks down beside the paramedic, taking his hand. He squeezes her palm. Despite the cold, his hair is matted down with sweat. His eyes are wild, full of terror. Kath wants to tell him it's going to be okay but they need to clear the mouth of the river first.

Jorge lies along the inflated sidewall with his chest resting on the bow, keeping his profile low and reducing the chance they'll be spotted. He swings the paddle from side to side, dipping it into the water and pulling them along in silence. Water drips between each stroke, falling back into the river. To Kath's ear, it sounds like torrential rain. She's sure they can hear them. She wants him to start the engine. Gunning the motor and racing away across the bay seems like the best option, but Jorge continues to stroke at the water.

After a distance of a hundred yards, she expects him to start the outboard but he continues paddling further out into the bay. After what Kath's seen of his courage, she is not going to question him.

"Can they swim?" he asks her sitting up and getting more leverage with the paddle.

"I don't know."

Jorge laughs, whispering, "And I don't want to find out."

It takes almost half an hour for them to reach the dark outline of *The Santiago Apostol.* Veronica is waiting for them as Jorge paddles alongside the trawler. She says, "You had me worried."

To which Jorge replies, "I had me worried."

He throws her a line.

"Get the first aid kit," he says as she finishes tying up the longboat. Kath has doubts about the ability of a civilian first aid kit to help the paramedic, but Veronica returns with a backpack that's almost as big as she is.

"My daughter, Maria," Jorge says by way of explanation. "She works for *Médecins Sans Frontières.*"

"Oh."

Kath and Jorge carry the paramedic on board. He's slipping in and out of consciousness. They rest him on the raised hatch leading to the hold.

Kath pulls on the Velcro straps, opening the pack. To her surprise, it unfolds like her dad's old toolkit, opening out into five different sections.

"Okay," she says, sweeping her hair behind her head with a bloodied hand. "I'm not a doctor—well, I am—but not that kind of doctor."

She searches through the various items under the watchful eye of Jorge and Veronica. They're looking for direction from her. Kath sets up a battery-powered heart monitor, clipping it onto the paramedic's index finger. His pulse is erratic.

She picks up a bag of saline solution along with an insertion needle and looks at it carefully. "This kit is very well stocked. Is your daughter always this prepared?"

"She takes no chances," Jorge says.

"Even with all this, there's not a lot we can do for him," Kath says. "We need to get him proper medical help."

She pauses, thinking about her options. A few hours ago, she was ready to burn Houston to the ground along with everyone in it. Now, she's exhausted. Her conviction has waned. Perhaps there's another way.

Kath has no idea what they're going to find in the Sample Return Lab. Maybe there are answers hidden in that basement. Are there any alternatives to a scorched Earth? Is it foolish to hope for one? No, she decides, it's human.

Kath says, "I'm going to get on the radio and see if we can get a chopper to medevac him. Even if they can't get in here before dawn, at least they can tell us how we can help him with this kit."

"Okay," Jorge says. "Sounds good."

IN THE
DARK OF NIGHT

Andy whispers into his microphone, transmitting live to a global audience spanning hundreds of millions of people.

"To anyone out there in the darkness, this is just another abandoned house in the suburbs. The Rangers have taken up positions around the edge of the property, but they're as impossible to spot as the enemy that stalks them."

Andy's using battery packs in parallel in his camera, which allows him to swap out batteries without cutting the signal. It drains the charge quicker, but he's got enough juice to last until dawn and has spare batteries charging inside the house. Captain Winters, though, had him stick black duct tape over the LED indicators.

"No one speaks in anything beyond a whisper," Andy says as his camera struggles to make out anything in the grainy half-light.

Andy switches his camera to night mode. The light amplification module allows him to see in the shadows. If he accidentally sweeps the lens across a streetlight, the camera is momentarily blinded by the influx of light. Psychedelic trails appear, dragging over anything else that happens to be in the frame. It takes about fifteen seconds for the electronic circuitry to recover. Even in the night mode, he can barely see the soldiers moving around in the shadows.

The Rangers have camouflaged their hides with bits of foliage, loose bricks and timber from the woodpile. Occasionally, Andy spots someone crawling slowly between positions. They keep to the shadows and move with care.

"The airport has fallen," he whispers from the lounge behind the glass sliding doors. He's sitting inside what the Rangers call a pillbox. Someone found a large cardboard box in the garage. Originally, it held an 85-inch television. Now, it's folded on three sides with a tiny slit cut into it, allowing him to see out. It looks like a World War II machine-gun nest from Normandy. The Rangers mocked him for getting a comfortable armchair to sit in while they lie on cobblestones and the cold grass, but he's got to keep a certain height or the camera on his helmet can't see through the slit. Andy can exit out the back if he needs to use the bathroom, but he's been told not to flush. Andy didn't ask about the Rangers. He's not sure what they do when they need to go.

"It's eleven in the evening. We can still hear fighting to the north, but we've been told that's not from the airport. The front has shifted four miles north to the Spring-Mercer area. We're lost. Stranded in the south."

Hand signals are exchanged in the darkness. Andy catches it on camera. He has no idea what is being said, but it's the most movement he's seen in hours.

"We're trapped behind the lines. Thankfully, we haven't seen any action since sunset. Hopefully, the night is quiet as the battle has moved past us.

"The plan is—once dawn breaks—to leg it over to the interstate and then head northeast to the City of Woodbranch. Hopefully, we can—"

A hand reaches around from behind his head. Fingers close over his mouth.

"Shhhh," is whispered in his ear.

Against his will, his head is turned. His eyes are directed up to the left, over by the kitchen.

"Thereeee... In the shadowssss."

Andy can't see anything. His view is restricted by the thin, half-inch slit in the cardboard. A block of knives sits on the marble bench top, glistening in the moonlight. Beyond them, starlight catches a chrome tap curling over the sink. Out through the glass, there's an elegant brick wall surrounding the entertaining area and swimming pool. The roof of the next house is visible only as a dark shadow with sloping sides.

He points the camera on the helmet at the roof, glancing at his smartwatch to help his aim. The brightness on his watch is dialed down. He can barely make out anything in the grainy image beyond the moon visible through the trees.

In front of him, the screen door slides open. Rangers slip inside, moving like ghosts. They peel away, treading softly on the carpet and disappearing into the shadows.

Winters holds him still in his chair. Andy wouldn't move anyway. He understands what she's doing. She's ensuring there's only one person in motion at a time. Her troops retreat inside, avoiding conflict.

Andy still can't see anything outside.

Tree branches sway in the wind.

The stars beyond them move. The effect is subtle. It's as though someone's running a magnifying glass in front of a picture. They shift one way and then return back to where they were as a creature creeps along the top of the brick wall.

"Garage," she whispers. "Now."

Andy goes to move, but she's got her hand on his head, ensuring he remains crouched and doesn't accidentally tap the cardboard, causing it to sway. He grabs his shotgun, slinging it quietly over his shoulder.

Andy doesn't want to turn his back on the kitchen windows but he's got no choice. He leaves his batteries charging. Before he can walk toward the hallway and into the garage, Mahatma stops him with a hand on his chest.

311

"You need to crawl through this area," he whispers. "We need to be like them—invisible. If you walk past the front door, your silhouette will break the light from outside."

The frosted glass window in the door reaches down to waist height. Andy takes no chances. He drops to his hands and knees. His helmet keeps slipping down over his eyes, forcing him to use one hand to push it back. Slowly, he crawls across the carpet. Another soldier waits in a darkened doorway. The man extends his gloved hand, helping Andy to his feet. A second hand on his back makes sure his shotgun doesn't bump the wall.

Andy's chin strap is loose. He unclips it, tightens the straps and pushes the black clips back together.

Clunk!

The sound itself is innocent enough and barely audible but it cuts through the silence. Nobody moves.

Glass breaks in the kitchen.

Mahatma squeezes past Andy in the darkness, rushing into the garage.

Winters opens the front door. She's got something in her hand. Whatever it is, it's cylindrical. She tosses it out onto the footpath. A plastic garbage can bounces down the driveway. She turns away from the door, pushing Andy back into the garage. Someone closes the door quietly behind them, easing up on the knob without making a sound.

The garbage can bounces until it reaches the road. There's a change in pitch as it leaves the steep driveway. Garbage spills out as it rolls, adding to the confusion. Aluminum soda cans join in the cacophony of sound outside. They scuff against the concrete like steel drums.

Tiles break on the roof above them. A leg punches through the sheetrock. Claws pierce the roof of the garage as the creature scrambles back up in pursuit of the garbage can at the bottom of the drive.

Barrels point up, waiting to unleash hell.

Bits of sheetrock come loose, falling to the floor.

312

The creature leaps from the roof.

Timber beams groan under the shifting weight.

"It took the bait," Andy whispers, determined to continue his commentary.

A fist grabs his shirt, twisting it up in front of him and tightening it around his throat. Gloved knuckles rise into his neck, pushing under his jaw. Captain Winters is inches from his face in the darkness. Her eyes are on fire, burning with anger. Gritted teeth and flared nostrils tell him everything he needs to know. That was beyond stupid. This isn't one of his fucking parlor games. Dumb shit like this will get them killed.

She shakes her head in disgust and lets him go.

Moonlight comes in through dozens of glass panes in a set of fancy French doors at the far end of the garage. Those doors lead to the pool area. Skimmers and pool toys lie to one side next to gym equipment looking out at the entertainment area.

Winters points at the way the pale light falls on the concrete, indicating that no one—absolutely no one—especially not Andy—should step there. It's the glare she gives him after pointing at that portion of the garage floor that makes it abundantly clear. Andy swallows the lump in his throat.

The captain crouches on one side of the doors. She's on her haunches, right on the edge of the light, but she keeps to the shadows. Winters peers across the tiled outdoor entertainment area, staring through the glass at an angle. Mahatma does likewise from the other side of the doors, taking care as he crouches, avoiding the coiled pool hose. They communicate with hand gestures, letting each other know what they see.

Andy can't see anything out of the ordinary. The creature that leaped from the roof hasn't come back. It tore the garbage can apart, that much was obvious from the sound of plastic being crushed and ripped. The noise then receded down the road. He's sure it's gone.

There's a kidney-shaped swimming pool in the middle of the entertainment area outside. It should be fenced, but it's not.

313

Cobblestones lead from the edge of the pool to the house. A barbecue and outdoor table sit under the cover of a sunshade. Grapevines wind their way over a trellis. A six-foot-high brick wall surrounds the property. Next door, there's an acacia tree. Its branches hang over the wall.

"Options," the captain whispers.

One of the Rangers holds up a gas can for the lawnmower. He gives it a gentle shake. Liquid sloshes around. He and Winters exchange hand signals.

Andy looks carefully at all the junk at the back of the garage. He's embarrassed himself. He was so damn focused on his stupid broadcast he almost cost them their lives. He wants to redeem himself.

The garage is huge. It's big enough for four vehicles parked two abreast, but the owners have used the extra space for storage and a home gym. There are weights, an exercise bike, a treadmill and a cardio-stepper. The pool maintenance gear is neatly stacked.

No one else comes forward with any other options. What options are there? They're trapped.

What is Andy supposed to be thinking? If Kath or Nolan were here, they'd have some brainstorm that saves the day, but him? Not a chance. Andy's good at coming up with ideas the next day. If he makes it out of here alive, he'll wake in the middle of the night and realize the exercise bands could have been converted into a trebuchet or some stupid shit like that. His mind won't let him rest. It'll demand answers no matter how dumb they might be—no matter how late they might be.

The reality is, the Rangers are bristling with weapons, but how do you kill something you can't see? Then there's the size of the goddamn things. Hit them with an elephant gun and they'll keep going. Andy once heard of a hunter that shot a Grizzly through the heart. The bullet penetrated the left ventricle but the bear tore him to pieces before it succumbed to its fatal wound. These creatures are even bigger. How many bullets did it take to kill that one by the lake? The fifty-caliber machine gun fired a helluva lot of rounds before the Humvee was flipped.

314

Winters looks at him. She shrugs, holding her hands out wide. She's open to suggestions.

His eyes settle on some painting equipment by the door to the house. Even to his untrained eye, it's obvious this is for renovating rooms. There's a roller, a couple of brushes, a folded sheet covered in drips of paint, and a few plastic buckets of white paint.

Nolan would improvise an explosive device using the pool chlorine. Kath would fashion a rudimentary rail gun using the treadmill and the paint roller as a hyper-velocity spear. Andy would paint the spare room.

He feels spectacularly dumb.

Captain Winters seeks him out. It seems she's trying to balance her anger with leadership. She points at the moonlight coming in through the French doors.

"We're stuck," she whispers. Andy notes she's come around the right side of him so she's close to his microphone. "Originally, there were two of them. We think there's still one out there. We can't kill it, but I think we can scare it off."

Andy can't help himself. He was determined not to say anything in case he demonstrated his stupidity yet again, but he's got to ask, "You think you can scare one of those things?"

"Yes," she replies, pointing at three Rangers lined up beside the French doors, poised with their rifles pointing down at the concrete in front of them. They're standing just beyond the light spilling in through the windows, but they're ready for action. They look as though they're about to charge through the french doors regardless of whether they're open.

"Why do you think they're invisible?" the captain asks. "We've seen a carcass, right? Their natural color is blue/grey, so they have to deliberately turn invisible—just like an octopus changes color, but why?"

"I—I don't know," Andy whispers in reply.

"They're vulnerable," she says under her breath. "We all are. And

315

anything that's vulnerable knows fear. Even a tiger knows fear."

"You're mad."

"The unknown," she says, raising a finger in objection to his point. "Everyone's afraid of the unknown—something new. We've got to exploit that. Bullets aren't going to kill these things out there. Fear is the only weapon we have left."

Andy would rather sit tight and hide, hoping the aliens move on by dawn. Winters seems determined to take the fight to them. In some ways, it makes sense. If she's right and they can scare one of these things, they'll avoid them during the daylight rather than attack. To him, though, it seems like an impossible task.

"I need something to distract them," she says.

Andy points at the painting equipment, gesturing to the drop sheet. It'll hide their human outline if nothing else. Are aliens afraid of people dressed up as ghosts?

"Genius," she whispers, ignoring the sheet and picking up one of the plastic pails. "It's time to play a little paintball."

"Play what?"

"Matte white finish," Winters mumbles, squinting as she struggles to make out the writing in the dark. "That'll work."

She holds the pail in two hands, saying, "You're going to shoot this for me. Understood?"

Andy nods. He understands—but understanding a simple directive doesn't mean he comprehends what she's doing or why. His fingers tremble. He wants to tell her this is a bad idea, but he's already been the instigator of enough dumbass acts of his own. Andy's not a coward, but he'd rather cower in the corner than provoke one of those things again. His bladder feels as though it's going to explode. Okay, he's a coward. He's man enough to admit he's afraid. He taps her on the shoulder as she edges toward the light streaming in through the door.

"Ready?" she asks, turning back toward him.

Ready?

What the hell?

No. He's not ready.

He'll never be ready.

Andy fumbles with his shotgun, swinging it down from his shoulder. His finger pushes gently on the safety, pushing the button back. There's already a shell in the chamber. He thinks. He's not sure. Yes, he pumped the action back when they were setting up in the yard, just before he flicked on the safety. He's sure he felt a shell load into the breach. If he didn't, he's about to look pretty damn fucking stupid pulling a dead trigger. Fuck. Fuck. Fuck!

Andy wants to pump his shotgun one more time just to be sure, but the idea of making any more unwanted noise is terrifying. That he's about to fire a shotgun and wake the dead hasn't quite registered in his mind. He knows it intellectually, but his mind is caught up on the soft sound of his chin strap clicking moments ago. If he was to cycle the pump-action, he'd draw another creature to attack.

Winters reaches out into the moonlight and slowly pulls on an ornate brass handle. She edges the door ajar. It opens outward. On the other side of the French doors, Mahatma reaches in as well, grabbing an identical brass handle and pulling it down. Once the catch releases, he removes his hand. Like Winters, he pushes on the outside of the frame to gently rock the door open without being exposed to the moonlight.

The French doors open from the middle, with both soldiers staying out of sight as they ease the doors wider. Neither is in a rush. Behind them, soldiers stand in the shadows with their guns leveled at the door, ready to fire if one of those things pounces.

Winters and Mahatma take their time, allowing the doors to move as though they were never locked and have been caught by the wind and blown open. They move with a natural motion, like the swaying of branches.

A cool night breeze swirls within the garage. Over the course of a couple of minutes, Winters and Mahatma push the doors wide, exposing themselves to the courtyard surrounding the pool. An inflated beachball floats on the surface of the water. The wind pushes it gently around. It bumps into the tiled edge of the pool and rebounds softly, drifting further along the pool in the darkness.

Branches sway on the tree beyond the far wall of the pool. It's just the wind, Andy tells himself. Now, it's no longer his bladder he needs to contend with, it's his bowels. Moments ago, he was fine. Now, he wants to squat in the corner and take a dump. His lower bowel feels as though it's under pressure and about to burst.

Winters makes eye contact with him. She holds the pail of white paint up, making sure he's got a good look at it. At a guess, it only holds a couple of gallons of paint. Andy's still not sure what she's going to do. The door opens roughly five feet from the pool. At a guess, she's going to put it down on the rim and he'll shoot it. Paint will go skidding across the surface and that'll somehow scare these creatures—that's not going to work. He's going to die.

Andy steels himself to shoot the plastic pail. Like the Rangers, he keeps his shotgun pointing at the concrete floor. It's already pulled hard into his shoulder. He's ready to swing it into action. To his mind, this is madness, but it's the Rangers that are keeping him alive. He trusts Captain Winters. If she thinks this will work, he'll do it. She stands out of sight with the pail hanging from her right hand. With her left hand raised, she counts down from three. Andy sets the shotgun hard into his shoulder and stares down along the barrel. He's a condemned man on death row. There's nothing to be done now but to go through with the inevitable. Andy's ready to step out beside her into the moonlight.

Two fingers.

One finger.

None.

Winters steps into the courtyard, swinging the pail of paint with all her might. She throws it high, sending it sailing over the swimming pool.

Andy walks out beside her, tracking the pail with the bead at the end of his barrel, leading the shot. Several Rangers rush past, but he ignores them. He squeezes rather than pulls the trigger.

Bamm!

The shotgun recoils, slamming into his shoulder and catching the side of his cheek.

The pail explodes.

White paint sprays through the air.

The peppered bucket spirals through the night, sending paint swirling over the pool area. To Andy, it's like fireworks going off minus the color. He's mesmerized by the fine drops soaring through the air like tens of thousands of shooting stars falling to Earth.

A hand grabs him from behind, yanking him back into the darkness.

There, on the brick wall, are two alien creatures—only they're covered in a fine coat of white dots. Their heads and front legs are visible. Most of their bodies are hidden from sight, being draped over the wall on the neighbor's lawn.

"You can't hide," Winters whispers from the shadows in the silence that follows.

The aliens seem perplexed by the sudden crack of noise. They flex, but they don't attack. This act of violence wasn't directed at them. They're baffled by the fine white mist settling around them. It must sound as though thunder broke from the sky and rain is falling. They have no idea they've lost their invisibility.

In response to the motion by the garage, one of them leaps down into the courtyard. It straddles the pool. Andy can see its front legs but not its entire body. Claws dig into the tiles surrounding the pool.

"Let's do this," Winters says, only she isn't whispering anymore. She's speaking out loud with no fear. She steps in front of the massive alien creature, blocking the doorway behind her. She's got an old-fashioned lighter in one hand. It's made from either silver or polished chrome. The shiny metal catches the moonlight, reflecting it back at them, making it obvious in her fingers. She flicks the flint. A flame appears. Winters tosses the lighter through the air, saying, "Fuck you!"

The lighter somersaults from her fingers, landing in the shallow end of the pool almost fifteen feet from the creature.

319

Whooooomp!

Fire races across the surface of the water. The pool erupts in flames. An orange fireball billows into the night, scorching the alien as it straddles the pool. It leaps, jumping onto the far wall and then onto the roof of the neighbor's house. Flames trail from the animal's legs. Pungent black smoke rises into the air, billowing as it rolls above the house.

"What the?" Andy says, seeing the empty gas can floating on the surface of the pool. The Rangers must have dumped it there as he was shooting the paint.

For the first time, there's a cheer from the troops. They roar with excitement, but it's more than a celebration. They're sending a warning, yelling into the night. They may not have killed either of those aliens. They may not have even hurt them. But they scared the crap out of them. Those things have no idea what just happened. They won't be back. And if they do return, the Rangers will see them coming.

DAШN

The sky lightens.

Dawn is approaching.

After raiding the dive shop, there was no way Kath was going back to sleep. She was too hyped. Besides, the paramedic needed a lot of care. She was happy to do whatever the doctor told her over the radio. After providing a detailed description of his injuries, his vital signs and his wavering consciousness, the doctor at the forward base had them put the paramedic on a drip. He told them to give him basic painkillers and apply antiseptics to the bandages. Veronica was a spare set of hands for Kath, helping where her fingers lacked dexterity. Jorge helped where he could and kept the coffee coming.

It's been a long night. It's going to be one helluva long day.

Smoke rises from the city. Five helicopters approach from the north. At first, they're black dots above the horizon, drifting in the pink hues of the coming dawn. Then they're a swarm of angry hornets shattering the quiet of the morning. Finally, they're a storm raging overhead.

Kath spots the familiar shape of a Blackhawk but she doesn't recognize the other helicopters. They're smaller and thinner, with pylons extending from their sides like tiny wings. Missiles bristle beneath the fuselage. A large radar dome extends above the rotors. Each helicopter has a crew of two—a pilot with the copilot sitting directly behind instead of beside each other. If Blackhawks are the Chevy Suburban of the skies, these are the motorcycles. There's no room for anyone else onboard the smaller choppers.

The Blackhawk hovers fifty feet above *The Santiago Apostol.* Hurricane-like winds swamp the deck. Jimmy, Veronica and the pilot watch from the wheelhouse. Kath and Jorge brave the artificial storm. They squint as they peer up at the Blackhawk, watching the loadmaster.

The paramedic is awake. Jorge wraps him in blankets to keep him warm. Kath places her hand on his chest, keeping the blankets from blowing away.

A member of the aircrew descends on a cable with a recovery basket beside him. It's an aluminum frame in the shape of a stretcher. Loose straps flutter in the downdraft. A red cross on his white helmet designates him as a medic. The soldier's boots have barely touched the deck before he unclips and rushes over to the injured paramedic. He talks with him, but Kath can't hear what's being said over the thumping rotors.

He yells at her, giving her a thumbs up. "Okay. He's good to go. Let's get him in the basket."

Jorge and Kath help transfer the injured paramedic onto the stretcher. Once he's strapped in, the wire is reeled in by the helicopter's winch. The medic hooks on and returns to the Blackhawk with his patient. He keeps a firm hand on the stretcher, preventing it from spinning with the rush of air around them.

The door to the trawler's wheelhouse slides open. The downed pilot beckons the two of them over. As they get close, he yells above the noise of the Blackhawk engines. "They want you to clear the deck for the SEAL deployment."

"Oh, okay," Kath replies. She and Jorge slip inside.

Kath has no idea what *SEAL deployment* means. From where she is within the wheelhouse, she can no longer see the Blackhawk. It's hidden by the roof of the trawler. The water around the boat ripples outward under the steady beat of the helicopter's four massive rotors.

Thick black ropes fall into view. They strike the deck like thunder. Barely a second later, black rucksacks slide down the ropes, thumping the deck. Behind them, soldiers appear, descending the rope as though it were a fireman's pole. No sooner have they cleared the ropes than another set of soldiers descends.

The first soldiers already have their rifles up. They move to the side of the trawler, looking out across the bay for threats. Once eight black-clad soldiers are on deck, a ninth soldier comes down the rope, but he's dressed in camouflage.

"No, no, no," Kath says, storming out of the wheelhouse and past a surprised Navy SEAL dressed head-to-toe in black. She yells over the sound of the Blackhawk, directing her voice at the ninth soldier, "What the hell are you doing here?"

"It's good to see you again," Nolan calls out over the noise of the rotors. He marches over to her, straightening his black gloves. Like her, he lost several fingers and toes during the initial encounter with *Anduru* and hides his prosthetic fingers from sight beneath a pair of gloves. Sliding down the rope was risky—no, foolish. Kath's not sure whether she wants to berate him or hug him.

Somewhere high above them, the loadmaster releases the heavy ropes. Gravity does the hard work and the ropes collapse to the deck, coiling themselves into a mess. Within seconds, the Blackhawk rises hundreds of feet into the air and Kath can finally think and hear again.

"You shouldn't be here," she says.

"You really don't understand how the military works, do you?" Nolan says, grinning. "It's not like an opt-in kind of thing."

Kath ignores him. "Your wife is going to kill me."

"You'll have to survive first," Nolan says, winking at her.

"You're a general," she says. "You're supposed to be leading from a command bunker, not joining troops on the front line."

"I always hated that," Nolan says, reaching out and giving her a hug. For a moment, a sense of calm washes over her. Touch is important. It's not logical, it's human. She returns the embrace, feeling at ease with her old friend.

She says, "It's good to see you again." Although they're his own words echoed back at him, they come from the heart.

Nolan smiles, saying, "You too."

He was never going to leave her to do this alone.

The SEALs begin unpacking and sorting their equipment. The others come over from the wheelhouse. Nolan introduces himself and shakes hands. Jorge beams with pride. Veronica and Jimmy are excited at the sight of soldiers on *The Santiago Apostol*. The injured pilot has fractured his right arm so he can't salute. He grimaces as he tries to lift his arm from the sling.

"Easy, captain. It's okay," Nolan says, squeezing his good shoulder and smiling warmly.

"You really didn't need to come here," Kath says.

"What? And let you have all the fun?"

"Okay, so what's the plan?" she asks as the sun breaks over the horizon, casting long shadows across the bay.

Nolan introduces Kath to one of the SEALs. "This is squad leader Lieutenant James Jackson. He'll be taking the lead."

"Ma'am."

"It's an honor," Kath says, extending her scarred hand and shaking his gloved hand—and she means it. Anyone that is willing to risk their lives along with her has her respect.

Nolan says, "The lieutenant is commanding two fire squads of highly trained Navy SEALs."

"This is it?" Kath says, surprised. "This is all we're going in with? I was expecting a cavalry charge."

"Without heavy armor this far south, we need to be cautious," Nolan says.

Jackson adds, "We're big enough to fight, small enough to avoid attention."

"And we have considerable air support," Nolan says.

"We'll cover the flanks as you head to JSC," Jackson says. "Once inside, we'll take forward and rear positions. Don't worry. We'll get you into that lab, ma'am."

"And those?" Kath asks, pointing at two of the SEALs with long, bulky rifles. The magazines protruding beneath them are absurdly thick. To her mind, the rifles are bordering on cannons.

"Those are sniper rifles. We'll have one with each fire team."

"Sniper rifles?" she asks, curious at the SEALs' choice of armament. "Like for long distances?"

"The Barrett fires 50 caliber rounds. In war, they're effective against light armor."

"And against people?" she asks, not being familiar with the term *light armor*. How light is light? Kath's trying to understand how effective a sniper rifle will be against the alien creatures.

"They leave a smudge, ma'am. Just a fine red mist hanging in the air. Not a body."

"Oh," she says, surprised by the notion. "Thank you, lieutenant."

Nolan looks at his watch. "In about three minutes, Operation Fire and Brimstone goes into effect."

"Fire and Brimstone?" Kath asks, raising an eyebrow.

"It was your idea."

"My idea?" Kath says, pointing at herself in surprise. The lieutenant smiles. It seems he likes watching Nolan torment her.

Nolan points toward the skyscrapers. "Somewhere out there, about forty miles north of the city, two and a half thousand M1 Abrams tanks and around five thousand Bradley Fighting Vehicles are poised ready to mount a counterattack. They're waiting to advance along a front curling around a hundred and eighty miles. These creatures have struck a hornet's nest. They're about to learn how wars are fought on Earth."

"Nice," Kath says.

325

"Our strength doesn't come in planes and tanks alone," Nolan says. "Modern warfare is about logistics. It's about coordinating assets. It's about striking with overwhelming superiority. By itself, even an Abrams can be defeated. When used in unison with artillery, close-air-support and ground troops, though, the damn things are unstoppable."

"But *Fire and Brimstone*?" she asks.

"We've established an air corridor in a triangle stretching from San Antonio to Dallas and on to Baton Rouge. There are four AWACS up there and a rolling presence of air refueling planes in support of a fleet of over two thousand aircraft. They're going to provide the *fire* while ground troops sweep through and clean up with the *brimstone*. Nothing is getting out of the isolation zone. Nothing."

Kath smiles. "I like it."

Nolan points. "The only thing that worries me is whatever started all this. We debated bombing the lab, but the consensus is—you're right. We need to understand what the hell we're up against."

"And that's where we'll find it," Kath says, liking their reasoning.

Nolan turns to Jorge. "I need you to take us into Clear Lake. That'll put us within a mile or so of the lab."

"It's dangerous," Jorge says, pointing at the bridge spanning the mouth of the river. "Those things. They're watching."

Kath gestures to the scuba gear and air tanks lined up against the gunwale of the trawler. "We got ambushed while we were in the dive shop."

"They're using the bridge," Jorge says. "They stalked us like a jaguar."

Nolan has a combat radio on his belt. A flexible cord winds its way up behind his back and over his shoulder to a microphone clipped onto his shoulder boards. He squeezes the transmit button.

"Oscar Zulu, this is Romeo. I need the bridge over the river mouth cleared. Over."

"Copy that."

In the background, over the military radio, there's considerable discussion between an AWACs aircraft coordinating their air support and the various helicopters hovering nearby. Kath is fascinated by the discussion. What for Nolan was a single sentence unwinds into numerous details she would have never considered, including the approach and exit flight path, the current distance to the target, the heading used for the attack and confirmation of the location of friendlies even though the pilots know the SEALs are in the trawler below them. Nothing is assumed. No piece of information is too trivial to be skipped. Even the elevation of the bridge is given along with its grid reference.

"Romeo, Oscar Zulu," the AWAC says once the discussion is complete. "Bravo One-One is locked on target and requesting to be cleared hot."

"Oscar Zulu, Romeo," Nolan replies. "Bravo One-One is cleared hot. Over."

One of the helicopters descends, racing in toward shore. A machine gun opens up but it's unlike anything Kath's ever seen before. Tracers are visible in the soft morning light. Hundreds of rounds tear through the various vehicles on the bridge, shredding steel panels and shattering glass. Even from where they are, chunks of concrete are visible, being torn up from the road. Dust swirls in the aftermath of barely fifteen seconds of fire. It's a flex—like the roar of a lion on the savanna. It doesn't matter whether any of the creatures were actually hit. It's enough to demonstrate the sheer intensity that can be brought to bear at a moment's notice. If there are any creatures in the area, they won't be using the bridge any time soon.

The helicopter continues hovering near the bridge, watching the approaches on both sides.

"That'll do," Jorge says. He works with the SEALs to retrieve the anchor and get underway.

"Romeo?" Kath says, raising an eyebrow. "That's your call sign? Really? Does Jan know about this?"

"It's the letter R—that's all," he says, knowing she's ribbing him. "And it was assigned to me by the ops team. It's not my choice."

"Sure," Kath says, trying to suppress a smile.

The Santiago Apostol approaches the coast. It passes beneath the bridge with a wary SEAL team covering all angles. Rifle barrels bristle outward. If an alien was to approach from shore or drop from the bridge, it would be cut to pieces by gunfire. Even so, Kath and Nolan join Jorge and the others in the wheelhouse during the passage through the narrow channel leading into Clear Lake.

Tensions ease once the waterway opens into the lake.

Nolan points, telling Jorge, "Bring us to a halt in the middle."

"Yes, general."

Nolan turns to Kath, walking out onto the deck. "I have a present for you. A surprise."

Kath looks at him as though he's gone mad. No one's sure whether to take him seriously.

"Come," he says, checking his watch. "It's seven twenty. They should be here by now."

Over by the hold, the Navy SEALs are changing from their night combat fatigues into scuba gear.

Nolan's radio squawks. "Romeo, Oscar Zulu. Alpha-Zulu 104 is on station four miles out, circling to your east."

"Bring them in," he says into his handset.

"Bring who in?" Kath asks, wondering who else is going to join their team.

Nolan points back at the bridge. The wetlands across the bay are visible. In the distance, a commercial airplane banks, showing its vast wings. The plane drops altitude, making as though it's turning sharply to land somewhere nearby.

Kath squints, fighting the glare of the rising sun. "What is that?"

"A present—from Jacinta. It was her idea," he says. Nolan addresses Veronica and Jimmy, gesturing to the wheelhouse as he adds, "Climb up there. Make sure you get a good look at this thing. It's something you'll never see again."

The kids scramble up onto the wooden roof of the bridge. They're excited even if they don't know why. Jorge walks out, wondering what all the commotion is about.

Kath walks forward to the edge of the trawler. She rests her hands on the old, worn wooden gunwale. Out across the bay, beyond the bridge, a 747 approaches, coming in low. The distinct bulge of its second-story cockpit is visible as are its massive engines hanging from beneath its wings. Its landing lights are on, competing with the sun for attention. From its heading, it seems it's going to make a low pass barely a quarter-mile north of them on the far side of the lake. The aircraft looks as though it's coming in to land, but it hasn't lowered its landing gear and there's no airport.

"What am I looking at?" Kath asks turning to Nolan.

"Ah," he says, pointing across the lake, wanting her to watch. "AZ104 is a decommissioned commercial passenger jet operated by the US Forestry Service to fight fires."

"I don't understand," she says, shaking her head in disbelief. "You're going to put out the fires you've started?"

"Paintball," Nolan says. "Think of it as one gigantic paintball going splat!"

The 747 races over the suburbs to the north of them barely a couple of hundred feet in the air. It's so low and loud it's scary. Veronica and Jimmy have their hands over their ears, but they're jumping with excitement on the roof of the trawler.

A fine pink spray begins falling from the underbelly of the aircraft. Within a second, there's a torrent of red rain streaming behind the 747. The jet rises as it drops its load. A wall of what looks like red paint falls from the fuselage, being dragged along in the wake of the jet. Four massive turbofan engines scream as the aircraft gains height. The cloud of red descends, drenching the Johnson Space Center along with the surrounding roads, fields and suburbs. It's as though there's been a micro cloud burst and torrential rain has been unleashed, only it's bright red.

Veronica and Jimmy are cheering, bouncing around and

hollering. Even the SEALs have stopped to watch the dump. The large boxy buildings within the space center are covered in red spray.

"That's twenty thousand gallons of bright red fire retardant dropped with pinpoint accuracy."

"Paintball, huh?" Kath says, genuinely impressed by what she's just seen.

Nolan talks into his radio. "Oscar Zulu, Romeo. Do you have target acquisition? Over."

"Copy, Romeo. We have identified fourteen targets in range."

"Oscar Zulu. You are clear to engage. It's time to plow the row."

"Copy that."

Up until this point, the helicopters had been hanging back on the south side of the trawler. Two of them fly forward. Missiles roar away from their pods. Smoke trails curl through the air. Explosions rock the fields. Several of the NASA buildings are struck. Smoke billows into the air. The sheer number of missiles fired is overwhelming. Kath can't keep track of where they all went.

"Romeo, you are clear to continue."

"Copy that, Oscar Zulu," Nolan says.

"You're not taking any chances, huh?" Kath says.

"War is about taking opportunities, not chances," Nolan says. He addresses Jorge. "Can you bring us into the western pier, then wait for us back here."

"Yes, yes," Jorge says.

Veronica beats him to the helm. Jimmy is by her side. Jorge stands back and watches as Veronica brings the boat in toward the dock with a deft touch.

"You didn't want to ferry us by chopper to the space center?" Kath asks as they get changed into their scuba gear.

"The joint-chiefs are a little nervous about anything touching down inside the isolation zone. This boat makes for a great platform."

"Opportunities, not chances, huh?" Kath says, sitting on the hold of the trawler, struggling to pull a wetsuit up over her legs.

"Can I help?" one of the SEALs asks. It's only now they're in wetsuits, Kath realizes two of the SEALs are women.

"Ah, yeah," Kath says, holding up her scarred hands with their stubs, making the reason for her difficulties obvious. The two women help her don her suit along with a pair of foam-padded wetsuit shoes and the headpiece covering her hair and neck. The SEALs carry their full-face masks slung low around their necks so Kath does likewise.

Once they've pulled up to the dock, the SEALs offload the trolley and stack their air tanks and equipment onto it. They carry their rifles.

"Here's the gear you asked for," Nolan says, handing Kath a backpack. She opens it. There's a laptop and a satellite dish sealed in thick plastic. She rummages around. There's also the collection kit she asked for. If she can, Kath wants to collect samples along the way so they can better understand how this alien biosphere is interacting with their terrestrial biology. Whether anyone's going to let her take samples out of the isolation zone is another question. They may demand they're incinerated. Even if that's the case, the act of collection will get her to pause and think a little deeper instead of walking on by—so to her mind there's still value in the process.

"Ready?" Nolan asks, distracting her from her thoughts.

Kath glances around the deck of the trawler. Something's missing. No. Not some piece of equipment. Someone.

Jimmy.

"Hang on," she says, walking away from the soldiers waiting on the dock.

Veronica's in the wheelhouse of the trawler, but she's focused on keeping the boat steady in the shallow water. Mud swirls around the hull of the trawler, being kicked up from the bottom of the lake by the engine screws. Jorge has looped a thick rope over a support pillar on the pier but he hasn't tied it off. Given the two of them were attacked on this pier, it's no wonder they're nervous about returning here. That focus, though, means both of them are ignoring Jimmy.

Kath sticks her head through the hatch leading below deck.

"Hey, there you are," she says.

After the water bomber flew over Houston, it was easy to become swept up in the euphoria of the moment, but being back in this lake is traumatic for Jimmy. They sailed past the boom of the sunken Blackhawk without so much as a comment. To Kath's mind, it's a gravestone, marking where the copilot is buried. She'd rather not think about what the alligators have done with his body. It seems Jimmy saw the tail boom as well. She can see it in the pained expression in his eyes. He sits on the edge of a bunk bed, trying not to cry.

"It's okay," Kath says, climbing down below deck. She sits next to him, wrapping her arm around his shoulder. "Listen, I know this is scary. I'm scared. I don't want to admit it, but I am. This time, though, things are different. This time we've got General Nolan and the soldiers. We've got Jorge and Veronica. We've got water bombers and helicopters. We're not alone."

She squeezes his shoulder, asking, "Are you going to be okay?"

"I guess," he replies, and Kath finds herself on the verge of bursting into tears.

These are the first words he's spoken to her. Ever since they arrived on *The Santiago Apostol*, Jimmy's only ever spoken to Veronica. Kath's seen them huddled together, comforting each other, but he's been quiet and withdrawn from the adults. And understandably so. Jacinta's been trying to track down his mother, but in the chaos surrounding the exodus from Houston, it's like looking for Waldo. Jimmy's world hasn't been turned upside down so much as inside out. Nothing is recognizable anymore. Change has been his only constant. Even positive things, like helicopters flying overhead and soldiers sliding down fast-ropes, are disconcerting. It's a lot to process. And the helicopters are loud—too damn loud. Even for her, they're intimidating.

"Are you going to be okay?" she asks, repeating herself, wanting to draw more out of him.

"Yes," he says, looking up and staring deep into her eyes.

"I'm proud of you," she says. "You're very brave."

Reluctantly, he nods.

Kath says, "I'm coming back. You know that, right?"

"I know."

"Come on," she says, rubbing his hair affectionately. "Come up on deck and see us off. This is the good part. This is where we win!"

Ah, lies. Sweet, sweet, lies. Well, hopes—perhaps that's a better term.

Jimmy smiles and follows her up the ladder and back onto the deck of the trawler.

Kath steps onto the dock, stretching over the watery gap between the gunwale and the pier. She waves back at Jimmy. He smiles, returning her wave. It's an image she holds in her mind. It's a sight she wants to see again.

"Thank you, Jorge," she calls out as the trawler backs away from the dock.

Bits of grit and weeds swirl around the boat, being kicked up from the bottom of the lake. The wounded pilot secures the ropes with his one good arm.

For Kath, it's strange being surrounded by soldiers. To her mind, they want to be in control and shoot things. That might be an oversimplification, but it doesn't exactly scream curiosity. For Kath, it's science that's going to save the day, not grenades or sniper rifles.

"From here, we walk," Nolan says, looking at a line drawn on a map. "This way."

The Navy SEALs spread out, keeping to the sides of the road as Kath and Nolan walk down the middle. The SEAL at the rear pushes the cart, coming up the center of the road behind them. With the exception of Kath and Nolan, the soldiers maintain twenty to thirty feet between them. If any one of them is attacked, they'll lose a single soldier, buying the others time to respond. Given the red goo covering the ground, Kath doubts anything could get close without being spotted. As it is, the attack helicopters trail them, forming an outer perimeter. Occasionally, there's machine-gun fire from the choppers as they peel away to deal with a threat. As dangerous as it feels walking into alien-held territory, Kath knows she's safer than she's ever been in her life.

"Jacinta's giant paintball worked really well," Kath says as they walk past the severed remains of a creature in the field to their right. The missile that killed it dug a small crater. Smoke lingers in the upturned dirt. As best she understands, it was struck with a high explosive rather than an incendiary bomb, but if the plan plays out, eventually this place will be scorched from the air.

Bits of bloody blue flesh lie scattered about on the red grass.

"You're not worried about this place being covered in flame retardant chemicals?" she asks.

"If you saw the list of munitions designated for the space center alone, you wouldn't worry. This place is going to be covered in liquid fire."

"Good," Kath says, walking along the road to the space center.

An abandoned guardhouse is visible at the end of the avenue.

"What are you doing for Thanksgiving?"

Kath turns and looks at Nolan. "Are you serious?"

"I'm serious," Nolan says, looking anything but serious wearing a scuba wetsuit on dry land. "Jan and I would love to have you and your partner over."

"It's March," Kath says dryly. "We're marching toward an alien-infested building and you're thinking about Thanksgiving?"

"Everything requires planning."

Kath laughs. She knows what he's doing. He's distracting her. Hell, he's distracting himself. What are the odds of them getting out of this alive? Once they go inside those buildings, they're on their own. Kath could have insisted on an entire battalion, but Jackson is right. Once they're in those narrow corridors and small rooms, numbers become irrelevant. Out here, they can negate the alien advantage with air support. In that massive building at the end of the road, everything changes. All they'll have is their wits—and bullets and grenades—but mostly wits.

"You know," she says, playing along with him, "if this were a movie, this would be one hell of an anticlimax. It's right about now they up the ante on their special effects budget and go for the big bang explosions. And here we are—walking. How boring is that?"

"If this was a movie," Nolan says, "we would have hot-wired a car."

"Why didn't we hot-wire a car?" Kath asks as though it's an option. That might have been possible in the 1980s, but since then, electronic ignition and built-in security systems have made it all but impossible. Without saying anything, she's answered her own question.

Nolan ignores her, asking, "Who's going to play you in the movie?"

"Me?" she says. "I was joking about the whole movie thing."

"They always make a movie out of these things," he says. "Always."

"Ah, not if we don't survive they won't."

"Especially if we don't survive."

"Not if there's no one left to make popcorn and run the projector."

"I'd like Brad Pitt to play me."

Kath bursts out laughing. "You look nothing like Brad Pitt!"

A few of the SEALs snigger quietly. Nolan doesn't seem to care. If anything, he's working his charm on them too.

"I know," he says confidently. "Looks don't matter."

Kath clarifies. "Looks don't matter but you want a Hollywood *Dionysus* to play you?"

"I think he'd do a good job with the role."

Kath shakes her head. She loves it. She can't hide the grin on her face. They're walking to their deaths and Nolan's lightening the mood for everyone.

"Claudia Black," she says, playing along and answering his

question.

"Who's that?"

"Ouch," Kath says, faking her outrage. "She's only the greatest SciFi heroine of all time!"

Nolan clears his throat. "Sigourney Weaver would like to talk to you about your choice for queen of the xenomorphs."

"Okay, Sigourney is pretty cool," Kath says, granting him that.

"And Jennifer Lawrence and Grace Park and Emily Blunt and Summer—"

"All right, I'll admit it. They're all awesome, but I grew up watching Claudia in *Farscape*."

"Never heard of it," Nolan snaps back, but the side-eye he gives her is telling. He's baiting her. Kath simply shakes her head, grinning.

They walk past the JSC Materials Evaluation Lab. Overturned police cars block most of the road. Empty ambulances lie in the ditch. The mood turns. Reality sinks in. They're walking into the heart of the initial attack. The SEALs spread out, checking behind vehicles as they walk on. They turn, confirming every angle is clear, making sure the team isn't walking into a trap.

A fine red spray coats everything, but it's lighter this far into the Johnson Space Center. In some places, the grass is knee-height, springing up beside the road. Kath's only been to the JSC on a handful of occasions. She's never seen the grass over an inch in height. In summer, it's almost dead, being brown rather than green.

"We need to get to JSC Building 32," Nolan says. "It houses the spaceflight vacuum test chamber. The Sample Return Lab is in the basement."

The metal roof on the Space Vehicle Mockup Facility has been peeled open. Bodies lie scattered on the grass. Kath's heart sinks. They never stood a chance. Birds peck at the remains. Flies buzz around the rotting corpses. The eyes, nose and mouths of the dead are covered in what could be aerogel. It's not, but it looks like that, being a semi-transparent, white foam. Kath suspects it's some kind of alien fungal growth, but even that would be an oversimplification. It's feeding on human remains, of that she's sure, but its role and its function within the alien ecosystem is a huge question mark for her. Somehow, these lifeforms infect planets and go on to spread into space. This could be stage one of ten thousand, but how do they progress?

"We need to start breathing our own air," Kath says. She kicks at the dirt, noting the red fire suppression chemicals barely reached this area. They're on the outer edge of the region covered by the water bomber, which is going to make spotting the larger creatures difficult as the team won't be able to see their footprints.

The SEALs retrieve their air tanks from the trolley and slip on their full-face masks. They've got their own radio headsets. They select an open channel so Nolan and Kath can hear them on the radios from the dive shop.

Kath can get her face mask on, but she struggles to tighten the straps with the stubs of her fingers. One of the SEALs helps, making sure there's no exposed skin. They also help her slip on a pair of gloves. She positions her backpack on her front. It's not heavy enough to act as a counterweight for the air tank, but it keeps her equipment accessible.

"I want to get a sample," she says, pointing at a corpse.

"Okay," Nolan replies. The SEALs spread out, watching the approaches to their location.

Kath kneels beside one of the bodies in the long grass. She pulls out a collection kit. To anyone nearby, her process must look like a high school biology project in the local creek. There's nothing high-tech about her approach. She opens a plastic bag, retrieves a pipette and plastic sample jar. It's been a long time since she's used a pipette, but Kath gets her dodgy hands to comply. She retrieves some of the alien fungal growth, carefully places it in the jar and seals the lid. The pipette is discarded on the ground to avoid any further contamination. At the moment, littering is an acceptable strategy. She seals the bag and writes the location, subject and time on the plastic.

Nolan and the SEALs wait patiently for her to finish.

No rush, Kath. Nothing else going on here.

337

Ah, science. It's not for the impatient.

Kath takes a few cuttings of long grass, sealing them in a sample jar and writing down the details as well. She pops the plastic bags in her pack and gets back to her feet. The weight of the air tank is absurd on her small frame.

"I'm feeling like an astronaut again," Nolan says with the sound of heavy breathing coming through at the start and end of his sentence.

"I'd rather be floating in space," Kath says, grabbing at the straps on her scuba gear. She leans forward, shifting the weight of the tank as she walks on.

An Orion capsule lies crumpled in the street beside JSC Building 9. It's been thrown through a sheet metal wall. The heat shield is broken. A steel girder has punctured the cabin. Moss is growing on what should be the pristine outer white skin of the craft. Rather than lying here for a few days, it looks as though the Orion has been exposed to the elements for years.

"See this—this is not good," Kath says pointing at the moss. "As bad as those creatures are, they're a known entity. They're alien. This worries me. This is alien stuff screwing around with our stuff."

Nolan crouches beside the open hatch, letting the camera on his chest get a good view inside. Moss is growing over the support struts, seats, cables and control panels. The camera is broadcasting as well as recording, allowing the command group in Washington to see precisely what they encounter. If anything should happen to them, there will be at least a partial record to work from.

"But this is just like fertilizer, right?" Nolan says from behind the confines of his mask. "How is growth bad?"

Although it seems as though it's just the two of them talking, Kath knows every frame of video will be scrutinized by scientists and politicians alike—not to mention trolls. Her words need to be carefully measured. This is the kind of fertile ground in which conspiracy theories grow.

"It may seem normal-ish. It's not until we look under a

microscope that we'll know exactly what's going on and why."

She takes a sample of the moss and the grass, sealing them in a plastic bag and labeling them.

"I saw stuff like this within the hotel. It killed a rat and a human. It might not disrupt plant life, but could be fatal to more complex organisms like animals." She looks around. "I sure would love to catch a few of those flies."

The flies are interested in the moss. They buzz around, landing occasionally. Kath holds a collection jar with a little moss inside. She rests it against the rail by the open hatch of the Orion. Nolan stands beside her. He points at the next building but doesn't say anything to distract her. Kath knows what he's indicating. This is a sideshow. That's the problem with science. Something that looks insignificant could hold the answers. As much as she knows she should walk on, she can't. She's sure the President and the Joint Chiefs are getting frustrated. To their credit, no one's passing along a *for-gods-sake-hurry-up*. Monroe will know. He'll understand. Maybe he's providing commentary, helping them understand what she's doing and why.

"There was a study that looked at exotic peptides," she says, keeping her hands still as flies buzz around her, ignoring her collection jar. "Now, don't be fooled. Biology has lots of terms for lots of different stuff. It's easy to get lost in the distinctions but it's quite straightforward. DNA provides the blueprint for building proteins out of amino acids. When you get something like fifteen to twenty amino acids strung together you've got a peptide. String a few peptides together and you've got a protein. Biology's like LEGO but way cooler."

A fly lands on the rim of her collection jar. As tempting as it is to shove the lid on, she knows the fly's reactions are far faster than anything she can muster. She waits, watching as it crawls around.

"So these exotic peptides?" Nolan asks.

"They tested them against the immune system of mice," Kath replies, edging the cover closer to the specimen jar. The fly crawls over the moss at the bottom of the plastic container. "And the immune system response dropped from 80 to 90% down to about 20%.

Basically, the immune system was useless when faced with the unknown."

"Okay, that's bad," Nolan says. "That's really bad."

"Gotcha!" Kath says, screwing the lid closed with the fly inside. She stows the sample and gets back to her feet.

"What's that?" Nolan asks, walking forward a few feet and pointing at the rear of the capsule. The Orion is lying partially on its side, having sunk into the soil. Thick purple goo oozes out of the shell of a crab, only this is no terrestrial crab. Its body is the size of a dinner plate with thin legs stretching over a meter in length.

"Now *that's* really bad," Kath says, echoing his earlier sentiment. She pulls out another collection kit. "It's a form of alien life we haven't seen before. They're creating their own ecosystem." She crouches, using a pair of tweezers to pick bits of the crushed shell and innards for collection.

Over by the nearby building, the long grass sways. Alien crabs shuffle in the shadows, scurrying away from them—or so she hopes.

"Okay, that's enough for me," Kath says, freaking out at the motion of the grass.

Nolan helps her back to her feet, saying, "You don't want a live sample?"

He's joking—that's obvious from his tone of voice—but her response is serious.

"No."

She walks back onto the path, wanting to get out of the long grass. Kath's sucking in deep breaths. She's aware they've only got about an hour's worth of breathable air in their tanks—and they need to get in and out in that time. She says what everyone else is thinking but won't utter. "We'd probably best keep moving, huh?"

"Probably," Nolan says.

They walk along the road leading to JSC Building 32. Far from being a single building, it's a conglomeration of different buildings in a variety of shapes and sizes. The northern end of the building has

340

collapsed. Part of the roof has fallen into the parking lot. The reception area is only recognizable by the sheer amount of broken glass and a torn NASA logo.

Nolan says, "Drone footage has revealed significant debris in the north. We think that's where they exited. We're going to blow this fire door on the south to gain access."

Kath is horrified. "You're going to blow open a door? With explosives? Won't that attract these things?"

"Hopefully," Nolan says, pointing at an attack helicopter hanging back easily a quarter-mile behind them, facing directly at them. "It would be nice to draw them out because once we're inside, we're on our own."

"Ah. Okay, then."

The team takes shelter behind a smaller, nearby building. One of the SEALs jogs forward in their scuba gear and sets the charges. Once they've returned, there's a thundering explosion. Kath's heard a lot of gunfire and explosions—far more than she'd like—but this one rattles her bones.

Nolan and the SEALs talk to the attack helicopters watching over them. One of the helicopters is covering the door while the others are looking for anything approaching from other directions. Kath reaches down and picks up some dirt in her gloved hand. If she rubs it between her fingers she can find traces of the fire retardant chemicals, but it's not obvious. They're too far into the JSC complex. They've walked behind the main buildings. This region was sheltered from the dump. Kath suspects any aliens approaching from the north will be utterly invisible—and that makes her heart race.

"We're good to go," Nolan says. The two of them jog toward the door for no other reason than the SEALs are jogging. To Kath, rushing doesn't seem wise but she hurries along regardless.

"Oh my god," she says, stepping into the room behind the SEALs. "This is a cleanroom."

"*Was* a cleanroom," Nolan replies, pointing at the mud that's fallen from the scuba shoes of the soldier in front of him.

Kath is horrified. They've emerged inside one of the spacecraft assembly rooms. The door they blew open was an emergency exit that has probably never been used as it would allow contaminants inside. If anything, this is an old cleanroom as the newer, more modern rooms would use a dual access anteroom even for emergency egress.

The power is off. The SEALs flash the lights on their gun barrels around, illuminating the darkness.

Kath points at a smoking steel fragment embedded in the solar panel of a space telescope. It's one of the hinges from the door.

"You know what that is, right?" she says, gesturing to a tall, folded mechanical structure. A mixture of shiny chrome pipes and gold-plated solar panels catches the light.

Nolan looks at her, at the space telescope, and then back at her. He doesn't say anything.

"That's the Descartes' Exo-Atmospheric Detector. It's four hundred million dollars worth of hardware. I know of scientists that have worked on this project for thirty years just to get to this point. That's their careers sitting there on that stand."

"Oops," he says, trying not to laugh.

"This isn't funny," she says.

"DEAD?" he asks, ignoring her. "They gave it the acronym DEAD?"

"It's DED," she says, indignant. "Exo-Atmospheric is hyphenated. It's one word. DED is Latin shorthand for *daring* or *devoted*. We get the English word *dedicated* from *dedi*."

"Well, it's dead now," Nolan says, looking up at the gash running across the glistening solar panel.

Kath sighs, examining the spacecraft. The other door hinge has severed several pipes before becoming embedded in a bundle of wires. Green antifreeze drips onto the pristine white floor.

Nolan rubs his glove on the golden solar panel, saying, "It'll buff out."

Kath shakes her head. She knows somewhere someone's watching this in horror. Aliens aside, their life's work is sitting on this scaffold. She faces the camera on Nolan's chest, saying, "I'm sorry. I'm so, so sorry."

"Hey, Doc," one of the SEALs says. He's standing in front of the internal airlock leading to the main building. "You coming?"

FIRE AND BRIMSTONE

Out of the darkness, a voice asks, "Are you awake?"

"No," Andy replies. Well, he is now but he wasn't. *No* seems more appropriate given his groggy mental state. He goes to move. His neck seizes. He's lying on a sheet of cardboard in the garage with a jacket rolled up as a pillow.

"Coffee?" one of the Rangers asks, handing him a cup.

"Sure," he says, sitting up with his back against the drywall. The smell of burned fuel still lingers in the air.

"Captain gave us coffee privileges. The power's still on and these guys have a serious coffee machine. It's Italian—a Concordia. Mahatma reckons it's like fifteen grand new. Who spends fifteen cold hard ones on coffee?"

"I don't know," Andy says, still trying to catch up with the reality of waking.

"Hell, that's more than I spent on my pickup," the Ranger says, smiling from behind the smeared camo paint on his face.

Andy sips the coffee. There's no creamer, but it does have a bit of sugar. The taste is smooth rather than bitter. There's no nasty aftertaste. It has a slightly nutty flavor.

"Good, huh?"

"Really good," he says, feeling his head clear.

"Captain says we're rolling in five. She let you sleep as long as possible. If you want to shit or piss, now's the time to get that out of your system. Once she starts marching, she won't stop."

"Understood," Andy says, getting to his feet with his coffee in hand. It's lukewarm so he chugs it rather than enjoys it. He needs the caffeine hit more than the pleasure.

"Just past the laundry," the Ranger says.

Andy leaves his helmet outside the bathroom. He places it on a side table facing the open front door, sparing his viewers the call of nature. Last night, he set it on a box pointing out of the fancy French doors. He has no idea what it transmitted, but his primary battery is flat while the secondary is on 10%. His watch is almost dead. It's sitting on 3% charge. He's probably got about ten minutes left and then he'll lose his monitor feed. He should have taken it off and charged it overnight.

His watch aggregates the most common words and terms used in the insane flood of comments being left during the broadcast. If he taps the *comments* icon he gets to see a summation of the most common phrases overlaid on the screen.

asleep

he's awake

he's alive

good morning

about time

The counter showing the number of people watching continues to climb. If only that were his bank account.

The bathroom is a mess. It looks like a herd of rhinos has stampeded through in the middle of the night. The floor's wet, although that seems to be from the basin rather than the toilet. He relieves himself. From the greasy stains around the mirror, it seems some of the soldiers have washed off their camo. Andy heads into the lounge and swaps out batteries. As he's running them in parallel, he can change

346

them one at a time without cutting the live feed.

"Good morning," the captain says with a cup of coffee in hand. "You want one?"

"Oh, I just had one, thanks," Andy says.

She raises her mug, saying, "There are very few deployments where we get decent coffee."

"I bet," he says.

The Rangers look relaxed this morning. There are soldiers on the wall, looking out across the street, but their late-night barbecue seems to have worked. For now, there's no immediate threat. Andy doesn't say as much but he can see they needed some downtime. No one can maintain a constant state of vigilance. Even soldiers in the special forces have to breathe. Gourmet coffee has been the perfect *pick-me-up*. It's given them something to think about other than those that have fallen.

"How did you end up in the Rangers?" Andy asks.

Winters begins with, "Well, I—"

Andy points at the camera on his helmet. Although his motion will be lost on his audience, he wants her to talk to them and not just him.

"Oh, right," she says, remembering everything is being transmitted. "This is *The Interview*, right?"

Andy tries to downplay the formal side of things, saying, "Everyone knows someone who served, but few people talk about it. Oh, plenty of fakes will brag. The real heroes, though, go unnoticed."

"Ah, no, no, no," Winters says, waving her hand in front of her coffee cup. "We don't use the H-word. My great grandfather hated that word."

"Your great grandfather?"

"Major Dick Winters. He served in the 101st Airborne during World War II. He was such a kind man. He died when I was about fourteen."

"So that's why you joined the Rangers?"

347

"To avoid the 101st Airborne—yes."

Andy's perplexed. "To avoid them?"

"When people hear the surname Winters, the first thing they ask about is *Band of Brothers*."

"The HBO series?" Andy asks, surprised. "That was him?"

Winters nods. She's holding her coffee cup up near her lips, ready to take another sip, but Andy gets the impression she's hiding behind it.

He asks, "What did he think of the show?"

"Oh, he liked it," she says, lowering her mug. "But he didn't think he'd done anything special. All he wanted was to do his job and look after his men. He used to tell me, the only reason to fight is to live in peace. You don't fight out of anger or hate. You don't fight because you want to kill someone. You fight because the other asshole wants to kill someone and you're not going to let that happen. You fight so you can get it over with and everyone can go home."

"Huh," Andy says.

Winters knocks back the last of her coffee. She sets the mug down with a thud, saying, "Okay. We're leaving in ten."

"I'll be ready."

Ten minutes is better than five and will give him some time to check over his equipment.

"Captain Winters?" he asks, pausing by the hallway leading to the garage.

"Yes."

"What are our chances out there?"

She smiles. "Better than zero."

"That good, huh?"

"Well, the barbecue trick worked a treat last night, but it's going to come down to how many of those damn things we run into along the way."

"Have you heard from anyone?"

"No one," she says. "We lost contact when the airport went down.

Our LR comms was in the Humvee when it rolled. The damn thing tumbled out of the side window and was crushed by the chassis. Normally, we'd deploy with HOOKs—a GPS enabled combat survival radio, but this was anything but normal."

"So we walk," Andy says, putting on his helmet and adjusting the camera position.

"We walk," she says. "It's good for the heart."

Andy carries his chargers back to the garage and stuffs them in his backpack. His watch is down to 2%. He hits the *comments* icon and checks the most popular phrases over the last thirty seconds.

dying

watch battery

losing us

flat battery

goodbye Andy

"Yeah, I'm losing you," he says, responding to their concern.

With his boot, he kicks at a pile of combat gear loosely stacked against one of the walls in the garage.

"This is body armor. These are the ceramic plates we were wearing yesterday. And look at all those helmets. I think the captain and I are the only ones still wearing helmets. Once you've seen a man sliced in half by one of these monsters, you reassess your need for ballistic inserts and kevlar. It's the weight. It slows you down. You're better off being that little bit more nimble and agile. There's no defense from those teeth or those paws. The only viable strategy is to dart away and that means being light-footed. Besides, it'll make our march north a little easier."

He walks out through the French doors into the pool area. The image on his watch is dull. The energy-saving algorithm has automatically reduced the brightness to conserve the battery. As it is, Andy can barely see anything on the screen in the sunlight. If he steps back into the shade, he can still see the transmission.

"In a few minutes, I'll lose your feedback. Don't worry, though, I'll continue transmitting for as long as possible. I just won't see your comments."

Andy is fascinated by the damage to the outdoor entertainment area. The ornate brick wall separating the properties has partially collapsed. Bricks have fallen into the pool. They lie broken on the bottom. The surface of the water has an oily film. Claw marks reveal where the alien straddled the pool during the night. Andy crouches, letting the camera on his helmet focus on the damage. He watches the feed, making sure he gets good coverage.

nasty fucks

alien claws

nope, nope, nope

fuck that shit

hell no

"Hah, yeah, these things are nasty, all right," he says, enjoying the virtual conversation.

In the distance, there's the rumble of thunder. Andy looks up. The deep blue sky is clear of clouds.

"And still the battle rages," he says.

out

get out

run Andy

leave now!

they're coming

Panic seizes his mind. Andy turns through 360 degrees, looking carefully around him. Nothing. The messages on his smartwatch are alarming.

"Is there one of them?" He mumbles, unsure of himself. Has he missed it? Was there some clue those watching picked up on? The aliens are invisible so they're easy to miss, especially when they stay still. What have his viewers seen? Andy's blood runs cold. The hairs on the back of his arms stand on end. Thunder continues to roll through the air, rumbling around him.

burn

bomb

incendiary

scorched earth

fire and brimstone

"I don't understand," he says, looking at his watch. "What do you mean?"

Captain Winters walks out of the kitchen, coming up beside him. She looks at him talking to his watch and raises an eyebrow.

Planes buzz the suburbs north of them. Four aircraft roar over the roofs north of them, forming a staggered line. If Andy didn't know better, he'd think they were rehearsing for an airshow as they're flying low and screaming in across the city. Behind them, there's a string of explosions. Fireballs billow into the sky. The kitchen windows behind him shake as pressure waves roll over the suburb. Black smoke rises in the air.

"Jesus, that's close," the captain says.

Another trio of planes rushes in, dipping from the sky and dropping yet another load of bombs further to the northwest. The effect, though, is to form a continuous wall of overlapping fire.

Andy looks at his watch. The power indicator flashes at 1% but it's the cloud comments that trouble him. There are hundreds of millions of people watching his live feed. It takes a few seconds before he sees the fireballs appear on the tiny screen, but the comments are all saying the same thing.

Andy's automated software routine scans user comments in real-time. It uses machine learning to ignore outliers and only presents him with text that makes the top 20% of phrases in any 30-second block. In milliseconds, it filters those further, only giving him the top five phrases rather than everything that's being said. When Andy's broadcasting from his garage studio, this allows him to read the room, as it were. Feedback is important. It lets him feel the reactions of his audience and

351

tweak his tirades as appropriate. Here, though, in Houston, it's useless.

Now, there's only a single comment. That shouldn't be possible. He's never seen this before. Everyone agrees on this one thing. It seems they know more than he does.

"What's it saying?" Winters asks.

"I—I don't get it," Andy says, lifting his wrist so she can see the feed. "This can't be right."

Winters stares at the tiny screen. The words at the bottom of the image read:

you're next

"Fuck," she says.

"They know we're here, right?" Andy asks as she turns away from him and marches toward the kitchen door. "I mean, Nolan and the others back at base. They're not going to bomb us, are they?"

"They think we're dead."

"What? No!"

"Either that or they don't know our location."

"But they wouldn't bomb us," Andy says.

Winters isn't going to stand around and debate hypotheticals with him. She runs back into the house yelling, "On the street! Now! Drop everything! Everyone out on the street. Move! Move! Move!"

Andy follows her, more so as a professional cameraman than anything else, wanting to catch all the action. He looks at the monitor feed on his smartwatch. The screen is blank. The battery is dead.

Winters shouts at the soldiers on sentry duty in the front yard. "On the street! Leave your gear! Go! Go! Go!"

Andy's never seen anyone move as fast as the Rangers. Orders are followed. No care is taken. Mugs are dropped on the tiles. Black coffee splatters across the floor. Boots pound on the floorboards. The coffee table is flipped as someone brushes past. Backpacks are discarded on the carpet.

"Run! Run! Run!" Winters yells with the intensity of a drill

352

sergeant.

Andy darts along the hallway, wanting to grab his backpack from the garage. He can't stray more than about thirty feet from the uplink with its wireless router and satellite antenna. If he does, it won't just be his watch going blank.

Andy doesn't make it. Mahatma grabs him by his collar and swings him out through the open front door. Andy sprawls across the concrete. The padding built into his borrowed fatigues spares him from grazing his knees. His palms don't fair as well.

"My gear! I need my—"

One of the soldiers grabs Andy, planting his hand in the middle of his back. He hauls the YouTuber to his feet, forcing him to run to the bottom of the drive.

"Sound off," Winters yells from the grassy median strip on the street. The various squad commanders respond with their names and number of troops. Behind her, the sky is black. Hundreds of houses are on fire. Explosions rock the suburb. Glowing fireballs billow into the air, turning on themselves. Flames leap into the sky.

Mahatma comes running up behind Winters. He's got his rifle in one hand and the clunky satellite array in the other. He shoves it into Andy's chest.

"This what you were looking for?"

"Yes."

More planes roar overhead, drowning out their words.

Bombs fall. Flames swell through the trees, consuming them in a wall of fire. The aircraft are working in unison, forming an impenetrable barrier. In the distance, black dots line themselves up with their avenue.

"Look," Andy yells. "They're coming!"

Winters isn't looking at the flames or the approaching aircraft. She's looking around. Her eyes settle on the disabled Humvee, the broken tiles on the roof opposite the intersection, and the collapsed brick wall. Andy understands. She's looking for options. As much as he doesn't want to, as much as he'd rather focus on the sensational, he

353

follows her lead, checking his surroundings—bricks lie scattered on the road, oil soaks the concrete, the dead alien lies on the edge of the park, beyond the carcass, there's an empty slide and a set of swings. There are no ducks on the lake—not today. It seems they got the memo.

"The lake," he says, pointing. It's not a suggestion. It's his mind scrambling for even the most remote, outside possibility. If anything, he's asking a question.

Captain Winters points, yelling, "Grab a cinder block and jump off the end of that goddamn pier!"

No one questions her. No one hesitates, not even Andy.

The Rangers run, discarding their M4s, their jackets and magazine clips as they sprint down the road. Andy runs hard. His auto-correction software struggles with the extreme, shaky-cam footage, sending out a blurry image. He clutches the satellite uplink under his right arm.

Explosions ring out behind them, shaking the concrete beneath their boots.

Winters darts toward the park. She screams at the top of her lungs, "Phosphorus floats! Fuel floats!"

It's almost impossible to hear her over the sound of explosions rocking the neighborhood. She grabs a chunk of broken cinderblock from the road. To Andy, it makes no sense. It's going to slow her down. They still have fifty yards to cover. She tosses it to him. He tries to catch it, but with only one arm free he fumbles and it falls to the street. He stops, grabs it with his left hand, and then turns and runs on. Boots pound on the road behind him, closing on him.

Winters yells to her troops, "You need to stay under for at least a minute!"

Andy shoves his left arm inside the hollow of the cinderblock, holding it against his stomach as he runs. He keeps the satellite relay with its thick black antenna under his right arm. It's their only link with the outside world, but it slows him down. Winters overtakes him with a large cinderblock held in front of her. All of the Rangers are ahead of him, including one guy with a wounded soldier doubled over his shoulder. They charge down the wooden pier and off the end, jumping into the deepest part of the lake.

Behind them, flames billow into the air, consuming everything in their wake. Jets roar overhead. They're so close and loud Andy ducks, grimacing as they scream past. More bombs fall. Fireballs erupt into the sky. The radiant heat scorches the back of Andy's neck, but on he runs. His lungs are burning. Sparks fly through the air. The sky above him darkens.

Andy's boots hit the pier. He runs as hard as he can. His eyes are focused on the end of the wooden planks. The lake reflects the flames surrounding and engulfing it. Andy's about to jump when he's struck by a wall of fire, lifting him off his feet and throwing him into the lake. Flames curl around his face, singeing his hair.

He sinks into the depths. On instinct, he turns, cradling the cinderblock on his stomach. It weighs him down, dragging him into the weeds. Above him, flames lick the surface of the lake.

The sky is on fire.

JELLY

"Take these," Kath says, having grabbed two fire extinguishers from inside the cleanroom.

"We're here to start fires, not put them out," Lieutenant Jackson says over the radio linking the team together.

"They're not for fires," Kath says, still getting used to talking inside her face mask. She puts the extinguishers down next to her so she can talk over the radio. Being in scuba gear, she has to *squeeze-to-talk* and *release-to-hear* over the radio. As they're next to each other, if she forgets, she can still hear the others, but they sound muted. "These are CO_2 extinguishers. They'll provide you with a smokescreen. You'll be invisible to these things. Or, better yet, spray them down a corridor and watch how the vapor curls. If there's anything blocking the way, you'll see it even if it is invisible to our eyes."

"I like it," Jackson says. Kath hands off the extinguishers to the two soldiers by the door. They've been peering through the glass, planning their move once they get through the doors.

"Okay," Jackson says, returning to Kath and Nolan, who are standing further back inside the anteroom. "Once we're inside, we're going to break right and move behind the control panel. Jacobs is going to lead Fire Team One to the left, laying down a cloud of CO_2."

357

"He's bait?" Kath asks. Her comment about the fire extinguishers was supposed to be as an option of last resort, not something they would lead with as billowing white clouds are going to attract attention.

Although she can't see Jacob's lips behind his full-face mask, she can see the way his cheeks rise. He's smiling at the prospect.

"He's providing a diversion," Jackson says. "We'll be moving with Fire Team Two. If there's contact, stay by me. Do not leave my side. Understood?"

"Understood."

Nolan's found another fire extinguisher in the anteroom. He's holding it with both hands in front of his waist, probably because the damn things are so heavy, but he looks like he's about to throw it at someone.

The lead SEAL holds up three fingers, then two, then one—and slips quietly through the door. Each soldier leaves the anteroom with their rifle pointing in a different direction, covering all the angles. As they're entering a large, open space within the building, they scan the walkways and gantries. The two fire teams break in different directions. Before Kath and Nolan get to the door, a cloud of CO_2 obscures the room. The SEALs aren't taking any chances. Nolan's got his hand on the shoulder of the soldier in front of him. Kath does likewise, keeping her hand on his shoulder. Barrels protrude around consoles and tables, peering out at the vast warehouse.

No one moves.

Sunlight streams in through a gaping hole in the roof. The building has been torn open, but the damage is from within. Steel panels have been ripped from the ceiling. Previously, they saw how the spacecraft mockup facility was opened like a can of tomatoes, but this is different. Aliens exploded from *inside* JSC Building 32. Claw marks scar the walls. The industrial crane stretching overhead has been mangled. These things treated its steel girders like a dog's chew toy.

Pipes run along the walls. Severed electrical conduits hang from the ceiling. Blood stains the floor, having splattered across the concrete. There are no bodies.

JSC Building 32 houses the vacuum test chamber. Although it looks like a furnace, the massive cylinder reaches four stories in height. Thick steel supports surround the chamber. The door is large enough to drive a truck inside. Over the decades, the chamber has been used to simulate the vacuum of space for everything from the Apollo Command/Service Module to the James Webb Space Telescope.

The door is partially closed, but the hinge is bent outward. The top hinge has popped off its mount. It's been forced open at the top and has fallen forward. The bottom section has become jammed in place. The thick, plate steel is wedged against the chamber seals. From where she is, Kath can see the top half of the chamber is open, but she can't see inside.

The SEALs talk in their own form of sign language with strict, precise motions. Fists are raised. Fingers point. Symbols are flashed. Responses are given. They could use their radios but it seems they'd rather minimize noise.

Jackson makes eye contact with Kath. He whispers into his radio for her benefit. "Stairway. Thirty feet. East wall. Leads down to the SRL."

Kath shakes her head. "I need to get up there."

"What?" Jackson says, looking back over his shoulder at the cylindrical chamber in the heart of the building. From where they are, it's obscured by a raised platform and all the debris that's fallen from the roof. "You're kidding, right?"

"No."

"General," he says, addressing Nolan under his breath. "This is a deviation from the plan."

"Can we work it in?" Nolan asks.

"We can't provide effective cover. Not from down here. We don't have a direct line of sight. The angle's all wrong. This carries a high risk of compromise."

"Understood," Nolan says, looking at Kath.

"It's important," she says, craning her neck and trying to see up

359

on the platform beside the chamber without exposing herself above the control console.

"What's up there?" Nolan asks.

"Answers," she says.

Nolan nods.

Jackson looks at Nolan with eyes that seem as though they're about to explode out of his skull. He's exasperated. What seemed like a simple in-and-out operation has been complicated by a whimsical and insanely curious astrophysicist.

Kath says, "If I can get on that platform, I'll be able to see inside the chamber."

"We need to make it happen," Nolan says to Jackson. Kath notes Nolan doesn't tell Jackson *how* to make it happen, just that it has to happen. She respects that. Nolan might be in charge, but Jackson has the combat experience.

The lieutenant looks down at his feet for a moment and then turns, looking up at the raised platform. His eyes dart around the wreckage within the massive facility. Kath watches as he identifies the stairway, the access ladder on the far side, and the observation deck at the rear of the facility.

"Two, I need you to provide cover fire for One. We are proceeding to the platform. I want converging fields of fire in a V-formation. Keep a damn good eye on the open roof. Over."

The radio crackles with a hasty, "Two on the move."

On the other side of the floor, black scuba gear blends in with the shadows. The soldiers creep toward the rear stairs.

"I need your laptop," Jackson says.

Kath doesn't hesitate. She pulls it from the pack hanging in front of her and hands it to him along with the satellite uplink.

Jackson hands them to Nolan, saying, "I'll take her up there. If anything happens, you and Two need to complete the mission."

"Agreed."

"With me," Jackson says. Before Kath can key her radio to reply, he's turned his back on her. The four SEALs rush forward with their rifles raised. Jackson doesn't look back. The assumption is apparent. She's supposed to be in the middle of the arrow-like formation they're creating as they rush across the open floor. Kath scrambles after them. She crouches, mimicking them as she runs toward the metal stairs, keeping her head low.

Jackson stops at the foot of the stairs and looks back. The others don't. They keep their eyes outward. Kath follows his gaze. One of the SEALs from the other team has climbed up on top of the observation deck. He unfolds a tripod and lies prone, peering through the scope of his sniper rifle. The rest of his team creep out wide, taking up other positions at the back of the building. One of them leans into the corner of an I-beam supporting the roof. Within seconds, all that's visible is a dark barrel pointing at the raised platform.

Jackson whispers, "Two?"

From somewhere at the rear of the building comes a reply over the radio. "Two in position."

"One is green."

"Copy that. One is green."

Jackson creeps up the open metal staircase. Although his rifle is pointing up at the next flight of stairs, the rest of the support team backs up the staircase with their rifles pointing down and out to the sides. As these things are invisible, they take no chances.

The lieutenant turns on the landing. "One approaching platform."

"One is in sight."

"Copy that."

With his scuba wetsuit, Jackson is as quiet as a ghost. His feet seem to glide up the steel grating. Kath remains close behind him. On reaching the top of the stairs, he turns again, surveying the massive vacuum chamber from the side. Steel handrails lead to maintenance points on the pumps that draw out the air.

The lieutenant signals with his gloved hands. Two of the SEALs on his team remain at the top of the stairs. One of them has a sniper rifle. He lies prone beside a generator and sets up his tripod, pointing his rifle back at the other team. He's providing them with cover fire if needed.

Jackson and one other SEAL escort Kath to the edge of the vacuum chamber. Although they could creep across the steel grating, they don't. They keep to the shadows and move around the edge, coming up to the cracked door from behind. Neither looks at the chamber. The lieutenant has his rifle pointing at the gaping hole in the roof. Blue skies look down on them. The other soldier is looking at the far wall. Between the three of them, they're covering as much ground as possible. As Kath isn't armed, she grabs a fire extinguisher from the railing, more for comfort than anything else, and creeps toward the massive, bent door.

The door to the vacuum chamber is made from half-inch plate steel. There are two layers. The strength required to wrench this open would have been immense.

Kath peers into the darkness.

The inside of the chamber has been painted black, which doesn't help her eyes. With sunlight streaming in through the gaping hole in the roof, it's difficult to see anything in the shadows.

"What are you looking for, Kath?" she whispers, but she's not transmitting. "Why are you up here?"

The lieutenant was right. They're horribly exposed on the platform.

Kath puts the fire extinguisher down. She steps up on the railing and leans over, taking a good look inside the darkened chamber.

"Can Monroe hear us?" Kath asks, keying her radio.

"Yes," Nolan replies. "Everyone can hear you."

"Well, I think I've solved the mystery of how these things got out of the cleanroom."

"How?"

"They were never in there to start with," she says. "They hitched a ride on the *Aquarius* module."

"So that's where they came from? Not the lab?"

"I think so. There's a lot of jelly in there. It's coating the walls. This is the same stuff I saw in the hotel. It's clear. Almost entirely transparent. Ah, I can see the *Aquarius* sample return module. The heat shield has been ripped off. Something's been chewing on it. The rear of the craft still has its comms dish and fuel tanks, but there are lots of teeth marks. The inside of the chamber is scratched up."

"How could they hide on the *Aquarius*?" Nolan asks. "They're too big."

"There are a lot of places to hide on that probe," Kath replies. "They may not have even hatched yet. Remember, nothing starts out big—not even elephants. We're huge. And yet a fertilized human egg starts out no bigger than the period at the end of a sentence."

"We could have brought back hundreds of them," Nolan replies. "Thousands—without even realizing it."

"The heat of reentry may have started the process," Kath says. "Judging from the claw marks, they were small when they broke out. Much smaller than the ones we've seen. About the size of a rodent."

"And nobody saw them?"

"No one was looking for them. The recovery team stored the *Aquarius* in here as a precaution, but they would have never seen these things growing inside the chamber."

"And they broke out of here?" Nolan asks. "They busted through half-inch plate steel?"

"They bent it," Kath replies. "Looking down, I can see the latch mechanism on the edge of the door. It's open. There's a scissor lift pushed hard against the bottom corner. The front wheel has ridden up onto one of the crossbeams. Someone was trying to ram the door shut. There are bloodstains on the concrete directly below me, but the door has closed over them. Someone was trying to close the chamber after the initial attack. They must have opened it to check something and been ravaged by these things. They did their best. They tried to get it closed but it was too late."

She rummages around in her pack and pulls out a collection kit.

"There's jelly around the rim. I'm going to get a sample."

Kath climbs onto the upper rung of the railing and leans against the mangled steel. Her scuba boots don't have any grip. Her foot slips and her shins hit the rail.

"Ouch!"

She pushes off the outside of the chamber, reaching for the darkened interior, trying not to slip. If she falls, there's nothing between her and the concrete floor forty feet below.

Thick goo has been smeared around the bent door. Kath stretches, scooping some into a sample cup. She screws on the lid. She's so busy slipping it back into her pack she's only barely aware of the changing light around her.

A growl comes from the shadows.

Kath looks up.

Teeth glisten in the darkness inside the chamber. Beyond the thin glass on her face mask, just inches from her black, gloved hands there are thousands of needle-like teeth snarling at her.

Two words are spoken over the radio.

"Don't. Move."

DEATH IN THE APOCALYPSE

Andy's lungs feel as though they're being ripped apart cell by cell. He lies on his back in the mud at the bottom of the lake. Water swirls around him. Weeds reach up toward the fires burning on the surface. Bubbles slip from his lips. He tightens his grip on the broken cinderblock resting on his chest, weighing him down.

How long has he been down here?

Seconds feel like hours.

How long does he need to stay beneath the water?

How long can he last?

Andy looks around. The water is a blur. Reds and yellows roll over the surface, pushing the waves in patterns that leave no doubt about the scorching temperatures above. It's as though someone's unleashed a blow torch on the lake.

Every muscle in Andy's body screams for oxygen. He squeezes his eyes shut. Dots appear before his eyelids. He's stalling, trying to keep himself busy, wanting to distract himself from the fire raging in his veins, demanding oxygen. The urge to suck in a lungful of air is overwhelming. Reason is meaningless. He has to breathe. He has no choice.

Andy pushes the cinderblock off his chest, watching as it settles in the mud. Rather than swimming to the surface, he allows himself to float up. It's a compromise between what he wants and what he knows. Winters said they need to stay under for at least a minute—but from when? From when the first bombs fell or the last?

Andy's desperate. He can't fight himself any longer. His arms reach for the surface. He drags the satellite relay with him. Does the damn thing even work underwater? Does it even matter anymore? Heat radiates through his fingers. The top foot of the lake is as warm as a bath. The air feels like the inside of a blast furnace.

His helmet breaks the surface and he gasps, drawing in a deep breath. The air is hot and dry, scorching his mouth and throat.

Sparks dance around him. Burning embers fall from the sky. Flames rage along the shore.

The pier is gone. Charred stumps mark all that's left. Smoldering planks drift on the surface. Andy swims to one of the submerged support columns that once held the pier aloft. His clothing is sodden, making it difficult to float. His boots feel like lead weights pulling him back into the depths. The satellite array drags him down, but he can't let it go. What if it's still transmitting? What if it's not and he's clutching it like a child with a comfort blanket?

Flames rise from the water at various points around the lake. Whether that's because of burning oil or some exotic phosphorus compound, he's not sure. The effect though is unnerving. He could have emerged in one of those regions and set himself alight.

Andy wraps his legs around the pole and draws himself in toward the blackened column. He keeps his head low, with just his nose protruding above the muddy water. Occasionally, he dips beneath the waves to quench the burning debris falling on him.

The sky is black. It was a rich, vibrant blue just moments ago. The contrast is startling. Flames reach hundreds of feet into the air. The trees surrounding the lake are either splintered husks or they've fallen and are on fire. The houses that surround the park are nothing but rubble. The sun has descended on Earth, burning the world to a cinder.

Dark shapes appear beside him, bobbing in the water. Rangers call for each other. They band together and swim toward shore. Most of them lie on their backs, with only the outline of a face breaking the surface as they kick in toward land. Andy follows them.

No one is in a hurry to get out of the lake. Several of the Rangers sit in the shallows with just their shoulders emerging from the filthy water. Others stagger onshore and collapse.

Andy drags himself out of the lake. He crawls on his hands and knees, dragging the satellite array with him. The thick black antenna has melted, leaving the stalk looking wilted.

Hot ash drifts past, burning his hands, but he's beyond caring. He turns and collapses on the smoldering ground, lying on his back. Steam rises from his clothing as he lies in the ash. Tens of thousands of tiny burning embers swirl in the wind, lighting up the darkness high in the sky. Smoke chokes the air. Heat radiates on his face.

"We made it," a familiar voice says, touching his shoulder.

Captain Winters is drenched. Mud covers her face and hair. She slumps to the ground beside him.

"I—am—fucked," Andy manages. He coughs up blood. His throat feels as though it's closing up. His lungs hurt. His back hurts. His ribs hurt. Every breath is painful.

"But we're alive," Winters says.

"Either that or this is hell."

"You wish."

Bombs continue to fall. Explosions ripple outward, compressing the air, but the action is on the far side of the lake.

"What is happening?"

"Scorched Earth," Winters says. "Looks like they're going to carpet bomb these things into oblivion."

"What are we going to do?"

"Get the fuck out of here," Winters replies. She reaches up, touching his helmet. "Are you still transmitting?"

"I don't know."

She peels back a small strip of duct tape, exposing an LED on the side of his camera.

"You are! Well, I'll be damned."

Someone comes rushing through the water at the lake's edge. They're manic, kicking up waves even though they're still in waist-deep water. It's Mahatma. He has someone draped over his shoulder. He pumps his legs, lifting his knees high as he struggles to push through the mud and reeds. Black water splashes around him. Several of the Rangers rush back into the lake to help. They drag a body to shore. One of them begins CPR, clenching both hands together and driving hard into the man's sternum as he lies in the burning ash.

Mahatma checks for a pulse. He pushes his fingers hard into the side of the man's throat. Water drips from his clothing. Steam rises from those points where droplets land in fresh ash.

Andy doesn't recognize the soldier lying on the ground. He can't. One whole side of the man's face is burnt and blistered. His hair is matted with blood and mud. The black, charred skin on the man's right arm tells Andy all he needs to know. He's dead. If not from shock then from drowning. The Rangers, though, won't give up. Andy thought he was the last one to reach the lake but from the burns on his clothing, this guy must have been ten to fifteen feet behind him.

Captain Winters kneels beside the man's head. She's gentle, moving his hair from what's left of his brow and sweeping it to one side. Dead eyes stare up at the dark clouds. Embers glow, drifting on the wind. With two fingers, the captain closes his eyes and gets to her feet. The Ranger providing CPR comes to a halt. He's out of breath. He rocks back on his knees, letting his hands fall to the ash.

"I'm sorry," Winters says, bowing her head as she towers over the dead body on the shore of a burning lake.

Mahatma comes up beside her. Andy's expecting some discussion about what just happened or questions about what they should do with the body. Mahatma, though, has moved on. He's done all he could. It wasn't enough, but he's ready for more.

"Orders?"

Captain Winters looks around. "There's only one way we're getting out of this hell hole. Check to see who can walk and who needs help. If anyone's immobile, we're going to need to improvise a stretcher. I want to be ready to move in five."

"Understood."

Something falls into the far side of the lake. Something big. A wall of water races across the surface. The splash sends bits of debris flying. Spray hangs in the air. Everyone turns. It's as though a brick wall has collapsed into the water, but, apart from the burnt trees, there's nothing near the edge of the lake. The surrounding homes are all easily fifty feet back from the water's edge, allowing the park to wind around the lake.

The captain doesn't hesitate, "Weapons check!"

She pulls out her Beretta and pops out the magazine, tapping it on her clothing to drain any water. She opens the breech and blows down the barrel, mumbling, "That's going to have to do."

The other troops do likewise. Those that don't have a handgun grab burning branches or bricks. On seeing them improvise, Andy does likewise. He tosses the satellite array on the bank and grabs a branch, wielding it like a club.

A bow wave is kicked up by the creature swimming just below the surface of the lake. Its tail swings back and forth like an alligator propelling itself through the water.

"Semi-circle on me," Winters says. "We need to keep that thing in the water for as long as possible. We need to deny it access to the land where it can maneuver and turn invisible."

Mahatma says, "Aim for the head."

Ripples race across the surface of the lake. There's a small sandy beach beside the remains of the pier. A few of the Rangers came in through the shallows there. Like Andy, most of the soldiers took the more direct route to the bank, wading through the weeds, but the beach stretches for almost fifty yards. From the motion of the creature in the water, it's clear it's heading for the beach with its gentle slope.

The Rangers wade into the lake. Their boots stir up mud and

sand. Burning branches fall around them. Sparks swirl through the air. Captain Winters stands in the middle of the beach, blocking access to the shore. She holds her Beretta in an outstretched arm. Her left hand grips a spare clip, ready to swap it in when needed.

The submerged alien creature comes to a halt thirty feet from shore. Bubbles break the surface of the lake.

Andy whispers, "What is it waiting for?"

Winters says, "Us. It wants to draw us in closer. It's trying to assess our strength."

"Which is?"

"A lie. A bluff. We've got nothing."

A trail of bubbles runs in toward shore.

Winters calls out, "Don't fire on the creature. We're not going to penetrate that hide. We've got to hit soft spots. We need it to open its mouth!"

"Understood."

Mahatma steps forward with a smoldering branch, using it like a spear, holding the burning tip just above the water.

The alien emerges slowly. It's injured. It tries to turn invisible but it's only partially successful. Water drips from thin air, but the burnt sections of its body remain visible, outlining its flank and hindquarters. Teeth emerge from the water. Winters steps back, moving slowly through the shallows, drawing the creature toward her as the rest of the Rangers surround it on both sides.

Mahatma pokes the animal, jabbing his stick into its side. A massive claw swats the branch from his hand, snapping it in half. The alien lunges at him, opening its mouth wide. In unison, five Rangers open fire, aiming inside the creature's mouth. They unload four or five rounds each. The alien reacts, wheeling away from them and grimacing.

Andy's standing beside the captain. He raises a cinderblock over his helmet, holding it as high as possible. He steps forward, bringing it thundering down, throwing it at the creature's head.

The block smashes in mid-air, breaking as it hits the invisible, scaly hide of the animal. Fragments break off, falling into the water.

Andy loses his footing in the soft sand. He slips to one knee. He's close—too damn close. He can see that from the way the charred skin of the animal moves. Water laps around invisible legs. He shuffles backward, but it's too late. Teeth appear inches from his boots. Andy scrambles. Shots ring out.

Andy pushes back through the water, kicking and splashing. He's on his back, driving with his legs, reaching behind himself with his hands. Blood swirls around him. It takes a moment before he realizes the alien has grabbed one of the Rangers rushing to his aid. The creature swings the soldier like a rag doll, slamming him into the water on one side and then the other.

Winters and Mahatma hold their ground. Water laps at their boots. They've got handguns leveled at the creature but they don't fire. They're waiting. The alien drops the soldier and lunges at them, opening its mouth wide. They fire, emptying their magazines, hitting inside the animal's mouth and enraging it further. The two soldiers back up, allowing the creature to follow them onshore, slowly surrendering their ground. They fire whenever there's an opening. From either side, Rangers continue to throw rocks. Several of them club the animal, but without effect.

Andy scrambles to his feet. He's knocked onto the withered grass by one of the creature's paws. He tumbles, coming to a halt on the path winding around the lake. He watches in horror as the alien rushes Captain Winters. She fires but it's too late. Teeth clamp down on her outstretched arm. She tries to pull away. Bones break. Blood drips from the alien's mouth. The monster is toying with her, playing with her, refusing to let go. Mahatma stands beside her, firing at the creature. It shakes its head, severing her arm above the elbow. She screams. Blood sprays across the smoldering ash. The captain rolls across the ground in agony, clutching her arm, unable to stop the bleeding.

One of the Rangers pulls a belt from his waist. He wraps it around her upper arm and pulls it tight, but his back is to the massive creature. The alien bites, reaching over his head and shoulders. Blood sprays from its teeth, turning the ash on the ground a brilliant red.

Mahatma grabs Andy, dragging him by his collar.

"With me. Now!"

Andy doesn't want to turn his back on the melee, but he does. The two men scramble over a fallen wall into the yard of a house overlooking the lake.

Flames lick the sky.

Smoke rises from the ruins.

"What are we looking for?" Andy asks.

"Anything we can use as a weapon."

Rocks crunch beneath Andy's boots. Only one of the four walls of the home is still standing. The window frames have been blown out. Broken grass lies strewn over the driveway. The house is nothing more than a pile of rubble. Even if they could find something useful, it would take hours to dig it out.

"This is madness," Andy says. "Hopeless."

Mahatma ignores him, lifting a burning beam and rolling it away. A crushed refrigerator lies on its side.

"Great," Andy says, having given up looking. "We can choke it to death with curdled milk."

Mahatma snaps. "What do you want to do? Huh? Just fucking give up?"

"No. I just—there's nothing here."

"We have to do something."

Beyond the fallen wall, Rangers lie strewn in the ash. Bloodied bodies litter the ground. A soldier crawls toward the lake only to have an invisible paw pin him to the blackened grass. Claws extend, puncturing his body. Brilliant red blood runs down into the water.

It's futile. There are no solutions to be found in the rubble. There are no good ideas. Mahatma is keeping the two of them busy while they wait their turn to die.

"There!" Andy yells, pointing.

The crumpled remains of a garden shed lie beneath a collapsed brick wall. The handle of a lawnmower is visible. The plastic padding has melted.

"Yes. Yes. Yes."

Mahatma drags the lawnmower out, but he can't get it free.

Andy throws bricks to one side. He pulls on the metal roof of the shed, allowing Mahatma to wrestle the lawnmower out onto the grass.

The alien turns its attention to them. Footprints appear in the ash. One side of the creature has been scorched during the bombing, leaving that portion of its body visible. Claws appear as the monster stalks toward them, climbing the collapsed wall.

"Get it started," Mahatma yells as Andy pulls on the cord.

"I'm trying."

The blades turn, but the engine doesn't start. Andy adjusts the throttle, setting it midway, not wanting to flood the engine, and jerks at the starter cord. Again, the blades turn, but the engine doesn't fire. Andy jerks so hard at the cord the lawnmower is lifted off the ground by his effort. He reaches down over the engine, pumping the fuel line. Claws appear in front of him. Teeth loom beside his head.

Mahatma brings a clump of four concrete bricks crashing down onto the alien, distracting it. Andy pulls on the cord again. The engine splutters into life. He feathers the throttle, willing the lawnmower to accelerate from an idle without flooding it with fuel.

The alien turns on Mahatma, knocking him to the ground. He scoots backward through the ash, desperate to escape.

The engine roars at full throttle. Andy lowers the handle to the point it's almost touching the ground, raising the deck of the lawnmower on an angle and exposing its blades. He charges forward at the invisible creature, screaming at the top of his lungs.

Andy clips the creature just behind its front legs. The blades of the lawnmower catch the scales, ripping them off and causing blue blood to spray outward. The engine whines as the blades dig in. They slow as they carve chunks out of the alien. Andy pushes hard, rocking the lawnmower higher, wanting to get the blades to strike the body of the animal.

The alien swats the lawnmower, tearing it from his hands and sending it tumbling over the rubble. It comes to rest almost thirty feet away, lying on its back with its blades still madly spinning.

The creature backs away. Blood drips from its wounds. It circles on the driveway of the house, examining them from a safe distance.

Andy bends down, lifting a long hollow pole from the debris on the front lawn. At first, he thinks it's a drainpipe but it's made from quarter-inch steel. It's still warm to touch. A blob of molten black plastic hangs from one end. Flames crawl over the plastic as it drips to the driveway.

"This is it," he yells.

"What?" Mahatma asks, climbing onto the bricks beside him. "You're going to attack it with a basketball hoop?"

"Is that what this is?" Andy asks, looking back and seeing the round hoop behind him at the far end of the pole. "Oh."

"What are you going to do exactly?" Mahatma asks. The creature lines them up. It scratches at the ash, clearing it away so it can grip the concrete. It's wounded but angry.

"I don't know," Andy says. The basketball pole is too heavy and bulky to swing as a club. With no other options available to him, he says, "How about a bit of jousting? It's Saint Angry Andy Anderson against that *fucking* dragon!"

Mahatma steps behind him and grabs the pole, cinching it up under his armpit. "This is the dumbest *fucking* idea I've heard all day."

"Yep."

Andy's delirious. He's going to die. He accepts that. They've got nothing left. There's nothing else usable around them in the rubble, but it's human to try something, regardless of how desperate it may be.

Thousands of teeth glisten in the light of the burning buildings along the street. The alien charges toward them, pounding up the driveway. The two men charge, running toward the alien with all their might. Andy raises the pole, wanting to knock some of those goddamn teeth out of its mouth. The alien opens its jaw. The pole plunges deep into its throat, sinking down its neck. Andy and Mahatma yell at the top of their lungs, screaming as they drive the pole hard into the animal.

It chokes.

The alien swings its head, whipping it around with the pole protruding from its mouth. Mahatma tumbles over the bricks on the lawn. Andy tries to hang on. His body flails back and forth until the creature flicks its head. Suddenly, Andy's soaring through the air. He lands in the weeds at the edge of the lake and sinks into the mud. Water sprays out around him. It takes a few seconds, but he staggers to his feet, hearing the sound of gunfire.

The creature is on its back, writhing in agony and kicking with its legs. Mahatma has the captain's bloody Beretta in his hand. He lines up the pole and fires shots down through the hollow pipe. Bullets ricochet off the metal as they plunge deep inside the creature. Four, five, six shots and he stops to change the magazine. By now, the animal is lying still. It grimaces with each round Mahatma sends into its gut. He's yelling, calling out the names of the fallen Rangers with each shot. As the animal dies, its invisibility fades, leaving a sullen grey carcass on the driveway.

Andy climbs out of the lake. Every muscle in his body aches. Water drips from his clothing.

Winters is on her feet. She stabs at the ground with her boots, struggling to walk. Ash scatters around her. She locks her knees together, on the verge of collapsing. Fires burn in the distance. Blood drips from her severed arm.

"Easy, captain," Andy says, coming up and taking her good arm. He hauls it over his shoulder and helps her walk.

Mahatma joins them. His face is white with ash.

"What a fucking mess," the captain says.

They stagger to the intersection where the burned-out Humvee lies on its side. The wind swirls around them, picking up scolding hot ash and driving it at them like snow.

"Which way?" Andy asks.

"Doesn't matter," Winters says. She points with the bloody stub of her arm, which confuses him at first as if it doesn't matter why point? It's then he sees it. Bricks fall from a wall on the far side of the road. Claws grip the crumbling remains. Another alien climbs into sight. It's covered in dirt and ash. Iridescent blue blood drips from its mouth. Its tail whips up embers, sending dust soaring through the air behind it.

Andy comes to a halt.

"Fuck."

Mahatma falls to his knees in the ash. They've made it all of fifty yards before running into another one of these damn things. The shooting is probably what attracted it to them.

Captain Winters says, "It's been nice knowing you."

"Yeah. Well. Like you said. We were never getting out of here alive, were we?"

"Nope."

The creature steps down from the wall, turning toward them.

Thunder breaks overhead. The sound is deafening. As it is, Andy's ears are still ringing from earlier. Now, he can't hear anything.

Bullets tear through the creature, leaving streaks of blue as they punch out the other side of the animal. Every tenth round is a tracer, producing a yellow streak that looks like lightning. Hundreds of bullets fly down the street. A Bradley Fighting Vehicle comes through the smoke. Headlights illuminate them. The gunner continues firing, unloading on the creature until it's little more than a glowing blue pile of mush seeping out on the burned grass.

Troops run in toward them, grabbing them and hauling them back into the armored vehicle. Before Andy knows what's happening, he's sitting inside the rear of the Bradley. A medic pours clean water on his face, washing away the ash. Andy grabs the bottle from him and drinks. Plain old room-temperature water in an aging plastic bottle has never tasted quite like champagne before. Andy cannot get enough of it.

Water dribbles down his front.

Another medic shines a penlight in the eyes of Captain Winters. She bats his hand away, saying, "Well, you guys took your sweet ass time!"

THE LAB

Thousands of needle-like teeth glisten in the darkness. The vacuum chamber is shrouded in shadows, but the torn roof allows sunlight to reach the bent door.

Through her earpiece, Kath hears, "Stay still. Don't move. Don't speak. Don't even blink."

She doesn't recognize the voice. It's one of the SEALs from the back of the building. Kath holds her gaze. She wants to turn away, but she doesn't. Instinct tells her to run. Her mind lies to her, telling her she'll make it. She won't. Her legs shake. It takes all her resolve to fight the tremors consuming her feet.

Jackson says, "Two, do you have a shot?"

"Negative. I do not have a shot. Two on the move."

"One, I need cover on this platform. Go wide with the fifty."

"Copy that."

Out of the corner of her eye, Kath can see Jackson climbing up above the vast door to the chamber. His boots tread lightly on the reinforced steel beams welded onto the bulkhead to give it strength. He's slow, taking his time, making sure nothing bumps against the steel, giving him away.

Kath needs to pee. Her bladder feels as though it is about to burst.

Jackson is above and beyond her. He's pulled off his scuba gloves, allowing better grip. Besides, what's the point in following hazmat protocols if you're going to be torn apart by a monster? His soft, squishy diving slippers allow him to creep along in utter silence.

The crossbeams surrounding the chamber are designed to prevent it from collapsing when the air inside is reduced to a vacuum. They're not designed for parkour. They're barely an inch wide and lack handholds. To turn around and face her from the other direction, Jackson has to turn toward the chamber or he risks his rifle bumping the steel casing. His ass protrudes into the open space some forty feet above the concrete floor of the building. His bare fingertips grab at the slick, painted steel. To make things worse, he's only using one hand. He's got something hanging from his left hand but Kath can't make out what—not without taking her eyes off the teeth flexing in front of her.

Sweat beads on her forehead.

Good news: she no longer needs to pee.

Warm fluid runs down the inside of her suit.

Nolan is noticeably quiet. Kath has no doubt he wants to talk to her, but he must realize now's the time for the SEALs to shine. The last thing they need is a distraction.

Jackson shuffles with his feet, getting in position directly above her.

A whisper comes across the radio.

"Here's the plan. I'm going to distract the creature. Kath, you'll roll to the right. Don't step. Don't jump, just push off the rail and spin to your right. I need you to clear the path it's going to take to get to the platform. Once it's there, we'll unleash hell.

"As soon as we open fire, it's going to react. It's going to head for cover. It'll break for the stairs. I want a claymore down on the first landing. At point-blank range, it'll turn that thing into an interstellar hamburger patty."

A single word is spoken in reply.

"Copy."

For its part, the alien seems curious rather than aggressive. What is this monstrosity in front of it? Confusion demands caution. It must see that there are eyes behind the glass, but no face, just the sharp angles of molded plastic and rubber seals. Is this earthly creature even alive behind the layers of black Neoprene?

Animals on Earth use multiple senses to detect their prey. It may be that sight and some other sense have failed it, leaving it wondering about her. Hopefully, it's not like a shark, exploring with its teeth.

Kath swallows the lump rising in her throat.

"Two in position."

"Claymore set. Blast zone clear. One in position."

Jackson doesn't respond immediately. It seems he's human after all. After a few seconds, he says, "On my mark. Three... Two..."

Kath wants to ask, what mark? How the hell is he going to distract this thing?

"One."

Clouds of smoke swirl around her. A massive paw claws at the steel door. Kath rolls to the right, staying up on the railing and shuffling back beside the vacuum chamber. The creature climbs out of the chamber. Jackson is above it, unloading the fire extinguisher on it. White vapor swirls around the alien, ensuring it's visible in outline.

The SEALs open fire, but it's the fifty-caliber sniper rifle that shakes the building. The report from each shot is deafening, echoing around her. Whereas the regular rifles fire rapidly, there's a second or two between the thunder unleashed by the snipers. Blue marks appear where bullets slam into the creature. The fifty-caliber bullets cut clear through the animal, leaving horrendous exit wounds. Flesh explodes, spraying the outside of the chamber an iridescent blue.

The alien leaps to the steel grating on the platform, which brings it in sight of the second sniper. More shots ring out like cannons being fired. Deep gashes crisscross the animal's back. It's wounded but still lethal. The alien darts for the stairs, seeking cover. Its tail whips across the deck, missing Kath's legs as she balances on the railing.

The creature is fast, disappearing down the broad, open metal staircase in barely a heartbeat. It triggers the claymore and the building shakes under an almighty *boom!* Kath slips from the railing, falling to the steel grating. Jackson jumps down, landing beside her.

Blue blood erupts from the landing, spraying across the concrete on the lower floor. Bits of severed flesh hang from the metal rails. The body of the creature slumps, sliding down to the ground.

"Are you okay?" Jackson asks, squeezing her shoulders and arms, working his way down her body. It's only then Kath realizes how much of the splatter is sticking to her dive suit. Thick bits of blue sinew lie draped over her shoulders.

"I'm fine," she says as Nolan comes rushing up the stairs.

Kath pulls a sample container from her front pack and squishes the blue goo inside.

"Really?" Nolan says. "That's what you got out of this? Another goddamn sample?"

"Science," she says, trying to hide the quiver in her voice. "It's all about the data."

Her hands are trembling. She's distracting herself, trying to ignore how close she came to dying. Nolan leads her down the stairs. Their feet stick in the blue goo coating the metal. At the bottom, there's a chemical shower. Standing beneath it, Kath pulls on a large steel ring and is doused with water. It's as though someone's turned a fire hose on her. Within a second, she's washed clean. Nolan does likewise, but he has far fewer alien strands draped over him.

"We need to keep moving," Jackson says, pointing at the roof. Sheet metal flexes thirty feet above them, revealing a creature approaching from outside. Although there are attack helicopters out there, this thing must have come from the north, avoiding the red fire suppression fluid in the south.

Claws appear where roof sheets have been torn open. Another

creature is approaching from the west, having scaled the outside wall.

Both teams meet in front of the fire door leading to the internal, concrete stairs that wind down to the basement.

Jackson talks to his troops. "I want a chokepoint. Set the remaining claymores on the various approaches to this door."

"Yes, sir."

Kath, though, finds her mind running at a million miles an hour. Water drips from her wetsuit. She wants to get into that lab and yet rushing seems like a mistake. Another alien climbs the outside of the building. Claws punch through the sheet metal, marking how it's moving up toward the opening. She watches, wanting to see it round the torn edge of the roof. As best she can tell, it holds still by the opening.

"How many of them are there?" she asks, putting her hand out and stopping Jackson before he steps into the stairwell.

"How many what?" he asks, propping the door open with his foot.

"Claymores and aliens?"

"Three claymores and, I don't know, four of five of those things. Why?"

She points. "They're watching us. Look at how they're waiting. They're not charging in here."

"Doesn't matter," he says. "We need to get down to the basement while we still can."

"They can see it," she says, absentmindedly. "The danger."

"Kath," Nolan says, taking her by her forearm and leading her to the stairs.

Kath, though, won't be deterred. She pulls away and addresses Jackson. "Set one charge on each landing."

"No," Jackson says. "That's madness. We can't let them in the stairwell. Once they get in there, it's game over for us. We lose all ability to maneuver in a confined space."

Nolan says, "Kath, we've only got three claymores. We need to use them to maximum effect."

"We need a kill zone," Jackson says. "We've got to take out as many of those damn things as we can."

"I don't want to kill them," Kath replies with a chill in her voice.

"What?" Nolan says, taken back by her shift in attitude.

She rests her hand on the steel frame surrounding the door, looking back at the claws that have punched through the steel frame of the building, noting how the alien is waiting on the outside. From what she can determine from the placement of its claws, it can see over the lip of the wreckage. It must be looking at the blue-blood-soaked landing.

"They're intelligent," she says.

"So?" Nolan says.

"I want to teach them."

"Teach them what?" Jackson asks, cocking his head sideways.

"That to follow us means pain and suffering."

Neither man understands, not at first. Kath points. "They've seen what happened up there. We need them to realize that following us into the stairwell means death. Put one claymore on each landing and they'll figure it out."

"You," Jackson says, shaking his head and struggling not to laugh. "You scare me more than they do."

Jackson turns to Nolan, who shrugs, saying, "Hey, I'm just glad she's on our side."

"All right, you heard the lady," Jackson calls out. "One charge on each landing. Let's teach these *fuckers* a lesson they won't forget."

They jog down the stairs.

The trailing soldiers set up tripwires and claymores on each concrete landing.

The basement is comprised of four rooms divided by a central corridor. The lights are on. Cables run along conduits on the ceiling. Machinery hums.

"What the hell is that?" Nolan asks, pointing at a steel door at the far end of the corridor.

"Ah, an emergency exit?" Kath says, reading the sign on the door. She looks at him as though he's mad.

"I can read," Nolan replies. He's annoyed, but not at her. "I know what it is. What I want to know is why wasn't it on the goddamn building plans? It would have been a lot easier to come in through there!"

He turns to Jackson. "Get on the radio and figure out where that door leads. If it takes us directly outside, we may have a viable alternative to fighting our way out."

"Yes sir."

The SEALs check the storeroom, the meeting room and the break room. They're all empty. They drag a couple of tables into the corridor, allowing the snipers to lie prone on them. They set up the fifty-caliber rifles on tripods, pointing them at the fire door leading to the internal stairs. Three of the SEALs lie beneath the tables on the concrete with their rifles leveled at the door. The rest of the SEALs stand back, ready to provide support. Backpacks are stacked to one side. Spare magazines are placed within reach. They're ready for one helluva fight.

An explosion rocks the building. Smoke blurs the view through the thin glass panel in the fire door. Dust billows within the stairwell. The snipers peer down their sights. Fingers rest beside the trigger guards, ready to slip in and squeeze the thin curved metal when needed.

Jackson mutters, "One."

Less than twenty seconds later, there's another earth-shattering explosion. The SEALs ready themselves, waiting for the third explosion. After that, it's going to get messy. Kath, though, isn't worried. She knows there won't be a third explosion. The others may not believe it, but she's seen enough of these creatures to understand their predatory behavior. They prefer to lie in ambush rather than chase their prey. Suffering losses is not in their nature. They're not like ants, bees or wasps which are willing to sacrifice themselves for the hive. To Kath's mind, the closest analog on Earth would be a jaguar. These things hide in the shadows. They want a clean kill without the possibility of injury.

Kath heads for the lab. Large signs adorn the walls outside the anteroom airlock, providing clear instructions on the process of ingress. There's a warning about federal laws and unauthorized entry along with a bunch of surveillance cameras, but there's no breach.

"Nothing got out of here," Nolan says, confirming her thoughts.

She peers in through the double-glazed reinforced glass windows in the sliding door. The anteroom is full of positive-pressure suits hanging on racks. Three-foot-high yellow arrows on one wall all point in the same direction, indicating this room is not for egress. She leans back, looking further down the corridor, spotting the egress door. It too is intact. There was no escape from the cleanroom. The contamination they've seen is from the space probe itself, of that Kath is sure.

"It's locked," Kath says, seeing a distinct black keycard reader on the wall.

Nolan pulls a jack out of his bag.

"What are you going to do? Change a tire?"

From behind his full-face mask, Nolan glares at her. He holds the jack sideways and wedges the blades into the gap between the doors, pushing the rubberized seals apart. A few cranks of the handle and the door starts to open.

"Nice," Kath says as a gap widens. He keeps going until it's wide enough for them to slip through wearing their scuba gear. As it is, Kath still catches her air tank on the edge of the door.

Once they're inside the anteroom, Nolan says, "Look for something we can use to wedge this door open and I'll shift the jack to the far door."

Kath says, "We could just knock."

"What?" Nolan says, looking at her as though she's mad.

"Aliens wouldn't knock, right? If we knock, they might let us in."

"There's someone in there?" Nolan asks, joining her by the window in the far door.

"I think so."

Kath raps her knuckles on the glass. It takes a few seconds, but a bleary-eyed scientist in a pressure suit comes up to the window. He speaks through an intercom on the wall. His voice is raspy and broken.

"You made it."

"Yes. Can you let us in?" Kath asks.

"No," he says, shaking his head at her misunderstanding. "*Who* made it?"

"Who?" Nolan asks, surprised by the notion, but Kath intuitively grasps what must have happened. After they lost communication with the outside world, the team must have drawn straws to see who would stay and who would go and seek help. They probably loaded up all the relevant information they had on a bunch of hard drives, wanting to get their data out.

"No one," she says from behind her mask.

The man in the inflated suit on the other side of the glass hangs his head. Tears land on the inside of his clear plastic visor. He straightens.

"Why are you here?" he asks. "You're not here for me, are you?"

"No," Kath says, being brutally honest. "We need your data."

"Of course. Of course."

"Don't worry. We'll get you out of there," Nolan says, being more aware than her of the need for empathy.

"Oh, yeah," Kath says, feeling bad at her sterile approach.

"You need to suit up," he says. "Close the outer door, get into a suit, and I'll flush the lock."

Kath already has her face mask off. The prospect of shedding the heavy steel air tank on her back was enough motivation for her. Nolan gets one of the SEALs in the hallway to remove the jack and the outer door shuts. Peeling off Neoprene scuba suits with barely any fingers is arduous. Kath sits on one bench. Nolan sits opposite her on another.

"Just like old times, huh?" he says with red marks running across his face, highlighting where the scuba mask seals sat moments ago. His hair is sweaty and matted.

"At least we're not going to freeze to death in there," Kath says, referring to their time on the Orion spacecraft.

"Well, this is another first. I've never gone into a cleanroom before."

"You're already in one," Kath says.

"What do you mean?"

"This *is* a cleanroom," she says, pointing at the floor. "It's just not as clean as the next room."

"Ah."

The positive-pressure suits are lightweight. A zip extends from the upper left leg to the top of the right shoulder, allowing them to climb in and enclose themselves within the blue plastic suits.

"I'm not sure how this is supposed to work," Nolan says as the hood and visor built into the suit flop around on his head, leaving him looking at his feet.

"You need to hook up to an air line on the roof," Kath says, handing one to him. She shows him how to plug it into the valve on his waistband. Immediately, his suit inflates. The hood rises above his head, being held aloft by the pressure inside.

The scientist within the cleanroom watches them through the glass in the door. He activates a control panel and a bright UV light washes over them.

"Just waiting on the PPM to equalize."

"PPM?" Nolan asks.

"Parts per million," Kath says.

"This is an ISO class 1 room," the scientist says, pointing at the floor of his room. "We filter the air to ensure nothing over a micron makes it inside."

Nolan says, "So that's a very clean cleanroom, huh?"

"Cleaner than anywhere else on the planet," Kath says.

"If you need to bring anything in here, you'll need to flush it or bag it," the scientist says, pointing at a workstation on the wall.

388

"Of course," Kath says. Nolan hands her the laptop. She sits at the workstation and begins cleaning it. A brilliant blue/ultraviolet light shines on the table, sterilizing any equipment placed there. Kath runs a vacuum hose with a bristled end over the laptop, working it around the screen, over each row of keys on the keyboard, over the mousepad and across the various ports. She repeats the process with the satellite dish.

Nolan has his back to the door so the scientist inside the lab can't see his face. He mouths the word, "Really?" It seems he's questioning the need for cleaning their equipment in the middle of an alien invasion. It's a fair point. Given they're one claymore explosion away from being overrun, it does seem tedious, but Kath understands. Science is about eliminating noise. It's about getting clean, clear data and there's nowhere that's more apparent than in a cleanroom. Cross-contamination could lead to confusion and incorrect conclusions.

She nods, bagging the samples she's collected on the way to the lab. It's now a bunch of sample containers inside a plastic bag that is inside yet another, more sturdy plastic bag.

"Okay, we're good to go."

"Flushing the lock and opening the door," the scientist says.

The door opens and they step through an air curtain. An invisible wall of air hits their suits. It comes from the floor, the ceiling and the walls around the inner door, but it's no more than half an inch in width, pushing back toward the anteroom, away from the lab.

Nolan looks up, unsure if he should proceed.

"It's an air shower," Kath says. "One last process to protect the cleanroom."

"Okay."

"And now we switch air lines," she says, releasing her line and watching as it retracts into the anteroom. The scientist hands her a new line coming down from the ceiling. The tube is shaped like a slinky, giving them the flexibility to move around the room. There are several other air line stations, allowing scientists to switch as needed.

"Dr. MacKenzie," the scientist says, offering to shake her hand even though her hands are full. Fame has at least some benefits. She smiles warmly, putting the laptop, satellite dish and sample bags on a nearby table.

"And you're?"

"Dr. James Mahoney—lead investigator on the astrobiology research team here at JSC."

They shake rubbery gloves, only Kath doesn't have fingers extending to the end of her tips so the soft, squishy ends are easily compressed.

"And this is Brigadier General Nolan Landis," she says.

"Yes. Of course."

"Please, call me Nolan."

"And Kath."

"And James."

"What have you learned?" Kath asks, setting up her laptop and powering it on. Nolan unfolds the satellite dish and positions it on the desk.

"Will that even work?" James asks, pointing at the dish. "Down here?"

"Military-grade," Nolan says. "This will work under a hundred feet of water."

"What have you discovered?" Kath asks, repeating her question. "What data do you have from the original sample?"

"Oh, lots," he says, bringing over a portable hard drive. "It's fascinating. Revolutionary. It's a bioarete—a perfect biological specimen. It uses polychromatic groups that overlap with terrestrial DNA."

"You're going to have to explain that," Kath says, plugging in his portable hard drive.

"There are over five hundred amino acids. Life on Earth uses only twenty-two, while DNA has just four bases."

"Right," Kath says. "So different combinations of the four bases form the instructions to make proteins out of these twenty-two acids."

"Yes. And we call that grouping monochromatic. It's life in black and white. The organic material from *Anduru* has multiple groupings. Some are similar to ours. Most aren't, but they're all consistent with each other."

"Polychromatic," Kath says. "Lots of colors."

"Yes. It's an analogy. The groups are like complementary shades on a color wheel."

"Ah," she says. "I get it. Not every color goes together, but those that do need to be in harmony with each other."

"Exactly," he points at a series of folders on the portable hard drive. "This is all the raw data. There are also a bunch of subfolders with my work in them. You can have it all."

"Thank you," Kath says, connecting to a remote file server on the internet and starting the upload. "How many color groups did you detect?"

"Seventeen," James says. "No group has more than thirty acids. There's some overlap, with bases like adenine and guanine being shared by ten of the groups—including ours. The phosphate and sugar groups used to form nucleotides differ slightly, but not by much."

"What do you make of these colored groups?" Kath asks, barely understanding the concept but curious about the implications.

"Johan thought they reflected different lifeforms on different planets. Several of them are close to ours."

"Huh?" Kath says, stunned by the realization they're indirectly gaining insights into life on multiple planets throughout the galaxy.

Nolan says, "What does all this mean in plain English?"

Kath says, "These things have infected at least seventeen other planets—probably far more. They carry with them the blueprints from these different worlds."

"Seventeen different types of life!" James says, throwing his arms wide. "And across all of them, there are the same basic patterns. They may differ in chemistry, but there's the same basic scaffolding. Genetic

391

information is stored in either pairs or triplicates. Oh, and the start/stop codons are remarkably similar."

"You can distinguish individual genes?" Kath asks, surprised by the notion. "I didn't think that would be possible."

"Oh, yes," James says. His eyes light up. "It's a case of pattern matching. My work has identified over five hundred thousand genes. We have no idea what they do, but their length and placement is duplicated across the various color groups."

"That's astonishing," Kath says. "So this stuff is like a Swiss Army Knife."

"Yes."

"And half a million genes? That's a lot?" Nolan asks.

"Humans have twenty-five thousand," Kath says.

"Genes are deceptive," James says. "Tomatoes have almost thirty-two thousand. Crazy, huh? No heart. No brain. No nervous system. And yet they have more genes than us—seven thousand more!"

"Life as we know it is an illusion," Kath says, watching as the upload progress passes 10%. "Here on Earth, there is only one type of life—DNA. Oh, we see lions and crocodiles, peacocks and cockroaches, but all that's a mirage. We're judging a book by its cover. Zoom in and all life has roughly the same cells, the same DNA structures and often the same genes. Pick a gene at random from an elephant and there's a 99% chance you'll find the same gene in a mouse! On the surface, it seems preposterous, but the diversity we see between animals is smoke and mirrors. At a cellular level, they're often indistinguishable."

"But here," James says. "Here we get to see seventeen ecosystems all at once."

"Wait a minute," Nolan says. "What about those things out there? Are they multi-colored or whatever? I mean, how are they? None of this should be possible."

Kath hands James her sample bag, saying, "Can you sequence these while we're uploading your data?"

"Sure," he says. "The data gathering process is quite quick. It's the analysis that takes time."

He leads them over to an isolation chamber on the side of the lab. It's a cleanroom within a cleanroom. Three pairs of gloves reach into a transparent box the size of a chest freezer. Beyond the Perspex screen, there are a bunch of pipettes, an autoclave, a gene sequencer and several devices Kath doesn't recognize. James opens the side panel and inserts the sample bag into a mini-airlock. He has to slip his already gloved hands into the gloves on the box to retrieve the bag from the other side.

"Would you like to assist?" he asks.

"I'd love to," Kath says, sitting next to him and slipping her hands into another pair of gloves protruding from the Perspex front panel. She can feel air circulating inside, being drawn down into the sterilizing unit beneath the chamber.

James extracts each of the samples with the care of someone disabling a bomb. He labels each pipette sample, handing them off to Kath who puts them into one of the sequencers.

"Your talents are wasted in astronomy," he says, joking with her.

"Give me a supernova over aliens any day," she says. "Less mess."

"Okay, I've heard from Jackson," Nolan says, pressing his hand to his earpiece and scrunching his suit up against the side of his head for a moment. "That fire door leads to an external stairwell that emerges behind the main building. The Apache attack helicopters are watching those stairs. We should be good to exit that way."

Kath says, "Sure beats tangling with those creatures again."

"I—I don't understand. There was no breach," James says. He sounds nervous. "I don't know how they got out. We heard screams—explosions."

"It was the *Aquarius* probe," Kath says. "Some of the viable material from the artifact hitched a ride on it."

"Fertile eggs?"

"I guess so," Kath says, hating her use of the word *guess*. Guesses are for sports commentators, not scientists.

"And they grew from there?"

"Heat. Atmosphere. Moisture in the air," Kath says. "I don't know what the catalyst was, but all they needed was exposure to the conditions on Earth."

James is quiet, nodding within the confines of his positive-pressure suit. He fiddles with the samples in the isolation chamber, making sure everything is tidy and ordered. He's distracting himself. Kath can spot OCD a light-year away.

"Has there been much damage?" he asks as the first results come back from the gene sequencers. Several screens mounted on the bank of computer servers are suddenly flooded with information. Text scrolls faster than anyone could ever read, but Kath pauses. This is the first time James has asked about the outside world.

"They've run riot," Nolan says, which is an understatement.

"They," James says, lingering on that one word. He stops himself from going further. It seems he's trapped by a question he can't or won't articulate. Kath can't imagine the doubts running through his head. If she'd been down here for days, the isolation would have driven her mad. She doubts she would have had his staying power. It's the uncertainty that would have got to her. Waiting for two days is easy. Waiting with no end in sight is torture. Kath would have buckled. Curiosity would have driven her mad. She would have gone up for a look and been killed along with the others. It took courage for James to keep going with his research while waiting for a rescue that might have never come. Now, everything has changed. A rescue party has arrived. Thousands of questions must be flooding his mind and yet he halts on that one word *they*.

They personifies the aliens. *They* aren't microbes. He must sense the enormity of the situation above, but he remains professional. "And our data. You think it will help?"

"It's bad," Kath says, ignoring his comment as to her the answer is obvious. She wants to focus on his unspoken question. She feels she needs to tell him about all that's happened but it's impossible to compress the sheer magnitude of the devastation into just a few sentences. At the least, she owes him clarity. He lives in Houston—lived in Houston. Given his age, he probably has family scattered throughout the city. Kath can see it in his eyes. He's burying his worry beneath his work. He understands the importance of what he's doing for humanity as a whole—and that takes precedence over him as an individual.

"We're evacuating the city," she says, picking her words with care, trying to give him hope. James has been down here for almost three days. He must have suspected the worst. He would have had access to a bathroom and water in the egress room, but no food. Kath struggles to describe all she's been through.

"We..."

Nolan is succinct. "We can fight monsters. We can't fight microbes. Bullets and bombs aren't going to win this war."

"Of course," James says, getting up from the isolation chamber and walking over to a bank of fifteen computer servers stacked on top of each other. He folds out a keyboard and mouse, and starts examining the results of her samples on the two main monitors. Kath and Nolan watch over his shoulder, but to them it's gibberish. James flicks between screens, looking at a variety of graphs and stops suddenly. He double-checks the details, saying, "Wait! This can't be right."

"What is it?"

"It's the same?"

"As what?"

"As my samples."

"Hang on?" Kath says. "All of them?"

"Yes."

"Check the timestamp on the sequences," she says, assuming there's been a mistake. "Mine should all be from today, but they'll be slightly different, even if only by seconds."

"Oh, these are different samples, all right," James says, tapping the screen. "This one is the moss. This is the grass—although it's not our grass as under a microscope the cells are shaped like hexagons. This is the red fungi-like growth. That's the purple gunk. This is the blue organic material. And that's the transparent goo."

Nolan says, "That blue stuff is entrails or something. We got it off one of the creatures we killed upstairs."

"The goo is from a nest," Kath says.

"And the red foam?"

"From the mouth of a dead man," Kath says.

"And the funky stuff with bits of shell?"

"Some kind of crab," Nolan says.

James shakes his head. "Well, at a genetic level, they're all the same as my original sample."

"Where are your samples?" Kath asks, feeling a little worried at the thought of what happened to the original biological material.

James points at a large cabinet with a transparent door. Frost lines the edge of the glass. A red temperature gauge at the bottom of the fridge reads -196 F.

"I used liquid nitrogen to refreeze the samples. This is the same temperature and process we use to store human eggs to keep them viable. The samples need to be cold enough to prevent cellular replication but not so cold as to destroy their cell contents."

He rocks back in his chair, pointing at the screen. "But this? I would not have predicted this."

Nolan asks, "And in English, what does *this* mean?"

Kath says, "Ah, the plain English translation of this would be—I have no idea—this makes *no* sense!"

James laughs, nodding within his pressure suit. "Yep."

He taps away at the keyboard, entering a series of commands. "I'm going to run a Matlab plot to overlay all the results and remove any terrestrial fragments. We're dealing with protein strands that reach into the hundreds of billions of atoms so this is the quickest way to find exceptions."

As he types, his commands are highlighted in different colors. The computer predicts commands from the context, with just a few letters being typed, allowing him to hit *tab* to complete them and add parameters. The effect is he's able to rattle through dozens of commands in just a few seconds, adding data from various files and setting the plot variables.

"Okay," he says, clicking on the *run* button.

The computer brings up a series of graphs that look like the Himalayas.

"And if we zero the baseline, we should see genetic variations as spikes."

He clicks a few buttons and a straight line runs across the middle of the screen. The graph legend shows ten data sets, including some from his previous runs.

"There's no variation at all," he says.

Kath leans forward with her hands on her knees, taking a good look at the screen as she mumbles, "Unexpected results are the best kind of results."

"Yes, yes," James says. "But what does it mean?"

"You're the astrobiologist," she says, examining the graph. There's not much to see, but her eyes catch the x and y-axis markings and the legend. Everything looks correct to her—not that she would necessarily know otherwise.

James zooms in on a section of the line. It's slightly bumpy when viewed up close, with some of the colored lines departing slightly from being dead flat.

"Okay, that's to be expected," he says, tapping the screen. "There are always going to be some transcription errors from mutations and things like cosmic rays, but this is minor random variations in individual amino acids, not at the gene level."

"Is that good or bad?" Nolan asks.

"There are slight genetic differences between all of us," James says, "but we're all still the same. We're still *Homo sapiens*. These variations are similar. They're slight changes, but there's no material difference—not at the macro scale."

"Great," Nolan says, clapping his gloved hands together. "So not good or bad."

Kath has gone quiet. She knows they're in need of a paradigm shift. They're thinking about this like Earthlings. For all the scientific advances of the past hundred years, humanity has only ever had one ecosystem to consider. Just because something doesn't make sense to her and James doesn't mean it doesn't make sense at all. Perhaps it makes sense in some other context.

"Everything's the same," Nolan says, squinting as he looks at the graph. He may not have said anything profound, but he's trying to remain engaged. He might be an Air Force general and completely out of his depth when it comes to astrobiology, but he's pushing himself to reason through the problem. Stating the obvious is his way of trying to stimulate thinking. Kath appreciates his interest. For her, these results are baffling.

James checks parameters that make no sense to her. Kath watches his screen, hoping something will click in her mind.

"Maybe we're thinking about this all wrong," Nolan says. "Maybe it's the same because that's the way this stuff works. You said it yourself—all of life on Earth is just DNA. We even share the same genes as—what? Tomatoes and mice, right?"

James holds his hand up, raising his fingers slightly as he looks at a screen full of chaotic text. Nolan's distracting him. Kath raises a finger to her lips, wanting Nolan to give them some time. James leans forward, peering through both his glasses and the thin plastic dome of his suit. There are no words or paragraphs on the screen. Capital letters run in pairs, forming columns. As he scrolls, it's apparent he's visually comparing two sets with each other.

"An illusion, that's what you called it, right?" Nolan says, oblivious to the way he's breaking their concentration. "A mirage that hides similarities. Like a mouse and an elephant having the same genes."

"Nolan!" Kath says, wanting him to be quiet. He's right, though. She can't fault him for echoing her own logic back at her. As annoying as he may be, he's got a way of centering her rationale. When she goes off down a rabbit hole, he's always there dragging her back to the basics. Kath smiles as the realization hits.

She laughs, lightening up as she says, "Sometimes we get too close to the problem."

"Can't see the forest for all the goddamn trees," James says, pushing his seat away from the table and turning to look at Nolan. "Say that again. The last thing you said. What were you were thinking exactly?"

"Ah," Nolan says, suddenly unsure of himself. "We share genes. Maybe they do too."

"It's more than having the same genes," James says. "It's the exact same genetic code across vastly different organisms—with no differences at all."

Kath laughs, pointing at Nolan. "But he's right. We're looking at the magician's trick. We're seeing the rabbit being pulled out of a hat and scratching our heads."

James shakes his head, not quite agreeing. "But we get to look behind the curtain. We get to see the setup of this particular magic trick."

"And we need to accept what we see," Kath says. "Think about how many genes you've identified—far more than anything we've ever seen on Earth."

James nods. "Okay. So how does it work?"

"How do we work?" Kath asks, holding out her arms and displaying her own body as an example. "We have a single genetic package that results in eyes, arms, legs, livers, whatever. Each organ is different even though the code is the same."

"Huh?" James says, nodding. He likes the comparison. "Okay. A single strand of hair contains the blueprint for the entire body. It's redundant, but that's just the way life on Earth evolved."

Kath says. "Yes. The same DNA that makes toenails can be used to make a brain cell even though they're radically different."

"Is that what we're seeing here?" James asks. "One genetic package that can be activated in different ways, resulting in what we would think of as different species?"

Kath says. "I mean, it's possible, I guess. It's an idea worth exploring. It's not what I would have expected."

James laughs. "Since when are expectations good science?"

"Exactly. And this changes everything," Kath says. "It answers a question I've had since we were in orbit."

That gets Nolan's attention. "What?"

"How they can be so effective at spreading between star systems. This explains how they can dominate a planet. Trees drop thousands of seeds for every sapling that grows. In the same way, they only need one seed to germinate and the whole system unfolds."

"So just one of those creatures or one bit of moss?"

"Yes."

James says, "They must be like a caterpillar morphing into a butterfly."

"There has to be a lifecycle," Kath says. "First, they overrun the local ecosystem. Then they yeet themselves back into space, probably in multiple stages and over an excessive period of time as I can't imagine that is quick or easy."

Nolan says, "Then they take aim at the next planet."

"Yep. We need to send these results out as well," Kath says, sitting in front of her computer and typing an email. "We need to give our scientists a working hypothesis to test."

"I like it," James says, handing her a USB stick with the results. "And the first upload is complete."

Nolan is impatient. Kath can tell that from the way he paces behind her. It takes her a few minutes to finish composing her email with James. She attaches the additional files and hits *send*. As they're raw text they upload quickly.

"Okay," Nolan says, clasping his gloved hands together. "So we know what they are. We know how they operate. How do we win this war?"

"I think we just did," James says. "Now, it's just a matter of time."

"I don't understand."

"This isn't about us anymore," Kath says, pointing at her computer screen. "It's about them out there. It's about what they can figure out."

"They who?" Nolan asks.

"Everyone. Anyone. I've told my team to make this available online to scientists all around the world. None of us is as smart as all of us working together."

James says, "No Lone Ranger riding in to save the day, huh?"

"No. And I think it's quite fitting," Kath says. "We've won with the click of a mouse button. There's no Will Smith blowing up the mothership. No Jeff Goldblum chewing on a cigar."

"No fat lady singing," James says.

Kath enjoys the banter, adding, "No Chris Pratt coming in with guns blazing to save the day."

"Hey," Nolan says, faking indignation. "Some of us like shooting guns and blowing up motherships. Personally, I enjoyed seeing Tom Cruise and Emily Blunt doing parkour in mech-suits."

"Not this time," James says.

"This time it's a bunch of scientists poring over the data," Kath says.

"Hundreds of thousands of scientists," James says.

"So that's it?" Nolan asks.

"That's it," Kath says. "Now we let science go to work."

"Well, I want to blow something up."

"If it'll make you feel better," Kath says, laughing. "But the real battle has just been won."

"You seem pretty confident about that."

401

"I am," she says. "As a species, we've never been the strongest or fastest. We've succeeded because we work together."

James says, "As long as the army keeps those things bottled up, our scientists will find a weakness."

A low rumble shakes the lab. Lights swing above them.

"Is that anything we should be worried about?" Kath asks, realizing this is different from the bone-shaking explosions of the claymores in the stairwell. If anything, this feels violent but the tremor isn't on top of them. The motion is dull, bordering on what she feels at home when an earthquake rocks LA.

Nolan wanders away from them. He hears her, but he raises his hand, wanting a moment. After a quick chat over the radio, he returns to them.

"That was a missile strike," he says. "Jacinta brought the water bomber in for another pass. That's allowed our Apaches to clear out the area."

"Is it safe outside?" James asks.

Nolan says, "For now." He's distracted. He's holding two conversations at once. He looks at Kath and says, "Okay. Jackson is ready to take us out the rear of the building. If there's anything you need to take with you, now's the time to grab it. Once we're on the surface, the Apaches will escort us back to *The Santiago Apostol*. From there, we'll head out to join the fleet gathering offshore and watch the fireworks as Houston goes up in flames."

Kath folds up her laptop, saying, "See, you still get to blow shit up."

Nolan grins.

"And these samples?" James asks.

"Burn them," Nolan says.

For a moment, Kath hesitates. Perhaps they should keep some of the organic material for future study. This is the first time humanity has seen the evolutionary result of life beyond Earth. She wants to say, '*Wait.*' She wants to find some compelling reason to keep just a few vials, but then she remembers how humanity squandered the opportunity to destroy smallpox. Both Russia and the US retained samples—samples that got lost and misplaced. It's good luck, not good management that has saved millions of lives. And now it's too late. No one will ever destroy their stocks. Uncertainty has crippled what should have been a clear-cut decision. She looks at James. He doesn't say anything but she's sure he can read her mind. He nods. He too seems to realize this is a pivotal moment. They have a unique opportunity to end this before anyone objects. It's better this way. There's no squabbling between countries, no conflicts of interest, no ambiguity. Kath tightens her lips.

"What temperature can you get out of that autoclave?" she asks.

"Six hundred degrees," James says, transferring samples from the freezer into the kiln-like device. Kath does the same with the samples in the isolation chamber, moving them into the smaller autoclave within the miniature lab. She smiles as the inside of the autoclave glows through a glass panel in the door. Golden yellows and flickers of red mark the demise of these extraterrestrial organisms.

"Done," James says.

Nolan bundles the hard drives and laptops into a bag and walks over to the egress airlock. James stands beside the door, waiting for Kath and Nolan to lead the way through the air curtain. He turns off the lights as they leave.

The End

EPILOGUE

"I'm not drunk," Kath says, slurring her words.

"Kath!" Jacinta says, taking her arm and leading her to one side within the White House. "What are you doing? You're about to go on stage."

"No one will know," Kath says, pulling a small plastic case out of her purse and shaking it in front of Jacinta. "I've got breath mints."

Jacinta shakes her head in disbelief.

Nolan rushes over from the seats on the side of the room, seeing Jacinta waving for him from behind the edge of the stage curtains. He's in parade dress.

"What's going on?" he whispers, coming up beside them.

Kath looks at him with tears in her eyes. "He lied, Nolan. He said the decision to collect samples was not political. He told the press corps he had no involvement, that the decision was made before he took office."

"You can't call the President a liar," Nolan says. "Not on national TV. Not without evidence."

"Oh, I wouldn't dream of such a thing," Kath says. "Besides, he's only a liar if he comes from the Lyon region of France. Otherwise, he's an absolute bastard!"

"That's the champagne talking," Jacinta says.

"That's not any better," Nolan says, gently taking Kath by her shoulders. "Look. I know you're upset, but let's just get through this in one piece, okay?"

"He wouldn't even meet with me," Kath says, tugging on her formal dress to straighten it. "Not until the presentation." She points on an angle at the lectern on stage as a speech is being delivered about America's resolve to rebuild Houston. "She was so much better."

"She was," Jacinta says, referring to President Aston. "But she's not here now."

"Nope," Kath replies, looking whimsical. "Do you think you could get me another glass of champagne?"

"Later," Nolan says.

Kath wipes her tears. After all she's been through, she's now got to smile and go on stage like a high-wire circus performer and pretend everything's okay.

Nolan says, "We'll get through this—like we always do."

Jacinta tries to be upbeat, saying, "Richardson, Michaels and Cheung have been nominated for the Nobel Prize in Biology for their work identifying an enzyme that inhibits *Anduru* at a cellular level."

"And they deserve it," Kath says. "They've given us a biological forcefield. Finding a mechanism that attacks these things and not us was a stroke of genius. We need never fear these creatures again!"

For Kath, that finding was an immense relief. Everyone that had been in the isolation zone within Houston showed signs of extraterrestrial contaminants in their bloodstream—including Kath and Jimmy. The enzyme became the basis for a vaccine that provoked an immune response, cleansing the infection.

Jimmy was reunited with his family while the military action was still ongoing. Nolan had them flown to the forward base in Austin. Jimmy's mother said she thought her husband, Phil, died of a heart attack. With the stress of all that was happening, he'd been experiencing chest pains. He'd gone back to the room to get his medicine while she waited for the evacuation. One of the creatures attacked a bellhop in the hotel lobby and chaos ensued. As Phil and Jimmy were in the back tower, she hoped they'd made it out but gave up hope on day three. When she learned her son was alive, she couldn't wait to be reunited with him. Kath was there when they met. Everyone was in tears, including Nolan.

Kath's distracted. She wanted Jimmy and his Mom at the ceremony but her request was turned down.

Jacinta stutters. "Y—You know, you've been nominated for the Peace Prize, right?"

"Oh, no, no, no," Kath says, waving a 3D-printed finger at her. "I torched a major US city. That hardly qualifies as bringing peace. Tell them to give it to someone that actually deserves it—someone deescalating conflicts or pushing for climate change."

"The committee seems pretty intent on you," Nolan says.

"I've got enough participation trophies to last me a lifetime," Kath says. "And I'm about to get another one."

"But it's an honor," Jacinta says.

Kath tries to stand still but she sways like a tree in a storm, saying, "If I win, I am totally selling that thing on *Craig's List*."

Jacinta says, "No, you're not. Now, behave."

Kath looks down at her feet like a scolded schoolgirl. She's regretting knocking back four or was it five glasses of champagne on an empty stomach. Her head feels as light as a cloud drifting through the sky.

Kath's been in the stateroom at the White House before. This time it's with a different President, but it's the same podium, the same Baroque-era portraits on the walls, the same heavy curtains hiding them until the last moment before they walk on stage, the same champagne on tables off to the side, ready to be snatched by the same media contingent. Kath's the last one standing between them and alcohol.

"Deep breaths," Jacinta says. "You can do this."

She peeks around the curtain. It's the paintings that fascinate her. They're clearly influenced by Rembrandt. Moody, dark surroundings give way to a fleeting ray of light catching each historic face. There are plaques beneath the paintings, telling the viewer a little about each portrait. Each is a long-forgotten story. Each tries to capture something of the past for the future. Each simplifies the complexity of life into a few words. Is that what will become of her in the centuries to come? Will she too be a byline in history? Maybe they'll name a school after her or hang her portrait on some wall somewhere.

The President introduces Kath, announcing she's been awarded the Presidential Medal of Freedom for her heroism during the outbreak in Houston. Kath notes he doesn't say, *again*. What is she going to do with two of these damn bits of metal? How much could she get for one on *eBay*? Ah, Jacinta's right. She needs to be nice.

The stage manager gestures for Kath to walk out in front of the lights. Nolan and Jacinta offer a thumbs-up as encouragement.

Kath greets the President with a handshake and dozens of camera flashes. She even smiles. The President waffles on about the importance of scientists to America's future and then presents her with the medal, draping it around her neck. He steps back, offering her an open microphone.

Kath walks forward. Silence descends on the room. She clears her throat and adjusts the microphone. For all of the differences between them, President Wilson has given her a platform. He didn't have to let her speak. He could have kept things *"more ceremonial."* As late as it may be, she appreciates his trust.

There's a lot Kath could say. She's thought long and hard about what she should say. Yet again, conspiracy theories are rife. Why destroy all of Houston? What was the government trying to hide? Supposedly, there were experiments on human-alien hybrids in the basement at JSC. Kath's been accused of burning evidence. The Illuminati were involved in yet another *Great Reset*. Apparently, the aging Q exposed *"The Lie."* She suspects Q is a front for any asshole with an axe to grind. Oh, and pedophiles. That's the one addition that always gets Kath. There were human-alien hybrids *and* a child sex ring in that basement. For those on the fringe, there's always got to be a play to emotion. There's nothing like sexual perversion to stoke the fake fires of outrage.

"Be kind to each other," she says. It's not the greatest opening in the history of speeches. It won't go down with the Gettysburg Address, but it's what she feels rather than thinks. The first time she was here, logic ruled her mind. Now, emotion holds sway over her heart. She sees humanity in a different light. Earth is the lucky planet. By saving themselves, *Homo sapiens* have saved every other species on this tiny rock. Given the damage caused by fossil fuels and greed, that's a surprising step in the right direction for an otherwise self-indulgent species.

All eyes are upon her, but she's in no rush. She wants that point to sink in.

Angry Andy Anderson is sitting in the front row along with a number of dignitaries. He looks uncomfortable next to them, but she's glad he's there. He called the online trolls "*a generation of vipers!*" He's right. For all the threats humanity faces from without, it's those that come from within that hurt the most. In the months following the incident, Kath reviewed his footage from the northern suburbs of Houston. It's astonishing how far he's come from those early days when comet *Anduru* first appeared in the night sky. His *plus-one* is a captain in the US Rangers in formal military dress. She's got her arm in a sling. The lack of any forearm screams of the agony she's endured and yet she's looking up at Kath with admiration.

"Listen to science," Kath says. "Don't fight it. Just listen. Sure, it may not be what we *want* to hear, but perhaps it's what we *need* to hear."

As tempting as it is, Kath avoids any discussion about conspiracy theories. From her perspective, they get too much damn airtime as it is.

"I know. I get it. I understand. It's natural to defend your position, but that doesn't make your position right. Listen. Just listen. Maybe, just maybe—perhaps, there's some merit to what scientists are telling us. Don't fight reality. Take a deep breath and listen.

"Think of scientists like a dentist. Ignoring them and delaying action is only ever going to hurt."

She grips the lectern with plastic fingers reaching out inside a pair of white lace gloves. Walking out on stage has had a sobering effect on her.

"We all have opinions. We all have an agenda. You do. I do. We all do. We can't help it. It's human. And we're tribal. It's in our nature to back our side in a fight. Whether that's a sports team or some pet idea floating around on the internet, we love nothing more than to get passionate about a cause—our cause.

"The only difference when it comes to science is the goal is clarity. The goal is to get rid of our human biases and look at things honestly.

"Scientists are human. Sure, they make mistakes. And when they do, there's a whole line of other scientists like me ready to pounce and call them out. That's what we call peer review. It's the way science works—by demonstrating transparency. It's not enough to make a bold claim, you have to prove it. You have to be able to back it up.

"All of science—in every field over the past five hundred years— can be summed up in one phrase: *put up or shut up!* If you make a claim, you had better be able to prove it or a hundred thousand other scientists are going to jump down your throat and call *bullshit!*"

Kath clenches, feeling bad about letting a curse word slip out. Perhaps that last glass of champagne was a mistake after all. She tries not to pause too long, wanting to recover and move on.

"And that's okay. That's how science advances. Suggest an idea. Test it. Throw out what doesn't work. Refine your idea and strive for consistency.

"People think it's a sin to be wrong. It's not. It's human. The problem arises when we refuse to accept we're wrong. That's when shit gets dicey."

Oops, she thinks, there goes another one!

Tighten it up, Kath.

"Mistakes are part of life," she says, tacitly acknowledging her own bloopers in this speech. "Mistakes are normal. Remaining in them is the real problem. That takes pride and arrogance. And I'd argue, those are the worst mistakes of all.

"The grand lesson of science is simple: *accept reality, don't fight it because you don't like it.* Push the boundaries but don't live in a dream. We've got to accept the challenges that face us, not ignore them. We've got to work together. And above all, we have to be patient with each other."

She pauses, looking down at her lace gloves and the scars on the back of her hands, adding one last sentiment.

"We need to be kind."

With that, she turns and steps back from the lectern.

When there's no applause forthcoming, President Wilson says, "Well, thank you for those kind words." It seems everyone's stunned. They were expecting her usual rant. They were waiting for a fiery Dr. Mackenzie sermon from the pulpit. They expected anger, but Kath's tired. She can't inspire change alone. No one can. Yelling might make her feel better, but it's ineffective. It might embarrass some, but it'll only harden others. She hopes her words are heeded, but the only person she can change is herself—and she accepts that.

Kath steps back into the shadow of the President. She stands beside three other recipients of the Presidential Medal of Freedom, including a doctor who continued operating on someone while an alien prowled the hallway outside. He turns slightly, offering her a smile.

The ceremony ends and Kath joins Nolan and Jacinta for a glass of champagne.

"Hey," Nolan says, knocking back the last of his drink. "Do you want to split and go grab some dinner from *Old Ebbitt's*?"

Food sounds like a very good idea to Drunk Kath. "Sure."

They slip out of the reception at the White House and onto Pennsylvania Ave. *Old Ebbitt's* is a restaurant across from the Executive Office. They used to have lunch there during the Aston administration.

Kath's never been there for dinner.

After ordering, they sit in a booth drinking soda water and lime rather than champagne. It's a good decision.

"That was close, huh?" Nolan says.

"Too damn close," Jacinta replies. "I prefer my aliens in space—deep space."

Nolan replies, "Me too."

Kath is quiet. She sips at her water before saying, "It was kinda cool, though."

"Ah, here comes Drunk Kath," Nolan says, chuckling.

"No, I'm serious," she says in her defense. "I mean, think about what just happened. We had First Contact. Okay, it wasn't the kind of contact we wanted, but it opens entirely new fields of study for us—and the hope of reaching others out there."

"I dunno," Jacinta says. "For a while there, it was touch and go as to whether we'd make it out of that mess alive."

"Those monsters were scary as *fuck*," Nolan says.

"See," Kath says, raising her glass and staring through it at him, mimicking the presence of one of the transparent aliens before her. "You see an alien. I see an organism. You see a creature standing before you. I see *billions* of years worth of evolutionary selective pressure arriving at a single point in time."

"Are you sure that's soda water?" Jacinta asks, pointing at her glass.

"Look at the Grand Canyon and what do you see?" Kath asks with eyes as big as saucers. "Sediment laid down over hundreds of millions of years, forming cliffs and rocks and outcrops. When I look at DNA, that's what I see—layer upon layer of genetic change accumulating over eons.

"I remember taking a helicopter into the Grand Canyon as a tourist. We flew in from the west, tracing the Colorado river as it winds through the gorge. With each foot, we descended through tens of thousands of years. These are periods of time we simply cannot imagine and yet our helicopter passed through them like a time machine.

"The colors were magnificent. There were bands of red and grey, orange and pale yellow. Ridges, mounds and buttes lay scattered throughout the labyrinth of gorges forming the canyon. Limestone and shale had fallen as rubble on the slopes. I found it astonishing that the history of all complex life on Earth lay beneath the clear Perspex dome of our chopper.

"I remember we landed on a plateau a couple of hundred feet above the river. At a guess, it would have been somewhere in the Permian, perhaps on the edge of the Triassic. I watched in horror as our rotor blades kicked up fine sand, scouring fossilized microbial mats laid down in an ancient swamp two hundred and fifty million years ago! Once, dinosaurs grazed beneath the skids of our chopper."

Kath is lost in thought, reminiscing on that moment. Nolan and Jacinta don't care. They're held captive by her comments.

"We were given champagne and strawberries. We had fifteen minutes to walk around. Then we were back in the air again, returning to Las Vegas.

"As astonishing as that was, DNA is even more magnificent. It's a living fossil record that is every bit as complex and layered as the Grand Canyon. And it reaches back deeper in time, stretching for *billions* of years! All that history is captured within the cells of our bodies. We think of our DNA as here and now, but it's not. We're a palimpsest—a sheet of paper that's been reused and written over time and again, constantly being recycled.

"We're the graffiti in a subway tunnel. Behind the oversized letters and the splash of color, there are hundreds of other tags—only our tags extend back to the Romans and the Greeks. They blend with the cave paintings of Neanderthals and extend even further, winding back through hominids to primates and mammals, vertebrates, chordates and the simplest of animals. By that point, we're spanning easily seven hundred million years, but the layers of graffiti in our DNA continue for at least 3.8 billion years. We're just the latest stencil on the wall. We're like someone standing on the rim of the Grand Canyon not realizing it describes the history of complex life."

"Well," Nolan says, charging his glass and offering a toast. "Here's to us stencils on the wall."

They knock their glasses together and sip their soda water.

Jacinta says, "Ah, drunk Kath is the best Kath."

AFTERWORD

Thank you for supporting independent science fiction.

I broke my own rule with this book, writing a sequel within the First Contact series. At the conclusion of *Wherever Seeds May Fall* there was still so much to explore I felt it deserved to be the exception to the rule. Whereas *Seeds* is First Contact in space, *Vipers* is First Contact on Earth.

Here's some background information on various aspects of this novel.

Logistics

Novels are a delicate balancing act between character and plot. Endings have to resolve the various threads woven throughout the narrative. When it comes to *Generation of Vipers*, I deliberately avoided the classic *god-among-men* trope where the hero/heroine stands victorious as no other could. Instead, the protagonists pass the torch to others, getting scientists around the world involved. To me, this is more realistic than the *lone hero* trope so often used in science fiction. I'll give you a historic example.

World War II lasted from 1939 to 1945 but Winston Churchill considered the war a foregone conclusion as soon as the Japanese attacked Pearl Harbor.

On December 7th, 1941, he wrote:

"Silly people... might discount the force of the United States. Some said they were soft... [that] they would fool around at a distance... [that] their democracy and system of recurrent elections would paralyze their war effort... [that] they would be just a vague blur on the horizon to friend and foe... [but] once the fire is lighted under [the US] there is no limit to the power it can generate."

On recalling that night in his memoirs, Churchill said, *"I went to bed and slept the sleep of the saved and thankful."* A week later, when talking about the Japanese, Churchill said, *"Let the raider come—what does it matter?"* He understood that *"many disappointments and unpleasant surprises await us,"* but he knew the war was now a numbers game. The Second World War raged for another four years, but there was only ever going to be one outcome.

Churchill understood the importance of logistics and the economic might of the US being brought into the war. He realized neither Germany nor Japan could compete with America's industrial might. In the same way, I had Nolan buying time for the US Army to establish a counter-attack in this novel—and I framed the ending as requiring scientific cooperation rather than heroics. In this story, humanity wins because it works together.

We all love a good alien invasion movie with mech-suits and machine-guns firing on full auto, but the reality is that wars aren't won on the battlefield. They're won in factories. They're won by scientific/engineering breakthroughs. General Omar Bradley famously said, *"Amateurs talk strategy. Professionals talk logistics."* All too often, everything is just magically available to the Hollywood protagonist—not so for Nolan, Andy and Kath. The reality is, it would take time and effort to bring everything together for a counterstrike and to find a scientific resolution to the threat. I thought that sense of realism was an interesting angle to work into the novel.

Misinformation

After publishing books like this, I inevitably run into a bunch of 'too woke' reviews so I wanted to address why misinformation is a recurring theme in my recent novels.

Disinformation is easy to deal with. It's hostile by design and thrown into the debate by bad-faith actors wanting to manipulate people to their own advantage. Misinformation is different. It's sincere. When someone stuck an anti-vax poster on the back of a road sign at the end of my street, it wasn't out of malice. They've been conned. They think they're defending what's right. They feel as though they're fighting for civilized society, not against it. They're genuinely concerned. They've been fed disinformation from trolls or perhaps misinformation from other sincere people they know, but they're perpetuating lies—and that's tragic.

As I write this, there's a *truth about covid* book sitting in the top 500 books on Amazon—only it doesn't tell the truth at all. It's full of lies. I get harassed on social media because Australia is apparently a *covid prison*—when, for a while, at least, Australia escaped the worst of the pandemic. I've even been told helicopters were preventing me from leaving the house—at a time when I could move about freely.

What's the best way to counter blatant lies?

I don't know, but staying silent isn't a solution.

Will speaking up change people's minds?

Probably not, but it's irresponsible to pretend the problem doesn't exist. With the advent of the Internet, we moved into the Information Age. With the advent of social media, we stepped across into the Age of Misinformation.

Why are we in this mess?

Money.

Oh, there's nothing in it for the misinformation folks. They're disciples of the cause. But those spreading disinformation make a lot of money. Fox News famously set up a vaccine passport while publicly ridiculing the concept. In the words of Andy Anderson:

If you can turn a molehill into a mountain, you'll make money.

It surprises me how easily people can be misled and how stubborn they are once they've accepted a lie. When the blind lead the blind, both fall into a ditch.

Logic does not play a part in these decisions. Questions are not allowed. When it comes to conspiracy theories, logic is only useful to confirm what's already believed. Present a logical reason for someone to question their beliefs and they'll tack, changing course like an ocean-racing yacht sailing off in another direction, avoiding the point entirely. *"But,"* they say, and any honest objections are ignored in favor of protecting one's pride and position.

So why bother?

Because it isn't harmless. Misinformation kills.

And it's only getting worse.

Memories

One of the examples used in this novel is the false memory of a hijacked plane hitting a grassy field outside of Shanksville, Pennsylvania on 9/11. Although this did happen, no one saw it. There was never any footage of the event, but a lot of people think they've seen it. In her non-fiction book *Remember: The Science of Memory and the Art of Forgetting*, Lisa Genova uses this as an example of how memories can be misleading.

Selective memories are one way unscrupulous people manipulate others. Some people are all too willing to lie about the past, gaslighting what actually happened during various historical events and injecting different ideals and motives from those of that time. It's too easy to gloss over or romanticize the past. If we want to learn from the lessons of the past and avoid similar mistakes in the future, the past must be preserved and understood. The past cannot be changed or ignored. It needs to be accepted.

Easy Company

In this novel, Captain Winters recounts her grandfather's comments about fighting Nazis in World War II. Although this recollection is fictitious, it's based on a comment then First Lieutenant Dick Winters made on D-Day, saying, "My dear God, if I live through this, all I want is peace and quiet."

After retiring, Major Dick Winters was reluctant about telling his story for fear of being depicted as a hero. When historian Stephen Ambrose began writing a book on Easy Company, Winters got involved to make sure Ambrose got the details correct. This book then became the basis for the HBO mini-series *Band of Brothers*.

The nature of the aliens

The description of the aliens in this novel is modeled after the idea of convergent evolution being extended to life on different planets.

On Earth, various species have arrived at similar body types even though there's no direct relationship between them. Sharks and dolphins both have dorsal fins and streamlined bodies even though one of them is a mammal. Bats and birds both have wings because wings are astonishingly effective for flight—and not because these species are related. In the same way, evolution has settled on the crab with its exoskeleton as a common design for a variety of different species from lobsters to scorpions.

When it comes to mammals, the body shape of weasels is astonishingly prevalent, with 70 different species using a similar, streamlined, flexible body (ferrets, minks, prairie dogs, beavers, meerkats, cats and even non-mammals like lizards, geckos, etc). These similarities arise because natural selection converges on the most efficient forms, so this became the basis for the body shape of the aliens in *Generation of Vipers*.

Although the idea of invisibility is a stretch, camouflage is common on Earth. Natural selection has led to spotted deer that mimic the terrain they inhabit. Grasshoppers resemble the tip of a blade of grass. Stick insects look like, well, sticks. Some butterflies are adorned with the color of the flowers they favor. Tigers and leopards have disruptive patterns making them difficult to spot in the undergrowth.

Evolution has even led to active, adaptive camouflage with cuttlefish blending into the background. Flounder have the ability to change the color of their skin to match different parts of the ocean floor in under a second. Blink and they're gone! Octopus can change both the color and texture of their skin to mimic rocks and coral. They can even change each hemisphere of their bodies independently, so they appear different from either side!

When it came to *Generation of Vipers*, I felt there was something distinctly unnerving about knowing these aliens were out there, but not knowing precisely where they were.

DNA

One of the key points at the end of this novel is how misleading physical appearances can be when it comes to DNA. Mice and elephants really do share 99% of their genes. For that matter, mice and humans also share 99% of their genes. Most people realize we're closely related to chimpanzees. What they don't realize is we're closely related to *all* mammals. It's not a question of what genes differ, but how they're used. And it's not just mammals. We share genes with ants, tomatoes, birds, bacteria—you name it—just to a lesser extent.

We all learned about DNA in high school. We all understand it provides the blueprint for our bodies. But what most people don't realize is that, out of the three billion base pairs that make up our DNA, only 2% is actually bundled into the roughly 25,000 genes that code for proteins and make our bodies. Our DNA is mostly *"other stuff"* sometimes called junk DNA because it doesn't seem to do anything. It's not junk, though, as it seems to help indirectly in other ways. If that's not surprising enough, though, around 8% of our DNA (an astonishing four times the actual useful DNA we carry in our cells) comes from the retroviruses our ancestors survived!

Our lives are an extraordinary Rube Goldberg machine. Life is far more complex than it seems. We are a patchwork quilt of biological interactions, which is why extraterrestrial contamination could easily upset the apple cart.

In *The Varieties of Scientific Experience: A Personal View of the Search for God*, Carl Sagan said, *"with trivial exceptions, all organisms on Earth use... proteins as a catalyst... to control the rate and direction of the chemistry of life. All organisms on Earth use... a nucleic acid to encode the hereditary information to reproduce it in the next generation. All organisms on Earth use the identical codebook... And while there are clearly some differences between, say, me and slime mold, fundamentally, we are tremendously closely related. The lesson is, don't judge a book by its cover. At the molecular level, we [as in all species] are all virtually identical."*

Quantum Biology

Quantum biology is an astonishing field. In this novel, I used it to juxtapose our reliance on technology and the ability of nature to surprise us with innovation. This is used to make the point we shouldn't assume anything about alien life being reliant on technology. Animals flew for hundreds of millions of years before we figured it out.

One example from our own bodies is that our noses can detect differences at a subatomic level! The vibration theory of olfaction suggests the nose uses quantum tunneling to detect isotopes (that is it can distinguish between the same atomic element with an extra neutron). As isotopes are chemically indistinguishable, it's an astonishing feat of evolution! Nature mastered the quantum realm long before we even realized it was a thing.

Too often, we underestimate biology to our own detriment. Yes, the Arctic Tern really does fly 90,000 km a year between the poles. Over the span of their lifetimes, they average around 2.4 million kilometers— that's to the Moon and back six times!

Cleanrooms

The cleanest places on Earth are the NASA/ESA clean rooms where spacecraft are assembled, and yet even there we find microbes. Not only do we find microbes, we find microbes that don't seem to live anywhere else other than in those cleanrooms. We have no idea how they got there. They eat cleaning products like bleach and hydrogen peroxide for breakfast. Oh, and they've spread between cleanrooms separated by hundreds of miles. Again, we don't know how.

There is no place on Earth where microbes can't survive—even inside nuclear reactors. Earth is a microbial planet. We're tourists.

Panspermia

Panspermia is the idea that life might be able to survive drifting between worlds in much the same way as iguanas made it from South America to the Galapagos by clinging to branches, but there are limits to the theory, including the time involved in transit and the likelihood of reaching fertile ground.

The Galapagos Islands are a good example of how invasive species can take over an ecosystem in a manner similar to *Anduru*. These islands have an odd imbalance in that there are 22 species of reptiles, no amphibians, and just six mammal species. The reason for this is reptiles are more suited to surviving the 600-mile journey clinging to vegetation as a raft. Most would have died, but over millions of years, only a few crossings were needed to survive to give us the diversity we see there today.

Alejandra Traspas and Mark Burchell produced a peer-review paper entitled *Tardigrade Survival Limits in High-Speed Impacts— Implications for Panspermia and Collection of Samples from Plumes Emitted by Ice Worlds*. This places strict limits on the survivability of microbes hitchhiking on asteroids.

The average asteroid enters Earth's atmosphere at upwards of 20 km/s. Even such hardy microbes as tardigrades cannot survive these speeds. Bacteria can survive impacts at 5 km/s, but tardigrades will be turned to mush by anything over 1 km/s.

Depending on the size and composition of the asteroid, one possibility is that the deceleration may happen in phases. As the parent meteorite breaks up, individual parts may remain below these thresholds. Once within the atmosphere, such fragments would fall like a stone rather than a meteorite, landing at little more than terminal velocity, and would be survivable by microbes.

Our inability to contain pathogens

Yes, vials of smallpox were found at the back of an FDA storage room in Maryland in 2014. No one knows how they got there, but the samples date back to the 1950s. Although they hadn't been opened in sixty years, there was evidence of growth, indicating the samples were still viable. Mistakes happen. Keeping pathogens like these around isn't smart.

In another example, inactive anthrax was sent between labs with low-level security for research purposes, only the anthrax wasn't dead. It was very much alive and capable of becoming airborne.

It's not a question of if these things will leak out, it's a question of when and how bad it will be. So far, we've been lucky. Luck, though, isn't a good strategy when dealing with bioweapons.

If we find life on other planets we will have to think long and hard about whether we ever return samples to Earth. One option would be to establish a lunar base as a planetary quarantine facility. Even then, it would have to be carefully managed to prevent two entirely separate biospheres from coming in contact by accident.

Alien Pathogens

Could alien pathogens even infect Earth-life?

Professor Neil Gow from the University of Exeter has conducted research into this idea. "[After Covid] The world is now only too aware of the immune challenge posed by the emergence of brand new pathogens. As a thought experiment, we wondered what would happen if we were to be exposed to a microorganism that had been retrieved from another planet or moon where life had evolved... Would our immune system be able to detect proteins made from these non-terrestrial building blocks if such organisms were discovered and were brought back to Earth and then accidentally escaped?"

It's a good question.

And the answer?

Dr. Katja Schaefer notes, "Life on Earth relies on 22 essential amino acids. We chemically synthesized 'exo-peptides' containing Earth-rare amino acids, and tested whether a mammalian immune system could detect them."

As Adam Temper notes, the results were startling. Taking the most common amino acids found in space and incorporating them into exotic peptides cause T-cell activation to drop to 22% (it's normally up around 80% to 90%). In short, our immune system would fail to recognize them as a pathogen.

This would *not* be good.

The closest historic analog we have for a clash between pathogens from different biospheres is smallpox. As devastating as smallpox was for Europeans, for native Americans it caused a mass-death event on a scale never seen before or since. The virus tore through the population like a scythe.

In 1781, the native American Saukamappee raided a Shoshone village, but said, "*our war-whoop instantly stopped, our eyes were appalled with terror [at the smallpox outbreak]; there was no one to fight with but the dead and the dying.*" In 1792, George Vancouver wrote, "*The skull, limbs, ribs and backbones, or some other vestiges of the human body, were found in many places, promiscuously scattered about the beach in great numbers [after a smallpox outbreak].*" While in 1776, Lord Dunmore wrote, "*we were struck with horror at the number of dead bodies, in a state of putrefaction... about two miles in length.*" This is not what we would associate with a disease. It is the kind of description we would expect in the aftermath of a holocaust.

As Michael Crichton wrote in *The Andromeda Strain*, an extraterrestrial infection could be devastating. And it need not be intentional. Although there were cases where smallpox was used as a weapon during the colonization of the Americas, being spread on infected blankets, the vast majority of infections were incidental. The result, though, was the same.

When it comes to the danger of cellular interactions with extraterrestrial organics, we need to apply the precautionary principle and avoid the possibility of contamination or the effects could be disastrous. All of these TV shows and movies where colonists land on an alien planet and walk around outside in a t-shirt and shorts are laughable—*I'm looking at you, Prometheus!*

The Danger of Ignorance

As much as possible, I try to entertain and inform through my stories. I enjoy actual science in my fiction. Science can be intimidating, but you don't have to understand every aspect of science to appreciate how it has enriched our lives. I can watch both ballet and basketball and appreciate the athleticism and skill without needing to experience it myself. The challenge arises when people demean excellence. It's too easy to be critical. Armchair quarterbacks might talk a big game but they never get off the couch.

The same scientific method that sent astronauts to the moon and allows airplanes to fly safely through the sky powers my home, has given me my computer and my smartphone—as well as lifesaving vaccines. To me, that's something to celebrate.

In 1980, Isaac Asimov wrote an article called The Cult of Ignorance. In it, he laments how we have been taught to distrust experts—the competent, he says, have been unfairly recast as elitists. It's madness. It makes knowledge the enemy. Anyone that tells you elitists are manipulating you is simply projecting their own actions on those that are trying to help. It's sleight of hand. By labeling others as elitist, they avoid questions about themselves.

There is a cult of ignorance in the United States [and around the world], and there always has been. The strain of anti-intellectualism has been a constant thread winding its way through our political and cultural life, nurtured by the false notion that democracy means that "my ignorance is just as good as your knowledge." — Isaac Asimov.

His solution is simple—*read*.

He says, "*...what we badly need is social approval of learning and social rewards for learning. We can all be members of the intellectual elite, and then, and only then, will... democracy have any meaning.*"

The future is ours.

The future is what we make of it.

We can embrace the astonishing scientific advances of the past couple of hundred years or we can bury our heads in the sand, but make no mistake—there's no equivalence between ignorance and information. Ignorance is not bliss, it leaves you naked and alone. To be ignorant is to be stripped bare before those that would manipulate you for their gain.

Beware of the generation of vipers.

Thank You

I hope you've enjoyed this novel as much as I have. It takes an astonishing amount of effort to make a book effortless to read, but for me, it's a labor of love.

Take the time to leave a review of *Generation of Vipers* online. Your opinion of this book is far more important than mine, but please, no spoilers.

I'd like to thank my wife Fiona for putting up with my crazy ideas. I'd also like to thank the following beta-readers for their enthusiasm, support and encouragement: John Stephens, Didi Kanjahn, Chris Fox, Bruce Simmons, John Larisch and David Jaffe. Observant readers will notice these beta-readers have been helping me catch typos for years, which is something I deeply appreciate. Oh, and if you're curious, the order in which they're listed is randomly generated from one book to the next as they're all equally valued by me.

Ian Forsdike, Commander Mike Morrissey (USA, Retired), Dr. Tris Kerslake and Terry Grindstaff helped review this novel for accuracy.

Any mistakes that slipped through the cracks are mine and mine alone.

This is the 19th novel in my First Contact series. I have at least 25 stories planned, so subscribe to my email newsletter if you'd like to learn more about upcoming novels. Next up is a rather unusual look at First Contact in a story called *Clowns*, due out in mid-2022.

You can find all my novels on Amazon, and you can find me on Facebook and Twitter.

Peter Cawdron

Brisbane, Australia

Printed in Great Britain
by Amazon